THE
ENGLISH
AGENT

Clare Harvey's debut novel, *The Gunner Girl*, won the 2016 Joan Hessayon Award. Her follow-on novel, *The English Agent*, was inspired by the bravery of the women agents from the Secret Operatives Executive (SOE) in wartime France. Clare lives in Nottingham with her family. To find out more, get in touch on Twitter @ClareHarveyauth, Facebook: clareharvey13 and at her website: www.clareharvey.net

By the same author
The Gunner Girl

THE ENGLISH AGENT

Clare Harvey

**SIMON &
SCHUSTER**

London · New York · Sydney · Toronto · New Delhi

A CBS COMPANY

First published in Great Britain by Simon & Schuster UK Ltd, 2016
This edition published by Simon & Schuster UK Ltd, 2017
A CBS COMPANY
Copyright © Clare Harvey 2016

1 3 5 7 9 10 8 6 4 2

Simon & Schuster UK Ltd
1st Floor
222 Gray's Inn Road
London WC1X 8HB

www.simonandschuster.co.uk

Simon & Schuster Australia, Sydney
Simon & Schuster India, New Delhi

A CIP catalogue record for this book
is available from the British Library

B Format ISBN: 978-1-4711-5057-9
eBook ISBN: 978-1-4711-5058-6

Typeset by M Rules
Printed in the UK by CPI Group (UK) Ltd, Croydon, CR0 4YY

MIX
Paper from
responsible sources
FSC® C020471

Simon & Schuster UK Ltd are committed to sourcing paper
that is made from wood grown in sustainable forests and support the Forest
Stewardship Council, the leading international forest certification organisation.
Our books displaying the FSC logo are printed on FSC certified paper.

For Chris, always

Conservez vos meilleurs amis proches,
mais vos ennemis plus près.

Keep your best friends close, but
your enemies closer.

Chapter 1

Edie

Edie sat on the edge, legs dangling into the rushing darkness. The hatch was a circle of obsidian, the reverse of the full moon that shone, somewhere up there, picking out silvery skeins of tracks and field-edges lacing the shifting ground below. At least now her parachute cloche was on the noise wasn't so loud, more of a vibration, right through her bones, into her teeth, which chattered against themselves.

There was still time to back out. Even at the last moment; remember you are a volunteer, Miss Atkins had said. If you don't think you can hack it, come back: the boys will still get their Stens and plastic explosives, and we'll send another operator in the next moon period. But Edie said she would be absolutely fine, thank you. Miss Atkins leant towards her then, brushing her cheek against Edie's, her breath warm, and whispered in French, '*Conservez vos meilleurs amis proches, mais vos ennemis plus près,*' pressing a package into her palm as they shook hands before take-off.

She'd opened the package once she got in the Lockheed

Hudson. The black tissue paper was tied with a single white ribbon, and fell away to reveal a silver powder compact, with a creamy circle of powder already inside, pristine and unblemished, like a baby's forehead. She smelled it – a musky, flowery scent – and it reminded her for a moment of her mother. What would Mummy be doing now, she wondered? Knitting in front of the fire, with the BBC Orchestra on the wireless, thinking that her only daughter was in London, doing translation work for the Inter Services Research Bureau, instead of on her way to Occupied France. Then the plane had coughed and roared into action, and she'd clicked the compact shut and put it away. It was in the breast pocket of her flight suit now, clattering against her compass.

There was a tap on her shoulder, and she turned to see the dispatcher, who was showing her that he'd attached her static line. He raised his bushy eyebrows and she nodded to show that she'd understood. Her legs were getting cold, the wind biting through her bandaged ankles and the bulky flight suit. She thought she could see intermittent flashes below. It must be time, now?

It's not too late to back out, Miss Atkins had said. But Edith replied that she'd be fine. What was there to go back for, after all? The shame and chaos of last year: she wanted to leave it all behind her. '*Adieu*,' she'd said to Miss Atkins, giving a final wave before heaving herself up into the fuselage. 'Don't say *adieu*, say *au revoir*, dear girl, because I'm quite sure we'll see you again,' Miss Atkins replied.

The dispatcher was now kneeling next to the two lights opposite the hatch. His lips were pressed tightly together, as if he were trying to hold in a cough, and his face was tinted red by the red light next to him. She kept her eyes on him. It must be any moment now, and she couldn't afford to hesitate.

It felt like her first hunt: fear and exhilaration mixed. She recalled the feel of the horse's flanks between her thighs, the baying of the hounds, and the rushing wind. Afterwards there was the blood from the vixen's tail, sticky and strange-smelling on her cheeks. She hadn't been hunting for years – couldn't bear the killing these days.

The dispatcher lifted his hand as the red light turned off.

'*Au revoir*,' Edie mouthed as the green light came on. She pushed herself off into the inky vortex and was gone.

Vera

'Well, that agent seemed raring to go,' said the driver, holding open the car door as Vera walked towards it. The girl was new: obviously nobody had told her she shouldn't speak unless spoken to. Or perhaps it was Vera's lack of uniform that made her feel she could be so familiar. Vera sighed and didn't respond. It had been hours since she'd seen off the new wireless transmission operator – there'd been all that nonsense with Major Wishaw to attend to – she simply wanted to get back to London now.

But as she approached the car in the darkness, she was transported momentarily back to another black car, the door being held open for her by another driver – a man in uniform – and a solid presence at her shoulder, a hand resting lightly in the small of her back, guiding her forward. The air was warm, and she was wearing a navy silk dress, and in the background a gramophone was playing Stolz's 'Im

Traum hast du mir alles erlaubt': In the dream you allowed me everything.

'*Come, Vera, I must take you home, or I will be in trouble with your mother, again—*' That deep voice, rich as black coffee.

'*I'm not getting in your car with the flag up, I've told you.*'

'*As you wish, Vera.*'

And the driver removed the swastika from the stubby flag-pole, which poked like a finger from the bonnet of the car, as they got inside. She remembered the feel of the silk dress against her bare legs as she slipped onto the leather seat, and the hand of her companion resting casually on her thigh as they drove off into the night.

Vera sighed again, banishing the memory as the driver slammed the car door shut behind her. She pulled her cigarette case from the pocket of her fox fur coat. The driver was fiddling with the ignition, and stalled twice before getting the car started, so Vera decided against offering her a cigarette – the girl was having quite enough trouble as it was. She clicked the lighter, and the flame curled up over the tip of her cigarette. She sucked, watching the little orange bonfire. She took the smoke in, but didn't inhale, swilling it like a good brandy round her mouth and looking out of the car window as they pulled away from the old farmhouse buildings that bordered the airstrip and onto the pitted track. You could barely make out the empty ploughed fields in the darkness – a veil of cloud covered the moon now, and it had started to drizzle.

'Are they always like that, the agents?' said the driver, catching Vera's eye in the rear-view mirror as they stuttered along.

'Like what, exactly?'

'I don't know. Upbeat, I suppose. I mean – she can't be

much older than me, can she?' said the driver, turning onto the main road.

She wasn't, Vera thought. She was the youngest agent they'd sent so far, and the first woman – just a girl, really. Too young, Vera thought. At her age, Vera had been – but the image of the black car appeared again in her mind's eye. She tutted. 'That agent was very well trained and she is fully aware of the risks,' she said with finality.

'Oh, quite, Miss Atkins, I didn't mean to imply – I just meant that if it were me ...'

'Well, thank heavens it's not you, then,' said Vera, flicking ash into the little metal tray in the doorframe. It needed emptying; someone should have a chat with these wretched FANY drivers about standards, Vera thought, as the car growled and swerved. The airfield was gone, now, vanished between hedgerows and darkness.

She checked her watch, the gold watch that he'd given her, letting her finger rest on its pale cream face for a moment, cool to touch. Midnight already – she leant forward to speak to the driver.

'My dear girl, could you possibly put your foot down? Some of us have work in the morning, you know.'

Edie

Edie struggled to break away, but she was being dragged bodily across rough clods of earth, stones scraping her back, her body twisting. She kicked out with her feet, trying to catch hold of something, anything, but it was no good.

At last she remembered, fumbled with the clip on her flight

suit. She stopped moving as the parachute floated free, pulling the harness with it. She sat up, pausing momentarily to catch her breath. She could still hear the plane's drone, and see its moving silhouette, black against navy, shooting away towards the low-slung moon. In the distance the parachuted crates of equipment spun earthwards like sycamore seeds on the wind.

The parachute had been carried up into a tree by the wind, so she got up to retrieve it, tugging at the harness and loose straps. Where were the reception committee? she wondered. The local Resistance had flashed out the drop signal on torches. Why weren't they here? She hauled in the cords, pulling until it ripped away, leaving just a scrap of parachute silk fluttering madly in the branches, as if asking for a truce.

The sound of the Lockheed Hudson had all but gone now, just a faint distant thrum. Other than that, there was just the sigh of the wind in the bare tree branches, and the smell of winter earth. She looked around; she needed somewhere to dispose of the parachute, which she held bundled up, slippery and tangled, like a huge jellyfish in a net. She walked to the edge of the field; the icy sods of earth were hard as cobbles beneath her French-style shoes with their cork soles. There was her flight suit and cloche hat to get rid of, too. Bury it, they'd said in training. There was a miniature shovel with a detached handle in her thigh pocket. She put down the parachute, standing on it so that it wouldn't blow away again, and took out the shovel head, fixing it to the wooden handle. The whole thing was no bigger than a seaside spade. She tried digging with it, but the ground was frozen solid, and she couldn't even make a dent.

The wind made her eyes water, and sliced her throat with each breath. She chewed a fingernail briefly, and then made up her mind, shoving the parachute underneath the bushes.

She took off her cloche and suit and bundled them on top, weighing it all down with stones and loose clods of earth. She left the useless shovel in the bushes, too. The wind was bitter, slashing through her good wool suit as if it were nothing more than thin silk. The wind must have blown her off course, she reasoned. She turned, facing it full on, and began to walk, counting her paces so that she could return to retrieve the parachute if necessary. If she walked in the direction of the wind, she'd find the reception committee eventually, she thought. Unless the Germans find you first, said a voice in her head, but she ignored it, walking along the hedge line – surely this field must have a gate at some point?

Until now, she'd been able to see by the light of the moon, silver-plating the tree branches and chalky earth, but a cloud passed over, and suddenly everything was dark. She walked on blindly, stumbling a little, still counting. Something plucked at her sleeve. She gasped, turning, but it was just a branch. Of course it was just a branch, not a hand on her sleeve, not a Nazi to fight off – not yet, at least. She breathed out and walked on, remembering her first day of hand-to-hand combat training, all those months ago.

Edie tumbled awkwardly for the umpteenth time onto the matting that had been placed on what had once been a croquet lawn, in front of the old manor house. She paused for a moment, breathing in the musky coconut-husk scent, not wanting to see the judging faces of the other agent recruits who were grouped round. Why couldn't she do it properly? The others had all managed it – the others were all men.

'All right, miss?' The training sergeant's voice roused her. She saw his chunky hand and reached out to grasp it, letting herself be helped up. 'So you're gonna fight the war and beat the Germans, right?' he continued as she staggered upright. She nodded, looking down at her feet in the old canvas daps they'd given her to train in. 'I beg your blooming pardon, miss, I didn't quite catch that.'

She looked up into his round brown eyes, the scar scoring his left brow. 'Yes, Sarge.' The sun shone square into her face, and she could feel the sweat beginning to dribble down between her shoulder blades.

'Good. Now let's try again.' He moved back a few paces so they were facing each other across the brown rectangle. In the distance she could hear shots from the rifle range, and shouts from the assault course. But it was quiet here in hand-to-hand combat training, the others waiting to see whether the girl could hack it, or if she'd just funk it, again.

The training sergeant shoved a Brylcreemed lock of hair off his forehead and began waving his right hand about. 'I'm a Jerry, see, and I'm coming towards you, and I've got a big knife in this hand.' He spoke slowly and loudly, cockney vowels drawn out and rubbery. 'So this is the hand you got to watch, right?' Edie thought she heard a suppressed snigger from somewhere behind her.

She knew what she had to do. She'd watched the demonstration, seen the others do it: grab, twist and pull – capturing the weapon and hurling the man to the floor. In her periphery she glimpsed a figure approaching from the house, but there was no time to see who it was, because the sergeant had already begun to stride across the mat, waggling his invisible German knife. She rushed towards him, determined to do it right this time, reaching for his right forearm, getting the full weight of her body behind her as she twisted and – she fell backwards, where he'd shoved her, crying out, despite herself, as the air was forced out of her lungs when she hit the ground.

'For Gawd's sake, miss, if you're going to fall, fall properly, like I taught you.' He put out a hand to help her up. But this time she refused to take it, pushing herself up onto her feet. 'All right, get back into line.' He rolled his eyes and she shuffled back to join the group, catching her breath, still winded from the fall. 'You're up next, sunshine.' The sergeant pointed to a tall man with blond hair, who stepped forward.

'Hardly your most edifying moment, my dear girl,' muttered a voice in her ear. Then Edie realised who the figure had been, walking from the house. It was Miss Atkins who'd come over to observe the training session – Miss Atkins had witnessed her humiliation. 'I didn't come all this way to see you let the side down,' she added, flicking ash onto the grass.

Edie walked on through the French fields, remembering how her cheeks had burned with the shame of it: *I didn't come all this way to see you let the side down.* Well, she wasn't going to let the side down now, she thought, as she strode on through the icy air, blinking in the blackness.

What was that darker smudge up ahead? Could it be a gateway? If she could get to a road, and if the moon came out again, she could check her compass. There was a safe house in the village just to the east of the drop zone, near a bridge. Her thoughts slipped back to her training, that night exercise with Hugo and Vic.

Edie shoved the box of matches back in the pocket of her slacks as the fuse caught, a sudden rip of sparks in the darkness. She ran back into the woods that bordered the stream, feet slipping in the wet autumn leaves.

They'd been sent out in pairs on sabotage training, the brief being to evade capture and blow up a bridge. Except there'd been an odd number of them, so she'd been told to tag along with Hugo and Vic. As she made her way through the trees she could just make out the tips of their cigarettes, dancing orange spots in the black. It had taken her a while to clamber along the bridge joists, attach the explosives and run the fuse back. She'd thought it pretty decent of them to let her do the sabotage ops for a change – especially because it wasn't really part of a wireless operator's role – but she supposed the real reason was that they were glad of the excuse for a fag break, after the eight-mile walk to get here.

She was almost at the track now, could make out Hugo and Vic as shadows separate from the tree trunks they leant against. It would be another minute or so before the bridge blew, and then if they were lucky they'd make it back to the training centre in time for breakfast.

But what was that? A sudden engine roar, a vehicle with no headlights, skidding to a halt on the track in front of her. Edie ducked behind a log, crouched down, watched as the incandescent dots of Hugo and Vic's cigarettes arced groundwards and were extinguished, heard the car door slam, footfalls on the muddy track.

'Good evening, lads. You quite comfortable? I suppose you're just biding your time, waiting for the bang?'

'Yes, Sarge,' Hugo and Vic replied in unison.

'And in the meantime, if I'd been a German sentry, I could've come over 'ere, knocked you two off, gone over to that bridge, unplugged the fuse, and gone 'ome and 'ad me dinner!'

Edie shuffled forwards until she was right underneath the passenger side of the Humber, close enough to see – but not be seen. Her breath was rasping, loud in her throat, but nobody had noticed her watching, waiting. The training sergeant was just a few feet away, his beret wobbling as he carried on shouting at her fellow recruits. Perhaps he'd forgotten that there were three of them in this group. Or perhaps he just assumed that she'd be snivelling in a ditch somewhere with a twisted ankle – like a girl. She shunted one knee up, into a sprint-starting position, readying herself.

'Got your revolver, lads?'

'Yes, Sarge.'

'Tell me where it is.'

'In my holster,' said Vic.

Edie's heart was pumping. If she was going to do this, she'd have to pick her moment.

'Oh, you're keeping your precious weapon warm, I suppose?' Vic didn't reply. The sergeant's voice rose to a bellow. 'The number of times I've told you – never leave yourselves undefended!'

Edie shot forward, head-butting the back of the sergeant's knees and simultaneously grabbing his ankles, a classic rugby tackle, felling the sergeant. They hadn't covered this one in hand-to-hand combat, but messing about with a rugger ball with Kenneth on his school exeat weekends had taught her something. She grabbed the sergeant's scrabbling hands and pinned them behind his back, holding him in position, face down in the mud. Vic had the revolver out, shoving it into the back of the sergeant's skull as he squirmed on the ground. 'What was it you were saying about not leaving yourself undefended?' Edie said.

Just then came the giant sparking crash of the bridge blowing up. In the light from the explosion, Edie saw Hugo and Vic's faces grinning down at her. But after it had blown, darkness pressed in on her eyeballs, and she could barely see at all. She let the sergeant's hands go. Despite the ringing in her ears she heard his sputtered expletives as he got to his feet. And in the awkwardness that followed, there was another sound, coming from the passenger side of the Humber: a slow handclap, and a woman's voice: 'Oh, brava, my dear girl, jolly good show!' – Miss Atkins had been watching all along.

Edie smiled to herself, recalling the older woman's pride, and the ribbing the sergeant had got in the mess at breakfast. But now the texture of the ground changed, she noticed, as she walked on in the dark: sharp stones had replaced the frozen earth. And there was an emptiness where the hedge bank had been. Perhaps she had reached the road already? She reached out a hand – there was something there: a gatepost? Suddenly a blinding flash, right in her face, and a voice: *'Qui est là?'*

'Je m'appelle—' She hesitated, but only for a moment. *'Je m'appelle Yvette Colbert.'*

Chapter 2

Vera

The sky was opalescent and clear by the time they reached Sloane Avenue. Vera thanked the driver as she pulled up outside Nell Gwyn Court, saying she'd let herself out. There was hoar frost like patterned doilies on the windows, she noticed, climbing the steps. She heard the car move off as she pushed through the glass doors into the vestibule. The concierge was nowhere to be seen, and the air smelled of boiled fish and floor polish. Vera waited for the lift to appear. Her eyes felt as if someone had sandpapered the insides of the lids. She had tried to sleep on the journey, but it had been no good, and now it was already daybreak.

The apartment door opened from the inside to reveal her mother: sage-green housecoat and accusing stare. 'Well, whoever he is, I do hope he'll make an honest woman of you one day,' she snapped. Vera pushed past and into the flat. 'Gadding about, at all hours,' her mother added, slamming the door.

'Oh Mother, please—' said Vera, putting her coat on the

hook and going straight into the galley kitchen. She filled the kettle from the tap and lit the gas. Early sunlight glanced through the dusty window. Outside grey slates and black drainpipes shoved up against each other towards the little triangle of empty morning sky. Her mother stood, hands on hips, in the kitchen doorway as Vera put the kettle on to boil, and checked her watch. Of course there was no time for sleep, even if she'd been able to.

'Any cigs in the house?' she said. Her mother sighed and passed an open packet of Sobranies from the sideboard in the hall. Vera lit one from the gas, and waited for the kettle to whistle. She drummed the fingers of her left hand on the windowsill, running through a mental checklist: the figures for Tonkin needed rechecking; the outfits from the French tailor needed collecting; the last set of ID cards hadn't really been up to scratch, so that needed attending to; there was the daily round-up of information to disseminate; and then of course there was the next-of-kin debriefing with Raoul's wife – how she hated those debriefings: the blanched look on the relatives' faces, and all those unanswerable questions. Vera swilled smoke out between her teeth. But before all of that, there was Buckmaster's morning meeting. She inhaled properly this time, pulling the sweet smoke right down into her lungs. Buckmaster's meeting to be got through, before she could even make a start on the rest of it. The kettle began its shrill whistle, and she looked over to ask her mother if she wanted a cup of tea, but she'd gone.

Vera poured hot water into an enamel bowl and took it across the hallway to the bathroom. She put the bowl in the sink, before going next door to her own room. Her bed was still made, pillowslip smoothed straight and floral eiderdown looking invitingly soft. She put her cigarette in the crystal ashtray on the dressing table, and took clean cami-knickers and stockings from the drawer. In the bathroom she quickly undressed – it was biting cold – and gave herself a strip wash with the hot water. She put a dash of talcum powder in her armpits and groin before getting dressed again. It would just have to do today. Back in the bedroom she took a last puff on the Sobranie, and ground it out. There was a little dribble of Chanel left in the bottle, so she dotted that behind her ears, brushed her hair and applied fresh lipstick, not even bothering to sit down at the dressing table. She could hear her mother clattering about in the kitchen, being unnecessarily noisy, Vera thought, making some kind of point. If her mother thought she was having a wild liaison, then so be it: it was safer than her knowing the truth.

She checked her watch, and it glinted, catching an early ray of sun. She sighed. Was it that time already?

She was taking her coat back off the peg when her mother called from the kitchen: didn't she at least want breakfast? Her mother appeared, proffering a plate of fried bread. Vera shook her head; there was no time. She did up every single one of the frog clasps on her fur – it was always so damned cold in this country – and pulled on her gloves.

Outside, the sun was fully up, washing the grey streets with cool yellow light. There was still that bomb crater where the bus stop used to be. She quickened her pace. If she hurried she might catch the 74 from further up by Exhibition Road. If only she had enough funds to take a taxi every day. She hurried on.

Edie

'You shouldn't have hesitated,' Justine said as they bumped along, the horse's hooves plodding softly on the track. 'If you stop like that, they'll know. They're not stupid; they can tell if it's an obvious lie.'

'I'm sorry. I had no idea you is there,' said Edie, watching the muddy road wind away through the fields behind them.

'Were,' Justine corrected. 'No idea you *were* there. Really, you have to at least use the right tense. Slip up on grammar and that's another thing that'll get you noticed. And just look at you, so English, *mon Dieu!*' Justine sucked her teeth, and Edie looked away, out over the empty French countryside. The last vestiges of night were a purple smear along the western horizon, and the sky was empty. The wind had died down now. The air was cold, but the morning sun warmed one side of her body. Her suitcase and the case containing her wireless set were beside her, and the pile of damp logs prodded her back at each jolt of the cart. 'So,' Justine continued, pushing her black curls off her forehead, 'let's try again. What's your name?'

'Yvette Colbert,' Edie replied.

'And you're from?'

'Paris.'

'And what do you do, Yvette?'

'I'm a piano teacher. I visit children in their homes, and teach them piano.'

'Do you live with your family?'

'No, they live in Honfleur, by the sea.'

'How long have you lived in Paris, Mademoiselle Colbert?'

'Since—' Edie paused.

'No, no, no. You must not just stop like that! You should

know these things. I thought you were supposed to be fully prepared. They said they'd send a trained operative, not an English schoolgirl.' Justine sucked her teeth again.

Edie turned her face away from Justine so that it caught the morning sunshine fully. She closed her eyes; the warmth made her feel sleepy. It had been such a long night. Justine elbowed her and Edie opened her eyes and turned back to her new colleague, seeing her clearly now the sun was up: small eyes with irises so dark they looked almost black; arched brows above a pinched nose. There was a vertical line in the middle of her forehead, etched deep into her pale brow. She reminded Edie a little of her old staff sergeant, back with the ATS. Edie wondered what Justine's real name was. She'd probably never find out.

'*Alors*, let's have a smoke and then try again,' said Justine, pulling out a leather tobacco pouch and beginning to roll a cigarette. When she'd finished she offered it to Edie.

Edie shook her head. 'No thank you – I don't.' Even the smell of smoke still reminded her of that night last summer; it made her feel sick to her stomach.

Justine gave an exaggerated shrug. 'So, you don't smoke, you don't know your background properly, and as for your hair – you'll never pass for French looking like that. We'll have to keep you hidden away in the Paris catacombs like some English ghost,' she said, puffing rapidly at the cigarette and flicking ash away onto the road that twisted below their dangling legs.

'What's wrong with my hair?' said Edie.

'No Frenchwoman would have a style like that.' Justine blew smoke through pursed lips. Edie wondered what on earth was wrong with it. She'd been under the impression that she was here to outwit the Nazis, to send coded messages so that the French Resistance could communicate with the SOE headquarters in London, to help win the war – not to discuss the latest fashion in coiffure with this prickly Frenchwoman. Would the Gestapo or the *Sicherheitsdienst* really be that perceptive, notice a slip in grammar, and an unfashionable hairstyle? Edie wondered. 'It's not just the SD, you know, there are plenty of informers. It's impossible to tell whose side people are on,' said Justine, reading Edie's mind, and flicking her cigarette butt into the road.

The horse's harness jangled and the gently trudging hooves gave way to clopping as the cart rumbled onto cobblestones. They must be nearly there now, Edie thought. They passed an orchard – ranks of arthritic apple trees, naked in the sunlight – and a water pump, then an empty barn, and then the white-plastered houses. The cart tipped as they began to go uphill into the town, and the pile of logs shifted, pushing into them. Edie held on to the handle of the case containing her wireless set. She heard the farmer grunt something at the horse and the swish of reins.

'So, Yvette, how long have you lived in Paris?' said Justine.

'Since early 1940, before the Occupation,' Edie replied, without hesitation this time.

'Good, now take this.' Justine undid the scarf that she was wearing. It had brightly coloured triangles on a cream background. 'Take it, take it!' she said, holding it out. So Edie took it; it was silk, she noticed, slippery between her fingertips. 'Tie it round your hair,' Justine ordered. Edie tried, but the jolting cart made her frozen fingertips slither. 'Here, let me,' Justine said, and smoothed Edie's hair off her face before tying the scarf neatly under her chin. 'Better, but not French yet. Don't you have any make-up? You're supposed to be a Parisian, you know.'

'No,' Edie began, then remembered Miss Atkins' gift. 'Yes, yes, I have powder.' She took the compact from her pocket and clicked it open. She squinted into the little round mirror, dabbing the powder over her nose and cheeks.

'You can have my lipstick,' said Justine, handing her a little gilt cylinder. Inside was the stub of a lipstick, cyclamen-pink. 'Use your finger; it will last longer.' Edie smudged pink over her lips with her forefinger, blotting her lips together to work the colour in and checking her reflection in the silver circle. She remembered the last time she'd worn lipstick, that night last summer. She remembered the GI with his mouth hard and wet on hers, and his thick, forcing hands. I'm not that woman any more, she thought. I've left her behind. She passed the lipstick back to Justine, but Justine told her to keep it. Edie thanked her and put it into her pocket, where it clinked against the powder compact.

The cart rumbled on. A fat woman in black was opening the shutters of a *boulangerie*. She could hear the sound of a baby crying from an upstairs window. Pigeons fluttered away from the cartwheels. 'Nearly there,' said Justine. A man was putting tables and chairs up outside a café in the town square. Smoke drifted from chimney pots. 'Do you have your ID papers and travel pass to hand?' said Justine. Edie nodded, as the cart stopped outside the station. 'Just remember not to make eye contact. And let me take this one,' Justine said, jumping down from the back of the cart and taking the case containing the wireless transmitter. Edie dropped down beside her, and heaved her suitcase off. It was dusty and scratched from the log pile. 'Let's go,' said Justine, pulling her towards the station entrance. The old farmer nodded at them as they thanked him for the lift. The horse snorted steam from its nostrils and stamped, impatient to move off.

There was a white wooden fence around the station, and a gateway to the platform. The slanting sunshine made long shadows on the station buildings, chunks of charcoal breaking up the glare. Because of this, Edie didn't see the man until they were at the entrance, a dark figure in the shadows: his grey uniform, black boots, weapon slung diagonally across his chest. Forgetting Justine's advice, she looked straight into his eyes: slate-coloured, bored-looking, glancing over her. He held out a large hand. *'Ausweis, bitte, Fräulein.'*

Vera

'I'm not signing the damn thing,' Vera said, sweeping past the ledger on Margaret's desk. She saw Margaret biting her lip. Buckmaster was trying to instigate some kind of log of who was in the office and when, making them sign in and out with the secretary. It was ridiculous, treating them like factory workers, clocking on. Vera tutted. She couldn't bear registers of any kind. It reminded her of that day in 1937, not long after she'd arrived in London.

'Sign here,' the bald man had said, pointing with a chubby forefinger at the space on the ledger. The queue snaked away behind her, a stream of huddled men and women in their drab, damp overcoats, all the way out of the doors of the police station, and right along the pavement towards Covent Garden. Vera had been stuck with them for hours, shuffling forward a few inches along the pavement every couple of minutes, feeling the drizzle seep through her good fox fur and trickle down her neck. She stared down at the line on the page, wedged underneath the mass of other signatures and details. The woman behind her was coughing loudly into her hand; she wasn't even carrying a handkerchief. Vera shuddered, thinking of TB.

'My dear boy,' Vera began, realising this was her last chance. 'Is this strictly necessary? Perhaps there has been some kind of mistake?' She opened her palm to reveal the wad of notes it contained – probably more than one month's salary for this officious little man. He cleared his throat and she watched as his hand moved towards hers, and for a moment she thought she was home and dry. But instead of sliding the money into his own hand, he curled his pudgy fingers round hers, so the money remained in her palm. Then he gave it a little tap with his fingertips, as if shooing away a fly. Vera felt herself flush. She pushed her fist deep into her coat pocket, underneath her handkerchief, and let go of the roll of notes.

'Sign here, please, madam,' he repeated, poking the thick cream paper again. So Vera picked up the pen and signed, filling in her date of birth and nationality. The man waved her on to the next desk, where she had to do the same thing again, in triplicate, but this time with details of her address, marital status and next of kin. After that a beaky woman with spectacles told her she was free to leave. Vera walked towards the big wooden doors, furious that an accident of birth had brought her to this. She thought of her elder brothers: lucky Ralph to have been born in Colonial South Africa and so be British by birth; lucky Guy to have been in England earlier in the decade, when naturalisation was as easy to obtain as a driving licence; unlucky Vera, the only one in her family not to belong. She pushed open the door and was in the street. The coughing woman followed her out into the blanket of London drizzle.

Vera crossed the road to distance herself from the unhealthy woman, and the disconsolate trudge of the other 'aliens' disgorging from Bow Street Police Station. She didn't even want to be near them. There was a ladder leaning up the side of the cobbler's opposite. A man in a flat cap swung a bucket and rag, cleaning the upstairs windows, whistling to himself. He looked down as she approached and broke off. 'Ruddy foreigners,' he called, looking down at her as she walked along the pavement towards him. She looked straight ahead, ignoring the horrid little oik. But his ladder spanned the pavement. To go round it would mean walking through the gutter: oily puddles and fag butts. 'Get back to where you came from,' he yelled, cockney vowels twanging. Vera continued along the pavement; she wasn't going to walk in the gutter, and to hell with the silly English superstition about walking under ladders. She heard the man clearing his throat. She felt a soft plop on the crown of her hat as she walked underneath his ladder. She walked swiftly on, pretending not to notice or care that she had just been spat on by a window cleaner.

Vera turned down a side street, and ducked into a shop doorway. She took off her hat. It was her best one: fine black felt dressed with a pheasant's tail. The gobbet of spit lay just off-centre on the crown: grey-green and shiny. Vera pursed her lips and took her handkerchief from her pocket. She rubbed the spit off, scrunching it up into the centre of the hankie. But there was still a faint stain, like a snail trail, where it had been. Vile man. How dare he?

Vera put the hat back on and walked out into the moisture-soaked London air, still so angry that she'd lost her sense of direction. Which way was it to the Tube? She scanned the buildings looking for a street sign. As she did so, a shop front caught her eye. Like a spilled jewellery case, it was a tangle of colours: garnet, ruby, emerald and sapphire. Frocks, hats and scarves jostled for space. Vera stepped up off the kerb and pushed the glass door. A bell tinkled as she entered. It was darker inside the shop, but still vibrated with colour. Vera's fingertips brushed the sleeve of a Schiaparelli-pink dress on a mannequin beside her: real silk – good quality, too. A bell-shaped woman who looked as if she'd been sewn into her royal-blue suit appeared from behind a counter. 'Is madam looking for anything in particular?' the woman said, her lip-sticked mouth shiny as a toffee apple. Yes, Vera replied, feeling the nest of notes in her coat pocket, yes she was, as a matter of fact.

Vera chose half a dozen silk scarves for herself in shades of amber, garnet and aquamarine – the colours of sunset on the Mediterranean. Then she tried on a red pillbox hat with a veil. 'Very Mayfair, madam,' the shop assistant said as Vera admired herself in the long cheval mirror. The shop assistant packed everything carefully in pale pink tissue paper tied with ribbons. Vera said she'd like to keep the new hat on, and when the assistant asked whether she would like her old hat in a hatbox, Vera said no, and told her just to throw it away, ignoring the upward jink of the saleslady's eyebrows at the waste of it.

The weather had started to lift a little by the time Vera left the shop, so she decided to walk with her armfuls of bags to Oxford Street, and take the bus home instead. When the bus arrived, it was exactly the same shade as the hat she'd just bought. Sitting on the top deck, looking down at the milling London crowds, she couldn't help but think how well she looked in her new hat, how she fitted right in. *Very Mayfair, madam*, indeed.

'As you wish, Miss Atkins,' said Margaret, drawing her back to the present. Vera liked Margaret; she was one of the best secretaries in F-Section. She had a way about her, something fierce behind those dark brown eyes – what a pity she didn't speak French, Vera thought, she'd be useful in the field. Vera remembered the agent she'd just sent off: Edith Lightwater – Yvette, they'd codenamed her. Her French accent was impeccable, but her grammar sometimes let her down. Thankfully, as a wireless transmitter, she wouldn't have to do an awful lot of local liaison, so she ought to be all right, Vera thought. Her heels clicked on the lino as she made her way towards her desk. She checked her watch. Ten to ten – still time to get a coffee before the meeting.

'Would you be a darling and make me a cuppa?' she turned to call to Margaret, who looked up from her typewriter and said of course, Miss Atkins, and got up to go through to the kitchen. Vera's phone was ringing. Neither Buckmaster nor Tonkin were at their desks, she noticed. She could see her in-tray. She'd cleared it last night; before setting off for the airport, but it was full again already, a manila file stamped *Urgent* toppling on top. And what was that on her blotter? It looked like an aerogramme.

'Nice of you to join us, Miss Atkins,' came a voice from behind her. She turned. Buckmaster's frame filled the office doorway. 'We're in Meeting Room 5.' He raised his eyebrows.

Vera checked her watch again. 'Oh, but, Buckie, it's not even ten,' she said.

'I sent a memo that the briefing would start early today,' he said, 'which you would have read if you'd been here on time.' He was smiling, his voice teasing, but still it rankled.

'I was at the airfield last night,' Vera said. 'But of course you knew that.' She could see Margaret hovering in the doorway behind him. 'Could you take my coffee through to Meeting Room 5, please, Margaret,' Vera said. Buckmaster cleared his throat and turned to walk up the corridor, and Vera followed him, leaving behind the overflowing in-tray, ringing phone, and unopened aerogramme on her desk.

The meeting took an age. Buckmaster was determined that the new Paris cell should set up sabotage of a prototype weapons development facility on the outskirts of the city at the earliest possible opportunity. He'd got wind that bomber command wanted to do a raid, but didn't have the necessary aerial intelligence; he was keen that SOE tackle it themselves. 'It will save lives and ammunition, as well as casting our organisation in a good light with those higher up the food chain,' he said, looking round and tapping the bowl of his pipe against the table in emphasis. To her left, Tonkin was nodding vigorously in agreement; head bobbing like an old Christmas tree bauble on a flimsy branch.

Outside, it had begun to rain. Vera lit another cigarette and sipped on her now-tepid coffee. The men were talking finance and logistics. She made a mental note of the salient points for future reference, but chose not to add anything to the discussion at that point – let them thrash it out amongst themselves for a bit, she thought, glancing at the window and watching the raindrops cling pointlessly to the glass as they fell. She was thinking of the full in-tray, Raoul's wife on her way right now to the next-of-kin debriefing at the Northumberland Hotel.

And thinking of that very young WT operative she'd just waved off, upon whose wireless-transmission skills this whole sabotage plan would rest. When the men had all stopped talking she took a final sip of coffee, and stubbed out her cigarette. 'It's far too soon,' she said. 'The WT was only dropped last night. She needs time to find her feet. Perhaps we should let bomber command take this one, and make other plans? There's plenty of lower-level disruption the cell can coordinate in the meantime.'

Buckmaster shot her a look. She held his gaze. Tonkin shuffled papers nervously. After a pause, Buckmaster cleared his throat and smiled. 'Given Miss Atkins' reservations, perhaps we should all double-check the details one last time, and re-convene before going firm on this one. Tomorrow at ten, then. Gentlemen, Miss Atkins.' He nodded at them, and there was a scraping of chairs as they all got up to leave. But as she pushed her chair back underneath the table, Buckmaster lightly touched her sleeve. 'A word, Miss Atkins?' She nodded, waiting for the others to disperse.

'That wasn't terribly loyal, was it, Vee?' he said, filling his pipe bowl with Old Holborn from the tin. Vera slowly lowered her lids and opened them again, saying nothing. If he thought she was just going to roll over and— 'Sometimes I wonder whose side you're bloody well on,' he said, pushing the tobacco down with the ball of his thumb.

'I'm not going to dignify that with a response, Buckie,' she said. 'Now, if you've quite finished, I have plenty to be getting on with.'

'Yes, yes, off you go then.' Buckmaster made a shooing motion with the stem of his pipe. 'Oh and, Vera, will you please start signing the register in the mornings?'

'I'll sign in when you have a signing out book, too,' she said. She might not make it to work by nine, but she rarely left before nine at night, either, six days a week – not to mention the nights when she did airfield runs – and he damn well knew it. He said nothing, merely frowned and lit his pipe. She left, not looking back, knowing that he'd be rolling his eyes and muttering 'Bloody woman' under his breath. She'd buy him a whisky some time. He'd come round. She checked her watch. But right now there was work to be done.

She went back to her desk and sat down. And there, on her blotter, was the aerogramme she'd glimpsed earlier. Her work address was written in that looping generous script she knew so well. A letter from Dick, at last. For the first time that day, she allowed herself a smile.

Edie

'Shh,' said Justine. Edie looked up. The guard was just coming into the carriage to check their tickets. The old woman opposite was still snoring; grey bun unravelling against the seat back, mouth agape to show blackly missing teeth. Empty fields of chalky earth pulled past the dusty train windows. Justine handed Edie the sock she was knitting: a triangle of needles dangling scratchy brown wool. Justine took out the train tickets and Edie tried, feebly, to carry on where she'd left off. She heard the guard getting closer, exchanging words with other passengers, and she tried to concentrate on the knitting. 'Remember what I told you,' said Justine.

Justine had told her not to make eye contact with anyone in uniform. And then what had Edie done? Looked directly at the official who'd checked their pass at the station. And not only looked at him, smiled at him, too – a nervous smile: she hadn't been able to help herself. 'Why did you have to draw attention to yourself like that?' Justine hissed as they got into the carriage. Justine had ordered her to keep her eyes down and her mouth shut whenever they came into contact with anyone official in future.

The guard was almost at their seats now. Edie drew a breath, feeling as if her heart was actually beating out loud, audible to the others in the carriage, as she fumbled ineffectually with the wool. The sleeping woman awoke with a grunt. Justine handed over the tickets. The guard clipped them, muttering '*Merci*', and was gone.

Edie let her breath out slowly. She saw the old woman staring at her fingers as they tangled the rough wool. Justine, looking down, tutted and took the half-made sock from her, saying something in rapid French slang to the old woman, who laughed. Edie flushed and looked back out of the window. The sunshine had gone now, replaced with a sky as pale and watery as spilt milk.

The train pulled into a station, stuttering to a halt, and the woman heaved herself up, bidding them both '*Au revoir*' as she picked her basket off the seat next to her and lumbered off, leaving behind the scent of unwashed clothes.

As the train pulled away Edie saw the woman stood on the platform, like a black stone thrown into a puddle, surrounded by ripples of people and luggage and crates of potatoes. The seat opposite them was empty now, and Edie judged it safe to talk. 'What did you say to her, just now?' she asked Justine, who was knitting the sock again.

'Nothing,' Justine replied. 'Just that you are a little simpleton.'

'Thanks,' said Edie.

'Well, what do you expect? You can't even knit properly – I had to explain it somehow.'

'Teach me, then,' Edie said. 'Teach me how to knit like a Frenchwoman.'

Justine sighed and said she'd try, demonstrating with exaggerated slowness how to loop and pull the wool around the stubby little needles. She seemed surprised when Edie got the hang of it almost immediately. *'Pas mal,'* she said.

Edie smiled. 'I have pianist's fingers. They are good at remembering patterns.'

'Well, maybe you're not a little simpleton. You can carry on a while longer – you need the practice.'

Justine rolled herself a cigarette, poking the ends of tobacco with a matchstick before lighting it.

'Who are the socks for?' Edie said, as Justine spouted a plume of smoke into the space where the old woman had been.

'My husband,' Justine replied. 'He's in Germany. Got rounded up for the labour camps. But I can post them.'

'How long has he been gone?' Edie looped the wool and shoved the pointed needle through, again and again.

Justine shrugged. 'A few weeks. They took him on Christmas Day.'

'That must be terrible.'

'No, being shot as a traitor is terrible. Being forced to dig your own grave and being shot on the edge, to save them the trouble of even having to toss your body in, that's terrible. This is bearable.' Her forced exhalation of smoke sounded like a sigh. 'And you? Are you married?'

'No,' said Edie, pulling and twisting the brown thread. She had thought, once, that she'd end up with Kenneth, her girlhood crush. She remembered a picnic, sheltering under a tree, as the clouds blotted out the sun, the rain slamming suddenly down, and in the distance the deep bellow of summer thunder. She remembered his arm slung over her shivering shoulders. But she'd never see him again, would she? And there couldn't be anyone else, not after the American, the terminated pregnancy, the shame of it all. There would never be anyone else.

'Engaged? Boyfriend?'

'No.'

'Good. No man. No children. Less chance of clouded judgement.'

'And you? Do you have children?' said Edie, remembering the face of a little girl peeping out of the window of the farmhouse as they'd prepared to leave. But Justine didn't answer, just frowned, sucked her teeth and looked away out of the train window.

Eventually the scenery outside the carriage began to change from fields to backyards, factories and sidings: the guts of Paris spewing into the countryside. The skies were overcast now, grey as the buildings shunting past. The train slowed to a chug.

'Here.' Justine held out a hand for the knitting and Edie passed it over. 'So, when we arrive, where are you going?' said Justine, putting the bundle of wool and needles into her coat pocket. Edie replied that they were meeting the others in a room above the Lucas Carton in place de la Madeleine. 'And who are you going to ask for when you get there?'

'Marie.'

'Is it Marie Leclerc you're looking for?'

'No, I'm looking for Marie Laval, with the blonde hair.'

'Good,' said Justine, satisfied that Edie had at least remembered the coded dialogue that would let the others know whose side she was on.

'We won't get separated though, will we?' said Edie, looking out at how the train cut through the stacked-up Paris buildings like an iron through crumpled sheets. Justine didn't reply, and just then the train ground to a hissing halt. Justine ushered Edie out of her seat, passing her the suitcase containing just her clothes, and keeping, as before, the one containing the wireless set for herself. The suitcase thudded awkwardly against Edie's leg as she got out of the train.

The Gare du Nord was as vast and cavernous as she remembered, a chaos of echoing noise and jostling crowds. She walked along the platform remembering the last time she was here, in 1939 with Mummy. She remembered buying two dresses in Molyneux: dove-grey and sky-blue, which Mummy said were 'decent' for entertaining. She'd felt quite grown-up, even though she was still just a schoolgirl, really. They'd helped Grand-maman Redette pack up a trunk, and her grandmother had cried when she gave her apartment key to the concierge, a wet rivulet forging its way through the rouge on her wrinkled cheek. Mummy had said not to worry, it was only a holiday really and she'd probably be back by Christmas, and they all took the boat back to England together. But in September war came, just as Pop said it would. When the first lot of evacuees came to stay, Grand-maman Redette went to live with a family friend in Bath, saying she didn't like children, never had.

Edie strode on, Justine behind her, as if it were 1939 again, and she was off to do some shopping and visit her grandmother, just as she'd done dozens of times before. It was almost a shock to see the guards waiting at the end of the platform, checking everyone's papers were in order. But she'd learnt her lesson from earlier, and didn't make the mistake of looking at them. This time she kept her head down, scurrying on with the throng, as if she were in a bad mood and a dreadful hurry. She flashed her papers as she passed, not even glancing up, noticing only thick fingers and a green-grey edge of cuff as her documents were momentarily scrutinised.

She let herself be carried on with the crowd, through the bottleneck at the barrier, and onto the concourse, not stopping until she was at the archway where the terminus opened out onto the street. She turned back to Justine, to ask whether they'd be better off taking the Métro in this weather – it had just started to spot with rain – but Justine wasn't there. Edie's eyes scanned the crowd for the dark-haired woman in the brown coat. But there were so many people, so many shades of brown and beige, shifting like a pile of autumn leaves in the wind. She couldn't see her colleague anywhere.

Justine had disappeared completely – and with her the precious wireless transmitter.

Vera

Vera checked her watch. If Mrs Neasbrook didn't arrive soon then the hotel would need their anteroom back and it would be awkward, very awkward indeed. She resisted the urge to pace across the tiled atrium and instead stayed where she was, arm resting on the reception desk, watching the hotel doorway.

Netty, he'd called her, Vera recalled. My darling Netty, Raoul Neasbrook said – but he'd never shown her a photograph, so she didn't know what to expect. They had a little boy; she knew that, a two-year-old. Would Netty bring Raoul's child with her? Vera hoped not. The hotel doors flapped like a gossip's mouth, but the only people coming and going appeared to be elderly gentlemen in dark suits. Vera checked her watch again – perhaps Netty's train was delayed.

At last the doors inched apart to reveal a woman in a stone-coloured coat and matching shoes. She looked nervously about, faltering just inside the entrance. Vera walked towards her. 'Mrs Neasbrook?' The woman jumped as if she'd been ambushed and nodded. 'How d'you do. Miss Atkins,' Vera said, reaching forward to shake her hand. Mrs Neasbrook pulled her slim hand away almost as soon as their palms had touched, as if she wanted as little contact with Vera as possible. 'Follow me,' Vera said, leading the way through the wooden doors and into the dining room, where waiters in floor-length aprons were laying cutlery on the white-shrouded tables. At the far end of the dining room was a discreet door, almost camouflaged, painted cream to match the walls. Vera ushered Mrs Neasbrook ahead of her, into the little room with the dark red carpet. There was a single wooden table surrounded by six high-backed chairs. A cream porcelain ashtray, empty of ash, lay in the centre of the table, next to the smooth cream teapot, milk jug, and pair of matching cups and saucers. There was no window, but mirrors interspersed the fanlights on the walls. Vera glimpsed herself from all angles, reflected into a greenish infinity.

'Do take a seat,' Vera said, and they both sat down. Vera offered a cigarette, which Mrs Neasbrook declined, but she agreed to a cup of tea. Vera was mother, adding the milk, pouring tea into the cup. She poured one for herself as well, even though she knew she wouldn't drink it. The crockery chinked. Steam rose. 'I expect you can guess why I asked you to come,' Vera said.

Mrs Neasbrook's face was almost as colourless as the teacup she sipped from, except for a brown-sugar sprinkle of freckles across her snub nose. Her hair, the colour of damp sand, was cut in a short bob, waving up, away from the pearl necklace that wound round her thin neck. When she spoke she sounded as if she were plucking pearls off her necklace and tossing them, one at a time, into her cup of tea. 'You're going to tell me that my husband is missing?' she said. Her clear little voice flicked up at the end of the sentence, with just the edge of hope. Vera shook her head. 'Dead?' said Mrs Neasbrook.

'I'm so very sorry,' Vera said.

'But, Miss Atkins, I had a postcard from him, just this morning.' Mrs Neasbrook's face pulled in awkward directions as she spoke.

How Vera hated this part of her job. She patted the poor woman on her forearm. 'It was very sudden.'

'But how?'

'He died for his country, doing the job he loved. I hope you can take some small comfort from that.'

'How did he die?'

'I'm afraid I'm not at liberty to say.'

'He said he was doing translation work for the Inter Services Research Bureau. He sent postcards every week. I got one just this morning, Miss Atkins.'

Oh Lord, Vera thought, remembering the stack of agents' pre-written missives she'd posted. How had she let one of Raoul's get in with the bundle? 'My dear girl, he's been in

Occupied France. The nature of the work means we can't tell the families, and I shouldn't even say he was in France, but I hope it will help you understand why I can't possibly tell you any more about your husband's work or the manner of his death. Please don't ask for more information as refusal often offends.' Vera couldn't look at Raoul's widow's face, didn't want to see the anger and disbelief she knew would be there.

Raoul's widow moved her arm so that Vera was no longer touching her. Her teacup chattered against her saucer. 'Where is he now?' she said.

Vera had prepared for this question. 'The body was buried in situ. However, I give you my word that after the war every effort will be made to repatriate your husband's remains.'

'After the war?' The woman spoke as if it were an impossibility.

'Yes. After the war we shall locate and return his body,' said Vera.

'And now?' Raoul's widow said, her voice rising.

'I beg your pardon,' Vera said, not understanding what she meant.

'What should I do now?' said Raoul's widow, her voice sounding quite loud in the small room.

'I have some paperwork to go through with you,' Vera said. 'I will of course ensure that you get your full entitlement, in terms of war pension, and so forth.' She took out papers and a pen, pointing out the places on the forms where Mrs Neasbrook should sign and fill in her details. As Raoul's widow wrote, pen scratching on the paper, Vera checked her watch, very discreetly, under the edge of the table. She could smell the scent of boiled vegetables and roast potatoes drifting in from the kitchens. At least the woman wasn't crying. That would come later, Vera supposed, upon breaking the news to their boy that Daddy wasn't coming home, or rereading one of Raoul's postcards.

Vera couldn't tell Mrs Neasbrook that she had plenty more of Raoul's cards in her office, stamped and ready to send. She couldn't tell her that her husband's work colleagues had no idea his name was Raoul, and that he had a wife and child back home in Apsley. She couldn't tell her that Raoul was known as Gilbert and that he had been the best wireless operator they had in Paris. She couldn't tell her that Raoul had been shot in the back and his body tossed into a makeshift grave with another member's of the French Resistance network. She couldn't tell her that Raoul had already been replaced, by a young woman codenamed Yvette Colbert.

'I'm so sorry for your loss,' Vera said as the woman carefully spelled out her name again and again on the form with her curly handwriting: *Mrs Raoul Neasbrook*. 'He was a brave man, and very well regarded by all who worked with him.'

Mrs Neasbrook's tea was left half-drunk in her cup. Vera asked if she'd like a top-up, or a cigarette, but the woman said she should go: the babysitter had a shift in the factory later, so she needed to catch an early train. Vera saw her out of the anteroom and through the dining room, which was just beginning to fill with lunchtime clientele. In the hotel lobby Vera said she'd make sure the paperwork was sorted out as swiftly as practicable, and that if Mrs Neasbrook had any questions in the meantime she shouldn't hesitate to get in contact. Vera gave her a card, with *Inter Services Research Bureau, Norgeby House, Baker Street, London* printed in blue ink, and her name and telephone number underneath.

Raoul's widow took the card and shook Vera's hand, as

before. 'Thank you for your help, Miss Atkins,' she said, before turning to leave. It felt like a slap in the face.

Edie

Edie blinked in the sudden daylight as she emerged from the Métro at place de la Madeleine. The Lucas Carton restaurant was round here somewhere. She didn't dare ask anyone. She sipped on the cold air. It felt as if there was a boulder resting on her chest. Buck up, she told herself. Stop fannying about and get on with it. But get on with what? She still couldn't see the restaurant, and in any case, how could she show up, without Justine, without the wireless set?

L'Église de la Madeleine dominated the centre of the square, as big as three aircraft hangars, surrounded by the black cars that spun endlessly round, as if trying to cocoon it in petrol fumes. Edie felt the rush of air from the Métro, the nudge of other passengers coming up the stairs behind her, fanning out onto the wide pavement in front, spatters of black, grey and brown, and the occasional startling amber or red, an exclamation of colour. Reflexively she looked down at her wrist to check the time. But she didn't have a watch. Miss Atkins had taken it from her before the flight.

'Let's have a good look at you,' Miss Atkins had said, gesturing for her to turn and show off her clothes like a marionette. Edie did a slow spin, taking in, as she did so, the vast hangar – an aircraft cathedral. The planes were on the runway, outside, engines revving intermittently with the flight checks. There were voices outside, too, and clunks and thuds as equipment was loaded. Inside, the hangar was almost empty, save for the fire buckets, and a spare plane wheel leant against a far wall. The curved rooftop was far above. Edie turned full circle to face again Miss Atkins' trestle table, with a lit lamp and Edie's open suitcase on top.

They'd had a good dinner earlier: shoulder of lamb, followed by lemon pudding, with port and Stilton to follow. But Edie hadn't felt hungry. There were other agents waiting for their turn to drop – some she knew from training – and boxes and boxes of rations and equipment stacked like sandbags beneath every window. Outside, the moon was full and the skies clear. Someone had decided it was her turn tonight, and Miss Atkins had arrived from London, resplendent in violet satin, earrings like twinkling stars. She'd insisted they toast Edie, everyone raising their glasses, pouring the ruby liquid down their throats, everyone joking – a sort of desperate, nervous cheer that seemed the norm in the SOE. Edie hadn't touched her port.

After dinner they'd come out here to the hangar, Miss Atkins still in full-length evening gown, cigarette waving like a wand in its ivory holder. And Edie had half expected to be told to be home by midnight, or risk her transport turning into a pumpkin, so like a fairy godmother did Miss Atkins appear. 'You look a little too clean,' she said as Edie turned back towards her, 'but I expect the journey will put paid to that. Now, tell me the drill if – heaven forfend – the SD boys get hold of you.'

'Don't tell them anything. Stick to your cover story. If they get your code, hold on to the security check as long as you can. Even an encoded message sent without the security check is evidence of agent compromise.'

'Good,' Miss Atkins said. 'Good girl. Now take off your jacket so I can check your pockets one last time.'

Edie slipped off her jacket and passed it over. As she did so, her watch face glinted in the light from the lamp.

'Ah, your watch. Let me see. We need to make sure it's set to Continental time.' Edie held out her wrist for Miss Atkins to see. 'Oh dear, it's a Harwood,' she said. 'You can't get these in France. I'm afraid it will have to go.' Edie undid the clasp and held it out. 'I would lend you mine, but—' Miss Atkins stroked the mother-of-pearl face of her own wristwatch with a forefinger. 'I'm afraid I can't possibly part with it. You'll just have to make do. Buy yourself a French make with some of the funds at your earliest opportunity, dear girl.'

Edie knew she couldn't wait here any longer; it would start to look suspicious. She picked up her suitcase and began to walk across the road, dodging and sidestepping the cars that honked and swerved. Reaching the other side she paused to give her hand a rest, switching the case to her left. She looked up at the church: a huge marble box encased in columns. There was no spire. Above the triangular roof the sky was low and grey, pregnant with rain. Occasional drops touched the back of her hand, her cheek. Soon it would start to tip it down. It's only Paris, she told herself, the Paris that you've visited dozens of times before. Except that it wasn't. The black cars that scurried like insects around the church contained uniformed Germans. The Métro passengers had sat quietly in the train, not making eye contact, pinched faces slashed with frowns as they stared into the middle distance.

Edie picked up her case and walked towards the church. At the bottom of the steps an old woman in a long black coat and a frayed brown headscarf sat, rocking, a battered tin cup in her shaking hands. The few coins it contained chinked like sleigh bells. She looked up at Edie, muttering something incomprehensible and raising the cup towards her. Edie felt in her pocket for her purse. Miss Atkins had mentioned that it was a devil to get hold of small denominations for the agents. All Edie had was notes; she peeled one off from the roll and placed it in the cup. It wasn't really hers to give: it was government money, for the war effort, for the French Resistance, but she argued that, if Winston were here, he'd give something to this poor unfortunate woman. And she made a silent promise to pay it back from her own funds, once she got back home again (*if*, the unbidden voice nagged in her head – *don't you mean if you ever get home?*). The woman's face broke into a grin; mouth a jagged cavern of missing teeth. Edie smiled back and continued up the steps and through the huge bronze doors.

The traffic sounds were muted and for a while everything was a blur as her eyes adjusted to the semi-dark. She waited just inside the doorway, looking at Jesus carved in marble far away beyond the altar, hearing the echoing seashell sound of the cavernous church. A line of votive candles erased the gloom on one wall. Huge columns were like giant versions of the German grenades they'd been shown in training – the ones with the handles – lined up as if the whole place were ready to blow. Edie walked down the aisle of the empty church, hearing her footfalls on the marble slabs as she went. She slipped into a pew, clasped her hands, shut her eyes and lowered her head.

Her only French contact had disappeared at the Gare du Nord, along with the wireless transmission set. Edie felt the hem of her jacket for the two pebble-sized bumps. Yes, they were still there. At least if the SD had Justine and the wireless set, they didn't have the crystals – they couldn't use the set on her frequency without the crystals, that was something. She'd been due to meet the rest of the cell in a room above the Lucas Carton restaurant at midday, with Justine. What to do? Could it be a trap?

There was the sound of steps on the marble floor. Edie looked up, convinced that someone had followed her, that she'd feel the heavy hand of a uniformed guard on her shoulder – but no, it was just two women, smartly dressed in suits and coloured turbans, holding hands and walking slowly up the aisle towards the sculpture of Christ. One of them began to cry. Edie thought she ought to look as if she belonged. 'Our father,' she muttered, clutching her fingers together in prayer as they passed. The woman who wasn't crying turned to look at her, face ghost-pale in the heavy air. Horrified, Edie realised she'd spoken the words in English. She quickly made the sign of the cross and got up from her seat. Silly girl: speaking English, carrying a suitcase. She may as well have been waving a Union Jack. Ready or not, it was time to leave.

As she emerged from the church the rain hit her with full force: fat gobbets of icy sleet. The beggar woman had disappeared. A black Citroën sped through a puddle, splashing her legs. She decided to walk purposefully ahead, and hope. The restaurant must be here somewhere. In any case, where else could she go? She walked away from the Métro stop. The church wall was a grey blankness to one side, like a denial. More cars shot past. She could hear some of them coming to a halt around the corner. Perhaps it was the sound of skidding brakes that meant she didn't hear the footsteps striding ever closer behind her, catching her up.

There it was: she saw it as she rounded the corner, a mass of cars parked outside, clustered like flies. There were two bay trees by the doorway, and ironwork knotted over the opaque glass frontage, like fishnet stockings. Beside the restaurant there was an archway to a passage, a black shout in the milk-and-honey stonework. Justine had said to meet in a room above the restaurant, but the entrance was up some steps to the side, down the passage. If it's safe to go inside, there'll be flowers in the window, she'd said. Edie looked up, past the silver lettering saying *Lucas Carton*, past the curled metal balconettes on the first floor, up – up. In a high window she could see what looked like lilies, and behind them, the faint, pale blot of a waiting face. She took a breath in and switched her suitcase to her other hand, ready to go. But just then she felt a touch on her shoulder; there was a masculine voice in her ear: *'Wohin gehen Sie, Fräulein?'*

Vera

Vera hailed a number 36 outside the hotel, and stepped on. As the bus pulled away, someone swung in behind her. She glanced back and saw a long dark coat. There was a slice of blue lining as the bus's slipstream caught the hem and flicked it upwards. Vera nudged past the ticket collector and up the spiral stairway, hanging on to the metal rail as the bus swerved and jolted through the potholes. Don't look back, she told herself, but as she reached the top step she couldn't help herself, half turning to glance downstairs. The man with the blue-lined coat was hanging on to the pole near the open back end of the bus. He had on a brown fedora, and a carried a folded newspaper. She couldn't see his face. She climbed the stairs to the top deck.

Vera swayed down the aisle, staggering to keep her footing, and fell into an empty seat. The old woman next to her was crocheting a toddler-sized pullover in French-navy wool. 'Turned out nice,' she said, nodding out of the grimy bus window to where a portion of sky appeared above the roof-tops. Vera thought of the blue flash of the man's coat lining. She thought of the face half hidden under the fedora.

'It'll be icy later,' Vera replied. She looked round the top deck of the bus, clotted with the grey-brown huddle of weary passengers, and her gaze returned to rest on the half-made blue jumper in the woman's lap. Vera thought of Raoul's boy, who must have been about the size to fit into it. She shuddered, turned away, looking outside, past the woman's profile, to where the bus passed the British Museum, that big box of stolen booty. As they passed the dark stone walls she caught her reflection in the glass bus window: pale face, eyes dark shadows – and then the bus moved on and she was gone.

At each stop she watched the passengers getting off, but she didn't notice the man with the fedora get off. He must still be downstairs, she thought. She checked her watch. The bus swung round the corner and the woman next to her shuffled and asked if she wouldn't mind terribly letting her pass, as this was her stop. Outside a film poster emblazoned a hoarding: *Air Force* – a blue rectangle on a red background, with images of square-jawed US airmen looking heroically into the middle distance. And Vera remembered the letter from her own airman, Dick, still unopened in her pocket. She hadn't wanted to open it at work, couldn't bear any sense of her private life slipping into the office. But here was a chance: there were still a few minutes before they'd reach Portman Square.

She pulled it out of her bag and slipped a long fingernail

underneath the gummed edge so it ripped open. It had been so long since she'd heard from Dick; one couldn't help but worry. But here it was at last, and amongst all the scrambled curls of his extravagant script, one phrase leapt out straight away: *Of course we should get married, darling, what a wonderful idea!*

She read the rest of the letter in a rush, in her excitement not really taking in the details as the bus jolted along and the chipped and blackened shop fronts edged past her periphery. He ended the letter, as usual: *My sweet, my darling, my love.* Vera refolded it carefully and put it back in her handbag, inside the zipped pocket, separated from Mrs Neasbrook's forms.

She had to get off at Portman Square because Buckmaster wanted her to meet some new agent he was taking on: Henry someone or other – Buckie could be so vague. But that wasn't important. Dick had agreed to get married; that was all that mattered. She rang the bell to request a stop. She was still smiling as she walked down to the lower deck. She noticed the man who'd followed her on board. He was sitting down now, with an open newspaper, his whole upper half obscured by newsprint. His coat fell open, the blue silk lining paren-thesising black trousers and black shoes. And Vera could feel her smile slip as she hurried past him and stepped off the lower deck onto the pavement opposite Orchard Court.

Gerhardt

'Adieu,' Gerhardt said – that was 'goodbye' in French, wasn't it? But the door had already closed. He would have been offended, back home, if he'd carried a girl's heavy suitcase across a busy road and up a steep stairwell and received not

one word of thanks. '*Merci*' was French for 'thank you' – he knew that one, at least. He walked back down the stone steps towards the side alley. She was probably just scared though, he thought, pausing under the archway to brush any stray dust off the sleeves of his jacket. She'd looked scared: white-faced and wide-eyed, wet hair grazing a cheek when he put a hand on her shoulder and asked where she was going. But his mother had taught him manners; you should always offer to carry a lady's bag, she said. (Mother – how pleased she'd been when she'd found out about the Count arranging his interview with the security services in Paris: *Thank God you're not going to Russia* – her face looking twisted and old.) He noticed a stray strand of hair on his sleeve – long and auburn – it must be that girl's. He plucked it off and let the damp breeze take it. Red hair: he wasn't sure if he found redheads attractive or not. Lisel's hair was blonde, pale as moonlight. But if he got this job with the *Sicherheitsdienst* he might not see Lisel again for months. He tugged his jacket down at the hem on both sides to straighten it out. The Count had said he needed to make sure he was as smart as possible. Apparently Boemelburg was a stickler for such things.

Gerhardt slipped out through the arch; the rain hit him full in the face. He broke into a run, cursing himself for leaving his coat at the hotel. As he pushed through the glass doors and into the Lucas Carton, he could see the Count sitting at a table in the window. The waiter offered to take his sodden jacket, but an interview in his shirtsleeves would be unthinkable. The Count was drumming his fingers on the table top, glowering out into the rain. He turned as Gerhardt approached.

'You're late,' he hissed as the waiter pulled out Gerhardt's chair for him.

'I'm sorry, Father, I—' Gerhardt began, but noticing the look on the Count's face quickly corrected himself. 'Uncle. I'm sorry, Uncle. I didn't realise the time.' He must never call him Father in public: that was the rule – had always been the rule – how idiotic to have forgotten it now, here.

'You didn't realise the time – what about the watch I gave you for your eighteenth birthday last year?'

'It got smashed in the air raid; remember, the night Franz—'

The Count waved an impatient hand. 'Even so, you should have made an effort to be early, on a day like today.'

'I was helping a girl with her suitcase,' Gerhardt said.

'A girl! Stupid, reckless, boy – we can't have you messing this up for the sake of a girl. Never mind. Luckily for you, Boemelburg is late, too. Ah, here he comes.' The Count's granite features cracked into a smile.

Gerhardt looked round. A rotund man in a thick coat and fedora had just entered the restaurant. Two waiters and the maître d' were already at his side, removing outer garments and proffering clean white handkerchiefs for him to wipe the raindrops from his puffy cheeks. Gerhardt stood, chair scraping, ready to be introduced to the man who could determine his future.

Edie

'You must be insane!' said Justine.

Before Edie could respond, the man with the blond hair butted in. 'A self-respecting Frenchwoman would never let a German carry her luggage, never. And you led him right to our door.' He ran his fingers through his hair, so it rose in tousled spikes. Edie opened her mouth to reply, but he continued, turning to Justine. 'What were they thinking about, sending her? She doesn't have the common sense she was born with!'

Justine nodded vigorously. 'If only Gilbert were here. If only he hadn't gone and got himself—'

'Please, let's not talk about Gilbert.'

'I'm sorry, but there is no kind of – how do you say – control in London. I mean, how was she recruited? Was she just plucked off the end of a line of schoolgirls waiting at a bus stop?' Justine snorted.

They continued talking about her as if she weren't there, jabbing fingers in her direction, gabbling in their outraged Parisian slang about her obvious shortcomings. Next to her was the suitcase containing her belongings that the very helpful young German had offered to carry for her, when she'd paused to look at the window above the restaurant. He couldn't speak French, but he'd made it clear: here was a young woman struggling with a heavy case in the driving rain, and here was a fit young man, offering help. Refusal often offends, she remembered Miss Atkins saying once, as she handed over the suitcase, handle slippery with rainwater. He'd smiled and nodded, taking it from her, lifting it high to show his strength. And she'd thought, glimpsing him sideways through the rain, that he didn't look an awful lot like she'd imagined an enemy soldier. He'd carried her case across the street, through the archway, and up the stone steps to the room, giving a short bow before leaving her as the door opened.

Justine and the other man were still talking about the parlous state of things in London, about how the agent handlers were a clueless set of morons, about how they had no chance against the invaders at this rate. Edie stood, listening, dripping puddles of rainwater onto the bare floorboards. She wiped the drops off her face, and with it came a creamy smear of Miss Atkins' powder. She looked round the room. It was small and square, with just one window facing onto the place de la Madeleine, the one she'd seen from the street. She noticed now that the lilies she'd seen weren't real. They were made of some kind of fabric, and shoved into a cracked jam jar on the sill. Justine and the other man were standing near the window, half blocking the light. There was a small, bare fireplace. In place of a fire, a camping stove hissed, a metal coffee pot on top just coming up to boil. There was a clock on the mantelshelf; tarnished metal cherubs slumped up against the face. From downstairs she could just hear the clatter and murmur of the busy restaurant, smell the faint scent of braised meat wafting up. In the middle of the room was a round café-style table with chairs, and on top of the table her other suitcase, containing the wireless set. There was an armchair in the far corner of the room, shrouded in darkness. As she looked, a shadow detached itself from the gloom, standing up from the chair and walking towards her. Her first impression was of height and length: a very tall man, with a long nose and dark hair slicked off a high forehead. As he came closer, she noticed he was limping, and there were dark half-moons underneath his eyes.

'Personally, I think it rather clever that you got old Boche to porter for you. And if anyone watching thought you were a collaborator, then frankly all to the good, eh?' he said in English, holding out a hand. 'How d'you do, Felix.' Edie shook his large hand. The handshake was firm and swift, his palm dry as paper. 'But perhaps Justine has a point, and we should continue our conversation elsewhere. Shall we?' He indicated with his head towards the doorway. He wanted to take her back outside, to the rain and the German soldiers, just when she'd finally thought she'd reached safety.

'The wireless,' she began, looking at the suitcase on the table.

'Justine and Claude will take it. You'll be staying at hers tonight, just for your first night. Didn't she mention it?' he said. No, Edie thought, blinking raindrops from her lashes, she didn't mention it. She didn't mention anything. And then she realised of course not: the less she knew, the safer she was; scooting off with the wireless transmitter, telling her nothing of the cell's plans was Justine's way of protecting her. 'And your suitcase too,' Felix continued. 'Claude has transport – one of the benefits of being part of a family that runs a garage is having access to spare vehicles, and better still, ones that belong to someone else, eh?' He chuckled and Claude joined in, looking across the room at him as if he were a god.

Felix embraced Justine in the French way before they left, and Edie did the same, kissing her on both cheeks, smelling the lemon-tobacco scent of her, feeling her bony fingers briefly grip her upper arm. As Edie pulled away from Justine she saw Felix kiss Claude on both cheeks, and then – surprisingly – on the mouth. 'Be careful now, *chéri*,' Felix said to Claude. 'After you've delivered the luggage, go straight to Café Colisee. I'll be there before curfew.'

'Promise?' said Claude, flushing, 'because last time you said that—'

Felix placed a finger over his lips to silence him. 'Shh, I promise,' he said.

Edie didn't know where to look. She glanced at Justine, who frowned hard, and turned away. When Edie said goodbye to Claude he merely grazed her cheek with his own, and she felt the soft prickle of his stubble as he released her, eager for her to leave.

Felix opened the door and followed her down the stone stairwell and into the alley – the same alley where just a few minutes earlier a young German had walked beside her, close enough to touch. Her breathing was shallow, and she was finding it hard to concentrate on what Felix was saying, but he seemed as relaxed as if he were on his way to a good lunch at his London club. 'Don't mind those two,' he said as they walked out of the side alley and into place de la Madeleine. 'Justine can be a funny old stick at first and Claude is jealous of just about anyone I spend time with, the darling boy.' Edie smiled as if she understood perfectly, even though she felt as though the whole world was disintegrating around her.

The rain was still sluicing down as they turned left past the Lucas Carton frontage. Edie wondered briefly about the young German who'd carried her case so gallantly. She'd been too petrified to even make eye contact with him, but she'd noticed his hands as he'd taken her case – how his fingernails were bitten right down to the quick, just like her own. Had he been on his way to lunch? she wondered. Was he in there now, drinking beer and eating sausages, or whatever it was they served in the Paris restaurants now the Germans were here? She followed Felix's lanky silhouette as he loped awkwardly onto Boulevard Malesherbes.

Gerhardt

The formalities over, the three men sat down. The restaurant was packed with officers and expensive-looking women.

Glancing round, Gerhardt noticed red lipstick and sculpted hairstyles, and he thought of Lisel's shiny plaits and freckled nose and wondered if he'd ever take her anywhere like this. Outside the rain pelted down. Boemelburg told the waiter they'd all have his usual, without even glancing down at the menu. Gerhardt was relieved. He didn't mind what he ate, just so long as he didn't have to choose from the curly writing on the vast cream card; it was all in French, and he understood barely a word. The Count scanned the wine list and ordered a burgundy.

Gerhardt sat still and upright, hands resting on the damp wool of his trousers. He looked out of the window at the grey-black mess of the wintry cityscape. The colours reminded him of the carriage full of newly conscripted soldiers he'd travelled down on the train with. The Count had come separately, from Berlin in his car.

'. . . isn't that right, young man?' The deep voice interrupted his reverie. Gerhardt started.

'Yes, Uncle,' he replied, not knowing what he'd acknowledged.

Boemelburg motioned to the wine waiter, waving a pudgy index finger. 'You never mentioned you had a nephew when we worked together in Moscow,' he said, watching the waiter pouring the burgundy into the glass. 'Such a handsome young lad, too,' he said, swilling the wine around before lifting the glass to his lips. He sipped it, made an 'Mmm' sound, and nodded his satisfaction to the waiter, before looking directly at Gerhardt. Boemelburg's eyes were small and very dark, almost lost in the folds of his face. Gerhardt thought of raisins in *Stollen* dough at Christmas time.

'I don't generally like to mix work with my personal life,' the Count replied as the waiter filled their glasses with the blood-red liquid. 'However, I thought a boy with his talents would be more use to you here than being sent to the Russian front,' he continued, picking up his glass.

'I don't think anything would be much use on the Russian front, the way things seem to be going. Not so?' Boemelburg replied, taking a large swig of wine.

'Yes indeed,' the Count said, and the two older men shook their heads and pressed their lips into hard expressions.

Gerhardt tried a sip of the burgundy. He didn't really like the taste of it, preferring the golden foam-topped beer they had back home. He stared down at where a drop of wine had landed on the thick white tablecloth, spreading like ink on blotting paper, turning it sunset-pink. The rain still pattered, making him think of the percussive arrangement to Holst's Second Suite in F. Boemelburg and the Count had started talking about him, almost as if he weren't there: discussing his school grades, his membership of Hitler Youth, his facility for music and singing, and, of course, his fluency in English. Staring out at the rain-swept place, Gerhardt wondered how his father – 'uncle' – knew quite so much about him. It wasn't as if he spent any time with them. He was always away with the diplomatic service. He'd been in Romania when Gerhardt was little – they used to holiday there in the summers – and after that he was Ambassador in Moscow, until the Russian conflict began, when he'd been pulled back to some desk-job in Berlin. They saw him occasionally, in passing between the castle he was renovating in the East – Burg Falkenburg – and Berlin. At least he'd made it to Franz's funeral, Gerhardt thought, watching raindrops running like tears down the steamed glass.

'. . . aren't you, Gerhardt?' The Count's voice was suddenly loud.

'I'm sorry, Uncle, could you repeat that?' Gerhardt said.

He'd stopped listening, thinking that either Boemelburg owed his father a favour, or the other way round. He couldn't be sure which, except that it was clear he was merely a commodity in this horse-trading.

'I was just telling Boemelburg about your English language skills,' the Count said. 'The boy's mother was born in Cape Town,' he added, turning to Boemelburg.

'British Colonial?' Boemelburg raised an eyebrow and tilted his head on its axis.

'By birth only,' the Count replied.

Boemelburg nodded. 'A demonstration would be nice. Can he speak some now? Can you speak some English, young man?' Boemelburg again fixed Gerhardt with his curranty eyes.

Gerhardt shifted uncomfortably in his seat. 'A demonstration?'

'Yes, yes,' Boemelburg said as the waiter arrived with steaming dishes of horseradish soup. 'Say something in English for me. I'd like to hear your accent.'

The waiter began to slide the soup in front of them. The Count was looking at him through narrowed eyes. Mother would be so upset if he messed up this interview, Gerhardt thought. She hadn't wanted him to join the Army – she'd already lost one son to the British. When the Count had suggested there might be something for him with the SD in Paris, she had almost smiled, for the first time in months.

Aware of the expectant silence, Gerhardt clawed back through memories: something in English to showcase to the SD boss: what, though? There was a poem that Mother taught him, he remembered, clearing his throat. Yes, that would do it: *'If you can keep your head when all about you are losing theirs and blaming it on you,'* he began.

'Stand up, boy,' the Count said. Gerhardt stood. It felt as if the whole room were watching him.

'*I-if you can t-trust*,' he started again. Nerves made him stammer sometimes. He could hear the Count's quiet tut of impatience. He mustn't get this wrong. He looked out of the window, into the watery-grey outside, took a deep breath, and continued: '*If you can trust yourself when all men doubt you . . .*'

Through the falling rain he could see the spot on the square where he'd caught up with that girl and taken her case, and where she'd looked up with her drenched, anxious face. '*If you can dream, and not make dreams your master . . .*' he continued, ignoring the crowded restaurant behind him, and concentrating on the English words as they formed and fell from his lips. '*If you can make one heap of all your winnings and risk it on one turn of pitch-and-toss . . .*' He wondered now where she'd been going with that heavy case. Visiting relatives? Moving house? Perhaps she was new to the city as well. Perhaps she was as nervous and awkward as he was. '*If you can walk with crowds and keep your virtue . . .*' A shadow was passing the plate glass in front of him: the figure of a man, walking quickly through the storm, limping. And, just behind him, the slight scurrying figure of a young woman, a rope of red hair escaping from underneath her patterned headscarf. It was *her*, the girl from earlier on. But where was her case now? And who was the man with her? '*If you can fill the unforgiving minute with sixty seconds' worth of distance run . . .*' The two figures sped past like ghosts and were gone. '*Yours is the earth and everything that's in it, and – which is more – you'll be a man, my son!*'

Gerhardt heard applause. He turned. Boemelburg was clapping him. 'Kipling, very good,' he said. As Gerhardt sat down he noticed the Count hiding a proud smile behind his unfurled napkin, and he knew he'd done well enough. The job of English interpreter for the *Sicherheitsdienst* in Paris was his for the taking.

Vera

'And this is the chap I was telling you about.' Buckmaster ushered her across the room to where a stocky man stood with one arm draped casually across the mantelshelf. The man was talking to Tonkin, who was leaning against the corner of a table. Winter-bare tree branches traced chaotic shapes beyond the large windows, as if Portman Square had been crumpled like paper and then hastily smoothed out again. The man was saying something to Tonkin, and Tonkin laughed, throwing back his head and hooting. The man looked over at Buckmaster and Vera, approaching across the patterned carpet. Vera's stomach rumbled. She cleared her throat to cover up the sound. 'Dericourt, this is Miss Vera Atkins. Miss Atkins, Monsieur Henri Dericourt,' said Buckmaster.

Dericourt held out a hand. 'A pleasure, Miss Atkins,' he said, holding her hand for a moment more than was necessary and looking into her eyes. His face was on a level with hers, but he had the muscular build of a weight lifter, and his bulk made him appear larger than he was. She ungripped her hand. '*Mr* Dericourt,' she said.

Vera took out her cigarettes and offered them round. Buckmaster and Tonkin – both pipe smokers – refused, but this new Frenchman, Dericourt, took one. His fingers were stubby and capable-looking, like a mechanic's. He rolled the cigarette between thumb and forefinger as if testing it for something. Vera found herself thinking that his hands were nothing like Dick's, which were long and tapered, then wondered why on earth she should be making that comparison. She kept a photograph of Dick in her cigarette case, but his face was hidden behind the ranks of cigarettes. She snapped the case shut and put it back in her handbag. Dericourt pulled out a silver Zippo lighter, with something engraved on the side. Vera had to lean a little towards him to catch the flame in his cupped palm. 'Sobranie,' Dericourt said, regarding the gold-banded cigarette filter as he inhaled. 'You have good judgement, Miss Atkins.'

Vera was thinking of Dick – darling Dick – finally coming round to the idea of marriage: yes, she had good judgement. 'Indeed,' Vera replied, giving Dericourt a nod.

'Dericourt's just come from France,' Buckmaster said, insinuating himself between them.

'Really?' said Vera, regarding Dericourt through a veil of smoke. He held her gaze steadily. His open face and thickly lashed button eyes gave nothing away.

'He says he's happy to fly Lysander flights into Occupied France for us,' Buckmaster continued, 'so we wouldn't have to rely entirely on parachute drops. Lysanders are small enough to land on improvised strips in farmers' fields. Imagine that!'

'Imagine,' said Vera, not turning to Buckmaster, still looking at Dericourt. He had the tanned, weather-beaten face of a peasant, but those workman's fingers were clean and manicured. 'So, you're a pilot.' Vera spoke French to Dericourt. 'Why us and not the RAF?' She was thinking about Dick: tall, fair and handsome in his smoky-blue RAF uniform that day. Could it be three years ago already?

Dericourt shrugged, and smiled. 'Someone told me you

were an interesting outfit,' he replied in French, but using the English word 'outfit'. 'I used to be a trick pilot, before I joined the French Air Force. I thought you could use my talents,' he added. And Vera remembered how it used to be: a man with a plane above a country fair, pulling corkscrews, screeching low over the crowd, showing off. Dick had taken her up in his plane once. And the countryside had danced and spun below them. She'd felt drunk with excitement afterwards.

'Thrills and spills,' she said, exhaling. 'What happened?'

'The war,' Dericourt said, with another one of those shrugs.

'And what brought you over here?' Vera said. She inhaled again, watching his response. A flicker crossed his wide brow before he answered, like a cat's paw ripple on a still pond.

'You could say that the wind blew me over to the right side,' he answered, opening his lips in a wide smile to reveal evenly spaced white teeth.

'He's willing to start immediately,' Buckmaster interrupted in English.

'Yes, good show!' said Tonkin, tapping his hand on the desk as if in applause. Vera had almost forgotten he was there.

'I've been thinking how it will really progress things for F-Section,' Buckmaster continued, chewing on his unlit pipe stem. His eyes were shining and a smile hovered about his mouth. 'It will give us so much more flexibility. We'll be able to bring agents back in from the field, if necessary. And we can even allow them to send letters to and from home.'

'Isn't that a security risk?' Vera said.

'How so? The agent gives a letter to our man Dericourt here, and he flies it back to us. We can post it from London. It will help morale no end for the chaps to have some contact with their wives,' Buckmaster said.

Vera thought of Mrs Neasbrook. Would it have helped her to have had more contact with Raoul? Or would it have made the whole sorry business even messier than it already was? She looked beyond Buckmaster to where Dericourt stood, listening to something Tonkin was saying. He pushed his wavy gold-brown hair away from his wide brow as he listened. His jacket was tight over his shoulders. Vera could almost see the shape of the muscles beneath the fabric. His nose was short and straight, like a boy's. Vera wondered if there was a Madame Dericourt, and how she featured in all this. Buckmaster was still singing Dericourt's praises, but Vera only half listened. She watched as Dericourt made a remark to Tonkin, and the two men chuckled like chums over a shared joke.

'I feel like this calls for a celebration,' Buckmaster said in a loud voice. 'Shall we see if someone can't find something a little stronger than tea, for a change?' He was looking at Vera, as if it were her job to conjure up some refreshments. She stubbed her cigarette out in the ashtray on the mantelshelf, contemplating how to tell Buckmaster in the nicest possible way that she wasn't employed as a waitress. As she did so, Dericourt turned to put out his own cigarette. Their fingers almost touched.

Then Dericourt spoke, in English. 'Do you like champagne, Miss Atkins?'

Vera nodded, thinking of a particular bottle of Bollinger she'd shared with Dick at the 400 Club that night – oh, that night. 'I've not had champagne since 1940,' she said, and as she said it her eyes flicked up, catching Dericourt's. Something flashed between them, and for a moment it was as if they were alone in the room. She forced her eyes away.

'Then perhaps it's time you did,' said Dericourt, reaching down to open the leather rucksack at his feet and pulling out a bottle of Brut. Buckmaster and Tonkin showed delighted surprise at the prospect of French champagne, wondering how on earth Dericourt had managed to bring it with him. There was discussion of his journey, the perilous trip across to the 'right side'. 'But one must always carry the essentials, no matter the danger. As I'm sure someone like Miss Atkins can appreciate,' he finished, placing the bottle on the table next to Tonkin.

Vera was dispatched to find champagne glasses, but of course they had to make do with beakers. Dericourt popped the cork and filled them. '*Vive la France!*' he said as they chinked tumblers against each other. It wasn't chilled, but nonetheless it was a good vintage, Vera thought, sipping slowly and letting the men's talk wash over her. Dick had agreed to marriage – champagne seemed more than appropriate. Darling Dick.

When Tonkin took Dericourt off to fill in paperwork, Buckmaster drained the last of his champagne and lit his pipe. 'Seems like that Dericourt chap has a bit of a soft spot for you, Vee,' said Buckmaster through clenched teeth as he sucked to ignite the tobacco in the bowl. Vera wondered if Buckie was jealous. She responded with a question: 'How exactly did Dericourt come our way?' she said.

'Got out through Marseille, with help from the Yanks. Took his chance when he could.'

'But why now?'

'Why not now? Does it matter? Think of his utility: a French-speaking trick pilot able to fly into Occupied France for us. It's a godsend, Vera, that's what it is.' Buckmaster exhaled a gush of smoke.

Vera considered Dericourt – the godsend – with his charm, firm handshakes and earnest eyes. 'And the vetting process?' she said.

'No time for that. We had to snaffle him up before someone else did. Besides, he's completely solid. Tonkin knew him in Paris before the war; he's totally onside. One can tell, don't you think?'

Vera remembered what Dick had said about the barn-storming pilots he'd known: charlatans and gypsies, every last one, he'd said; they'll take you for a ride in more ways than one. 'My dear boy, are you quite certain he's one of us?' she said. 'Don't you think he seems just a little hail-fellow-well-met?'

'Oh Vee, there's no time to be suspicious. There's a war to be won,' Buckmaster said, a frown beginning to form between his thick brows.

Let him think that, Vera thought, sipping her champagne. Perhaps it was better for Buckmaster not to dwell too deeply on people's motives or their backgrounds. She checked her watch. It was time she was elsewhere.

Edie

It was dark and smoky in the little bar, but they had seats near the fire, and Felix had ordered them something to eat and drink. It was a relief to be out of the rain. They appeared to be the only customers. 'Not quite on a par with the Savoy, but all things considered, it's not bad. The barman – Paul – is one of ours. This is one of the places we use as a letterbox, along with Claude's garage and various other locations, which Justine can fill you in on. We can't be seen coming to you – better that we don't even know your location, in fact – so you'll need to scoot around between letterboxes. But try not to be too sociable; don't draw attention to yourself. In retrospect Gilbert was out and about too much. Poor Gilbert.' Felix sighed and shook his head. 'But of course you know all this,' he said, stretching out long, tapered fingers towards the flames. 'They cover it all in training these days, don't they – I'm afraid I'm teaching my grandmother to suck eggs.'

'Not at all,' Edie said, finally feeling the warmth beginning to seep back into her as the fire leapt and crackled.

'We have to be safe,' Felix said. 'Odd as it seems, even though you'll be my mouthpiece to London, this could be both the first and last time we have a chance to talk to each other!' He laughed as he said it, and Edie joined in, rubbing her hands and feeling the heat from the fire on her face. The barman brought the tray of ersatz coffee and croque-monsieurs, and she listened to Felix as he filled her in on the details of the Resistance cell, and the ambitious plans he was formulating to scupper a depot he'd learned about on the outskirts of the city, where the Germans were developing a new type of weapon.

Afterwards, when the rain had cleared, Felix walked her across the river towards the area where Justine lived, where she'd be spending the night ('Just to help you get on your feet, eh? And after that we'll be throwing you to the wolves and you'll have to find your own way, I'm afraid') and they paused, halfway across, where there was no one about, to look at the Seine snaking glassily below, green-grey – the same colour as a German soldier's uniform, Edie thought. 'I much prefer Paris to London,' Felix said. 'Don't you? Even the Seine is freer than the stuffy old Thames. And the people; the French are just so much more, more accepting than the Brits, even with the bloody Boche in charge.'

'Your heart is here,' said Edie, looking at the sinuous water, thinking of the way Felix kissed Claude goodbye.

'Yes it is,' Felix said. 'And yours? Where's your heart, Mademoiselle Yvette Colbert? In London or Paris?'

'Me? I don't have a heart,' she said. 'It wasn't on Miss Atkins' list of requisite items to pack.'

At this, he guffawed. 'Quite right too. Miss Atkins, eh? What a woman! What was your first impression of the old girl?' Edie thought back to that afternoon at the end of last summer, when it all began.

'It's not for ninnies, you know,' the woman said, placing a business card in front of her on the table and sitting down opposite in the window seat. The late-afternoon sunshine streamed in through the window, putting the woman in shadow – all you noticed were her wine-red lips. Edie looked down at the card:

Miss Vera Atkins
Inter Services Research Bureau
Norgeby House, Baker Street, London

'I beg your pardon?' Edie said, looking up at the woman – this 'Miss Atkins', whoever she was.

'I said, it's not for ninnies,' Miss Atkins repeated, signalling to the waitress. A tired-looking woman in a cap and apron wandered over and said, 'Yes, madam.' There were dark circles of sweat under the armpits of her 'nippy' uniform. 'Two

coffees, if you would, please,' said Miss Atkins, and the waitress nodded and was gone. 'I don't know what they mentioned
in your interview at the War Box, but this line of work is
not everyone's—' Miss Atkins paused, just for a second, as if
having to search for the correct phrase. 'Cup of tea,' she finished. She took out a silver cigarette case and flipped it open,
offering it to Edie, who shook her head. 'As you wish,' Miss
Atkins said, clicking a lighter and taking her first inhalation
before speaking again. *'Vous parlez français?'*

'Yes, but . . .'

'Good. Then I should like you to respond to my questions
in the language in which they are framed. Is that clear?' Edie
nodded. 'Ah, here's the coffee.' The waitress had sidled back
with a clinking tray, and Miss Atkins directed her where to
put the cups, the sugar bowl and the milk jug, before saying
thank you, that will be all, and shooing her away.

'Miss Atkins,' Edie began, but she was hushed by the other
woman holding up a hand, like a schoolmistress requesting
silence.

'Coffee first, chat later,' she said, exhaling. Her cigarette
smoke curled up through the thick yellow sunshine. Edie
poured milk into her cup and took a sip of the coffee. It tasted
like watery liquorice. She looked over at the woman opposite
her. She wore a dull red frock with a bow at the neck. The
colour didn't quite match her lipstick. Why wasn't she in
uniform? Edie wondered. The interview in the airless room
at the War Office had been with a Colonel Potter, who'd
been very friendly, but rather vague, and after making her
wait for a very long time whilst he 'popped out to make a
call', returned and placed a card in her palm with an address
and a time and told her to 'meet one of the officers from the

team' in order to 'establish further communication'. If she were being interviewed for a military role, why wasn't the recruiting officer in uniform, and why was the interview taking place in the top-floor café in Lyons Corner House, Oxford Street?

She saw Miss Atkins tap her cigarette in the ashtray, take a sip of coffee, and make a face. 'I forgot they serve Camp coffee here,' she said. 'Atrocious.' She pushed the cup away and took another drag of her cigarette. Edie could hear the clatter of the crockery as the waitress cleared a nearby table, and a dull rumble from the traffic, four floors below, but other than that it was rather quiet, the café almost empty: too late for tea, too early for supper, she supposed. Apart from the four WAAFs at the table by the door, and the man in the corner camouflaged behind a copy of *The Times* and a cloud of pipe smoke, they were almost alone.

The mixture of smoke and steam from the urn and the sunshine-choked air was beginning to make Edie's head ache. She got up and went to the window, pushing up the heavy sash, glimpsing the tops of buses and scurrying figures on the street below. 'You don't mind?' said Edie.

'Not at all, dear girl,' said Miss Atkins. 'But, as the coffee is clearly too awful to drink, let's get to business.' Manicured hands flourished, urging her to sit back down. As Edie sat, she saw Miss Atkins' red lips part, ready to speak.

'*Qu'est-ce que vous voulez de moi?*' Edie said, getting in first. She saw a frown flick across the older woman's brow. She's annoyed that I'm taking the initiative, asking questions, choosing the language, Edie thought. But the frown was quickly replaced by a fleeting smile – what very white teeth Miss Atkins had between that burgundy slash of lipstick.

'What do I want with you? You have certain – how should one say? – qualities, which might be of great use for the war effort. But I must tell you at once that this post comes under the heading of "dangerous work", you understand.' Miss Atkins replied in French, and waited for Edie's nod of assent before continuing. 'I see that you're in the ATS – a gunner girl, no less – good. So, I can't imagine you'll be what the English like to call a "wet fish", no?' She took a long drag on her cigarette and regarded Edie across the café table.

'But I don't understand what I'm being asked to do,' Edie said, looking into Miss Atkins' eyes, soot-dark in the sharp shadow. She saw the woman's head turn slightly in the direction of the man at the corner table, parting her lips to let the smoke out. Then she smiled again, showing those beautiful teeth.

'I say, it's such a glorious day,' she said loudly, reverting to English. 'Shall we settle up here and do a little window shopping?' She ground out her cigarette into the ashtray. Edie nodded and the two women stood up. Miss Atkins checked the menu card and left a pile of coins on the table. 'Rather a generous tip for quite possibly the worst cup of coffee I've ever had, but no matter,' she said, ushering Edie ahead of her out of the café door.

They walked together along Oxford Street towards Marble Arch, squinting into the lowering sunshine, pausing occasionally to glance unseeingly at the paltry displays of merchandise behind the criss-cross of protective tape on the plate-glass windows – there hadn't been an air raid for weeks now, but the shopkeepers weren't taking any chances. They spoke rapidly, alternating between French and English, but to passers-by they would just have looked like two ordinary women, shopping and gossiping on their way home from work.

At Marble Arch they took their leave, shaking hands cordially, before Miss Atkins crossed the street to catch her bus. It was only once the bus had gone that Edie looked down at the compact pile of paperwork that Miss Atkins had pressed into her palm: a travel warrant, and a slip of paper with an address and time, written in tiny, pinprick writing.

'I didn't know what to make of her at first,' Edie said, answering Felix at last.

'Nobody does. And yet somehow we all end up doing her bidding, don't we? What a woman!' he repeated. They walked on together in companionable silence, and despite the speeding black cars full of uniformed men, and the street signs that had been translated from French to German, she felt safe beside him. She felt as if she could breathe again as he led her into a maze of small streets.

Felix stopped at a small junction, pointing the way to Justine's apartment. 'Best if I leave you here. Best for us not to be seen together at her apartment,' he said, leaning in to kiss her on both cheeks. He held her firmly before letting her go, swathing her in his long arms, and crushing her in tight to his thick woollen coat. 'It was a pleasure to meet you, Mademoiselle. Miss Atkins chose well when she chose you. I know you won't let us down.' And then he was gone, disappearing into the grey shadows of the alleyways.

Miss Atkins chose well, he'd said. Edie thought about this as she pressed the metal button next to the card that had *Justine Hescoet* printed on it in fading ink. She waited, shifting from foot to foot. There was no response from inside, so she pressed the button again. A shutter banged open from an upstairs window. *Miss Atkins chose well when she chose you*: Edie repeated the phrase to herself like a mantra as she listened to the dull thud of footsteps coming down the stairwell and waited for the click of the front-door latch.

Vera

'Not going out tonight?' Mother said, arching her brow. 'That man of yours – whoever he is – seems to think he can just pick you up and drop you off whenever he chooses!'

'Leave it, Mother,' Vera said. The blackout blind had come undone, and she could see the waning sliver of silver moon quivering like a distant barrage balloon in the darkening skies. She fastened the blind tight, and the moon disappeared. No airport run today – the Met predicted storms over the Channel tonight, although it should be clear again tomorrow.

Vera thought it strange that her mother had never connected her 'gadding about with all and sundry' with the phases of the moon. And – having signed the Official Secrets Act – Vera would never be able to breathe a word of the truth of it. Perhaps Mother would go to her grave believing she had had tempestuous love affairs throughout the war, Vera thought, turning on the standard lamp. Or was it time to finally tell her about Flying Officer Richard Ketton-Cremer?

Vera flicked the radio on. It began to hum and hiss its way to full volume. She thought about Dick's letter, waiting on her bedside table. No, she wouldn't tell Mother about the engagement until it was all settled, until she had a ring on her finger and an announcement in the papers, Vera thought, remembering the mess she'd got herself into with Friedrich, all those years ago. *No, don't think about Friedrich – it was a different life then, you were a different woman.*

'I think I'll turn in. I'm very tired, actually,' Vera said.

'I shouldn't wonder,' her mother said through pursed lips, squinting down at her embroidery.

'Goodnight, Mother,' Vera called over her shoulder, crossing the hallway to her bedroom. She hastened to bed, pulling off her clothes in the darkness, but she took out her best nightdress – the eau-de-Nil satin with the cream lace trim – and sighed as it slid over her thighs, remembering the last time she'd worn it: *My sweet, my darling, my love.*

The bed sheets were clean-cold, but her bare toes flinched from the boiling heat of the rubber hot-water bottle at the far end. She switched on her bedside light and pushed herself up against the padded headboard, plucking Dick's letter from the bedside table. *My darling Vee, Your letters are like oxygen . . .* He wrote about the airfield, his pals, especially 'Gu' who'd been at school with him. He wrote about daily life, the food, and the heat. He wrote about the sunset on the sea, and how it reminded him of when they'd first met, on that long-ago cruise. He referred to the suggestion in her last letter that perhaps, as they'd been together so long now – even if so much of the time apart – they should think about making their partnership a permanent arrangement: *Of course we should get married, darling, what a wonderful idea!*

That was what had made her heart contract on the bus earlier on, made her smile despite Mrs Neasbrook, Buckmaster, and that awful Dericourt chap. Smile even when she'd noticed the man on the bus, and sensed him looking at her over the top of his newspaper as she'd got off.

But now, rereading the letter, she focused in on the following paragraph:

I don't care who you are or where you come from, darling, but I do have a duty to the family, don't you see? I can only marry a British girl. That's just how it is, I'm sorry to say. So as soon as you can get the naturalisation nonsense sorted out, I will break the news to Mother and you two can start making plans.

'But won't marrying you make me British?' she whispered, frowning at the looping script. 'Isn't that enough?'

It's a question of being seen to be on the right side, my darling. I'm sure you can come up with something. After all if, as you say, both your brothers and your mother are British, and you're now working for the government – well, how hard can it be?

How hard can it be, Vera thought, remembering all that had happened in 1937: the last-minute flit to the overcrowded ship, the interminable questions when they finally docked in Portsmouth, changing her surname, her hairstyle, her accent, changing everything about herself. And holding her breath every time the conversation turned to foreigners or Jews. How hard can it be? Darling Dick, he had no idea at all.

I'm sure this blasted war can't go on indefinitely. When it's over, we can be together, and populate Felbrigg Hall with lots of little Dicks and Veras! Do you think you'll enjoy being Lady of the Manor, darling? Or will I need to schedule in illicit breaks to the Big Smoke so we can revisit our dubious past?

He joked about it, Vera thought. But he didn't really know about her past. Nobody did, not even her own mother, who honestly thought Vera had been working as a translator for Pallas Oil back in 1936, and who still believed that Friedrich had been just another family friend.

She let the aerogramme fall onto the counterpane, and touched her cool watch-face with an index finger. Dear darling, she'd thought that marrying him would be the answer to all her problems. To be married to Dick, to be British, that was all.

That was all – but asking for it felt like asking for the moon. Vera pushed herself down under the covers and shut her eyes, aching for sleep, as the tissue-thin aerogramme drifted to the floor.

Edie

Edie opened her eyes, suddenly wide awake. The moonlight cast silvery stripes across her blanket as it seeped in through the shuttered window. The floorboards were hard beneath her shoulders and spine. In the distance someone was playing the trumpet, and that was what had woken her, a lone trumpeter bellowing out the Marseillaise into the empty Paris night.

Next to her, on the thin cot, Justine was snoring gently. The moonlight lit up the edge of the metal bedstead. What was that wedged between the mattress and the springs? A slip of paper. Edie shifted up onto her elbow and tugged at it. It was a photograph. She held it into the moonlight for a closer look. There was Justine, smiling, a man at her shoulder, and in her arms a bundle of lace, a small face peeping out. Justine had a baby? Edie remembered the farmhouse they'd stopped at after she'd parachuted in the night before, and the little girl's face at the upstairs window. Justine had said to be quiet because the farmer's granddaughter was asleep. But she hadn't been asleep. Edie had seen her, waved goodbye as the cart rattled off in the pre-dawn.

She thought about her old ATS friend, Bea, and the fierce way she'd held her own little girl at the station that day. She thought about how she'd felt secretly jealous, because Bea loved the girl's father, had a future with him. Whereas Edie's own pregnancy had been the result of violence, and she'd let them kill her unborn baby. No, she mustn't think about it. She was Yvette Colbert now, had been ever since the biting cold morning when Miss Atkins had pulled her out of her wireless transmission exam.

'I'm afraid I'm going to have to call a halt to all this,' Miss Atkins said, beckoning Edie to follow her along the corridor.

Why, Edie wondered? She'd been doing well on the course – her instructors expected her to fly through the test – and she'd already completed the paramilitary course in the Highlands and parachute practice. There was just the final exercise to go and she'd be fully prepared for work in France.

Miss Atkins paused by the door opposite the stairwell, knocked, checked there was no reply, pushed the door open and ushered Edie inside. It was a bathroom: tiled floor, onyx bathtub, and loo – all sleekly black, apart from the gold fittings and the semi-circular mirror above the sink. A frosted window, high up, let in a shaft of pale light.

'It's the only room available at present.' Miss Atkins closed the door behind them and clicked the key in the lock. She flicked on the light switch, and shadowy reflections appeared on every surface. 'In any case, we don't want to be interrupted, do we? Take a seat.'

Edie perched on the edge of the tub, feeling it chill and slippery through the fabric of her skirt. The room was like an abattoir in reverse – slick-dark and empty: a place for bringing things to life, instead of killing them?

Miss Atkins sat on the ebony toilet seat, crossing her silk-stockinged legs and placing her clipboard on her lap. She began to leaf through the sheets of paper. 'Now, where are you?' she said. Up at the high window, a shadow flitted past on the ledge. 'Ah, here you are.' She cleared her throat and looked up at Edie. 'We urgently need a wireless operator and your course director tells me you're about the best of the bunch.'

'But I haven't completed my training yet.'

'It's true you're a few days shy, but if we wait until after the final exercise we'll miss this moon period, and we might not be able to drop you for weeks. It's hard enough to get a clear night at this time of year, even when the moon is full enough for the pilots to fly by. But the Met boys say it's set fair for the next week at least, so we'll have to take our chances.' Miss Atkins leant forwards, reaching across and touching Edie on the hand. 'It will be dangerous. I would rather not have to ask you, but a situation has arisen – we're very short of good people right now, and things are critical. But you are a volunteer. You can say no, and nobody will ask questions or think any the worse of you. So think carefully before answering. Are you willing and ready to go to Occupied France for us?'

'Of course,' said Edie, without hesitation. Backing out now was unthinkable, after all the work she'd done this far – after all the effort she'd made to leave her past behind.

'Good, then let's sort you out.'

Miss Atkins looked back down at the paperwork. 'We can use your personal history as much as possible – start from the truth and work sideways: your childhood holidays in Honfleur, your Parisian grandmother, all these things will be useful.' She cleared her throat. 'Let's see . . . we need to find a reason for your being in Paris . . .'

'Paris?'

'Didn't I mention it? Don't worry, I'll cover it all in greater detail in due course. But first, let's find out who you are. I've already had ID papers prepared. Your name is Yvette Colbert, and—'

'And I grew up in Honfleur,' Edie said, recalling seaside trips with innumerable cousins: gritty sandwiches and salt water in her eyes.

'But then why are you in Paris?'

'To study music at the Sorbonne, of course – I play the piano.' Edie remembered an afternoon lesson with a private tutor at the Sorbonne, arranged by her grandmother as a gift, and the pigskin attaché case for her scores her mother had bought her afterwards.

'So you do – but I'm not sure Jerry would buy that, especially if you're not on any registration lists there. However it's not a bad idea – being a student would explain your mobility, out and about between classes . . .' Miss Atkins tapped her pen on the side of the clipboard and frowned.

Edie thought about the piano in her grandmother's apartment, and then a picture came into her head of Bea's little girl, with her chubby toddler's fingers and wide, blinking eyes. 'I'm a piano teacher,' Edie said. 'I moved to Paris to tutor the children of wealthy parents, and ended up staying there when the Germans arrived. I'm always moving from house to house to teach spoilt little children their scales, carrying my music with me in my attaché case.'

'Perfect,' said Miss Atkins, scribbling down some notes. 'Yvette Colbert, piano tutor.' Edie glanced at the high-up rectangle of glass. The shadow passed again – only this time it froze, and Edie could see quite clearly the silhouette of a cat on the windowsill outside. Its tail quivered like a question mark. 'And we need a call sign, for when you're transmitting – a nickname, if you like – something short that will identify you immediately. I was thinking Halfpenny, or Mouse, because of your size, you see—'

'Cat,' Edie interrupted, as the shadowy silhouette wavered and disappeared again. 'My call sign is Cat.'

Edie pushed the picture back into its hiding place. She shouldn't have pried. Justine was entitled to keep her private life hidden; ignorance was safer. Everyone's past was a secret these days.

The trumpeter had almost finished his rebellious rendition now, working up to end on a crescendo. Good for him, Edie thought. But just then there was the urgent rattle of boots on cobbles passing the street below, and shouting, and the trumpeting abruptly stopped. Edie held her breath, wondering if the patriotic musician managed to get away. The shouts died off and eventually the Paris night was curfew-quiet again.

Edie concentrated on slowing her breathing, and shut her eyes, blanking out the moonlight. She needed to rest. Tomorrow she had to find a safe place to stay, and to transmit from, and then her work could really begin.

Chapter 3

Vera

'It's been too long, ducks,' said Penelope, brushing her cheek against Vera's as they embraced at the bottom of the steps. 'Whatever happened to our bridge afternoons?'

'Terribly busy with work these days,' said Vera as they began to climb the steps to the National Gallery. The barrage balloons were high up in the watery winter sky, like minnows, beyond the vast, comforting gallery façade. Coming in here, Vera always felt as if she were entering a palace, or a castle of some sort, with Nelson on his column like an oversized sentry at the gate. Friedrich had a castle, hadn't he? *No, don't think about Friedrich. That book is closed forever.*

'Oh yes, your marvellous job,' Penelope was saying, bounding along beside her. 'I remember you saying you had an interview with some woman called Nips or something. But that was ages ago.'

'Naps,' said Vera. 'I didn't much care for her. Said I'd give it a month's trial, but I found it suited me very well.'

'What is it you actually do?' said Penelope, her tin hat

banging against her hip as she took two steps at a time to keep up with Vera.

'Inter Services Research Bureau,' said Vera, 'in Baker Street.' (She often found that, if one answered with information, people were satisfied, even if the information didn't specifically answer the question asked. It was a tactic that had served her very well over the years.)

The sun was high and bright, and their feet made trip-trapping sounds on the stone steps. As they reached the top and were underneath the colonnades, the sunshine vanished, and the air was cold in the shade. Vera ushered Penelope in front of her through the revolving doors, noticing how slender her legs were. I'm not averse to a well-turned ankle, Dick had once said. Dick had never met Penelope. He'd been gone months before they were ARP wardens together in Chelsea. Vera decided it might not be wise to introduce them; at least not until the wedding. She'd invite the whole world to the wedding. Yes, even that vile Dericourt fellow, if he was still batting about.

They were inside now, and Vera steered Penelope in the direction of the shop. 'I just want to get a postcard,' Vera said, and Penelope agreed that was a good idea, seeing as they were here. There were reams and reams of postcards on rotary racks, prints of all the pictures that were no longer on show in the gallery itself, hidden away 'for the duration of hostilities' – however long that would be. Penelope said she'd heard the paintings had all been wrapped in newspaper and shoved down an old coal mine in Wales somewhere, as she spun a carousel. Vera fingered the glossy postcards, toyed with a Titian, knowing how Dick liked redheads (another reason not to introduce him to Penelope), and was reminded of that new wireless operator she'd seen off. She had red hair, too. Vera sighed, scanning the racks of postcards. In the end she settled on Velázquez's *The Toilet of Venus*.

After she'd paid they sat down on a stone parapet near the entrance and took out their sandwiches. 'What've you got?' said Penelope.

'Spam,' said Vera.

'Lucky you. Mine are cress,' said Penelope, making a face. 'Funny picture,' she added through a mouthful, pointing at the postcard, which was between them on the stone. 'You can only see her face as a reflection in the mirror – don't you think it makes her seem sly?'

Vera looked at the print: the sensual rump of flesh laid out invitingly on the rich silks, chubby Cupid holding the mirror, and the woman's face reflected in the glass: beguiling yet secretive. 'Dick will love it,' she said.

'Oh, it's for Dick.' Penelope spoke as if she knew him, even though they'd never met. 'Do you hear much from him?' She picked up a second sandwich. There was a piece of cress lodged between her front teeth, but Vera didn't mention it. 'My John writes every day, but the letters don't arrive for weeks, months sometimes,' Penelope said. 'He always complains about the heat, but I have to say, I have very little sympathy – my flat is a perfect ice box at the moment!'

Vera felt a sudden, unexpected urge to confide. 'Dick's proposed. We're engaged,' she said.

'Oh, congratulations. How marvellous!' said Penelope. Vera could see Penelope scanning her hands as they held the limp slices of national loaf.

'No ring yet,' said Vera. 'There's a family engagement ring – ruby and diamonds – but it's still in the safe, and he'll get it next time he's on leave. That's when we'll make the official announcement, in *The Times*, naturally.'

'Naturally,' Penelope echoed, wolfing down the rest of her sandwich. 'How wonderful. I say, d'you think we've time for a cuppa before the concert?'

Vera checked her watch. 'Not if we want a seat, dear girl.'

As it was, they had to stand. Myra Hess was playing, and it seemed as if half of London had turned out. They managed to get a spot down the side, near an empty gilt frame and a fire bucket. A woman with a fake-diamond brooch and a sad expression wedged herself in behind Penelope. Next to Vera, sitting on one of the precious seats, a soldier with a bandaged head and one arm in a sling was reading the programme. He offered his seat to Vera, but she motioned him to stay sitting, and read the programme over his shoulder: *Mozart's Concerto 453. The Orchestra of the Central Band HM Royal Air Force with Myra Hess, Pianoforte.* The band were already in position, their uniforms a blue smudge, like good cigar smoke, up on the dais. Next to them, by the archway and the marble statue, the huge Steinway piano waited for Myra Hess. Penelope had started to knit. 'Scarves for prisoners of war,' she said, looping the wool round the twitching needles. 'Hope they don't send one to John – he'll only complain about how ruddy hot he is.'

Vera took out a cigarette. The smoke mingled with the scent of people's woolly winter clothes, and their bodies, gradually warming in the packed room. It smelled like the upstairs of a bus. The band were warming up, squeaking and twittering like a flock of birds. Vera looked round. Some people were waiting patiently, hands folded in their laps. Others were talk-ing, smoking, reading, knitting. A man in a fedora a couple of rows in front appeared to be writing something on the back of his programme. When he'd finished, he folded it up, and put it down underneath his seat. Then he took off his hat. He had fairish hair and a bald spot at the back of his head, Vera noted. He kept his coat on – she couldn't see what colour the lining was.

The orchestra stood, and the room descended into hush. Vera nudged Penelope, who looked up from her knitting. Myra Hess glided through the archway and anchored herself in front of the piano. She was in some kind of cream, flowing dress, but her arms were bare. Ripples of calm extended from where she sat. She nodded at the conductor, and the orchestra sat. The conductor stood, paused, then began his baton-less conducting, using just his index fingers. The band struck up. You could tell it was a military band, Vera thought; they even managed to reduce Mozart to marching music. But then Myra joined in, sculpting the score with such exquisite curves and cornices that even the RAF band began to play like men inspired. Vera shut her eyes and let herself sail away with the music. How she loved Mozart. She'd write about this concert on the postcard, reminding Dick of another concert, in 1939, before he'd gone and joined the RAF and flown away from her. She listened to the violins and the oboes and Myra's deft constructions of sound and for a moment she was back with Dick, after a promenade concert at the Albert Hall, summer sun on the footpath, the air drowsily warm, her arm looped through his, when it was still possible to pretend that the war would never come: *My sweet, my darling, my love.*

The sound of applause jolted her back into the present. She opened her eyes. 'Oh brava, brava,' Penelope said. 'Wasn't she just marvellous. Thank you so much for suggesting this, ducks.'

As the applause died down and Myra left, people began shuffling in their seats and collecting their things, ready to leave. Vera noticed the man putting back on his fedora. She watched as he sidled into the aisle, but lost him in the river of people exiting at the same time. 'I suppose we'd better be on our way,' Penelope said, stuffing the purple wool and needles into her gas mask case.

Vera and Penelope shifted with the others towards the door. As they fanned out with the crowd into the winter air outside, Vera checked her watch, letting Penelope get in front of her. Penelope was already at the steps when Vera called her. 'Penny – you go on ahead, I've just remembered something.' And when Penelope said she'd wait, Vera said not to worry; they'd catch up again soon. Penelope waved goodbye, and tripped off into the swirling crowds of Trafalgar Square.

Vera turned on her toe and went back, pushing against the tide of people, all in a rush to get back to their desks: 'I'm so sorry, I do apologise,' she said, nudging and shoving until she reached the now-empty room where the concert had been held. Two women were just beginning to clear away the chairs. Vera rushed to the row where the man with the fedora had sat. His carefully folded programme was still there, underneath the chair. Vera leant over to pick it up. I am merely collecting a memento of the concert, she told herself as she plucked up the sheet of paper and folded it again and again until it was a tiny rectangle, which she pushed deep into the pocket of her coat, underneath her handkerchief.

She paused to check her watch, then walked swiftly out.

Edie

If she hurried, she could finish in time, Edie thought. Her needles rattled against each other and the red wool pulled through her index finger, cutting into the ever-present blister: it was her Morse finger. But she was trying not to think about coding, for once. When she was out of the apartment, in these brief snatches of daylight and conversation, it didn't do to dwell on what lay waiting for her on her return: the hours of squinting at scribbled messages, laboriously transposing the letters into code from her poem-crib, and then putting the whole thing into Morse, struggling to get through it all in the scheduled time. Felix's lists of questions got longer each day. And the replies from London, decoded in the same exhausting system, took forever. She struggled with the cold, the hunger, the sleeplessness, and the dread that enveloped her like a shroud every time she opened her wireless transmitter. How long could her luck last?

She looked up at the clock above the bar. Justine wasn't late. There was no need to worry – not yet, at least. And out here in a café, with her knitting and her French identity card, she was safer than she was alone in her apartment, Edie reasoned. And it was warm, here, with the sun streaming in through the café windows, much warmer than her coffin-cold room. Her needles clacked on, the almost-finished wool a tangled red nest on top of the round café table, next to her half-drunk *café au lait*.

Usually Justine left messages for London in agreed 'letter-boxes' scattered throughout the city: behind a loose brick in an alleyway, inside prayer books in church, or newspapers left on a park bench at a designated time. Edie, in turn, left the decoded replies in other places: a hole in a tree trunk, underneath a loose paving slab, under the wheel of a car parked outside Claude's garage. It wasn't safe for her to be seen with Justine very often, but sometimes they agreed to meet in person, and today was one of those days. Edie looked forward to these encounters; the rest of the time she felt so alone, with just the dots and dashes to connect her with Miss Atkins, London, and home.

She began to cast off. There would be just enough wool, she judged. The last of it was like a trickle of blood, twisting down from a cut finger onto the mirrored table top. When she'd finished, biting off the wool and pocketing her needles, she held up her creation and had a good look at it: a dark red pixie hat – perfect for a little girl. She remembered her mother reading 'Little Red Riding Hood' to her as a child. The girl in the dark forest never stood a chance against the cunning wolf, did she? As a child she'd had Perrault's Fairy Tales in French and *Grimm's Fairy Tales* in English on her nursery bookshelves. The two versions of Little Red Riding Hood muddled together in her memory. No matter – this knitted red hat would do very nicely for a little French girl, left alone in the countryside with her grandparents, whilst her mother—

The bell jangled as the opening café door announced a customer. Edie looked up. The open door let in a gust of chill air, bringing Justine with it. Edie watched her stride over, a moving silhouette against the bright winter sunshine that flooded in through the plate-glass frontage. Edie stood up, and the two women embraced, kissing on each cheek. Edie fizzed at the touch of another human being. For days all she'd felt was the cold coding contact against her fingers. Justine's cheeks were soft, her embrace definite and strong. She smelled of some kind of lemony soap, and smoke from the cigarettes that were never far from her lips.

Justine called to the waiter to bring her a coffee and they both sat down at the table. Justine took out her tobacco pouch and immediately began creating one of her usual skinny roll-ups. Beyond her, outside the café windows, occasional cars and bicycles passed. A seagull shot upwards in the empty blue sky. In that moment they could be just two young Parisian women meeting for a coffee and a gossip. Edie could hear the chink of metal against china as the waiter prepared Justine's coffee.

'I've just finished this,' said Edie, holding out the hat.

'Very nice,' said Justine, her eyes darting over the red wool as if searching for dropped stitches. Her match flared against her roll-up. 'A little small, no?'

'It's not for me, dear,' Edie laughed. 'It's for you – for your daughter.'

'How do you know about my daughter?' Justine said, eyes narrowed, cigarette halfway to her lips.

How do you think I know, Edie thought. A mother knows a mother. Even a murdering mother like me, who let her child be killed before it had the chance of life. Aloud she said, 'The little girl at the farmhouse window, the night I arrived?' The café was empty; it was safe to talk.

'But I never said—' Justine broke off, frowning.

'You didn't need to. I won't say anything. Don't worry.' Edie touched Justine lightly on the forearm. 'I had a friend with a little girl about the same age, back in—' She almost said England, but stopped herself just in time. 'Back home. And she was always worrying about the child, thinking she'd get cold in wintertime, and I just thought, when I saw this wool for sale, that it would make a perfect hat for a little girl.' She wanted to tell Justine more about Bea, and Bea's daughter, more about everything that happened in the summer of 1942. But she remembered that all that had happened to Gunner Edith Lightwater, a British soldier. That girl doesn't exist any more, she reminded herself.

Justine was still frowning, taking quick drags of her cigarette as if sipping soda through a straw.

'And I also,' Edie began. She had the sudden urge to confide, to tell Justine about her own baby, the one they'd sucked from her, in that squalid hotel. Was it a little girl? She'd never know. 'I also had,' she began again, thinking it might be easier to articulate, to unburden, in French. But just then the waiter arrived at their table.

Justine's coffee was small and black: a doll-sized cup. She knocked it back, the same way Edie remembered the men knocking back their glasses of port, after the speech, when they'd had her pre-departure dinner: hurling it into their open mouths and wincing, afterwards, as if it were a dose of medicine. Edie didn't drink. Not since that night at the 400 Club, not since the American soldier, with his grasping hands and wet lips, not since then – never again.

'It's very kind of you,' Justine said at last, putting her empty coffee cup down on the table. She looked away out of the window. 'You're a very thoughtful person,' she said. She remained turned away, so Edie couldn't see her face. Justine touched her nose with the back of her hand, cleared her throat, and took another drag of the cigarette before returning her gaze to Edie. 'Thank you,' she said, picking up the hat. 'She will love it.'

Edie sipped her *café au lait*, now just tepid. Justine put the red bonnet in her pocket, and Edie asked if her daughter knew the story of Little Red Riding Hood. Justine said yes, of course, it was one of her favourites. It was a relief to talk about something normal, to pretend, just for a few minutes, that they were just friends, meeting, drinking coffee, passing pleasantries. How did the story end, Edie wondered, confusing the two versions she'd read as a child.

'The wolf eats the girl,' Justine said, pushing the butt of her cigarette into a rusted ashtray in the centre of the table. Edie wondered if there wasn't a happy ending. Didn't the grand-mother and Red Riding Hood outwit the wolf? Wasn't there a woodcutter who helped? 'Perhaps in your version,' Justine said. And they were so engaged in their conversation about fairy tales that Edie barely noticed the bell jangle as the café door opened to let in another customer, who passed their table in a waft of cool air. 'You British are very good at inventing happy endings,' Justine laughed, leaning back in her chair. 'We French are more realistic,' she said, sparking up another roll-up. They'd moved on to discussing the Perrault version of 'Sleeping Beauty', which didn't stop with the happy-ever-after kiss, but moved on to darker themes – cannibalism and regicide.

They talked some more; Edie asked Justine about her daughter, left with her grandparents on the farm. 'It's safer. There's more food there,' Justine said simply. She tried to visit as often as she could, she said. When supplies were parachuted in, it was a good excuse to get out of the city. The night Edie arrived was the first time she'd seen her daughter for weeks, she said. Edie thought about the evacuees they'd had in the big house at home, and how Bea had left her little girl behind, a secret, when she'd joined the ATS. And she thought again about her own shameful brush with motherhood: the blood on the sheets, the grinding pain in her abdomen.

The waiter drifted past, flicking a cloth at the table tops, asking if they wanted another coffee. Justine, checking her watch, said no, she had to go. Edie had finished her coffee, the remains clinging like soap scum inside the cup. She asked for another one. Surely it would be safe to linger in this café just a little longer? Why not enjoy the winter sunshine, pretend the big bad wolf wasn't waiting somewhere out there. She stood up to kiss Justine goodbye and Justine thanked her again for the hat. As she was leaving, Edie called after her.

'I forgot to ask – your daughter: what's her name?'

'Violette.'

'Such a pretty name. Give her a kiss from me.'

'I will,' Justine said. And she smiled and waved as she passed in front of the wide glass frontage.

Edie imagined her going back to the farmhouse in the fields, imagined a little girl running towards her and shouting 'Maman, Maman!', arms outstretched. Justine must be wrong, she thought, picturing little Violette in the red pixie hat, walking hand-in-hand with her mother to the farmhouse door. The fairy tale can't end with the wolf; the wolf can't win.

As Justine disappeared into the morning street, Edie turned away from the window. Whilst she'd been waving goodbye, the waiter had brought her a fresh cup of coffee. The sun glanced off the table tops, and she realised how round and shiny they were, like the powder compact Miss Atkins had given her.

With that thought, Edie took the silver compact from her jacket pocket. She flipped it open and it lay coolly in her palm.

She wiped the puff onto the creamy powder. Frenchwomen had no qualms about putting on make-up in public, Justine had told her. Edie smoothed the velvety powder over her cheeks and nose, covering up her freckles. She took the lipstick Justine had given her out of her pocket. The colour didn't suit her – a bold cyclamen, which she would never have dared wear at home. It's about making an effort, Justine had said. Glamour is a kind of resistance. Those grey mice – that was how she referred to the German women who came to Occupied Paris to work – can never match us for beauty or charm, and that is our victory!

That is our victory, Edie thought, pulling off the metal top of the lipstick case and swivelling up what was left of the buttery-pink cylinder. 'Vive la France,' she mouthed at her own reflection in the circle of glass, smacking her lips together until they looked like the petals of forest flowers. The wolf doesn't win.

It was only as she was about to close the powder compact that she noticed the man in the long coat. She saw him in the periphery of her reflection in the mirror, standing at the bar, smoking. But when she caught his eye, he turned abruptly away.

She snapped the powder compact shut, and took out her purse. She unrolled a note, left it under the undrunk café au lait, and stood up to go.

The bell tinkled as she left, and she remembered then that she'd heard it earlier. It must have been when the man in the coat had walked in, walked past, just as Justine said – what was it? – *You British are very good at inventing happy endings*. Edie walked quickly away across the street, resisting the urge to break into a run – to run all the way to Grandmother's house.

Vera

'Exploding rats, whatever next?' Buckmaster chuckled. 'I say, Vera, come and have a look at this.' Vera's heels tip-tapped on the Natural History Museum's marble floor as she walked over to where Buckmaster and Fraser-Smith were looking at the new sabotage prototypes. Boys and their toys, she thought wearily, glancing round the demonstration room, which, despite the vaulted ceiling and stained-glass windows, had something of a garden-shed feel about it. She thought of the stack of paperwork piling up on her desk in her absence as she looked down at where Buckmaster pointed a curious finger.

'I don't think it will offer as much utility as the exploding bicycle pump,' she said, coming to a halt in front of the card table by the column. 'That's been very effective in the field, the agents tell me.' She prodded the matted fur of the stuffed beast, laid out proudly on the green baize like a royal flush. Ghastly thing. 'And what about the damp?'

'Damp?' said Buckmaster, chewing on his pipe stem.

'I'm only thinking of its efficacy. Rats live in damp places, like sewers and gutters. This weapon will have to be placed somewhere wet, therefore, and won't that affect the explosive material?'

Buckmaster turned to look at Fraser-Smith, who twisted his mouth down at the corners and tugged his moustache. 'She might have a point,' he conceded eventually.

'Well, don't take my word for it; I'm hardly an expert in this sort of bricolage,' said Vera. 'But I do know that the bicycle pumps pack up nicely with the Stens in the crates, and they have a track record of use in the field.' She saw Buckmaster and Fraser-Smith exchanging looks. It was as her mother had always told her, she realised: sometimes one had to try not to be so obviously right where men and their egos were concerned. 'But really, it's your decision of course – you men know far more about these Q-gadgets than I do,' she added, taking out her cigarettes.

She watched Buckmaster and Fraser-Smith in earnest conversation, and let her mind drift a little, with the cigarette smoke. Should she have told Penelope about Dick and the engagement, earlier on? It did force her hand, rather. Penelope wasn't one to sit tight on gossip. But wasn't that the point?

Fraser-Smith was nodding and making notes on a clipboard as Buckmaster gesticulated, creating invisible devices in the stone-cold museum air. Vera exhaled, thinking of that Dericourt chap. If ever there was an obvious rogue – but Buckmaster hadn't even questioned his credentials. If Buckmaster was prepared to be so lax about Dericourt then perhaps it was time to reveal the truth about her own background?

Afterwards Buckmaster, on good form, invited both Vera and Fraser-Smith to the Hoop and Toy, just round the corner. Fraser-Smith declined, saying his wife had invited people to supper, and disappeared down the rabbit hole of South Kensington Tube Station. 'Well, all I've got waiting at home for me is a Spam sandwich – it's her bridge night,' said Buckmaster. 'Care to join me for a snifter, Vera?'

Vera squinted at her watch – she could barely make out the face in the moonless night. There was no airport run tonight. It was already past six and home was just a few streets away. A chill winter drizzle had just started to fall. 'Why not?' she said, thinking that perhaps this was the opportunity she'd been waiting for.

'Do you play bridge, Vee?' Buckmaster said as they walked across Exhibition Road, dodging bicycles and scurrying commuters in the gloom. 'I imagine you'd be rather a bridge fiend, what with your memory,' he continued. 'The wife won't partner me these days, says I can't be trusted, and to be honest, I don't mind. Crosswords, that's the thing, eh?' Vera nodded. He was right. She had been good at bridge, very good in fact. But one particular afternoon had put her off the game for good, she remembered, as they made their way towards the pub.

She'd just led with a spade when Vera heard the van drawing up at the kerb. It was a warm day, and the window was open a couple of inches at the bottom. She could hear the street sounds: the tring of a bicycle bell, a cat meowing disconsolately and the van's engine turning off. She could tell it was a van because the sound was somehow more definite than a car, but not as loud and juddery as a bus or truck. Using the pretext of opening the window to let more air in, she got up from the bridge game and walked over to have a look. She pushed up the heavy sash, leaning out slightly. In the distance she could just glimpse the dark green of the plane trees on the edge of Hyde Park. Above, the sky was a dusty blue swathe, like a mohair shawl she'd once owned. She'd left it behind when they came – she wondered what happened to that lovely shawl: was some Iron Guard's wife swanking about in it these days?

Vera looked down. Yes, it was a black van. From this angle it was hard to see if it was a police van or not. But who else had the petrol coupons to go roaring about town these days? She pushed the sash even higher, taking in a gulp of air, tepid as the coffee left undrunk in the cup beside her bridge hand.

'Lucky us, Penelope's got the king, so this one's ours,' Vera heard her mother say from inside the room. 'Vee, dearest, do come in and join us. It's unnerving having you hanging out of the window like that.'

She hasn't heard, Vera thought. How can she not have heard? Vera took one last look down at the van, but nobody had got out – yet – and ducked back inside the room. They had the baize-topped card table out. Vera had invited Penelope and Vera's mother had asked Mrs Littlewood from the flat below to make up numbers. Vera slipped into her place opposite Mrs Littlewood. To her right Penelope flicked away an auburn curl from her forehead and laid down the ace of diamonds. 'Is ace high or low, dearie, I can never remember,' Mrs Littlewood said. Her lipstick had smudged onto her teeth so they clattered yellow-pink together like those rhubarb-and-custard sweets one could buy before rationing.

From outside Vera heard the sound of a van door slamming shut, footsteps on the pavement. Still no one else seemed to have noticed, not even Mother, who should have been listening out for such things. Distracted, Vera gave away the king of diamonds, and her mother raised an eyebrow in surprise.

Would they let her take her suitcase? Vera wondered. Would they give her a few precious minutes to pack: some perfume, her best nightdress, Dick's letters. Or would they just strong-arm her, hustle her out of the front door, into the waiting van and off to Holloway Prison?

Penelope led with the two of hearts. Vera heard the main door downstairs open and close. Mrs Littlewood heard, too. 'I wonder who that is? The postman's already been – what's trumps again, dearie?'

Vera's mother replied that clubs were trumps, and asked if anyone wanted a top-up of coffee. Penelope said no thank you, but she was gasping for a ciggie, so Vera took out her packet of Sobranies, wondering whether or not one could get hold of Sobranies in camps, or if this would be her last one. Her ears strained to hear the soft ping as the lift stopped at their floor.

Vera had only just sparked up when the doorbell rang. 'I'll get it,' she said, jumping up before her mother could, thinking to spare her some of the shame of seeing her daughter interned, in front of her guests. I'll go quietly, she thought, and maybe Mother can think of some kind of excuse. She wedged the lit cigarette in the gap between the index and middle finger of her left hand, exhaling smoke in front of her in the hall-way as she walked, approaching the door as if through a fine mist. There was another impatient buzz of the doorbell as she approached. Her fingers slipped, sweaty with fear, on the door handle as she fumbled to open it.

There at the door was a forest of uniformed men. Vera planted her feet firmly on the hallway floor and took another drag of her cigarette. She made herself count them: one, two, three, four – not a battalion of soldiers, just four police officers. The one in front was looking down at a piece of paper on a clipboard. 'Excuse me, madam, but we're looking for a V—' He paused. Vera couldn't breathe, felt as if her own smoke was drowning her. This was it. 'What does that say, George? I can't read it in this light.' The man next to him looked down at the sheet. The two at the back shuffled their feet.

'Who is it?' Vera heard her mother call from the lounge. Vera didn't answer, unable to speak, waiting. The other man – George – whispered something into the first police officer's ear. Vera couldn't hear what he said.

'Victor Carluccio,' the police officer said, looking up from the sheet at Vera. 'Mr and Mrs Victor Carluccio,' he said.

Vera exhaled in a rush, almost choking. 'The Carluccios are on the ground floor, dear boy,' she said, beginning to close the door.

'Thank you, madam, and sorry to trouble you,' said the officer, and Vera said not at all and shut the door softly in his face before he thought to say anything further. She stayed for a moment, looking at the shut door, listening to the muffled tramp of boots on the carpeted hallway as the phalanx of police moved away. She thought of old Mr Carluccio and his wife, geraniums on their kitchen windowsill, and how their tortoiseshell sometimes wound around her legs when she arrived home in the early hours after her ARP duties. Who'd have the cat, she wondered. Who'd have the cat when they got taken away?

'Who was that, darling?' said Mother when she went back into the lounge.

'Oh, nobody,' Vera replied, but her fingertips shook as she tipped the long chimney of ash into the ashtray. 'Just some people looking for the Carluccios.' Vera could hear thumping on a door downstairs. And there was still the mewing of that cat outside. 'Actually, I think I'll shut the window again, if nobody minds,' she said, getting up again before anyone answered and rushing over to slam the sash shut. But even as she did so, she could hear shouts from below, footsteps outside, and the sound of a woman starting to sob. This window fell with a thud onto the sill. Vera sat back down.

'It's you,' Penelope said. Vera checked her hand, not really seeing it, and plucked out a card, laying it swiftly down.

'I thought we had to follow suit. It's hearts this time, isn't it, dearie?' said Mrs Littlewood, looking at the two of clubs Vera had laid.

'I'm afraid I can't follow suit,' said Vera, imagining the Carluccios being shunted into the back of that horrid black van. 'I don't have any hearts left.' Even through the closed window she thought she could hear the sound of the van starting up again.

'You're heartless, ducks,' said Penelope, smiling at her own joke as the others laid hearts. 'And this one's yours.'

'Well, one has to play one's trump cards eventually,' said Vera, taking another drag, and bashing the trick into a neat pile in front of her. 'I suppose I was just lucky, that time, wasn't I?'

As Buckmaster held the door open for her and Vera slipped inside the old pub, she shuddered, remembering that afternoon. She nudged her way through a wedge of work-weary men towards the bar. They found a table squashed into a corner, next to the door where the landlord disappeared periodically to 'sort the pipes'. In the small space the air was an essence of stale beer and smoke. The floor was black, sticky under the soles of her shoes. Vera sat down, letting Buckmaster get the first round in. She rubbed her forefinger along the varnished wood and watched as the landlady caught sight of him and bustled over. She saw Buckmaster's gaze rest briefly on the woman's ample bosoms, solid as torpedoes under her pullover, before he ordered the gin and tonics. He came and sat down, necked his G and T in one, took his pipe from his pocket and cleared his throat.

'Good speech from old Winnie the other day,' he said.

'What, about it being the beginning of the end of the war?'

Buckmaster nodded, taking out his tobacco tin.

'D'you think it'll be believed though, what with the Tunisia debacle?' said Vera. 'I mean, Russia's all well and good, but it's hardly the end of the road, is it, dear boy?' Vera said, taking a sip of gin. It tasted like the first mowing of spring. And it took her right back to Crasna, to hunting parties in the forest, and tea on the lawn, and Friedrich. Dear Friedrich. She blinked the image away and took a larger swig.

'The right side will always win through,' Buckmaster replied, lighting his pipe and nodding, as if it were perfectly clear which side was the right side. And for him – for everyone in the crowded pub, except her – it probably was clear.

She noticed his glass was already empty 'Let me get you a whisky,' she said, getting up. 'They always have a good stock in here.'

'I doubt they'll have anything of a half-decent age. I haven't had an honest single malt since 1941,' he said.

'Let me try and surprise you.' She got up and went over to the bar. She'd been here before, with Dick. The night before he left. They'd drunk Laphroaig, she remembered. They'd drunk until the room swerved and tilted, and she'd almost forgotten that they were about to be torn apart.

The landlady was serving at the other end of the bar, but the landlord had just come up from the cellar, wiping his hands on a rag, red-faced, slightly out of breath. 'I swear those barrels get heavier every day,' he said. 'What'll it be?'

'Do you have any whisky?' she said. He motioned to the indifferent bottle of Bell's behind the bar. 'Anything older? A single malt?' She smiled hopefully, even as he began to shake his head. 'I've had some good news, you see,' she added. 'My RAF boyfriend has finally agreed to make an honest woman of me!' She leant forward over the bar and smiled, catching her reflection in the mirrored glass behind the bottles. Handsome, that was what Dick called her – not beautiful, but handsome. Was she? Was she still? Her teeth flashed white between her lipsticked smile. 'You probably don't remember, but we used to come here a lot, my fiancé and I, before he was deployed.' Her mind flicked back to those glorious nights: the pubs, the Proms, the 400 Club, and afterwards. 'You used to have such a marvellous selection of whisky, I remember.' She touched the landlord briefly on his hand, where it rested on the bar. He said seeing as it was such a very special celebration, he might manage to find something. He sucked his teeth and said it wouldn't be cheap though, what with anything over twelve years old being impossible to come by nowadays, even with his contacts, and Vera unrolled a note from her purse, trying not to think about the overdue electricity bill and the holes in her last pair of silk stockings.

Buckmaster thanked her for the drink. 'Dericourt brings vintage bubbly and you manage to conjure up single malt – almost feels like I'm back in my old job!' They clinked glasses and he reminisced a little about his work in public relations before the war. 'And what did you do, Vee?' he said. 'Before.'

And as he said it she realised with a kind of reverse déjà vu that that was how they'd always delineate their lives in the future, that there would always be a 'before' and 'after': the war a gaping rift in the centre of their lives. She sipped at her gin and tonic. 'Oh, you know, finishing school, secretarial college, and far too many parties,' she said, reaching for her cigarettes. She opened the case. There were only a couple left, so she could see almost all of him: the arched brows, the confident smile underneath the RAF cap. Her Dick: darling Dick. There would be an 'after', wouldn't there? There would be an 'after' and the wonderful man in the photograph would be her husband. She just had to make it happen.

'Buckie, I have a favour to ask, as a matter of fact,' she said, wedging the Sobranie between her fingers.

'Oh yes?' He was swilling the drink round in his glass so it clung thickly to the sides.

'It's rather a delicate matter,' she went on.

'You're not in some kind of trouble, are you?' he said, looking up and frowning. 'Because I'm dreadful at that sort of thing. Terribly squeamish, you see. One of the office girls got "appendicitis" a while ago – you know – and I couldn't bring myself to . . . I'd just rather not know, Vera, if it's all the same to you. Take as much time off as you need, to get better.'

'My dear boy, it's certainly not that,' she said, blushing at the very thought.

'Oh, good show. I'm not one to judge, but, you know . . .' He trailed off, taking a large swig, and not looking her in the eye.

'It's about where I'm from,' she said in a low voice, leaning forward. There didn't seem to be anyone close enough to hear, but one couldn't afford to take chances, even so.

'Yes, Hump did mention you'd been abroad, before the war,' said Buckmaster.

'Born abroad,' said Vera.

'Oh, I thought he'd said *been* abroad. And I did think it odd to mention, at the time, because of course you'd been abroad, otherwise how would you speak so many languages so very well? I mean, it sort of went without saying. So, *born* abroad, you say?'

'Yes. It's not a secret, as such, but it's not something I like to broadcast,' Vera said.

'Oh, quite.'

'And it didn't matter much before, really. But these days it would be so much easier if I were in uniform, the way things are – especially with spending so much of my time at airfields during the moon periods.'

'Not Commonwealth, then?' said Buckmaster, taking another swig.

'Not Commonwealth,' said Vera.

'I see,' he said slowly.

'And if things should develop, as they ought, as they will, when our aims have succeeded, then I might be needed elsewhere – across the Channel – and I couldn't possibly go, in my current situation. I would need to be in one or other of the services, in order to be deployed.' She spoke in a low voice, but she could see Buckmaster's eyes flick worriedly round the bar. Nobody could possibly have heard, though, could they?

Buckmaster cleared his throat. 'So where, exactly, were you born?'

Vera hesitated. She'd spent so many years not saying it that there was almost a physical block to getting the word out. It was like having a fishbone stuck in her throat. She took another sip of the bitter-fresh gin. 'Romania.' She spoke in such a low voice that it was almost a whisper.

'But Romania is—' He looked aghast, didn't even finish his sentence.

'On the wrong side. I know. But when I arrived here that wasn't the case. Romania didn't even take sides until—'

'November nineteen-forty,' Buckmaster interrupted, frowning.

'My mother and both my brothers are British,' she said. 'And as you know, I have signed the Official Secrets Act. My fiancé is an RAF pilot. I went to secretarial college in London. I'm British in all but name, Buckie. It was just an accident of birth.'

'I see,' he said, still frowning. He hasn't asked about Father, she thought. Thank goodness he hasn't asked about Father. And he won't ever know about Friedrich – no one will ever know about Friedrich. 'And Hump?' Buckmaster added.

'Of course Hump knows. Hump knows everything.' Almost everything, she added silently. Hump knows almost everything. But no one knows everything; no one can ever know everything.

Buckmaster, still frowning, took out a handkerchief and blew his nose. 'I'm at a loss to know why this hasn't been brought to my attention before,' he said.

'But you said Hump mentioned—'

'Only in passing, not . . . look here, this is very serious, Vee. If it gets out—'

'Indeed, if it gets out.' It was Vera's turn to interrupt. 'If it gets out that you have an enemy alien in SOE's employ, then I'll be off to an internment camp and you'll be transferred to some Home Guard unit in less time than it'll take you to finish that whisky,' she hissed, fixing him with a stare. 'Is that really what you want? You said yourself, it's the beginning of the end of the war and SOE's time is now. Do you want to miss all of that, just because my silly mother happened to be holidaying in Romania when I made an appearance?'

Buckmaster looked down into the whisky glass and shook his head, and for a moment she thought it was all over. She held her breath. 'No,' he said at last. 'It's not what I want. I'll make enquiries in the morning.' Vera exhaled, able to breathe again. 'But I'm warning you, Vee,' he said, looking up from his drink and straight into her eyes, 'I'm demanding absolute loyalty from now on. No more shenanigans like we had in the meeting the other morning. Is that clear?'

'Clear as sunlight, my dear boy,' Vera replied and plucked the last cigarette from the case so she could see all of Dick's face smiling up at her.

Chapter 4

Edie

There was so much to get through. In training they'd said not to transmit for more than a few minutes at a time, for fear of detection. But this little lot would take her aeons, Edie thought, as she slowly drew the curtains to her room. She nodded at Madame LeBlanc, who lived opposite her on the *passage*. The elderly Madame's front room was double-aspect: set on the corner of the main road and the side street where Edie was lodging, overlooking the steps that went down past the drinking fountain. Madame LeBlanc could see if the detector vans were approaching, and she knew that when Edie closed her curtains during daylight it meant she was transmitting. The old woman had promised to keep an eye out.

Edie locked her door, took out the suitcase from under her bed and placed it on the table beneath the window, hooking up the aerial, which slid under the bottom sash like a rat's tail and trailed up a bare wisteria vine that climbed the wall outside. The room was all shadows and gloom, but there was enough light from the table lamp to make out the messages she needed to code and send. She checked the clock on the mantelpiece: ten past – just enough time to set up before sending her messages at the scheduled time.

She pulled the chair closer in to the table, and clicked the set on. It began to hum and crackle. She slipped her hand inside her dress and pulled out her poem-code. She still wasn't able to transpose the messages without referring to it, even though she knew it was risky to have it written down. She picked up the pencil and licked the tip, metallic on her tongue. As usual, the table wobbled as she transcribed the messages into code, and for the umpteenth time she thought she really ought to find a bit of cardboard to place under one of the metal feet.

The gap in the sash window let the aerial out, but also the winter air in, snapping at her fingertips and down the neck of her dress. Cold – she hadn't remembered Paris being this cold when she used to visit her grandmother. She had on both sets of clothes: the cream blouse underneath the dress, which in turn was tucked into the charcoal-grey skirt – she'd lost so much weight already that it fitted underneath – and the jacket covering the blouse and dress. It was tight under the arms from all the layers of fabric. Lately she'd taken to doing what the French did, wrapping newspaper round her trunk for an extra layer of insulation. She rustled when she moved and the paper scratched her skin. She wore cut-off gloves that Justine had knitted her, keeping her fingertips free for tapping out transmissions. But still she was cold. She shivered, and shifted the dial. She should get started or risk being chastened by Miss Atkins again.

She'd picked up a long message in the café this morning. Justine had slipped it inside a copy of *Pariser Zeitung* before disappearing on her bicycle. Miss Atkins had asked for so many details last time about the planned depot sabotage: grid references, numbers of personnel involved, names even, and provisional timings. And Felix had responded not just with answers, but a whole list of requests: explosives, guns, grenades and luxury food supplies to keep their contacts sweet – chocolates, corned beef, cigarettes.

She picked up the little metal contact pad and began. Tap-tap-tap. In training they'd been taught to remember the Morse letters as musical phrases, just as the dot-dot-dot-dash of the letter 'V' for Victory was implied by the use of the opening bars of Beethoven's Fifth in the BBC's *Radio Londres* broadcasts. Edie imagined the decoder at the other end, sitting in his warm office in Baker Street, probably with a cup of tea next to him and a hot dinner to go home to. She paused, hugging herself and running her fingers up and down her arms, rubbing heat into her frozen limbs. Her fingertips were white, except for the index finger on her left hand, which was red and inflamed from the continual tapping of Morse on the metal contacts. She was concentrating so hard on getting the message out that she wouldn't have noticed the piano music if a gust of wind hadn't suddenly caught the curtain, sweeping her code off the table and onto the floor. It was only when she bent down, scrabbling to catch the little slips of paper, that she heard it: 'Au clair de la lune', thumped out rapidly, with the loud pedal held down – Madame LeBlanc's signal that the detector van was coming.

For a moment she felt like she was on the high diving board: breath squeezed clean out of her chest and vision narrowed to a pinprick. She gasped, gulped for air, then grabbed the stray sheets of paper and shoved them into her mouth, chewing as she slammed the suitcase lid down on the still-humming equipment, and ripped the cable from its umbilical attachment. Terror drove her on. She snapped the catch shut on the suitcase and heaved up the heavy sash. There was no time to untangle the aerial, take it with her. Her tight skirt and layers of clothing threatened to catch on the window, but she shoved herself out, pulling the heavy suitcase, and ran blindly up the empty cobbled passage, away from the sound of 'Au clair de la lune', away from the sound of a van drawing closer to the steps at the end of the street.

She ran without looking back, cork heels sliding on the cobbles, heavy suitcase thumping against her knees, skirt ripping at the seams as she forced her legs into a wider stride. Her mouth was still full of the crumpled messages, but she couldn't chew or swallow, her breath came in forced gasps, the wad of paper like an extra tongue restricting her breath. The street got narrower and darker, running up at an incline, like the entrance to an animal hole. She felt like a vixen going to ground. She ran on, almost choking on the paper stuffed in her gasping mouth. As she reached the far end, she could hear footfalls, loud on the steps running up to the street entrance.

She skidded sideways at the top, where cobbles turned to paving slabs. There were sounds of shouting in German from the passage she'd just turned off, and the thudding of fists on a wooden door. She jumped as a hand reached out to close a shutter on a window next to her: nobody wanted to witness what was about to happen. She leapt onto a pathway of slabbed steps between high-sided buildings, tumbling down the twisting walkway, which led to the market. She could lose herself there, she hoped, amongst the crowds and the stalls. The case was heavy, unwieldy. She kept having to shift it from side to side as she slipped and stumbled down the steps. Where the alley opened out into the marketplace there was a pile of rubbish: rotting potatoes, straw and horse dung. She spat out the gobbet of paper, stamping it into the pile with her foot, before rushing on. She'd thought she'd be safe here, but the market was all but empty: skeletal stalls like winter trees. There were just a few stall-holders packing up, faces pinched and sallow, and a handful of Jewish women, chests branded with yellow stars, as always forced to be last in the queue, having to make do with whatever was left behind after the rest of the population had taken their pick. Hunched up and hungry in the icy wind, they barely had the energy to notice her. Neither Jew nor stall-holder, she'd easily be spotted here: the girl with the suitcase. Edie rushed on, over vegetable peelings and splinters of broken crate.

She hurried out to the main road, where there were cyclists, a horse and cart and – thank goodness – an empty *vélo-taxi* winding disconsolately in the opposite direction. '*Monsieur!*' she yelled, as loud as her rasping lungs would allow. '*Monsieur, arrêtez-vous!*' The driver stopped pedalling and turned to look at her, his waxy face showing no emotion under his beret. He didn't bother to come and get her, merely motioned with his head. She thought she could hear the sound of boots on the steps to the market. With one last surge of effort she ran to the little cart behind the cyclist and threw herself inside, shoving the suitcase down at her feet.

'*Wohin?*' said the driver. With a start, she realised he was speaking German. And then she remembered what Justine had told her: only Germans and collaborators took *vélo-taxis*.

'Gare du Nord,' Edie said.

The driver grunted and started to pedal. The vehicle jolted

over the potholes as they moved off. She shrank down into her seat and pulled up the collar of her jacket. She could hear shouts coming from the marketplace, but the driver pedalled quickly, and they'd soon turned off onto the road towards the river. She let out a breath, no longer cold, but throbbing with the heat of panic and fear. She was just a young woman in a *vélo-taxi,* with a suitcase, going to the station. And the taxi driver spoke German. She'd be fine, wouldn't she?

Vera

'Still nothing from Cat?' Vera said. Margaret shook her head. Vera tutted. Her scheduled spot had gone hours ago. Buckmaster made it clear he wanted to get things moving now that new Lysander chap was on board. At his desk Tonkin was chuntering down the telephone to someone. Vera checked her watch: 12.45 already – Buckmaster must be down at lunch. The window was a depressing charcoal oblong – they said it was going to snow later. 'And have you disseminated the titbits already?' said Vera. Margaret said that she had. 'Very well, you may take your lunch break. I'll hold the fort,' said Vera. Margaret began to tidy her desk. She was a fastidious girl, Vera thought, never so much as a leaf of paper out of place. Perhaps at some point she could be useful with the airfield runs, if she were thoroughly briefed, of course.

Just after she'd left, Dericourt appeared, saying he was look-ing for Buckmaster. He had a new grey suit on, Vera noticed: Savile Row, if she wasn't very much mistaken. Tonkin, his over-oiled brown hair making his head look like a schoolboy's conker, glanced up from his phone, grinned at Dericourt and motioned for him to stay, all the while continuing to mutter into the receiver. Vera said to Dericourt that Buckmaster was most likely in the canteen and why didn't Dericourt join him. She had mountains of memos to attend to, and really wasn't in the mood to talk to 'the godsend' herself. 'Too early for me,' Dericourt said, sidling across to Vera's desk and leaning on the edge. 'I shall eat later, at the hotel.'

'Oh, where are you staying?' said Vera, slicing open an envelope with her ivory-handled paperknife.

'The Dorchester.'

'Nice,' said Vera, scanning the contents of the letter and deciding it could be dealt with later. She wondered where the money was coming from to put Dericourt up in the Dorchester. She knew exactly what was available for agents' expenses. Unless Dericourt had some kind of undisclosed private income? But if Henri Dericourt had the kind of money that would see him through a stay at the Dorchester, why on earth was he coming to work for them? 'If you don't want to meet Buckmaster then perhaps it's something I could deal with,' she said with a sigh, looking up.

'I have a few questions about how exactly I will be liaising with the agents,' he said, looking down at her from his perch.

Vera cleared her throat and stood up. 'I think that will be on a need-to-know basis. The wireless operator will send in grid references, which we'll let you know when you fly. The fewer details you know, the better.'

'And their training? Perhaps you could tell me a little about how they prepare for these missions?' Dericourt said. Vera shook her head. She remembered observing how even 'Yvette' had evolved from ham-fisted ingénue to calculating saboteur over the course of just a few months. If Henri Dericourt thought she was going to breathe one word about all the tricks the agents learnt up in the Highlands and at Beaulieu, he had another think coming. Who knew who he'd be hobnobbing with in France?

Dericourt stood up, his eyes on a level with hers now. They were grey, she noticed. Not blue, like Dick's. 'I just think that the more I know the more useful I can be,' he said with his disarming shrug.

'I'm afraid that's not how it works, my dear boy,' said Vera.

'But Buckmaster said—' he began. Vera had to resist the urge to roll her eyes. Buckmaster – why couldn't he see Dericourt for what he was?

'I don't know what you've agreed with Buckmaster, but my first priority is the agents in my charge,' she said. 'Security protocols are imperative to ensure the safety of the men and women in the field.'

'Naturally,' Dericourt said, pulling out a packet of Sobranies from his pocket and offering one to her. She took it with a nod, wondering who had told him about the under-the-counter arrangement at Fox's. She definitely hadn't mentioned it herself. Dericourt flicked open his lighter. The flame flickered between them as she sucked in her first drag. She was close enough to notice a faint scar below his lower lip – a flaw in the otherwise symmetrical face. He lit his own, and continued on his exhalation, 'But surely you wouldn't imagine that I pose a security risk – not after what I went through to get here?'

'I'm not imagining anything, dear boy,' Vera said.

'And then there's the question of payment,' he continued. 'Currency can cause problems. As you know I'll be operating both here and in France, depending on the moon.' She nodded, regarding him through an uncurling thread of smoke.

'Diamonds are easiest, but I can also take bullion,' he said. Vera almost gasped like a shop girl. Diamonds indeed.

'I don't know what you've heard, but that's not how we operate, here in F-Section,' she said, lifting the cigarette slowly to her lips again.

'What I've heard?' Dericourt said. Was that a smirk on his lips? 'Oh, I get to hear all sorts of things, Miss Atkins,' and he moved towards her, close to her neck, as if about to whisper something in her ear. She could smell his hair oil, like pine resin, feel his breath warm against her cheek.

There was a sudden chiming thump as Tonkin slammed the phone down. Vera and Dericourt turned to look, pulling apart. 'Ruddy idiot!' he whispered, glowering at the telephone. He stood up. 'Sometimes I think the RAF would be better run by a cage of monkeys. Pity all pilots aren't a bit more like you, Dericourt,' he said. 'Jolly good to see you. How're the digs?'

'The digs?' Dericourt looked quizzically at Vera.

'He means your hotel,' she translated.

'Yes, very nice,' Dericourt said. 'I am going there for lunch shortly. Would you like to join me?'

'Would I?' Tonkin said. 'After the morning I've just had, I may decide to book myself a room! You too, Miss Atkins?' Vera shook her head. The last thing she wanted was to spend any more time in the company of Monsieur Dericourt.

When the men had left, she checked again in the coding room. At last Cat's transcript was in, hours late, and full of inconsistencies. What was she playing at? Vera hastily formulated an immediate response, dashing off the words and handing the slip of paper straight back to the coder: *Keep to your scheduled times in future. Your delay has blocked other agents' transmissions. Get back on track. It's not all about you.*

She stalked back to her desk. The office was empty: Buckmaster still in the canteen, Margaret out, and Tonkin off to the Dorchester with 'the godsend'. Tonkin's phone was ringing shrilly, but she ignored it, sitting back down and ripping open envelope after envelope with the paper knife, and tossing the contents to one side. Out of the window she could see that the snow had at last begun to fall: fat white flakes like down. By the time she left for home they'd be brown sludge in the gutter, she thought. Dericourt came back to mind, his easy confidence, and his unnerving charm. He was a fraud, she knew.

It takes one to know one, nagged her inner voice.

Chapter 5

Edie

When it happened it was almost a relief. The door banged open and the room was suddenly full of them, a grey-black swarm. They didn't shout. She'd expected shouting, violence, but it was nothing like that. The tall one must've seen her take the crystals from her set, and he prised them from her fist before handcuffing her. But apart from that, they barely touched her.

She'd been lucky to escape when Madame LeBlanc's piano playing alerted her to the detector van's approach. She'd found a new room, across the river, in one of the *passages* in rue du Faubourg Saint-Antoine. It was small and filthy, but safe. She'd been told that the landlady, Madame de Jouvenal, had links with the Resistance, that she was onside. Even so, Edie had existed in a fog of fear, knowing it only took one whispered word or nod towards her doorway to alert the authorities, knowing that it was only a matter of time until the detector van triangulated her signal. And now it had happened. No less terrible for expecting it.

There were only four of them, but her little room was thick with bodies. It was like someone pouring a jar of ink all over a patchwork quilt, suddenly all the pastel colours blackened out and ruined.

It felt as if it were all happening with painful slowness. Her mind slithered like a climber's foot on a sheer rock face, feeling for purchase. There must be something she could do, some way out? No, nothing, nothing.

Three of them searched: knocking on walls; slashing open pillows; fingering windowsills. The fourth – the tall one with the bony hands – stood next to her, one hand circling her upper arm. He watched her intently, perhaps waiting for a visual tic, to show that his colleagues were close to finding something.

A fifth man appeared in the doorway carrying a wooden crate full of pairs of black leather boots. Edie looked down, realising how they'd been able to approach her room so silently – they had taken off their boots. The man with bony fingers said something to the others, and they all laughed, stopped what they were doing and went to put on their boots. Edie watched them kneeling down beside her bed. For a surreal moment it was as if they were saying their bedtime prayers. Bony fingers gripped tighter on her upper arm. One of the soldiers, the short one, had a hole in his sock.

Edie found herself thinking about sitting with Joan and Bea on barrack nights, mending uniforms. It was Bea who'd taught her how to darn. How far she'd come from that silly girl soldier, who couldn't even peel potatoes properly. Her memory of larking about with her pals on the gun emplacements was like looking the wrong way down a telescope: so far away, so insignificant. Now she was the woman who knew how to parachute, to code and transmit in Morse, and to assemble and fire a weapon. And who knew the snap of danger and the plummet of fear.

When they were up on their feet, the short man switched places with the bony-fingered one, gripping her upper arm. There was a moment when as they swapped two sets of fingers were around her arm at the same time, like fleshy bangles. Then the bony-fingered one went off to get his boots on, the only remaining pair in the crate. He had a long straight nose and a slice of close-cropped white-blond hair, so short it looked almost granular, like sand. When he'd finished tying up his laces he swapped places again with the short one. She could feel bruises starting to form where his fingers dug in.

The others were stamping on the floorboards now and listening with their heads on one side. Edie was reminded of the way seagulls stomp on rain-drenched ground, teasing out worms to eat. They pulled up a couple of floorboards, but found nothing underneath. There was nothing to find: they already had her crystals, and her poem-code was still hidden between the leaves of newspaper wrapped underneath her shirt for warmth.

The bony-fingered one barked out an order of some sort, and black-covered notebooks were taken out. Things were written down. She saw the short one with the hole in his sock was drawing a picture of the room's interior. The tip of his tongue poked out of the corner of his mouth as he concentrated.

They had her set, and the crystals to transmit on her frequency, but they didn't have her poem, the words she used to transform messages into code, before sending them in Morse. They could search as much as they wanted, but they wouldn't find the poem here, she thought, as she was shoved towards the doorway. The narrow stairs couldn't accommodate two abreast, but three of the men walked in front of her, and two behind. Bony-fingers kept a hand on her cuffs, and grabbed her upper arm again as soon as they reached the hallway at the bottom of the stairs.

Out in the courtyard at the end of the passage, Madame de Jouvenal was hanging bed linen on the lower branches of the lime tree. She shot Edie a sympathetic look as she was force-marched towards the black van, but Edie did not respond. She wondered, after all, whose side Madame de Jouvenal was on. The *Sicherheitsdienst* hadn't needed to break down the door to her room; someone had given them a key.

It was dark inside the back of the van, metallic-smelling. They made her sit at the far end, with her back to the cab. The equipment was in the middle, lights and dials stilled for now. They sat on seats on either side, legs apart, exchanging words in the guttural language she couldn't even begin to understand. It was odd that she didn't feel more scared, but there was something so coolly professional about the way they'd caught her, searched the room, made their field notes. Somehow she knew that assault wouldn't form any part of the process, not then, at least.

The man who'd held her fast with his fingers – he seemed to be in charge – had gone to sit at the front with the driver. But her hands were still cuffed behind her. There was a way of getting out of the cuffs; they'd covered it in training. It was fiddly, but not impossible, if you had a watch on. It was to do with using the winding pin from your watch to unpick the lock on the cuffs. But Edie didn't wear a watch, hadn't managed to replace the one that Miss Atkins had confiscated.

The engine had been running, but now the van lurched off suddenly, and she was flung forwards. Her cuffed hands were no good at protecting her, and she banged her forehead on the metal edge of the detector equipment in the middle of the van. The men stopped talking momentarily, but didn't offer any help as she struggled to get back up onto the seat, head throbbing. They carried on chatting. She wondered what they were discussing – the thrill of catching a 'terrorist', or what they were having for supper that night. She wondered if they'd celebrate.

Edie remembered when her ATS unit had shot down an enemy plane, and everyone felt so jubilant. They'd had bacon sandwiches for breakfast that morning, on CO's orders.

She felt a trickle run down from her forehead, all the way to her cheek. The metal edge of the detector must have broken the skin. She longed to be able to put up a hand and wipe it away. The van careered on through the Paris streets. The men lit up cigarettes, and the air got warm with their body heat. It was dark, but she could see their faces by the light of their cigarettes, swimming black-and-white masks in the dingy fug, like clowns'. She was shunted and tumbled as the van sped on, hearing the strange foreign sound of their voices and smelling the acrid scent of their horrible cigarettes.

She hadn't meant to vomit, but the sick just came, hurling up her throat, acid bile all over her dress, all down the edge of their precious detecting unit. But still they barely glanced in her direction.

Perhaps they had seen it all before.

Gerhardt

Gerhardt had been promised the night off. He was in the queue for the *Soldatenkino* when the car drew up at the kerb next to him. His arrival in the *Sicherheitsdienst* had coincided with Boemelburg's promotion and transfer to Berlin. The new boss – Major Kieffer – had rescheduled the pass system, and he'd only just got his turn. Gerhardt hadn't even bothered to check what film was showing, but he'd decided that he was going to see a film, grab something to eat in one of the street cafés near by, and then before curfew maybe head over to that little bar that Josef had told him about. It didn't really matter that he was on his own; there were lots of other young Germans he could hook up with – those girls in front of him in the queue, perhaps, with their shiny hair and carefully ironed civil service uniforms – the whole night stretched ahead. And then the car drew up.

The window wound down and Josef poked a head out: 'Kieffer wants you.'

'What, now?' Gerhardt replied. He was almost at the front of the queue. The brunette was nudging her plump blonde colleague, and they both glanced back at him, smirking.

'No, next Tuesday. Of course now, you idiot,' said Josef, winding up the window. The girl burst out laughing. Gerhardt felt himself flush, and walked quickly over to the car, getting in the passenger seat next to Josef.

'My first night out in Paris,' he said, slumping down on the black leather and slamming the door behind him.

'I know, but there'll be others, though, mate,' said Josef, jamming the car into gear and accelerating off. 'Next time, if we get a night off together, I'll take you to the sweetest little whorehouse I know, on the other side of the river. What those girls will do for a few Reichsmarks will knock your socks off.'

They swerved round the place de la Concorde, cutting past a *vélo-taxi*, causing the cyclist to wobble, and the smartly dressed woman in the cart to scream as her hat flew off into the road. Josef laughed. 'Cheese-eating fools!' he chuckled, accelerating away. Gerhardt, embarrassed, shifted down further into his seat.

Josef slowed down as they went up the Champs-Élysées. 'Take a look.' He motioned out of the windscreen. 'Say what you like about the cheese-eaters, they know how to dress their women.' They passed expensive-looking shops with mannequins in frozen attitudes staring archly out through plate-glass windows. Gerhardt imagined having enough money to take a woman shopping here – some impossibly smart Frenchwoman in a porcelain-white suit and very red lipstick, who'd demand a litre of Chanel No. 5, and a magnum of the best champagne, and afterwards . . . Actually the thought petrified him, and he found himself thinking instead of Lisel, his pretty neighbour from back home. But he couldn't imagine her here in Paris at all.

They'd reached the Arc de Triomphe, and Josef slowed down even more, easing round the iconic arch. 'And buildings,' Josef said. 'They do women and buildings well, but as for the rest—' Josef made a face. Gerhardt looked up. A vast red-and-black flag billowed from the archway. He thought about the swastika that had been on his father's car, when they used to go visit him in the holidays. The flag had flipped as the car sped through the dusty streets, the chauffeur dodging the potholes. He remembered people turning to look as they passed. He'd felt like royalty, asked his mother if Father was a king. She'd laughed: no, darling, just a diplomat, and remember, don't call him Father here, just Uncle, don't forget. There was one particular memory that was so old he wasn't entirely sure whether or not it was a dream.

The girl was standing in the kerb. The sunshine was so bright and her dress was white, so all he could see in the glare was the pinkish blob of her face underneath a bell-shaped hat, and one arm waving slowly. The chauffeur pulled the car in beside her. Gerhardt looked questioningly up at his mother, who shrugged. 'Hans must recognise her. Or perhaps she's in trouble,' she said.

Through the windscreen, the road ahead of them wound upwards, away from the river. Gerhardt had been down to see the boats with his mother. He liked being on his own with his mother, without the new baby, who always seemed to need her for something. The baby had been left behind with a nanny – the midday sun was too strong for him. When they were alone together, Gerhardt's mother talked to him in English, told him stories about her childhood in Cape Town, and girlhood in Beirut, where her father was a banker, and the handsome German diplomat who'd wooed her away from her family and set her up with her own house in Leipzig.

The girl walked over to the car and leant in towards the open window, smiling. Her broad mouth had lots of very white teeth. 'Yes?' said Gerhardt's mother . . .

Gerhardt heard some shouting from outside on the street. He blinked himself out of his daydream. His attention was caught by some French children, in those funny black overalls they wore, chucking pebbles at the pigeons on the pavement, and shrieking in hilarity as the birds flapped away. They were probably the same age as he'd been, when he'd been driven like a prince around Bucharest in his father's car that summer. How thin their arms were, he thought, how pinched their faces.

'So, what does Kieffer need me for?' Gerhardt said as they turned into avenue Foch.

'The detectors have picked up an English terrorist and a wireless set,' Joseph said, speeding up again, even though they were almost there.

'I bet Kieffer's pleased,' said Gerhardt.

'Like the cat that's got the fucking cream, mate,' said Josef, as they drove through the double avenue of bare plane trees, cutting between the huge blond buildings. 'So obviously, you're needed for the next couple of days. But like I said, next time we're off together, I'll show you the sights. And I mean the real sights, not this tourist nonsense, know what I mean?'

'Yes. Great,' Gerhardt said, not knowing if he did understand. From what he'd heard, Josef's idea of sightseeing involved absinthe and dubious side alleys near Sacré-Cœur. He looked out of the window, wondering what exactly he'd be asked to do. Would Kieffer question the agent himself, or would there be others involved? Nobody had really explained what his duties were, other than being available for translation at all times. He was glad they'd caught one of the British saboteurs, though. It was a British bomb that had killed his little brother, sent his mother dead-eyed and snivelling to shuffle through her existence as if she were herself a ghost.

Josef skidded to a halt. The gate guard told them there was a van in the driveway, so they left the car outside. The guard, recognising them, didn't bother to check their ID, but let them straight through the side entrance. The walls of 84 avenue Foch rose up like a white cliff face. The boxy black wireless-detector van almost filled the driveway. It had reversed in, so its back doors opened to the front of the building. The intelligence crew were just getting out, falling like shadows onto the little green square of lawn. The front door opened behind the van, and Kieffer strode out.

'Ah, Vogt, we found you, good, good!' He was smiling, and Gerhardt thought of what Josef said – like the cat that's got the cream. 'Sorry to drag you in from your night off, but as you'll see, an interpreter will be essential. She was caught in the act of transmitting. We've got her crystals, too.'

Gerhardt started. Had he heard Kieffer say 'she' and 'her'? Surely he must have been mistaken. But at that moment a figure emerged from the back of the van: slight, with long auburn hair, wearing a dark blue jacket. She looked straight at him. There was a dribble of blood, like a red teardrop, running down one cheek. There was something familiar about her. Then the intelligence officer shoved her inside the building and she was gone.

'But she's just a girl,' Gerhardt said.

Edie

When the door shut, there were just the three of them: the older man who seemed as if he were in charge, and a much younger man, who seemed somewhat ill at ease. Edie guessed he must be about the same age as her. The older man lit a cigar and said something seemingly casual to the younger man, who nodded.

A typewriter tapped in the adjoining room. The air smelled of smoke and wood polish. Edie looked around as the young man ushered her across the floor and towards the huge windows. The room had obviously once been some kind of drawing room. Maps and photographs of France were tacked to the panelling. A large desk stood on the left-hand side, near the door to the adjoining room, underneath a picture of Hitler. There was a lit fire in a hearth on the wall opposite the desk, with a piano near by. Two chairs had been placed near the windows: bloated brocade and toffee-coloured wood.

The older man motioned for Edie to sit, so she did, perching on an overstuffed chair, slippery beneath her thighs. He said something to the younger man, who sat next to her, tipped forward on the edge of his seat. The older man remained standing, puffing his cigar. Edie looked away, ignoring him. The less she said, the better.

'He just wants to know your name,' the interpreter said. His English was perfect, but he had an odd accent. Edie wasn't going to be caught out so easily.

Je m'appelle Yvette Colbert,' she replied.

The older man snorted and took a few steps across to the hearth to tap a head of cigar ash into the fire. 'He knows you're not Yvette. He knows you're not French, and that you speak English. That's why I'm here,' the interpreter said. Edie shrugged as if she didn't understand.

The interpreter looked up at the older man, who flattened his lips together and shook his head, walking back towards them, before saying something else in German. 'He says it will be easier all round if you just drop the pretence,' the interpreter said.

Edie looked resolutely out of the window towards empty

treetops and beyond. The older man knelt down next to her and began to talk softly in German-accented French. 'What's happened must be a terrible shock, I know. It can't be easy for you.' His eyes were searching for contact with hers, she knew, but she looked past the wavy chestnut hair, streaked with grey, and the forehead like a ploughed field, and thought about how on earth she could escape from this place. 'You have your job to do and I have mine. But in the end we are just doing our best in the situation we find ourselves in. We must help each other. Nobody needs to get hurt.' He patted her knee, and she flinched. Her stomach churned and the smell of her sick was putrid-sweet in her nostrils. Her forehead stung from the cut.

She heard the interpreter say something in German to the older man, who barked an impatient response. Edie stared at the scratchy branches cutting the pale-gold afternoon sky. If she could hold out then it might give Felix, Justine and Claude a chance to get away, she thought. But how would they know she'd been captured? She wasn't due to meet up with Justine again for days. If they didn't hear from her they'd probably just assume she'd had to find a new safe house, like last time. If only she could alert London.

When she didn't respond the older man stood up and began to pace around the room. 'There is a spy in your organisation. You may as well comply,' he said in French. Edie remained mute, focusing on the way the slanting afternoon sunlight gilded the trees, trying not to hear what was being said. 'Yes, there is. We are getting information direct from Baker Street, in fact.' It couldn't be true; it must merely be a tactic to get her to talk.

'We know all about your Miss Atkins, your Major Buckmaster,

everyone at Norgeby House,' the interpreter chipped in in English. She tried to keep her face as expressionless as possible, although it felt as if her innards were being clawed out.

'I don't know what you want with me. My name is Yvette Colbert and I am a piano teacher,' Edie said in French, deliberately avoiding eye contact with the English interpreter.

'Then why don't you come over here and play for us?' The older man gestured towards the piano, smooth as amber in the light from the big window. She held up her cuffed hands. He said something to the interpreter, who went to the desk and said a few words into the telephone. Moments later a large man heaved into the room, a set of keys clinking at his belt. He gave the Nazi salute, and the two men returned the gesture. He lumbered over to her. She watched his stubby fingers turn the key in the lock. He breathed heavily – he must have come up from downstairs – he had halitosis.

'Well, come on then, let's hear it!' said the older man as her hands were freed.

Edie pushed herself up from her seat. She saw the large man give the handcuffs and key to the interpreter on his way out. The door thudded behind him. She walked towards the piano; the older man stepped aside as she passed. She sat down at the piano stool. 'But what should I play?' she said, pointing to the empty music rack. 'There is no score here.' Even though she spoke in French her gesture must have made it clear what she was asking.

It was the interpreter who replied, 'Beethoven.' And the older man nodded his agreement.

Her fingers touched the keys. They think I'm going to play 'Für Elise', she thought. Anyone with even a few weeks of piano lessons can play that one, and hope to get away with it. But instead she began to play the Moonlight Sonata. She fumbled at first, hit a wrong note, saw the older man draw breath, ready to interrupt and humiliate her, but then she closed her eyes, continued, and she was good: not brilliant, but good – good enough to teach spoilt little Parisian children, at least. They let her finish the whole piece; a full fifteen minutes playing blind, filling the room with smooth, rich sound.

When she stopped, she opened her eyes and saw the older man stub out the remains of his cigar. He clapped, and the interpreter joined in. Did she know the Moonlight Sonata was Herr Hitler's favourite piece? the interpreter asked in English. Did she know the bombing raid on an English city called Coventry was codenamed 'Moonlight Sonata', on Herr Hitler's orders? The older man flashed her a wide smile as the interpreter spoke, watching her carefully, but Edie shrugged, said she didn't understand English, and shut the piano lid. She refused to even glance at the interpreter.

The older man walked over and stood behind her as she sat, so close that his uniform brushed against her hair. She shivered. 'You played very prettily, but it proves nothing. There's no evidence that you teach the piano. However, the evidence that you transmit coded messages to the enemy is incontrovertible,' he said. She could hear him breathing, feel the fabric of his jacket against the back of her head, smell his cologne, his cigar smoke.

Start from the truth and work sideways. Hide in plain sight. Those were the maxims they'd been taught in training. If they threw her into Fresnes Prison for non-compliance there would be no chance of alerting the rest of the cell, or Miss Atkins either.

'Let me explain,' Edie said, looking down at the smooth expanse of honey-coloured wood. 'I was asked to do this wireless transmission as a favour for a friend of a friend; I know Morse code – before the war I trained as a telegraph operator, you see. But the content of the messages has nothing to do with me. I just transmitted what I was told. I don't know anything about them; it's all just nonsense as far as I'm concerned. I do it for the money. There's no money in piano teaching these days. And the alternative . . .' She paused, turning on the piano stool so she could make eye contact with him. 'I'm sure you know what the alternative would be. How else does a girl make money in Paris these days?'

The older man smirked. 'Quite so. So who is it you transmit for?'

'Well, naturally I don't know his name. We were introduced via a mutual friend and I was told that it was best not to ask too many questions.' The half-truths came quite easily, once she'd begun. She didn't know Felix's real name, and they were introduced via a mutual friend, Miss Atkins. And really, she was only transmitting what she was told. As she spoke, she almost came to believe the lies herself. 'I'm not a saboteur at all, Monsieur. And if you don't mind, it's getting late. I should be getting home – it's not safe to be out after dark, you know,' she said, starting to rise.

His hands were on her shoulders in an instant, pushing her back to a seated position. The interpreter rushed over to handcuff her again. As he fumbled with the handcuffs, she noticed how his nails were bitten right down to the quick, just like her own.

The older man kept his hands clamped on her and leant down. 'How much does he pay you per transmission?' His breath was hot and wet in her ear. She plucked a figure from the air: the price Mummy had paid for the Molyneux dresses, that time in 1939. She heard him take a sharp intake of breath. He asked more details then, about her contacts and how she'd met them. Lies came more easily now she'd started. When describing her contacts, she gave descriptions of friends from her previous life. She took her dead friend, Bea, and muddled her into a composite of her and Justine. So Justine became what Bea had been, a working-class girl with a baby to support, a domineering mother, and not enough money coming in. And Bea, poor Bea, gained new life in Justine's black jumpers and slacks, with a roll-up permanently at her lips. Edie felt like the girl in the fairy tale 'Rumpelstiltskin', but instead of spinning straw into gold, it was her old life that she wove into the fabric of fiction for the SD boss.

Periodically the interpreter would interrupt with a question in English, trying to catch her out, but she kept her eyes turned away from him, fixing her gaze on where her palms rested, damp with nervous sweat, on the silken wood of the piano lid.

'So you really don't care who you work for – which side you're on. You're simply doing this for the money?' the older man said, and she nodded. 'Well, we have the set and the crystals. That's all we need for now. But perhaps we can do business together?' Edie inclined her head. Let him think that, if it bought her some time. His hands were still on her shoulders, but his grip was relaxing. The light was fading at the window behind her. Her mind raced with possibilities. If they let her go now, she'd surely be followed, but perhaps she could find a way to lose them: the streets were a rabbit warren in some parts of the city. But if they kept her here she could perhaps offer to help them use the transmitter, for a price, and alert London that way. And she could pick up as much information as possible on the internal workings of the SD whilst she was here. Her eyes scanned the room, taking in the pinboard with coloured string linking different locations on a map. She was so busy thinking of possibilities that she wasn't even really listening when the interpreter spoke.

'You played Beethoven so beautifully earlier,' he said.

'How very kind,' she replied, her English manners as reflexive as breathing (always acknowledge a compliment, that's what Mummy said). The hands on her shoulders tightened to a vice.

'I thought you said you didn't understand English, Fräulein?'

Gerhardt

Frau Bertelsmann's behind was like battleship on an ocean swell as she led the way. The girl prisoner followed her, and Gerhardt brought up the rear, closing the door to Kieffer's office behind him. Their footsteps pattered along the marble floor towards the stairs. Gerhardt wondered where Frau Bertelsmann had decided to put the girl. His own room was on the fourth floor, where the air smelled of dust and secrets.

The girl stumbled a little on the first step, turning on her funny French shoes. Gerhardt reached forward to stop her from falling, catching her sleeve, and she half turned, eyes wide, before regaining her balance and continuing up the stairs. As his arm fell back to his side, Gerhardt felt again a tug of familiarity – hadn't he seen her somewhere before? Maybe it was just déjà vu. He followed her up the stairs to the second floor. For this, they'd pulled his first night off – for this straggly girl with hair that trickled like a dirty stream between her angular shoulder blades. She doesn't look much like a terrorist, he thought. She looks like a child who's been in a playground fight – her matted hair, torn clothing, cut on her head – nothing more than a scrap over stolen sweets or a broken pencil case. They reached the top of the stairs and went three doors along the corridor, just opposite where the back stairs snaked up towards the fourth floor, where Gerhardt's room was.

Frau Bertelsmann's solid bosoms heaved from the climb as she took out a key. Gerhardt and the girl waited. He was standing quite close to her, could smell the disinfectant that had been hastily dabbed on her cut face when she was brought in, and something else, too: sickly-sweet, pungent. He glanced down and saw the dark stain on her skirt: the girl had been sick.

If they hadn't caught her, he might be sitting with the blonde and the brunette from the queue. After the film he might have asked them to join him for a drink, and the night would just be beginning. He shoved his hands in his pockets and tilted on his heels, resenting the girl for ruining his night off.

Frau Bertelsmann appeared to have jammed the key. She tutted and swore softly under her breath, ramming and twisting again and again, as Gerhardt and the girl prisoner silently watched. The girl turned towards him slightly in the gloom, brushing his sleeve with her own, and for a moment he thought she was going to catch his eye, and he wondered what colour her eyes were. Were they green like Lisel's? But she turned away, not looking at him.

At last the lock gave, and Frau Bertelsmann flung the door open, ushering the girl inside and following on herself. She left the door open for Gerhardt, and flicked the light switch on, illuminating the room: white-painted floorboards, a powder-blue rug, and a picture of a rural scene in a gilt frame. It would have been a girl's room once, before the war, Gerhardt thought. It was very like he'd imagined Lisel's room to be – not that he'd ever seen it, because Lisel's parents were very strict about things like that.

The girl prisoner slumped down on the end of the bed. He was aware that Frau Bertelsmann was frowning at him, waiting impatiently to close the door, but he stalled deliberately, taking a deep breath and setting his jaw before stepping across the threshold. He wasn't looking forward to what was coming next.

Edie

The woman with the face like a blob of grease garbled something in German and pointed at her. 'She says you are to undress,' said the interpreter. It was pointless trying to maintain the pretence of not understanding English. 'She says your clothes will be laundered, but for now you can wear these.' The woman swooped towards Edie, and for a moment Edie thought she was going to strike her, but instead she lifted the bed pillow to reveal a pair of black-and-white-striped pyjamas, just like her old Army-issue ones from back home.

'You'll need to undo me, or I can't undress,' Edie said, chiming the cuffs against each other. The interpreter came over. She'd avoided looking at him all through the questioning, scared of betraying her understanding of English. It didn't matter now. She looked at his head, bent over her handcuffs: ash-brown hair, parted on one side. He straightened up, holding the cuffs. There was something about his face: it was as if she knew him from somewhere, but she couldn't place him.

The woman spoke, pointing at Edie. 'Now you can undress,' said the interpreter. He moved across to the window and gazed out, his hands leaning on the sill, making it clear that he wouldn't look at her.

Edie bent over to unlace her shoes. The woman watched, arms folded across her ample chest, as Edie placed her shoes side by side on the rug. Edie had to get up to take off her stockings, hoicking up her dress to unclip her suspenders and rolling them down. She put them on the bed, then reached up again to unhitch the suspender belt. She picked up the pyjama bottoms, thinking she could put them on underneath her dress. The man was still at the window, seemingly engrossed in the bare treetops and lowering sun. He was hardly taller than the woman, and quite slight, but there was a tautness about the way he held himself, Edie noticed, like a bowstring – careful energy held under tension.

'*Unterhosen,*' the woman said. Edie paused. '*Unterhosen,*' the woman repeated, louder this time, pointing at Edie's groin. Then she said something to the interpreter.

He cleared his throat. 'She says you should also remove your under things,' he said. Edie pulled down her knickers and quickly stepped out of them: left-right. She reached for the pyjama bottoms.

'*Nein. Weiter.*' The woman gestured at her.

'She needs to see you naked before you can put on the

pyjamas,' the interpreter said. Edie took off her woollen jacket, stealing a glance at him. He was still looking outside, not at her, his profile sharply defined against the fading outdoor light: short nose, definite jaw.

Edie undid the buttons on her dress, and unbuckled the fabric belt, glad to be rid of the stench of sick, and threw it on the pile with the other things. But as she did so the pages of newspaper that she used for extra warmth, no longer held in place, fell out from the gap between her dress and her slip, whispering down and landing with a crackle at her feet. The woman snorted derisively. They'll think it's just rubbish, Edie thought, looking up. The interpreter had turned just slightly so his face was no longer in profile, but his gaze was still fixed on the window.

Once she took her slip off she'd be bare from the waist down. Edie faltered. The woman tutted and said something to the interpreter, who in turn muttered something to Edie. But he spoke in such a low voice she couldn't hear. 'I beg your pardon?' Edie said. 'I didn't quite catch that.'

'Hurry up and get your clothes off,' the interpreter said loudly. Edie reached and grasped the slip – navy-blue, satin – smooth under her fingertips. It slid off her body and she let it fall onto the bed. The chill air goosebumped her flesh. The woman pointed at her brassiere, and she didn't need to ask for translation, unhooked the back and plucked the twin triangles of cream cotton away from her shivering skin and threw them onto the pile with the other things.

Now she reached out again for the pyjamas. The woman said something to her in German, gesturing, and the man said something in English but at that moment there was the sound of the van leaving the driveway, and she didn't hear it. 'I'm sorry,' she said, trying to cover her breasts and groin with her hands, and shivering with the cold, 'You'll need to repeat that.'

'She needs to look at you. P-put your hands up and turn round slowly for her,' he said with the hint of a stammer. She looked at him as he said it. Was it just the sunset, or was his face flushed? The woman grunted and gestured. Edie stepped off the rug, away from the newspaper and the discarded slip, held out her arms and turned an awkward pirouette, whilst the woman inspected every inch of her flesh, making soft grunts as if verbally checking a list. The woman seemed unconvinced by what she saw, and said something to the man. His hands were balled into fists on the windowsill, Edie noticed, as he replied in German, his voice rising. The woman answered, loud guttural sounds like spitting out rotten food. Their disagreement volleyed, until finally the woman made as if to go to the door, calling something as she went. The man started, began to turn, said something, and turned back. The woman returned to Edie. The interpreter sighed, and said, 'You have to lie on the bed with your knees bent, so she can see you properly.' His breath was condensing on the windowpane, clouding it up.

Edie lay on the scratchy blankets, thinking of the last time she'd been forced to lie like this, naked in a strange room, with her knees up high. It had been different then, a hot summer's day, a doctor with clammy hands: the blood and the pain. Why couldn't they shout, shine lights in her eyes, slap her face – they'd covered that in training at Beaulieu: she could cope with that.

The woman had taken a pair of pale rubber gloves from her pocket and was putting them on, heaving her bulk towards

where Edie lay. The rubber was cool-slick against the flesh of her thighs as Edie's legs were pushed apart. The woman prodded, right up there. Edie winced. A sob escaped her mouth, despite herself, and the woman tutted, said something else and moved away.

'She says stop being such a b-baby and get yourself into the pyjamas,' said the man, his voice barely a whisper. Finally satisfied, the woman slapped off the rubber gloves, balled them up, and put them back in her pocket. Edie pulled on the pyjamas, the material thick and rough against her bare skin. She wiped the single hot tear away from her cheek – she wouldn't give them the satisfaction of seeing her cry.

The interpreter finally turned away from the window and faced her, a frown hardening his features. 'She will handcuff you and then we'll go,' he said. The woman shackled her to the bedstead and picked up her dirty clothes and shoes, leaving the newspaper on the floor. The interpreter opened the door for the woman, and she bustled out. He was halfway through the doorway himself, when he paused and stepped back into the room, crossing to the bed where she sat. She flinched. But all he did was bend down to pick up the sheets of newsprint from where they still lay on the rug. Edie held her breath as he lifted them up.

There was a metal bin by the door. He was just going to put the old newspaper in the bin, wasn't he? As he picked up the yellow-grey sheets of paper, something fell out, a small piece of writing paper. It drifted down, landing on the blue rug, like the tiniest of clouds in a summer sky. She thought he hadn't noticed. But he stopped and plucked it up, turning it over. He held it up, reading the handwriting – her handwriting.

'What's this?' he said.

Gerhardt

The piano music carried on even after he knocked. What was it? Mozart's 453, keys tapped precisely: accurate and unfeeling as if typing a memo. He knocked again. This time his boss heard. 'Come,' he called. Gerhardt pushed open the door.

Kieffer sat at the piano, far across the room by the big windows. The remains of the daylight seeped in through the empty panes behind him, but his face was in shadow. '*Heil Hitler*,' said Gerhardt, giving the Nazi salute.

'*Heil Hitler*,' Kieffer replied, his arm a swift moving shadow, raised and lowered in an instant.

'Ah, young Vogt! So sorry I had to cancel your night off, but as you've seen for yourself, a competent interpreter is critical in these situations. Everything all right up there?' He flicked his eyes up to indicate the English prisoner on the third floor.

'Yes, sir,' said Gerhardt, thinking of the girl in the room upstairs, huddled in the striped pyjamas, and shackled to her bed. He watched as Kieffer got up from the piano and walked towards him across the vast red rug that spanned the centre of his office.

'They tell me you're new to the job, too,' said Kieffer, referring to his own arrival in post, replacing the recently promoted Boemelburg. 'How are you finding Paris?' Kieffer was close now, smiling broadly. Gerhardt replied that he hadn't seen an awful lot of Paris yet, but that his colleagues had promised to show him the sights. 'Well, good to have you on the team,' Kieffer said. 'Once we've established the most efficacious use of our new resource,' Kieffer began, and it took a moment for Gerhardt to realise that by 'new resource' he meant the girl prisoner, shivering upstairs on the bed, 'then you can go and have some fun with the boys. As Herr Hitler is so fond of saying, everyone should visit Paris at least once in their lifetime.'

'Thank you, sir,' said Gerhardt, remembering the slip of paper in his pocket, the little snatch of English poetry he'd found on the girl's rug. Kieffer was smiling still, pushing his wavy hair back from his head. Then he gave a lazy stretch. Gerhardt put a hand in his trouser pocket and felt the piece of paper. It might be important, he thought. It might be some kind of message or code. But then again, it might just be something sentimental, a reminder of a lover, perhaps. He thought again of the girl. Did she have a lover, back in England, he wondered, someone writing poetry for her?

'I do like it when a plan comes together, don't you, Vogt?' Kieffer said. 'It's taken the team weeks to catch that agent at just the right time, so we get her crystals and her set. Now Dr Goetz can get on with transmitting back to London as if he's the agent himself. They'll never know they're sending messages to us. Cigar?' Kieffer walked over to the fireplace and took a wooden box off the mantelshelf. He waved it in Gerhardt's direction. Gerhardt, still standing awkwardly in the centre of the Persian rug, replied that he didn't smoke.

Kieffer raised his brows but didn't insist. The coals were glowing in the hearth, but the light had all but gone from the huge windows now, and the room was beginning to blur at the edges with night-time shadows. Only Kieffer himself was in sharp focus, outlined by the glow from the fire, brandishing his cigar like a conductor. 'They've been doing this with marvellous success in the Netherlands for months now,' he continued. 'Boemelburg mentioned it to me and I thought, that's what we have to do here. The British always think they're so clever. They never suspect that anyone might be equally intelligent. They think they're the only ones who know how to play games.' He blew out a rush of smoke and grinned.

Like the cat that's got the cream, Gerhardt thought, reminded again of what Josef said earlier. Kieffer seemed so certain of success that Gerhardt was embarrassed about the piece of paper. It was clearly of no importance at all. Perhaps he should just return it to the prisoner?

'Do you like her?' Kieffer said, gesturing expansively with the cigar. And Gerhardt thought of the girl: the pale silver reflection of her nakedness in the glass that he'd tried so hard to ignore. 'I brought her with me from Germany – although I do need to find a decent tuner: she's suffered from the journey.' Kieffer walked back across the room. Gerhardt realised he was talking not about the girl, but the piano.

'Very nice,' Gerhardt said, pulling his hand out of his pocket. The poem wasn't important, was it? He felt foolish for bringing it down here.

'Do you play?' Kieffer said, reaching the piano and stroking the woodwork appreciatively, as if it were the flank of a thoroughbred mare.

'A little. My singing is better,' Gerhardt replied.

'Ah, a singer, wonderful. We must get some scores, something modern, from the movies. Perhaps the English girl can accompany you – she plays well, don't you think?'

Gerhardt was about to answer with a question: how long was Kieffer intending to keep the girl and how would they make use of her – when the door banged open and the light came on, blanching the room suddenly yellow-white. Gerhardt blinked.

'We have to interrogate the prisoner immediately,' screeched Dr Goetz, scuttling in, not bothering to shut the door.

'*Heil Hitler,*' said Gerhardt, saluting, but Dr Goetz ignored him.

'What's the problem?' Kieffer said, exhaling blue-grey smoke through his nostrils, gazing down at the little man. 'You have her set and her crystals. Just get on with transmitting. If you leave it too long then London will start to suspect all is not as it should be.'

'But we need her code,' Dr Goetz hissed. 'I told you, they don't simply put the English into Morse, they encode it first, using something personal. You'll need to question her thoroughly to get the information we need. You need to get her down here right now.' Dr Goetz was wringing his hands, his pale hair almost transparent in the electric light, eyebrows twitching.

'Very well,' Kieffer said. 'But first, please explain exactly what we're asking for. What form will this code take, specifically?'

'A poem, or some such. Maybe a song lyric, or a prayer. I'm told they usually learn these off by heart, but they will also often be written down, before encoding, because they will need to match each letter from their crib with a letter from the alphabet – most of them find this too hard to do in their heads at first,' said Dr Goetz, pushing his gold-rimmed spectacles up to the bridge of his nose.

'I see,' said Kieffer. He took a side-step and threw the remains of his cigar into the fire, where it burst into a fist of orange flame. He turned back to Dr Goetz. 'Then call Frau Bertelsmann and ask her to bring the girl here. I know exactly what to do. My prediction is we'll have your precious code by midnight, if not sooner,' said Kieffer.

Gerhardt thought about the girl in the room, and what Frau Bertelsmann had done to her earlier. He thought about the slip of paper in his pocket. 'I found this,' he blurted, pulling out the poem.

'What's that?' said Dr Goetz, snatching it from Gerhardt's hand. He peered at the script. 'An English poem. Where did you find it?'

'On the prisoner's rug, sir.'

'Well, why didn't you say so before? This is precisely the kind of thing I've been after,' said Dr Goetz, frowning. 'I'll get to work straight away.' He almost ran out of the door, leaving it ajar. Gerhardt heard his footsteps scurrying up the stairs.

Kieffer slapped Gerhardt on the back, a couple of hearty thumps between his shoulder blades. 'Well, my boy, it looks like you've just saved the day.' His smile was very broad, white teeth stretched across his face. 'Boemelburg was right to take you on. Your uncle would be very proud of you, Vogt.'

Chapter 6

Vera

Would he never shut up? Vera resisted the urge to yawn as Buckmaster continued. Everyone else round the table seemed extremely interested in what he had to say, nodding earnestly as he mentioned such things as 'operational imperatives' and 'patriotic duty', and even, at one point, 'grateful acceptance of known risks', whatever the hell that meant. Vera didn't know anyone who gratefully accepted risk – what tosh. Still everyone else seemed entranced. Perhaps she was doing him a disservice, she thought, looking round the table at the very young men with their neatly slicked hair and polished medals. Perhaps he was a better rhetorician than she gave him credit for.

Flames curled at the logs in the huge fireplace. The silver-ware shone, the crystal glittered. Pipe and cigarette smoke floated upwards, misting out the chandeliers. Candles flickered in a stray scud of breeze. And still Buckmaster continued. Vera tried to listen. But her mind drifted off, rising away with the smoky exhalations of her dinner companions.

She felt underdressed here, even in her violet satin gown, with her white cotton gloves, and cigarette wedged into the long-handled ivory holder. Even with the diamond earrings. (There had been a matching choker, once. Surely not for travelling, Mother had said as they scrambled for their hand luggage that day in 1937, and Vera's fingers fumbled with the catch on the necklace. Diamonds aren't really suitable for a long voyage, darling, leave them in the safe – we can have them sent on, or come back for them, Mother had said. But Vera had known there would be nobody to send them on, and that she'd never go back.) Even dressed up to the nines, as Mrs Littlewood had said, catching her on the stairs on the way out that evening, Vera felt underdressed. Because everyone else here was in uniform: Air Force, Army, Navy – FANY, even. Everyone else here was part of the British establishment. Everyone – almost everyone. Scanning round the table she caught Dericourt's eye. He had on a dinner jacket, another Savile Row purchase, no doubt, and a lit cigar was trailing from his capable fingers. Seeing her, he gave a slow wink. She looked quickly away, fixing her gaze on Buckmaster, words still tumbling from his port-lubricated lips: something about the only good German being a dead German.

The boys had been knocking it back all night, all except for Dericourt, who'd be piloting a Lysander later, taking two agents – call signs Bombproof and Taff – to start up a new circuit in Pas-de-Calais. Soon, if Buckmaster ever finished his interminable diatribe, they'd change out of their mess dress and into their French civilian clothes. She'd check their pockets and wallets for anything obviously British. One couldn't have them turning up in Occupied France with two bob and a train ticket from Paddington. She remembered doing the same thing for Yvette, in the last moon period, as Buckmaster continued to pontificate, brandishing his port glass like a vial of holy water.

She'd been chatty, 'Yvette', friendly with everyone, so eager to please – wonderful manners, Vera thought, remembering her laughter, and that river of red hair. She'd taken the pre-departure checks with such good grace, even when Vera had had to take away her watch – you didn't get Harwood's in France, and one couldn't be too careful. Vera had given her the option to back out. They'd calculated that she only had about a fifty-fifty chance of making it back alive: heads or tails? The girl said that she'd won on horses at point-to-point races with worse odds. Then, almost under her breath, she'd added that it was better odds than the bomber boys got, and they didn't have a choice. Despite their differences in age, experience, background, Vera felt a connection with Yvette, because she, too, was running away from something. Hadn't she been the same, in 1937, leaving it all without so much as a backward glance?

Vera was startled from her thoughts by the scraping of chairs against the flagged floor. Everyone was standing up, holding their glasses aloft.

'Gentlemen – the King!' Buckmaster roared, finishing his after-dinner speech with the loyal toast.

'The King.' Vera added her voice to the rejoinder, and took a sip of port. She glanced across at Dericourt. He had a glass in his hand, too. Had he also toasted the King? Seeing her looking, he raised his glass to her. She saw his lips mouth 'Miss Atkins', silently toasting her, as the rest of the group began lighting cigars and coagulating into clumps of bonhomie. She turned away, pretending not to have seen, not liking the way the heat rose in her chest every time that gypsy pilot so much as glanced in her direction. Nothing more than a charlatan, she thought. No breeding, just swagger.

'Inspiring words, Buckie,' she said, turning to her boss.

'Yes, I think it went down rather well,' he said.

'It makes a change to have you with us for one of the send-off dinners.'

'Well, normally I'm happy to leave all that sort of thing to you, Vee, but as it's Dericourt's first time, I rather thought—'

'Oh, quite. My dear boy, I completely understand.' She understood that he was here to show off the outfit to 'the god-send' Dericourt. But she didn't say that, instead she continued to smile and offered to refill Buckmaster's glass. 'Say when,' she said, tipping the decanter, letting the ruby liquid pour.

'When!' he said at last as the glass was brimming. 'Oh Vee, in all the excitement, I almost forgot to say, I've heard back from the bods at the Home Office. Your form is being processed. Can't see it will be a problem. Although they'll need to interview you at some point.'

'That's marvellous, thank you,' she said, thinking of Dick. At last she could write with good news, just as soon as she'd got through tonight, and seen off Dericourt.

Dericourt

He'd have her one of these days, Henri Dericourt thought, pulling the Lysander up into the navy-blue sky: Miss Atkins, Miss-holier-than-thou-Atkins, with her over-enunciated

Kensington drawl – *My dea-ah boy!* and her pre-war fashion sense. I'll kiss those pursed lips and grab her uptight tits until she's begging for it. He dipped a wing, and the plane banked as they gained height. Down below he could glimpse Miss Atkins, a pale blur on the end of the runway, with one arm raised in a wave – although from this height it could equally well be a Nazi salute – saying a final farewell to 'her' agents, the two men he had in the back of the plane.

He pulled the Lysander round and felt the surge as the tailwind caught them. They'd make good time tonight. He turned to the two agents huddled behind him. 'Say goodbye to Britain,' he said, and they did, both of them saying 'Cheerio, Blighty' and waving out of the window as the darkened shapes of fields and houses slipped away below. Henri had come to realise that people generally did what he asked them, so long as he assumed their compliance in advance. Just like he'd asked Jeannot to divorce her husband, and asked the Americans to sponsor his safe passage from Marseille to Britain, and when he arrived in Britain, asked the British for a job with the SOE. They'd all done exactly what they were told. And one of these days, he'd ask Miss Atkins for a fuck, and she'd do as she was told, too, he decided, as the plane gained more height and they headed towards the Channel.

In the back he could hear the two agents chatting together as they passed a flask of brandy between them. They'd be drunk by the time they reached the rendezvous, drunk and so very easy for the *Sicherheitsdienst* to pick up, if someone had tipped them off. What was the English expression? Sitting ducks – yes, that was it. He heard the agents' laughter cutting through the engines' drone. They'd think that their shared secrets made them soulmates, when in fact it was nothing more than the proximity of death that made people feel close to one another.

The plane sped over the doodled line where the east coast met the sea, and everything became silver-blue and serene: star-dappled sky above, wave-crested water below, and the moonlit pathway like a threshold they could never quite cross. The moon was high up to the right of his vision: pulling, pulsing, and constantly drawing his attention with its irritating shimmer. Sometimes he could understand why it affected Jeannot so badly when it was on the wane. But now it was waxing and he was on his way to France, at last. Ah, it would be good to see Jeannot again, his little chicken. The engines purred, the course was set, and the conditions were perfect. Henri smiled. He felt like a god. He turned back again to check on his passengers. 'Okay?'

Their little faces were like twin moons. They gave him the thumbs-up and asked if he'd like some coffee from the Thermos. He declined. He'd had one of the obligatory 'wakey-wakey' pills before take-off, and in any case, British coffee tasted like mud. He'd wait. There'd be decent black market coffee soon enough, once he'd discharged his load.

The seascape slipped past like a pulled silk scarf. The stars were out, diamond chips scattered above. He thought about the diamond earrings he'd promised Jeannot early on in their relationship, when she was still married to the soldier. Divorce him and I'll buy you diamonds, he'd said. They'd been married two years already, but still he had no diamonds to give her. No diamonds from the SOE: Miss Atkins had put a stop to that, but the pay was adequate. Perhaps the SD? Boemelburg had promised diamonds. But he thought he'd heard that Boemelburg was no longer in Paris, had been promoted to a desk job in Berlin. Henri wondered what his successor was like.

Henri blinked, noticing that the moonshine was no longer tugging at his temple, and the sea had become a dull shadow. They were in cloud, and he hadn't even noticed. He pulled up the nose, thinking to get the Lysander up, and continue the journey above cloud-level, but as he climbed, the cover merely got thicker, until he was blindly hurtling upwards, the plane at such a sharp angle it was a miracle she didn't stall on him. Not too high, he reminded himself, checking the altimeter, wouldn't want ice on the wings, but climbing was the only way to get out of it now. It was silent in the back. He imagined the agents huddled together amongst the suitcases and Sten guns.

Without warning, the plane lifted up and sideways, hurling him about in the cockpit so that he banged his head against the instrument panel. He clutched the control column, cursing himself for losing concentration. There was a thud from the back, a stifled gasp. He was just beginning to regain control when, like a broken lift, they were gone, falling from the sky: an air pocket hurling them downwards. He heard one of the agents cry out.

With a lurch they were below the cloud, but they'd lost so much height he feared they'd ditch in the sea. He hauled again on the control column, lifting the nose up, away from the breaking surf, but as he pulled away a cliff face reared up, so close he could see the seagull nests in the chalky rock. He banked, pulling the aircraft sideways, swerving away and following the edge of the cliff round, on and on like a white ribbon, until it cut into the land. Ah, the estuary. Now he knew where they were.

Henri allowed the plane to gain a little height and steady herself before turning back to his passengers. 'People used to pay me good money for a ride like that,' he laughed. 'Back in my barnstorming days!' But they didn't answer, petrified into silence.

It had been close, he had to admit. But luck, as ever, was on his side. France unrolled beneath them like an expensive rug. And in the distance, towards Paris, there was a chink in the cloud cover, revealing two bright stars. Henri heard the agents rustling in the back, like hens in a coop. He smiled to himself. He'd get those diamond earrings, one way or the other.

Hail hurled down like insults as the two agents were scooped up and magicked away to safe houses near by. Henri managed to get the Lysander into an empty barn without causing too much damage. He stood in the barn doorway now, his aircraft like a giant dragonfly crouching in the gloom behind him. He looked out into the night that twitched and jerked with the falling ice. The sound of it on the barn roof was like machine-gun fire. The air smelled of old manure.

He'd been lucky to get them all down safely, he thought, when they'd hit the storm. He certainly wouldn't be flying back to Tempsford tonight, or any time soon, with the weather piling in from the north-east. He could be stuck in France for days.

Henri Dericourt drummed his fingers on the damp wood of the barn door, making uneasy percussion with the pelting hail. The obvious thing to do would be to make a run for his parents' house: the one-bedroomed cottage on the outskirts of the town. That would be the obvious thing to do. He pulled a packet of Sobranies from his trouser pocket. They'd got a little squashed in the journey, these cigarettes that were Miss Atkins' favourites: elegant, but rather the worse for wear – a little crooked. Like her, he thought, putting the filter to his lips and flicking his lighter open.

How long was it since he'd been home? Years – long before the war. But nothing would have changed, nothing ever did. The fire would be dead in the hearth and his father snoring upstairs. If Henri turned up now, there'd be a need for explanations. But it wasn't having to explain his long absence that caused him to pause and contemplate the storm. The Henri Dericourt from here – the son of the drunken postman and a maid from the big house, the boy who was regularly whipped at school for his lack of focus – that was not who he was any more. Nowadays Henri Dericourt was a dashing ex-French Air Force pilot, son of Picardie landowners: he'd left the snot-nosed peasant behind long ago.

He sighed on a smoky exhalation. Something will come, he thought, flicking ash out into the storm; something always does. Lightning flashed across the distant sky. Moments later there was a tearing roar. The storm was getting closer.

At first he thought it was another bolt of lightning, but then he recognised it as the twin beams of headlights, flashing up over the brow of the hill, parting the dark ahead of a vehicle. He threw the remnants of the cigarette into the night and ran towards the road.

Inside the van smelled of mud and blood. 'You've got a good haul, here,' Henri said, feeling cold feathers tickle the nape of his neck as they jolted forwards.

'They say there's good money to be made in Paris these days,' said the driver, his face dark and pitted as a pickled walnut as he frowned out into the driving hailstorm. 'They say the Boche like game. I've got rabbit, duck and grouse here.

I know you shouldn't, but how is a man to make a living, these days? My son's gone to the labour camps, and I can't manage the land on my own.' He squinted out of the mucky windscreen.

The van hit a pothole and a slaughtered bird slithered from the back and down into Henri's lap. He held it for a moment, stroking the cool feathers, feeling for the bullet wound. There it was: soft and sticky as a woman's hole. 'You're a good shot,' Henri said, turning to put the duck back on the pallet behind him. 'Who are you supplying?'

The man mentioned a couple of restaurants that Henri had never heard of. When the man said how much he'd expect to get for selling his wares, Henri sucked his teeth. 'You know you could get double that selling to the Ritz or the Lucas Carton or one of the other high-end outfits,' he said.

'Yes, but I hear they already have someone supplying them,' the man replied, hunched forward over the wheel. The road coiled snakelike into the valley below.

'Bladier?' Henri said.

'You know him?'

'We go back years,' Henri said, scratching an imaginary itch on the side of his nose.

'Then maybe you can help me,' the man said.

'Maybe we can help each other,' Henri replied. They'd be in Paris by dawn.

Chapter 7

Edie

Edie heard voices and footsteps but they went right past her door and on up the stairs. They'd be keeping themselves busy with her transmitter, she thought. There'd been laughter up the stairwells last night, as they congratulated themselves on their good fortune: a transmitter, crystals and code, all in one day. If only she'd been a better operative, hadn't had to keep her code written down for transposition. If only that interpreter hadn't seen – if he'd just thrown the old pages of *Pariser Zeitung* in the bin, where they belonged.

She hadn't slept last night, only slipped into fitful half-consciousness, waking with a jerk every time the moon shone in through the shuttered windows, mind feverishly working on how to deal with the situation. They didn't have her security check, that was something. Thank God they didn't have her security check, but she had to find a way to escape.

Edie sat up and stretched round so she could see outside. Her handcuffs chinked against the bedstead. Her wrists were red-raw from tugging against the metal. Earlier on the woman had cuffed her to the bed after opening the shutters and taking her to the bathroom to watch her urinate. Through the little rectangle of window there were treetops and a glimpse of the buildings across the boulevard. She pulled against the handcuff but it bit deeper into the flesh of her wrist. If only she had longer nails, she might just be able to reach the mechanism. But her nails were chewed to the quick, soft and raw as fillet steak.

Edie heard footsteps on the stairs and the click of a key in her door. She let go of the cuff. The door opened, but it was only a scrawny cleaning woman with a dustpan and a basket. Edie let out a breath. The woman began to sweep.

Swish, went the brush: swish-swish, and Edie remembered how Nanny used to brush her hair at bedtime: one hundred strokes and then kneel down for prayers. She looked down at the woman's back, her threadbare blue dress, knotted spine like a bicycle chain pushing up under the thin fabric. The sunlight slid in through the window, casting a triangle of beige on the brown blankets. Edie pulled her knees up to her chest as the cleaner swept, flicking the invisible pile of dust into a dustpan and straightening up. Her hair was streaked with grey, but underneath the old dress her body was upright and strong. Edie tried to catch her eye, but she moved swiftly away, emptying the dustpan into the metal bin. Edie lowered her feet and looked down at the blue rug, sliced diagonally into two tones by the shaft of sunshine: powder blue and deep sky. That's where it had fallen, her poem. That's where he'd found it: 'June Thunder', it was called. It was by a modern poet, Louis MacNeice. Miss Atkins had chosen it for her. A personal favourite, she said. And it was better to have something modern because it would be harder for them to guess – they'd be on to something like Kipling in a shot, she said. Miss Atkins didn't think the Germans would have heard of Louis MacNeice.

But the Germans hadn't had to guess at all, because Edie had practically given it to them. They had her set, her crystals and her code. Why had she never been able to code without seeing her crib written down?

The woman was whistling tunelessly, rubbing hard at smears on the glass. Edie remembered how the interpreter's breath had condensed just there, last night. The cleaner paused, catching Edie's eye in the reflection. She smiled – a crescent shadow on the empty pane. Edie thought about the interpreter. What had he seen in the glass, she wondered?

Edie heard a juddering rattle. Cool air washed in like a wave. The cleaner had opened the window and was wiping the outside sill. She'd begun whistling again, but you could barely hear it above the sound of army boots tramping along avenue Foch – a military parade was approaching. The windows open easily, Edie thought. There are no bars, either. She thought about the outside. The small patch of grass at the bottom held no hiding places, and anyway, there were high fences and the gate guard to contend with. But if she could climb up – she'd been good at climbing in training, she remembered: her small feet wedged well into tiny crevices, and her light frame meant it was easy to haul herself upwards – surely there would be a way of getting out over the rooftops? She'd glanced at the front of the building when she arrived: balconettes laced every window, and hadn't there been a lightning rod, and some guttering, too? If only she could get out of the handcuffs.

The cleaner shut the window with a thud, muting the parade. Edie heard footfalls on the stairs, someone calling up to a colleague, the flush of a toilet somewhere down the corridor: all the commonplace sounds of a working building. The cleaner was at the foot of her bed now, in the slab of sunshine, wiping the trellised bedstead with the vinegary cloth. Then she swept up past Edie to the head of the bed, passing so close that the fabric of her sleeve brushed Edie's face, and Edie could smell her: vinegar, raw onions, cheap soap and tobacco. A bit like Justine, Edie thought. She had to find a way to get out, warn Justine and Felix what was going on.

The cleaner wiped the bedhead, moving Edie's cuffed wrist so she could dust underneath. She'd stopped whistling now, and was muttering to herself: *How they expect me to make the bed properly with this girl tied to it, it's ridiculous. That Frau Bertelsmann can fuck herself if she thinks I'm going to be able to do a proper job on this room, what with everything else going on at the moment . . .*

She was speaking French, Edie realised. Of course. The Germans would hardly go to the trouble of bringing their own domestic staff, when there was a whole nation of cheap, desperate labour to be had.

'*Je m'appelle Yvette,*' Edie said. '*Et vous?*'

The cleaner clicked her tongue and stood up straight, looking down at Edie. 'Rosa,' she replied, hands on hips. She's young, Edie realised. The grey hair and old-fashioned dress disguise it, but her face is unlined – she's barely older than I am. 'My name is Rosa, but I'm not supposed to talk to you,' she said, running a hand through her frizzy hair, which was pinned back into some kind of low bun. It was a very natural gesture, simply a tired woman pushing her hair back, but as she did so a hairpin fell out and landed between Edie's bare feet. Edie quickly covered it, feeling the hooked piece of wire digging into the soft skin under the arch of her foot. Rosa turned, threw the rag into the basket by the door, picked it up and left.

Edie held her breath, thinking that at any minute Rosa might come back for the missing hairpin, but Rosa's footfalls disappeared downstairs. Edie lifted her foot. The hairpin was almost in the same place as her poem had been yesterday, when the interpreter had taken it. She put her right hand down between her knees and scooped it from the rug. It was perfect.

Vera

'Miss Atkins?' Margaret said, smiling beside the open ledger.

Vera shook her head. 'I've already signed it. I've been in since 8.30, dear girl.'

'It's not that. It's Jenkins. He wants to see you in Room 52.'

Vera nodded, checking her watch. It wasn't yet ten. She walked along the corridor. There was the muffled sound of typewriters tapping from behind closed doors. Figures scurried past clutching beige files stamped *Subject to confirmation*. A messenger boy was pushing a trolleyload of papers out of the cordoned-off area as she approached and, recognising her, left the signals-room door ajar. As she walked in she could see the call signs of active agents marked up on the blackboard: Taff, Bombproof, Cat, and all the others, along with their scheduled times. Five men in civilian jackets sat with their backs to her at five desks set against the wall, peering down at papers under the yellow glare of table lamps. It was silent except for the clack-chattering of the teleprinters on the far wall. Jenkins, F-Section's own, sat at the furthest end, near the permanently blacked-out windows.

'I thought you should see this, Miss Atkins,' he said, looking up as she entered.

'See what, dear boy?' She walked towards him.

Jenkins' chair scraped on the bare lino as he got up from his desk. He cleared his throat and put a pencil behind his ear. 'It's this message from Cat.'

'How's she getting on? Keeping to her scheds?' Jenkins showed Vera the decoded message. At first glance Vera didn't see anything out of the ordinary about it. It was asking for information regarding weapons drops and potential locations for a planned Lysander landing.

'I'm not sure about it,' said Jenkins. 'It was received hours late.' Vera had another look. Cat had been consistently keeping to her times, since that ticking off she'd been given. But who knew what was going on in the field? There could be all sorts of reasons why she couldn't stick to her exact timetable. A mistimed report didn't really signify anything.

'Nothing wrong with her coding?' Vera said. The paper Jenkins showed her was the decoded version. There were a couple of question marks – letters that he couldn't be certain of – but no more than usual.

'It's coded properly.' He pointed to the paper. 'But something in the phrasing sounds off, don't you think? Look here, where it says *Supply drop details at earliest convenience.'* Vera looked down to where his finger prodded the thickly typed capital letters. 'I've been decoding Cat since she dropped, and she's never used that phrase before. Normally she'd say *Supply drop details soonest.'*

'I see,' said Vera, taking the sheet of paper from him and scanning down through the message. 'And here,' she said, resting a fingernail on one word and holding the paper out to Jenkins. 'I'm sure you've already noted this?'

He nodded, frowning. 'Yes, her security check's missing, too. And that's most worrying of all. Her message was sent hours after her sched, with a different "fist", and she hasn't included her check, so—'

'So can we be sure it's her?' Vera said, finishing his sentence. She looked at Jenkins with his tousled hair, messed up where he'd been ruffling it in concentration, and his skew-whiff tie. It was how he looked that made people underestimate him, but he was one of the best decoders they had.

Jenkins looked back, his round eyes blinked owlishly. 'I just thought you should see it,' he said.

"Quite right. I'll fetch Major Buckmaster,' she replied, handing back the paper before walking out of the signals room and down the hallway. It was a worry, she thought, striding forwards. If Yvette's set had been captured, it changed everything. And what if it wasn't just her set. What if it was Yvette herself who'd been caught and taken in? It didn't bear thinking about. Buckmaster was at his desk, chewing on his pipe stem and frowning at a roll of blueprints that lay open in front of him. 'Buckie, there's something I need you to see,' she said.

'It's the morning briefing shortly; can't it wait?' he replied.

'No, I don't think it can, actually.'

Buckmaster sighed and pushed himself out of his chair. Vera walked ahead of him to the signals room. The other decoders were a line of mute jacket-backs against tables, but Jenkins still stood, holding the message, waiting for them.

'Tell him what you told me,' Vera said – there was no time for pleasantries.

Jenkins pulled his earlobe and cleared his throat. 'We've had a message from Cat, but it's not on sched and missing the check,' he said.

Vera looked at Buckmaster. He tapped his pipe stem against his lip.

'One of the Paris cells, isn't he?'

'She,' Vera corrected him. 'Cat is that new female WT we dropped during the last moon period to replace Sparks. Her codename is Yvette Colbert, remember?'

'The girl?' Buckmaster said. 'Silly thing. Tell her to remember her true check next time, will you?' He turned to leave. 'Now, we really should get on. There's a lot to get through this morning.'

Vera exchanged looks with Jenkins. 'But, don't you see, if she's been captured whilst transmitting, the Germans might have her code. How can we be certain this message is from Cat, and not a German Intelligence job?'

Buckmaster shook his head. 'She's just new to the post, that's all. I don't think we need to be overly paranoid.'

'With respect, I think we do. She's had months of training. You know as well as I do that the necessity to keep to the security protocols will have been drilled into her.'

Jenkins looked nervously from one to the other, the decoded message rustling in his hand.

'Well, let me take a look, then,' said Buckmaster, reaching out for the paper. He squinted as he looked down at it.

'Would you like me to fetch your reading glasses from the office?' Vera said.

'Not at all. I can see perfectly well,' Buckmaster said,

scanning through the words. 'Well, there's nothing really untoward as far as I can make out,' he said at last. 'The girl just got a bit flustered and forgot the check, that's all.' He handed the paper back to Jenkins, who put it down on the desk. 'Well, if that's everything?' Buckmaster turned to leave.

Vera placed a hand on his arm. 'No, Buckie – I mean, Major – if this agent is in a situation where she's been captured and the message comes back reminding her to use her check – well, that's just going to prove to the Germans that she's been lying; it will play right into their hands.'

Jenkins was looking at his feet now, tugging at a lock of curly hair that fell down his forehead.

'Um, a word in private, Miss Atkins,' Buckmaster said, pulling his sleeve away from her touch. 'Please excuse us for a moment, Jenkins.' Vera followed Buckmaster outside the signals room and into the corridor. 'In here,' Buckmaster said, ushering her in front of him into an empty meeting room and closing the door behind them.

'What the hell do you think you're playing at, Vera?' he said as soon as the door was shut. 'Undermining me in front of the staff – it's just not on, you know.'

'Oh, come on, it's not a question of undermining you, it's about the security of the mission, as you very well know, dear boy,' said Vera, returning his glare.

'I am not your dear boy, Vera. I am the head of this section, and as such I demand some respect. I do not expect to be let down like that. Where's your loyalty, woman?'

'Buckie, please don't make this about anything other than it is. I was only thinking of the predicament that poor girl could be in, and the future of the whole Paris network, not just her cell.'

'What utter tosh. That girl has just had one too many *vins rouges* and forgotten herself, that's all. I'm fed up with your games, Vera.'

His face was so red it looked almost purplish. Vera was reminded of beetroot sandwiches. She deliberately moved in closer to Buckmaster, leaning up and brushing a stray strand of cotton from one of his lapels. 'Don't let's fight, Buckie—' she began.

'Enough, Vera,' he said, pushing her hand away. 'You've asked me to sponsor your naturalisation and I shall do so – but only if I can be certain of your loyalty. I'm putting myself on the line for you. I don't expect to be undermined like that, in front of my own men, too. I need you onside, Vee. I need to know who you're with.'

'I'm with you, naturally,' Vera replied, smoothing the rejected hand against her skirt.

'Well then, go and sort this out,' said Buckmaster, his skin returning to a normal shade. 'And for goodness' sake, don't be late for the briefing.'

'As you wish, Major,' Vera replied. Buckmaster stayed behind in the meeting room, and she crossed the corridor on her own, checking her watch on the way.

Vera asked Jenkins for a clean sheet, and borrowed his pencil. The lead slid easily against the thick cream paper. It only took a moment to write out a response to Cat's message. It was the shortest message Vera had ever given Jenkins to send: death warrants probably took longer to formulate, she thought, passing the sheet to him as she finished.

She saw Jenkins' eyes widen as he read the words, and heard his intake of breath as if he were about to speak. Vera slowly lowered her lids, so Jenkins, the faceless coders, the teleprinters, and the black rectangles of the signals room-windows were momentarily out of sight. 'That will be all,' she said with finality, opened her eyes, and walked out, closing the door behind her. She sighed, and leant briefly on the doorframe. It was done, and the devil take the consequences.

Edie

'Major Kieffer and Dr Goetz request your presence immediately!' the voice rapped out as the door was flung open. Edie let the hairpin slip to the floor and kicked it under the bed with her foot. She'd almost had it that time, could feel the mechanism about to give. The interpreter stood in the doorway. She had that nagging déjà vu again. In daylight she could see his face clearly – dark brown eyes and a tip-tilted nose – where did she know him from? 'Hurry up!' he said, coming over and undoing her handcuff from the bedstead. He hadn't noticed the hairpin. He clipped the free cuff onto her right hand and ushered her out of the door and down the stairwell, dark after the sunny room. She feared she'd fall on the steep stairs – her handcuffs made it impossible to hold the banister – but he offered no help.

The building had a different feel in the morning. There was the sound of typing, and the smell of real coffee. A figure carrying a stack of manila files disappeared down the corridor. The interpreter nudged her through an open doorway into the room she'd been questioned in the previous afternoon. The office was as warm and welcoming as a drawing room today, the sunlight glancing off the prisms in the ceiling chandelier, making the room dance with pricks of light. The older man – Kieffer – who'd questioned her last night stood in front of the piano with another man: slight and pale, with gold-rimmed spectacles – he must be Dr Goetz. What did they want with her?

The interpreter closed the door behind them as Kieffer and Dr Goetz began to walk towards her. She glanced sideways at the gold carriage clock on the mantelpiece above the hearth, calculating: if they'd used her set to transmit a message last night, after they got her poem-code, then it would have been in London, decoded and with Miss Atkins, hours ago. But they hadn't had her security check. And a message received without a security check would alert Baker Street to the fact that either her set and code had been captured or she was being forced to transmit under duress, wouldn't it? Edie tried to breathe deeply and keep her mind clear. She'd been trained for this. There was a system: without the security check Miss Atkins and the others in Baker Street would have realised something was wrong and would not have responded. She told herself not to panic.

Even as Kieffer and Dr Goetz approached, Edie imagined Miss Atkins and Major Buckmaster noticing the absence of the check and sending telegrams and telephoning the boys at Tempsford. Perhaps they could get a direct message to Felix and Justine with that Lysander pilot who was flying over, warning them to lie low. It would ruin Felix's plans for the depot sabotage, but at least they'd be safe, wouldn't they?

Kieffer and Dr Goetz were in front of her now, their figures blocking out the sunshine. The interpreter stood just behind her, to her left. At first, nobody spoke. The pale little man – Goetz – simply held out a piece of paper. Edie's handcuffs jinked and pulled against her skin as she took it from him and held it up to read:

Cat – Sloppy work. Remember your security check and stick to your scheds.

Edie felt herself blanch, and the paper slipped from her cuffed grasp. It was like being kicked, hard, in the centre of her chest. She couldn't breathe.

Dr Goetz bent down to pick up the paper, his glasses slipping down his nose as he did so. Major Kieffer started to speak. Edie knew what he'd say even before the interpreter's low voice began to translate.

The radio game had begun.

Chapter 8

Gerhardt

Dear Father, Gerhardt wrote. He could call him Father in the letters, where nobody else could see – it was only in public he had to keep up the pretence of the Count being Uncle – Mother had told him the reason years ago: the Count's scandalous divorce from his first wife, his important diplomatic career, his position in the Nazi Party, the impossibility of admitting to a foreign-born mistress and bastard children. Mother seemed resigned to the situation, content to survive on scraps of love and attention foraged from the edges of the Count's ambitious life. But Gerhardt had always wished for a real father, one that came home for dinner every night, helped with homework and took him sledging in winter. But now he was a man, and it was too late for any of that, he supposed.

He paused, tapping the end of his fountain pen against his lip: cool and smooth. *I hope this finds you in good health,* he continued, thinking of the brisk morning walks the Count made them take when he deigned to visit (for your 'wellness', he always said). It was a relief when he left and they could return to their usual routine: Gerhardt only walking Loulou when the weather was warm, or when he needed an excuse to idle past Lisel's house.

I am settling down well here in Paris, Gerhardt wrote, the pen nib scratching across the pale blue, leaving an inky black trail. Was he, Gerhardt thought? Was he settling in well? Josef had been friendly enough, in his brash, slightly intimidating way, and the others, too. Even Frau Bertelsmann had smiled at him over the liver dumplings in the dining room. But it wasn't like home. If he was at home now he'd be sitting near the fire, Loulou at his feet, paws twitching as she dreamt of chasing rabbits. Mother would be doing her embroidery and the wireless would be on in the background. And Franz would be drawing cartoons – no, Franz was dead. The recollection was sudden as a fist in the face. And Gerhardt realised he was feeling homesick for a place that no longer existed. In reality his mother would be stony-faced and mute, playing the same record – Franz's favourite – over and over again on the gramophone. They would have had plain bread and cheese for supper, again, Mother either not noticing or not bothering to remove the blue-grey blooms of mould on the edges of the hard yellow cheese.

Gerhardt picked up the pen and started to write again. The top of his bedside locker wobbled, and he worried that the Count would complain about the illegibility of his handwriting. *Although at first there didn't appear to be much to do, the wireless detector operatives brought in a terrorist yesterday – a British wireless operator – and since then I have been quite busy.* He thought of his irritation at being called in from his evening off, his surprise at finding out the prisoner was a young woman.

The English agent is a girl, he wrote. *Can you imagine, Father, the British send their girls to do their dirty work for them. Either they have no men left in the whole of the British Isles, or they don't care about the safety of their womenfolk. It's a disgrace!* Gerhardt felt suddenly outraged at the very thought of it. What if Herr Hitler were to send the likes of Lisel to London as a saboteur? What would the island-monkeys do to her if they caught her? It was too awful to contemplate. He could only conclude that their Winston Churchill must be some kind of madman to send innocent young girls out into danger like that.

He slammed down his pen, realising he was breathing rapidly with the outrage of it. He scanned his room, slowing his breath, thinking about how to continue with the letter. It was much smaller than his room at home, with varnished floorboards and a single electric bulb under a plain red fabric shade. There was a tiny, empty hearth – only the fires in Kieffer and Goetz's offices were ever lit – and a cupboard to hang his things in. His trunk was at the end of the bed, underneath the window. The room must have belonged to servants when the house was a private residence, he thought. Now the domestic staff trudged in daily from – from where? Gerhardt realised he really knew nothing about the city that was his new home. He picked up the pen again.

We were very lucky that the English agent was caught in the act of transmitting. The operatives got her crystals as well as her wireless set, so Dr Goetz and his team hoped to transmit directly back to London, as if they themselves were the agent. It's a clever plan, which Kieffer says has had much success already in the Netherlands. I think it rather fine that we're doing such a good job of outsmarting the British, don't you?

Gerhardt was aware that he was showing off. But it had always seemed that that was what the Count wanted: a son – albeit an unacknowledged, illegitimate one – to be proud of. *Dr Goetz was worried that they didn't have the agent's personal code. Apparently they always use a poem or a song or something to encode their messages, before transmission in Morse,* he continued. It was rather nice to be explaining something to his father, to be an expert, for a change. He thought about the poem, how he'd discovered it, but almost not handed it over, for fear of it not being important. He wouldn't make that mistake again. In future everything he noticed about the prisoner he would pass up the command chain immediately. *Luckily I found the poem-code, and they were able to transmit to London that very evening,* he added. The muted sound of someone playing Kieffer's new piano began to filter faintly up from the first floor.

Gerhardt paused again, shifted position and yawned. He was exhausted. He hadn't been sleeping properly on this bed: the springs poked in awkward places. And it had been such a long afternoon: he'd never had to do that amount of simultaneous translation before. *The problem was,* he began writing again, but stopped, looked at the word 'problem' and scratched it out. He'd been switching between English and German so much that he'd forgotten what language he was even writing in. 'Problem' was an English word, wasn't it? No, it was a German word. The script looked like hazy scribbles to his overtired eyes. He said 'Problem' aloud, his voice sounding startlingly loud in the small room. It was both: an English and a German word. A problem shared is a problem halved, his mother used to say when he was little, worrying about the bullies at school.

The problem was that we didn't have her security check. We didn't even know the English agents had a security check as well as the code. But a few hours after we transmitted to London, Dr Goetz got a message back actually telling the agent off, and reminding her to include the check! So of course, then we had to interrogate her at length to try to discover this 'security check' and I have been quite busy, as you can imagine.

Gerhardt thought about the events of the afternoon, wondering how much to share with the Count. His father had said he wanted to know every little detail of the new job. *The interrogation took place in Kieffer's office,* he began, remembering how the questioning went on all afternoon, with Kieffer trying variously to catch the girl out and point out the rational choice she'd be making were she to help them. But the girl refused to even speak. *It was a long afternoon and still she hasn't given up her security check. We're going to try sleep deprivation tonight, and there's talk of sending her to the house prison tomorrow,* Gerhardt wrote, thinking that Kieffer had underestimated the girl's mettle, and wondering about what he'd do if he found himself in her situation. *I'd kill myself if I wound up in enemy hands,* he added. *I'd rather die than betray Germany.*

He needed to get the letter in the diplomatic bag for Berlin that evening. Write every day, the Count had exhorted. Write every day, and be sure to leave nothing out.

Gerhardt sealed the letter and got up. There was still the muted plink-plonk of poor piano practice from downstairs, which got louder as Gerhardt opened his bedroom door and began to descend: somebody murdering Mozart with clumsy, killing fingers. The dark stairwell opened out into the lower corridor. He had to pass the prisoner's room on the way to the main staircase. Frau Bertelsmann had left the keys dangling from the lock, Gerhardt noticed: a dull flash of silver in the gloom. The floorboards creaked, out of step with the piano, as Gerhardt continued along the passage.

Just after he'd passed the prisoner's door, the piano music downstairs abruptly stopped. And that was when he heard it: a scuffle-thud from inside the girl's room.

Edie

By the time she heard the door, it was already too late. There was no time to slide back inside, pretend she hadn't pushed open the window, tried to escape. So she stayed put, fingers grappling the rough stucco, feet sliding against the icy ledge with its wrought-iron balustrade. The footsteps came to a halt behind her. 'Don't jump,' said the voice in English. It was the interpreter.

He thought she was suicidal, she realised. Because she was just a girl, because she'd cried, in the end, worn out by the interminable questioning. He thought her incapable of escape. But the hairpin was still on the floor by her bed when he'd brought her back to her room. She knew she couldn't afford to wait, and she'd thought the sound of the piano would mask the slide of the opening window. Edie faltered, feet twisting awkwardly on the balconette. She caught the edge of the wooden shutter. The ground, far below, shifted in her vision. She looked sideways, up at an angle. If she could only reach the lightning rod, snaking up skywards, but it was too far away.

'Please don't jump,' the voice came again. That accent, not English – but not German, either. 'Think of your family.'

What about her family? About Pop drinking port in his London club? About Mummy, sighing and listening to Chopin on her gramophone? Her memories flickered like something at the cinema: ephemeral and unreal.

The ground swayed hazily below. She saw the gate guard, moon-faced, looking up, reaching for his holster as he walked across the lawn. If she tried to get away now, he'd shoot. Let them think she was suicidal then. She dipped forwards slightly, out into the chill monochrome air.

'Please don't!' he said. She could sense his presence behind her. 'The war won't last forever. You'll be able to go home one day.' Where had he learnt to speak English? Not in the beer halls of Munich with the other Nazi thugs, surely? 'Who do you have waiting for you? Brothers? Sisters? A sweetheart?'

She shook her head. She had none of that. No siblings, no lover – and why was there any reason to suppose things would change? She'd always be alone, she was certain of that. It was what she deserved. She stayed silent, shivering in the cold, holding on. She hadn't thought of suicide. In training they'd been told they had a duty to try to escape. But could death be a solution, after all? She looked down: just three floors – high enough to break her neck?

She could hear him breathing, and she remembered the way his breath had condensed on the window when she'd been stripped and searched by the German woman. 'If you touch me, I'll jump,' she said.

'I won't. I promise.'

It was hard to hold on. The ledge was narrow and her fingers pinched the wooden shutter edge, peeling paint beneath her fingertips. She swallowed, looking down at the garden to where a group of shadowy figures had joined the gate guard.

If she tried to climb now, they'd see, and they'd shoot. How silent they were, though. She couldn't even hear a whisper from below.

He was standing so close behind her that she could feel his breath as a touch of warmth on the back of her thighs. 'You can trust me,' he said.

Her hands were sweaty, her grip beginning to give. Three choices: climb and be shot; let go and fall; or go back inside. What should she do? What would Miss Atkins do? She thought of the older woman with her vivid red lips and steady gaze.

A lone motorbike buzzed down the boulevard and suddenly Edie felt exhausted, alone, and done with the drama. She started to turn, giving up, ready to go inside, but as she did so her ankle twisted, and her bare heel caught the rusted ironwork. The ledge gave way, dipping under her scrabbling feet. She tried to cling to the shutter but the paintwork was slippery beneath her fingers and she was falling.

His hand grabbed her wrist. Her dangling feet found purchase against the plasterwork. She caught the edge of the window frame with her other hand. She heaved and shoved herself upwards. His hands helped pull her in, wrenching her painfully through the open window and onto the floor of her room. As soon as she was inside, he let go, closed the shutters, and slammed the sash window down. She sat, panting, underneath the window, and he crouched down next to her.

'They'd kill me if I let you die,' he said. She heard a barrage of footsteps on the stairs, voices shouting, and he let go of her arms and shoved her into a sitting position. Then he slapped her face, just once, so her left cheek burnt with the impression of his palm. 'What do you think you're playing at, you silly girl?' he spat, his voice suddenly hard and empty.

But as the room filled with the uniformed figures and she was hauled roughly up, she couldn't help thinking: Girl? You're hardly more than a boy yourself.

Dericourt

'Hurry up, *chéri*!' Jeannot called.

'I'm coming, chicken.' The front door of their apartment slammed shut behind him as Henri Dericourt lowered the heavy pallet onto the floor behind the coat stand. The satchel was cutting into his shoulder, too. He couldn't wait to get it off. He looped it over a hook and hung his coat on top. It was dark in the hallway. He tried the light switch: nothing – another power cut. He'd been away from France for so long. He hadn't realised how much things had changed: rationing, power cuts – it was worse than Britain. But at least Jeannot was here. Yes, it had been wonderful to touch and taste his wife; it had been almost like being on honeymoon again.

'I can't see a thing,' he said. 'Why didn't you leave a lamp for me?'

'There's been no paraffin for weeks, and there weren't any candles in the shops today. I can't even get the basics. It's terrible, Henri. Can't you ask one of your friends to help?'

The apartment was so small it was possible to hold a conversation with anyone, anywhere, without even raising your voice. But it was in a very convenient location, Henri reminded himself. And besides, it wasn't as if he was having to pay for it. 'I'll try,' he replied, not feeling hopeful. Brandy, cigars, exotic fruit – Bladier was good for all that, but if he asked for candles he'd be laughed at. Jeannot would just have to get off her pert arse and get in a queue somewhere, like all the other little people.

He was fumbling with the camera in the darkness, winding on the film so that he could take it out and put it in the canister. It would be easier if he could see what he was doing, but still. At least he'd thought to get the Photostats while it was still light.

'I've been waiting up for hours for you, trying to knit in the dark. It's impossible. I've dropped about a thousand stitches. Your scarf will look more like lace than knitwear – you'll look like such a country bumpkin when you wear it!'

'As if a bit of lamplight would make any difference to your knitting,' he joked, slipping the film into the canister and wedging it underneath the fruit in the pallet. He would go to avenue Foch first thing. 'In any case, I *am* a country bumpkin,' he said, putting the camera back in the inside pocket of his coat. Hide in plain sight: wasn't that what the Atkins woman told her agents?

'Don't be silly, Henri. Everyone knows about Château Thierry, you're always talking about your childhood there. If you're a bumpkin, then I'm Monsieur Hitler! Now, will you please come to bed; it's so cold in here without you.' Her voice wavered like a child's. Even now she was the wrong side of thirty there was a vulnerability and an innocence about her. She still didn't know how he made a living. And she seemed happy not to know, skating along the surface of things, like those water boatmen he'd watched on endless summer days in the gardens of the big house, waiting for his mother to finish ironing the bed linen or blacking the ovens or whatever exhausting, thankless task the housekeeper had assigned to her that day. Jeannot was right: everyone knew about Château

Thierry, but nobody knew his mother was just a domestic servant. People believed what they wanted, and if it suited them all to think he was a dashing ex-Air Force officer, son of Picardie landowners, that was fine by him.

'Henri, please!'

'Yes, little chicken, I'm coming.' He plucked one of the fruits from the top of the pallet and began the three paces to the bedroom, remembering to sidestep so as not to trip over her shoes, which she always kicked off in the corridor.

He pushed open the door. She'd left the shutters open. Moonlight caught the edges of things: a mirror; a coverlet; a shoulder; a cheek. 'My love, my *chéri*!' she said. 'Ah, what's that smell? It smells like sunshine!'

He walked over to where she sat up in bed, propped up with bolsters and pillows, loose hair running like a silver stream over her bare shoulders. 'I have something for you,' he said, holding the orange behind his back and leaning towards her, 'but first you must pay.' She tipped her face up so her lips met his. He never tired of them: so soft and plump, like ripe plums picked straight off the tree. There were other women – of course there would always be other women, with firmer breasts, slimmer thighs – but Jeannot's lips . . . ah, no other woman had Jeannot's lips.

She pulled away. 'I hope it's my diamond earrings,' she said, laughing. It had become a bit of a joke between them.

'Not this time, I'm afraid, chicken,' he said, handing over the orange, 'but soon, I hope.'

'Oh *chéri*, thank you. How long has it been since we had oranges? Not since Marseille, and even then – oh, I can't remember. So sweet. Sweet like you, Henri. You are always so sweet to me. Shall we eat it now? Shall we be very naughty and have a midnight feast, like children, and not care about the juice on the sheets?' She laughed again, a gushing laugh, as if she were skipping home from school on a sunny day. How he loved her when she was like this. He wanted to keep her like this forever, even though experience told him that when the moon waned again she'd be all tears, and he'd have to lock the knife drawer. So it went with her: she was either deliriously happy or suffocating with despair, waxing and waning with the moon. Poor Jeannot.

'Let us feast on this orange first, and then I shall feast on you!' he said, beginning to unbutton his shirt. 'And if you are a very good girl, then perhaps tomorrow we can go shopping for something more exciting than black market fruit.'

He thought about the satchel with post for the agents; he'd leave it with the barman at Café Colisee, who'd pass it on to the agents. He thought about the Photostats he'd made of some of the London post, safely in the canister at the bottom of the pallet of oranges, which he'd deliver in person to 84 avenue Foch after breakfast, just as a taster, for Boemelburg's successor.

He unbuckled his belt. 'How would you like to have lunch at the Lucas Carton, and then maybe we could go to the Champs-Élysées?' he said. 'I have seen a frock in Rochas that would look perfect on you, chicken.'

Chapter 9

Gerhardt

The girl walked over to the car and, smiling, leant in towards the open window. Her broad mouth had lots of very white teeth. 'Yes,' said Gerhardt's mother.

'Oh, I do apologise. I thought this was the Ambassador's car,' said the girl, her smile dropping away.

'It is,' said Gerhardt's mother. There was a pause.

'I'm terribly sorry. I shouldn't have bothered you,' said the girl, beginning to turn away . . .

'Let's get this sorted out then,' said Josef, taking his hands off the steering wheel and rubbing them together. Gerhardt blinked himself out of the memory. The staff car had stopped outside one of the magnificent buildings in place des États-Unis: five-storey blocks with grey roofs like cloche hats above their giant cream façades. In the centre of the square was a small park: a smudge of green grass, an oily grey pond, and a scrawl of leafless trees.

'You can wait here, Josef,' said Norbert from the back seat, shunting the prisoner towards the door.

'No, no, I'm coming with, mate,' said Josef, pulling the key out of the ignition. A woman in a black coat hurried along the pavement beside them, pulling a little boy in a blue cap. She cast a worried glance at the car, and sped on, tugging the boy behind her. Other than that, the place was empty. Gerhardt got out of the car to join the others. Church bells were ringing in the distance. The sunshine had been bright on the way here, but the tall houses cast giant shadows over the square, and the air was cold as a crypt. The woman and boy had gone now.

Josef bounded in front as they began to walk towards what they called 'the house prison'. The English girl stumbled on the edge of the kerb, but Norbert grasped her arm and held her upright, then marched her towards the vast double doors in the curved stone surround. Gerhardt followed; until yesterday he hadn't even known that the *Sicherheitsdienst* had its own prison. But then, he'd only been in the job a short time; there were probably all kinds of things that went on in the SD that he didn't know about.

The doors opened from inside as they approached – someone had been watching, waiting for their arrival. A thin woman nodded curtly at them as they entered, and closed the heavy wooden doors softly behind them. They were inside a mirrored hallway, with black-and-white tiles on the floor and a marble staircase winding upwards. The air was very still, like a chapel. Gerhardt could see them all reflected again and again in the mirrors, as if there were a whole troop of them, instead of just three young men escorting a frightened girl. 'This way,' the woman said in a reedy voice, opening a door he hadn't noticed, concealed by a mirrored panel off to one side. Narrow steps led down into the darkness.

Josef sprang ahead, as if he could hardly wait. Norbert shoved the girl in front of him and Gerhardt brought up the rear. He had only descended a couple of steps when the thin woman shut the door behind him, and they were encased in gloom, footfalls loud in the darkness. Nobody spoke.

At the bottom, the stairwell opened out into a cool, white-washed space with low ceilings and alcoves, lit by a bare bulb. But there were no longer any bottles of wine or kegs of Calvados in the cellar; instead there was a chair with buckled leather straps hanging from the arms, and a bath full of water. To one side two men sat at a card table with what looked like a toolbox. They were reading through some documents. As the group arrived, the men got up, came over and shook every-one's hands except the prisoner's; they ignored her completely. One was short and wiry, with round spectacles perched on a long nose. The other was bigger and broader, with thin hair smeared across his pate and the complexion of an overripe peach. Nobody introduced themself: no names were men-tioned whatsoever.

The two men cross-referenced the information they had with the file Norbert had brought from the SD headquarters. They appeared satisfied and asked Norbert to escort the pris-oner to the chair with the straps. Gerhardt looked at the girl's face as she sat down, but it was as blank as the façades of the buildings in place des États-Unis: she didn't show any emotion at all. Norbert undid the girl's cuffs and strapped her arms to the chair, using the buckled straps that were attached. He had to do them up on the tightest notch because her arms were so slender. After that, Norbert asked whether he was still needed and the two men said no, he could go, they could take it from here; everything was in order. Josef wanted to stay and watch, but he had to drive Norbert back to avenue Foch, so they both left, boots ringing on the stone steps and door clicking shut at the top. The wiry man was ticking things off on the forms, and the big one was taking some tools out of the box and placing them on the green baize.

Gerhardt watched. He had a schoolfriend who had joined the *Abwehr*. He'd heard that the SD handled interrogation differently from the *Abwehr*, but just how, he wasn't sure. Next time he saw his friend, they could compare notes. The SD had an impressive record of agent capture and counter-intelligence work. It would be interesting to see how they worked.

He thought, briefly, about the girl's suicide attempt. Just for a moment, alone in her room with her, he'd almost liked her, felt sorry for her. She'd reminded him a little of Lisel. But that feeling had passed – she was a terrorist, after all.

The girl sat motionless in the chair and the interrogators checked their notes, muttering to each other and shuffling the pages. It was just a matter of process, Gerhardt thought. They would extract the information, and he would interpret. He really only had a passing interest in what was about to take place. He didn't care about the girl, and he certainly didn't feel complicit in anything.

Not then, not before it all began.

Edie

All night they'd kept her awake. Suicide watch, the interpreter called it, but she knew it was just a technique to try to get her to talk, waking her with a torch in her eyes and a slap in the face every time her head lolled forwards. But they'd covered that in training. She kept her mouth shut. At first light they'd bundled her in the car and taken her to this calmly impressive building in the diplomatic quarter.

In the cellar the interpreter said that all she had to do was to give her security check and it would all be over, but she kept her mouth shut tight as she'd done all night, so the other men rolled up their sleeves, pulled her out of the chair and pushed her into the bathtub. Icy water rose up and over her head. She gasped at the shock of the cold, drawing water into her lungs and choking, but as soon as she resurfaced and took a breath they pushed her down again. And again. And each time there was water in her ears and nose and the gargling rush of it as she came back up.

He said just tell me your security check and this will be over, but she shook her head. No. No! And the hands were on her shoulders, pushing her down again, and the water engulfed her. Hauled up, gasping, she saw his face through a liquid veil. You can make it stop, just tell them, tell them and it will all be over, he said, but she set her jaws and prepared to hold her breath again. The jab of their fingers in her collarbone. Down she went, thinking of witch hunts and ducking stools: if you float you're guilty; if you sink, you're dead.

The white enamel bath was like the whites of the interpreter's eyes and his chattering teeth as they pulled her up again, his face close to hers. Just say something, and I can make this stop, he said, and she saw that his hands were clutched together, as if in prayer. But then they had her down into the icy waterfall again before she'd had the chance to draw breath, and the pain bit her lungs and she remembered how it was, in the darkness with the sirens and the roar of the bomb blast and the rush of water and the American's dead weight on top of her and how she'd squirmed and struggled but couldn't break free. And she was there underneath him in the water, in the blackness. In the blackness.

Then she was in the chair where the buckles bit and tore at her wet flesh and the blood ran down to the floor, turning the stone pink-brown where it pooled. Her throat was raw from choking, lungs scoured. Please just tell me your security check – she could hear the interpreter's voice, but she couldn't see him. He must be behind her. You can make all this stop, he said. One of the men was reaching for something from the table. And she remembered the American with his greedy tongue and smoky breath and she thought that it couldn't be worse than that, nothing they did could be worse than what he'd done. So she shook her head. No. She saw the man pick up a pair of pliers. Dear God, just tell them and make it stop – the interpreter's voice was urgent, and she turned her head to look at him.

Gerhardt

It was only when she turned, hair flattened wet, eyes huge with fear, that he finally realised. How stupid he was not to have noticed before. '*Halt!*' he shouted.

The two men paused, open-mouthed and frowning. 'There's something I have to confirm with Kieffer before we can continue,' Gerhardt said.

The girl prisoner – she was the girl from place de la Madeleine, the girl he'd helped the day he'd come down for his interview with Boemelburg. She was the girl with the heavy suitcase and the petrified eyes, drenched in the winter rain. Gerhardt's eyes took in the scene in front of him now as if clicking the shutter on a camera: the drenched girl, the uniformed man leaning over her with the pliers. Gerhardt turned and ran up the stone cellar steps two at a time.

The mirrored hallway was empty, the narrow-faced woman nowhere to be seen. He called out, but nobody answered. A door opposite was ajar, so he scudded across the chequered floor and into a reception room, dodging a chaise longue and a coffee table to reach a telephone perched on top of a polished walnut tallboy in the corner. 'What are you doing?' A nasal voice from across the room. In his haste he hadn't seen her there, regarding him, crow-like, from her vantage point on the window seat.

'I need to contact Major Kieffer. It's a matter of great urgency,' he said.

'My orders were not to disturb him until the job was complete,' she replied.

'But some new information has come to light,' he said.

'So soon?' she drawled, raising her eyebrows and tapping ash from the end of her cigarette holder into a large shell that lay next to her on the seat. 'Well, that's quick work. Very well. But don't be long. I'm expecting a call myself.'

Gerhardt lifted the receiver and dialled.

'Kieffer speaking.'

'It's Vogt, sir.'

'That was fast. Well done. What's the check?'

'I don't have the check, sir.'

Suddenly Gerhardt realised how stupid he'd been. All they wanted was her security check, and he didn't have that. All he had was – well, what did he have? Evidence of a possible rendezvous point for herself and her cell, that was all.

'Well, why the hell are you calling me now? Get on with it and call me again when you have it. I'm going out now.'

'But I have other information, about her colleagues,' Gerhardt said. 'Her cell meets in a room above the Lucas Carton. There are three of them: a young man with blonde hair, a woman with black hair, and an older man with a limp.' He remembered it all now: glimpsing those three inside the room as the door opened, and seeing her walk off into the rain with the tall man later on.

'She told you all that, but didn't tell you her security check? God in heaven! As long as I live I will never fathom the British psyche. We need her check, Vogt. As soon as possible. We need to make this *Funkspiel* work.'

Gerhardt could sense that Kieffer was about to hang up on him. And if he did there would be no choice but to go back down to the cellar and witness – and be party to – no, it was intolerable. 'But surely you can use them – her colleagues – if you bring them in?' he said.

'Of course we could use them, but ... oh, I see what you mean.' Gerhardt hadn't really meant anything, hadn't paused to think of a strategy. He kept quiet. 'You mean we should bring them in and let her see we have them, use her instinct to protect her colleagues as leverage. Very good, Vogt. If we play our cards right, we might be able to get even more out of her than merely her security check. What is it the British say? Softly, softly catchee monkey or some nonsense like that? Right, tell the boys to pause, and I'll get Josef over with the car. Don't tell her what's happening, though. Don't tell her anything.'

'Yes, sir.'

'Oh, and well done, Vogt. I like a man who can take a situation and work sideways. I think you may have found your vocation.'

'Thank you, sir.'

When Gerhardt hung up, he told the crow-woman that a car was coming to take the girl back to avenue Foch. He had an uncomfortable feeling as he walked across the mirrored hallway towards the cellar door, seeing both sides of himself at the same time: endlessly reflecting. But interrupting the interrogation, passing on the information about the girl's colleagues – it was the right thing to do, wasn't it?

Dericourt

Henri touched Jeannot's thigh under the tablecloth. The fabric of her dress was as thin as flower petals, and he could feel her stocking tops. 'When Kieffer gets back, you need to make your excuses and leave, chicken,' he said, watching her scrape the last of her duck à l'orange onto her fork and into her pouting mouth. He watched her moistened lips as she chewed and swallowed the tender meat.

'But why, *chéri*? Can't I stay for coffee, at least?'

He lifted his hand from her thigh, reached into his pocket, took out a roll of notes, and peeled a couple off for her. 'Buy yourself a coffee in one of the cafés over there.' He nodded to the window next to their table, through which they could see all of place de la Madeleine, the circling black cars a jet necklace round a grubby décolletage. 'I'll meet you very soon, but first Kieffer and I have business to discuss. It would only bore you, chicken.'

Jeannot shrugged and put her knife and fork neatly beside each other on the clean plate, then dabbed at the side of her mouth with one of the thick white napkins. Only then did she pluck the notes from his outstretched hand, and tuck them inside her crocodile clutch.

Just then Kieffer returned, winding his way through the crowded restaurant. Watching him, Henri was reminded of a ball on a bagatelle board, ricocheting until gently coming to rest at their table. Kieffer smiled as if he'd just hit a top-scoring triple eighteen. He apologised for having to leave them for so long during the meal, claiming to have had a work issue to attend to, then took a seat on the other side of Jeannot, who was now applying lipstick, gazing at herself in her compact. She smacked her lips and clicked it shut. Then she checked her watch (a rather nice British Harwood – he'd found it in a box of discarded agents' things in the hangar at the airfield, and it seemed a shame to let it go to waste). 'It has been a very great pleasure to meet you, Monsieur Kieffer,' she said. 'But I'm afraid I have to run, as I have a hair appointment.' She glanced across at Henri when she said this, who gave a little nod of acceptance – a perfect reason to cut short her lunch date.

'Well, far be it from me to get between a Frenchwoman and her coiffeur,' said Kieffer, standing up. His French was heavily accented, but passable. 'It was a pleasure to meet you, too, Madame Dericourt,' he added, kissing her on both cheeks as she prepared to leave.

Henri also stood up, and Jeannot turned to him. She leant over to skim his cheek with her lips, but he pulled her closer, touched her earlobe with his tongue, whispered 'Later, my little chicken' in her ear. He needed to keep her thinking of him. Kieffer was a handsome man. It wasn't that he mistrusted Jeannot, he just didn't trust other men around his wife – after all, she'd been married to someone else when he first met her.

Jeannot fluttered her fingers at them and walked out of the restaurant. Henri watched Kieffer watching her. Both men sat down as the glass door swung shut behind her. Through the window Henri saw Jeannot disappear into the circling traffic, like a blown rose petal. Where is her coat, he thought distractedly. Why doesn't she ever remember her coat? A black Citroën van screeched to a halt right in front of the windows, and he lost sight of his wife.

Waiters' hands removed empty plates, refilled wine glasses and offered the cigar tin. Both men took one. Outside, a string of uniformed men oozed out of the van and disappeared up a side alley.

'Thank you for your delivery,' Kieffer said, once the cigars had both been guillotined and lit. 'Can I rely on regular deliveries of that nature from you?'

'It depends on what you're prepared to pay,' Henri replied. 'Do you have a figure in mind?'

'Boemelburg promised diamonds,' Henri said, poker-faced.

'As you know, Boemelburg has been reassigned, and I am the senior SD representative in the region now,' Kieffer said, narrowing his eyes behind the cigar smoke.

'Well, then you'll be interested in seeing more letters to and from English agents working undercover here,' Henri replied.

'Naturally, that's of interest to the SD. But as I'm sure you're aware, we have an English agent working for us now, a wireless operator, as part of a *Funkspiel*.'

'Yes, I'd heard that,' Henri lied, chewing on the tacky end of the cigar. When had that happened? Someone else was double-crossing London, and they had no idea. Damnation. He had so much less leverage if Kieffer already had a double agent. He'd need to be more persuasive. 'But do you know how much information will be sent *en clair* – uncoded – now the Tommies are using me?' he said, tapping cigar ash gently into the cut-glass ashtray and looking out of the window. He watched as two figures with bags over their heads were bundled into the back of the waiting van.

'Boemelburg did mention that you were being used as a postman as well as a taxi driver for the British, yes,' Kieffer said. 'Personal letters can prove useful in turning an agent, it's true, yet they hardly provide the same vital information that we get by direct contact with Baker Street.' He too tipped his cigar ash into the crystal dish.

The van doors slammed shut and it shot away, lost amongst the circling traffic. 'I may be able to get hold of other information,' Henri said at last.

'What kind of information?'

'Well, what are you looking for?' he replied with a question. He'd forgotten to arrange which café to meet Jeannot in. He'd have to check them all, and no doubt she'd be in the very last one he came to.

'I need actual plans, detailed information, not just letters home to wives and children. And for that I will pay, but the rate will depend entirely on the quality of what I receive. I'm not interested in love letters or postcards from seaside resorts, is that clear?'

'I'm sure that can be arranged,' Henri said, sucking on his cigar. 'And payment?'

'Cash only. No diamonds or gold,' Kieffer said, blowing smoke in Henri's direction. 'I'm afraid my predecessor was all too willing to make promises. I prefer to be a little more professional. It makes it easier all round. But do continue your little arrangement with the avenue Foch cook. We all appreciate that. Good food does raise morale, not just for the staff, but for any agents we pick up, too. The one we've just got was half-starved, and being offered a decent meal certainly helps do business, don't you think?'

Henri nodded, and stubbed his cigar out in the ashtray. No diamonds then. The Boche were even stingier than the Brits. Still, at least he'd got Jeannot a free lunch.

Vera

'Miss Atkins, do come in.' The man stood up and came out from behind his desk to shake her hand. 'Donald Brown,' he said. His handshake was rather weak, Vera decided. He had thinning hair slicked across his scalp, florid jowls, and a salt-and-pepper moustache. Brown suited him: brown, like his suit jacket and what was left of his hair. 'Take a seat,' he said, and they both sat down.

There was a picture of the King and Queen above the desk, and a sheaf of papers on the blotter. To her right, the sun shafted through the sash windows, and dust motes danced. It was a little on the warm side. A secretary bustled in with tea things. Vera waved her away. Even after all these years in England, she still couldn't bear the cloying way they took their tea. Vera took out her cigarette case.

'I do beg your pardon – I am remiss.' The man took the lid off a wooden box on the desk. It was filled with cigarettes, like tiny slaughtered bodies in a giant coffin, Vera thought, taking one out. 'I sometimes forget. I'm a cigar man, myself. Devil to get, these days,' he said.

'Have you tried Fox's in St James?' Vera said, lighting her cigarette with her own lighter. 'A friend of mine put me on to them,' she added, inhaling, thinking of Dick. 'If they try to fob you off, say you're a chum of Ketton-Cremer's, and they should see you right.' In her periphery she could just glimpse the traffic passing the window below: red streaks of buses. The sound of footsteps and engines filtered up to the first-floor room.

'I've had a look through your naturalisation papers, Miss Atkins,' said Mr Brown, glancing down and smoothing the paperwork in front of him on the desk. 'So we'll just go through it, shall we?' He looked up and Vera nodded. 'It says here that you were born in Romania, but your mother is South African?' he continued.

'She's British,' Vera said.

'She's from South Africa, it says here,' Mr Brown said, making a show of looking down at the papers.

'Yes, my dear boy, and South Africa is one of our colonies, which makes her British.'

'It does indeed,' Mr Brown agreed, ticking something off with his fountain pen. 'But why were you born in Romania?'

Vera exhaled and smiled before answering. 'Well, chiefly because my mother happened to be there when I came along.'

'She was holidaying there?'

'The family were staying in Romania, yes.' It was a holiday of sorts, Vera thought, watching Mr Brown's index finger following a line on the form. Crasna had been one long holiday, for all the years they'd lived there: the hunting and shooting expeditions; the dinners; the parties, especially when Friedrich . . .

no, not here. Stop it, you silly woman. She lifted the cigarette to her lips and inhaled deeply. 'We had many friends in Romania. My father advised the Danube Commission for a while.'

'And the family were resident there at the time of your birth?'

'My dear boy! My family were never resident anywhere. My elder brother Ralph was born in South Africa, and goodness knows where Guy was born. We have relatives all over the world, and I did seem to spend an awful lot of my childhood on ships and trains.' She blew smoke out over Mr Brown's shiny pate. It wasn't a lie, not really. She was just doing what the training chaps always advised agents to do: start from the truth and work sideways. Cat must have taken that training, she thought, down in Beaulieu with the others. In Vera's opinion a few hours being grilled by retired British Army officers in a hut in the New Forest barely seemed enough to prepare agents for encountering German Intelligence in Occupied Europe. One rather hoped Yvette hadn't needed to put her training into practice, Vera thought, remembering the strange message Jenkins had shown her.

Mr Brown turned a page on the form and made a note in the margin. 'And your father? He was from South Africa, too?' he said.

'He used to live in South Africa, yes. That's where he met my mother.' Again, it wasn't an outright lie. Father had lived in South Africa for all those years when he ran the mines.

'And he's living here in London with your mother, now?'

'My father died in 1933, as you'd know if you've read through the documents, Mr Brown.'

'Indeed. So it says. I'm so sorry.' He made another note in the margin.

Vera told herself not to be impatient. She couldn't afford to upset this Mr Brown. She smiled. 'But do carry on.' She needed this interview to run smoothly.

'There's a note here that says your father was German,' Mr Brown added, staring down at the form. 'He was born in Germany.'

'Really?'

'Yes.'

The air was thick with the heavy sunshine and her cigarette smoke. 'Mother never mentioned it. All I knew was that they met and married in South Africa.'

'You never thought to ask?'

'Is your father British, Mr Brown?'

He looked up at her, eyebrows lifting his broad forehead. 'My father? I don't understand what he's got to do with this.'

'You're saying that where you're born defines your nationality, aren't you? But, you know, birth is such an arbitrary thing, don't you think? Where was your father born, Mr Brown?' She leant forward, knowing the answer before he gave it – if they were going to delve into her background, she was going to make damned sure she'd done some research herself. Mr Brown hesitated before answering, but she gave him a smile and a nod, as if they were just exchanging pleasantries at a soirée.

'India, actually. Grandfather was in the Colonial Service,' he replied.

'Ah, India. I have always wanted to visit the Taj Mahal,' Vera said. 'However, one wouldn't call your father Indian, would one, Mr Brown?' Mr Brown shook his head, and opened his mouth as if he wanted to say something, but Vera continued. 'As I mentioned, Father was on the advisory board of the

Danube Commission before he passed away,' she said. 'It's through his colleagues there that we got to know Hump so well. You do know Hump, don't you? Leslie Humphries?' Mr Brown nodded again. Of course he knew Hump. Vera knew he'd know Hump – know him and know what influence he held in Whitehall these days. 'Hump was one of Father's good friends – a close friend of the whole family. In fact, it was he who suggested I apply for naturalisation. He said it was madness for me not to be British, as Mother, Ralph, and Guy already were. And, you know, Mr Brown,' she touched the sleeve of his jacket, 'Hump feels I'll be vital to work across the Channel, with the SOE, when the time comes. But the annoying thing is they won't be able to deploy me unless I'm in uniform, with one of the services or other. And to be in uniform, I need to get citizenship, it seems. It's a terrible bore, but that's the way the system works.'

She pulled back, flicking ash into the metal ashtray. Mr Brown took a gulp of tea, and shuffled the papers. He's not really looking at them, Vera thought. He's thinking about impressing Hump, and he's unnerved by being alone in his office with an attractive woman. He's just another man, after all.

Mr Brown gave a sharp intake of breath. 'Miss Atkins, you registered as an alien when you arrived in this country, and yet you were never sent to an internment camp. Why was that?'

'I really have no idea,' said Vera, stubbing out the remains of her cigarette in the ashtray. 'I can only think they didn't want me.' She sighed, remembering Mr and Mrs Carluccio being taken away, that bridge afternoon. The very next morning she'd gone to see Hump, in his large office with its view across the Thames.

*

Hump's secretary hadn't even wanted to let her through the door, but when she'd said to tell him it was Vera, she was ushered immediately inside.

'Marvellous to see you, Vee. How the devil are you?'

'Not good, I'm afraid, Hump.'

'How so? Not your mother, I hope?'

'No, Mother is very well. It's this beastly situation – my status, don't you see?' Hump held out a box of cheroots, and she took one. She wouldn't normally smoke cheroots, but still.

'Ah, the Romania connection. Shall I ask Pamela to bring some tea?' Hump said. But Vera declined with a wave of her hand. She was after something more than tea and sympathy.

'I had to register as an alien when I arrived in 1937. I haven't been allowed to work, except as an ARP warden – apparently it doesn't matter what nationality you are when you're pulling people out of burning buildings – and now it looks like Romania's going to end up on the wrong side, in which case I'll be classed as an "enemy alien" and they'll ship me off, Hump. I'll get carted off to Holloway with the rest of them.' She winced, thinking of it.

'What a pickle,' Hump said, patting her hand with his soft paw. 'I wish I could do something, Vee . . .' He trailed off, engrossed suddenly in lighting his own cheroot before turning to stare out at the barges and skiffs on the river below.

'Oh Hump, remember Bucharest?' Vera said, blowing an experimental smoke ring. Hump was still turned away from her, looking outside, so she could only see the flaccid edge of his jaw and couldn't make out his expression at all.

'Good times, eh, Vee?'

'No regrets, Hump?'

'No, Vee, no regrets. Although I have to say it's all a bit hazy at the edges – years ago, now.'

'I have an extraordinarily good memory,' Vera said, tapping the ash from the tip of her cheroot into the malachite ashtray on the desk. She didn't really like the taste of cheroots, she decided, there was something a bit mean and bitter about them. 'I can remember everything about those years.' She thought she saw him stiffen, tilt his head a little, as if sniffing the air. But he didn't turn back to look at her.

'Everything?' he said.

'Every tiny little detail. I kept a diary, naturally, as all young women do. I wrote religiously, every night, even if the end of the evening was sometimes breakfast time the next day.'

'A writer, eh? I never had you down as that type.'

'No, Hump, not a writer. Not in any professional sense. I just like to remember things. In fact I was looking at some of my old diary entries only last night, and it did make for interesting reading. Some of the people we used to mix with in Bucharest, some of the things we got up to – as you say, good times, dear boy.'

'But that book is closed now,' said Hump, still not looking at her, holding the burning cheroot up to his lips.

'Closed books can be opened,' Vera said, grinding the stub of her own into the ashtray. She'd had enough of it.

The next week she'd had the letter from that Naps woman, calling her in for an interview with the newly formed Special Operations Executive. And the van that had taken the Carluccios away never came back to Nell Gwyn Court.

*

A frown passed over Mr Brown's shiny brow, and he looked up. 'It says here that Atkins is your mother's surname. What was your father's surname?'

'When my father died, I took my mother's name, as did both my brothers.'

'Why did you do that?'

'Mother was . . .' Vera let her voice trail off, and tapped ash into the ashtray. 'It was something Mother asked us all to do, that's all. Grief does strange things to people, doesn't it?'

Mr Brown nodded, turning another page of the documents. 'Your father's surname was Rosenberg, was it not?' Vera couldn't bring herself to respond. 'Miss Atkins, I'm afraid I need you to answer.' Mr Brown's mouth worked, twitching his grizzled moustache.

'I beg your pardon? I didn't quite catch that, dear boy.'

'Your father's surname was Rosenberg. That's a Jewish surname, isn't it?'

'Is it?' Vera said. 'I wouldn't know. My mother is a Catholic, but personally I feel more at home with an Anglican service. What about you, Mr Brown?' Mr Brown replied that he was, in fact, Methodist, but that was beside the point. 'Quite so, Mr Brown, it is beside the point. Shall we move on? I expect you'll want to check when I arrived in England, and so forth?' Mr Brown shuffled the paperwork, moving his forefinger down the page. 'I arrived in 1937. We stayed in Winchelsea for a while, Mother and I, but then we moved to London. I worked as an ARP warden until the job came up in F-Section,' Vera said.

'And how did you hear about the SOE?'

'A letter came, out of the blue, inviting me to an interview. I said I'd give it a try, and it turned out to be quite an interesting position, so I stayed. I've no idea how they knew who I was. I can only suppose that someone mentioned me as being a good linguist. I was finished in Paris and Lausanne, as well as attending secretarial college here in London, you see. I speak four languages fluently, Mr Brown. Someone must have thought they could make some use of me, for the war effort.'

'I see,' said Mr Brown.

There, I have intimidated him, Vera thought. Mother always said I should try hard not to intimidate men, but in certain circumstances it is no bad thing. Mr Brown turned a sheaf of paper over. 'You'll want to know if I've been out of the country since I arrived, I suppose?' Mr Brown nodded. 'I went on a skiing holiday in early 1939, with my fiancé, Flying Officer Richard Ketton-Cremer.' She caught Mr Brown glancing down at her left hand. 'The ring is an heirloom; it is in the family safe at Felbrigg Hall in Norfolk,' she added.

Really, things were dragging on a bit. She checked her watch discreetly below the edge of the desk as Mr Brown made some more marks in the margins of her form. It was time to draw things to a conclusion. 'I'm terribly sorry, Mr Brown, but I promised to meet Hump for luncheon at his club. Would you mind if I borrowed your telephone to call his secretary to ask to reschedule?'

Mr Brown looked up. 'Not at all, Miss Atkins, but I believe we're almost finished here. What time is your appointment?'

'It's quite all right, dear boy. I'm sure Hump will understand your need to be thorough.' She reached for the phone. Let Mr Brown worry about upsetting Hump and disrupting his day. Let him worry about being thought an officious little oik.

'No, really, I think we're just about done,' Mr Brown said just as Vera began to lift the receiver.

'I wouldn't want to get you into trouble for not doing your job properly.' She caught up the receiver in her left hand and reached out her right forefinger towards the dial.

'Not at all. Don't let me ruin your luncheon. I think I have everything I need here. And give Mr Humphries my regards, will you?'

'Certainly, Mr Brown. It will be my pleasure,' she said, replacing the receiver in the cradle with a chiming click. 'If you're quite sure?'

'Quite,' said Mr Brown, tapping the pile of papers into a neat sheaf. 'Everything appears to be in order, here.'

Gerhardt

Kieffer's knee was almost touching the prisoner's as he leant forward to speak. Gerhardt noticed how she pulled her limbs into herself. She was pale as moonshine, her breath coming in rapid bursts. 'He wants to know if you'd like an English cigarette,' Gerhardt translated, but she didn't appear to hear him. He repeated the question, but she shook her head, clamping her jaws tight shut. He heard the office door open and one of the typists brought a tray of tea things and placed it on the table in front of them. The cups and saucers were made of porcelain so fine it was almost translucent in the late-afternoon light.

Kieffer patted her thigh. She jumped as if stung. 'You are well,' he said in heavily accented English. It was more of a statement than a question. Then he began talking in German again, pausing so that Gerhardt could translate, and pouring the tea. He said what a pleasure it was to have her back in avenue Foch, and how nice it would be if she decided they could finally do business together. Gerhardt looked at the girl's face as he translated. Her eyes looked glassy. Blue, he noticed now, as the light caught her: her eyes are china blue. But her pupils were huge and unfocused. Without asking, Kieffer poured milk and put two lumps of sugar into her teacup, using the little silver tongs. Someone must have told him that was how all English took their tea. The brown liquid streamed into the cup, and Kieffer handed it to her. She reached out to take it, but her hands were shaking so much that the cup rattled and tea splashed a puddle in the saucer.

'Let me help,' Gerhardt said. He held the saucer for her as she lifted the cup to her lips and drank greedily. His mother drank her tea like that, in the English way, with milk and sugar, Gerhardt remembered; she said it tasted of childhood.

Kieffer lit a cigar. The smoke snagged round them. Gerhardt looked at the girl's hand holding the cup as she gulped down the tea. Her fingernails were bitten right down to the quick. Just like mine, Gerhardt thought; she bites her nails just like me. When she put the cup back on the saucer, she thanked Gerhardt, and he placed it down on the polished table. Kieffer blew out another plume of smoke and checked his watch. There was the sound of a vehicle slowing down outside. 'That will be them, now,' Kieffer said. 'Tell her to look out of the window.'

Gerhardt told her. She was still shivering so violently that he had to help her out of the chair and over to the window. The lowering winter sun had already cast the garden into deep shadows, but occasional beams of light cut through the rooftops and sliced into the office, highlighting the edge of her shoulder, and turning a streak of her still-damp hair golden-amber. He watched her expression as the black van pulled up in the driveway and two figures were pulled out of the back seat at gunpoint. He saw her eyes narrow. When they were pushed into the middle of the little patch of grass, it was clear that the tall man was limping. They were both blindfolded.

'They can't see you. So don't worry, they don't know you're here,' Gerhardt translated for Kieffer, all the while scrutinising the girl's face, seeing the effort it took for her to try to maintain a blank expression.

'I don't know these people,' she said, and Gerhardt translated.

'What does she mean? She told you about them, about the room above the Lucas Carton,' Kieffer said. Gerhardt paused, unwilling to translate. It felt like a betrayal. But he'd done the right thing in telling Kieffer about the rendezvous point, about her colleagues.

'Th-they were picked up this lunchtime,' Gerhardt translated, unable to control his stammer. 'They are colleagues of y-yours.'

'I don't know them,' she said, shaking her head. 'These people are nothing to do with me.'

'Really?' said Kieffer. 'If they're nothing to do with you, then you won't mind if I have them shot?' Gerhardt translated. He'd expected the girl to look scared, but instead she looked confused. Gerhardt was aware of Kieffer watching her carefully. 'But you could save them, if you wanted,' he added. 'All we need is your security check, and a little support for Dr Goetz, too.'

But the girl said nothing. 'Fine,' said Kieffer turning to Gerhardt. 'Tell her you're going down to the garden to shoot the terrorists, then.' Gerhardt did as he was told. The girl still did not respond. 'Use my pistol; it's in my desk,' Kieffer said. Gerhardt walked over to the polished walnut desk that sat below the photograph of the Führer. Surely Kieffer didn't mean him to actually kill them, right there in front of her? The drawer slid out and inside there was an Astra 400, sleek and grey, with the textured coppery handle. 'It's loaded,' Kieffer said, as Gerhardt picked it up. 'Go down now, but wait for my command before opening fire.'

The weapon felt smooth-heavy in his left hand as Gerhardt went out of Kieffer's office and down the stairs to the front door, heart pounding like a kettle-drum. You're doing your duty to the Reich, he told himself as his boots thudded on the steps. You are obeying an order, that's all. His throat constricted. His mouth felt dry as dust.

There was a click as he released the safety catch. He looked up at the window, where Kieffer stood with the girl, but it was hard to see them properly: the sunshine caused spidery reflections of tree branches against the glass. Behind him the unit who'd brought in the saboteurs stood watching, waiting. Why hadn't Kieffer asked them to do this? Gerhardt wondered. Was it some kind of test?

It was cold outside, and he had no coat. His fingers were already white-numb over the trigger. It was all he could do not to shiver. He lifted the weapon and looked down the barrel at the saboteurs. Only two – there'd been three in that room, he remembered. He wondered if one of them had escaped. The woman was dressed in black, her dark curly hair escaping above the folded blue cloth they'd used to blindfold her. The man was taller: grey suit and wine-red scarf, thick brown hair ruffled out of place.

Gerhardt's breath was loud, sawing up his throat. His weapon arm was shaking. He tensed his muscles, lifting the pistol a fraction higher to shoulder height, waiting for Kieffer's signal.

He saw the man's handcuffed fingers reaching blindly towards the woman. One of the men from the unit shouted at them. Gerhardt lowered his weapon briefly as a couple of the team ran onto the grass and shoved the prisoners further apart, so they could no longer have any contact.

Gerhardt cleared his throat and looked up at the window again. With the sunshine reflecting on the glass it was hard to see, but it looked as if Kieffer was whispering in the girl's ear. Gerhardt's jaw tensed. He lifted the pistol back up and took aim again, staring through the sights at the figures in the centre of the garden: still as bronze statues in the fading light.

He waited for Kieffer's command, trying to keep his arm steady. If Kieffer told him to shoot, which one should he shoot first? The woman? He moved the muzzle to the right, centring on her chest. The buttons of her coat appeared to tremble with her breath. But would it take more than one shot to kill her? What if he missed?

Gerhardt wanted to cough, but gulped spit to salve it. His arm had started to ache. He looked again at the window, and as he did so a couple of sparrows landed on the lawn near by, making him jump, curl his trigger finger in surprise. That was close – a negligent discharge would be embarrassingly dangerous, here in the little garden, with all eyes on him.

He took a deep breath and trained his aim on the man. He was the same man he'd seen walking past the restaurant with *her* in the rain, on that first day. Where had they been going, he wondered? Were they just colleagues, or more than that – lovers, perhaps? He saw the man's hands clenching and unclenching, heard the handcuffs make tiny clinking sounds. He'd shoot the man first, Gerhardt decided, in the chest, and then the woman. Yes, that would do it.

His weapon arm was killing him, the muscles burning up with the strain. The sunlight hardened as a cloud passed, and the two figures turned from gold-brown to charcoal at a stroke. There was a sound from the building and Gerhardt turned his head, keeping his pistol arm still trained on the terrorists.

Kieffer was opening his office window. It must be time. Gerhardt steadied his arm, waiting for the command. There was a sudden rush of heat to his face. He swallowed. It wasn't murder if he was obeying an order, was it?

'Lower your weapon and come back upstairs,' Kieffer called, his voice cheery as a mother calling her children in for tea.

Gerhardt's arm dropped. His numb fingers fumbled to get the safety catch on. He walked towards the front door without looking back at the unit or the figures standing on the patch of grass.

It felt as if he'd just finished a hundred-metre sprint. Mouth parched, chest heaving, he pushed open the front door and began to climb the stairs back up to the English girl.

Edie

The heat battened down her exhaustion. But it felt as if she could have been at home in the drawing room, with the crackle of logs on the fire and the late-winter sunlight slant-ing in the window. There was a rug at the hearth and the BBC *Radio Londres* buzzed on the wireless in the corner. If she closed her eyes she could imagine herself back there, with Mummy entering invitations into the daybook, her fountain pen scratching on the thick paper. Perhaps that flapping at the window was the doves from the dovecote, not scrawny Parisian pigeons. Her lids drew down. Any minute now she'd smell a gust of Dior as Mummy swept past to make a telephone call. There'd be hot chocolate on the table. The sunshine caressed her shut lids and she felt herself begin to slide into a doze. Someone touched her shoulder. It would be Mummy, suggesting a hack – such a glorious day, and the horses needed the exercise after a winter cooped up in the stables. There would be snowdrops clumped round the tree roots in Windsor Great Park. But she was so very tired. She didn't feel like riding today. 'Actually, Mummy, I think I ought to go back to bed. I feel a little unwell. I'm going to give it a miss, if it's all the same with you.' That's what she said, but no sound came out. And Mummy was nudging her again, poking her hard in the shoulder.

'Fräulein,' Mummy said. Why was Mummy speaking German? The air was so warm. It felt as if her lids were gummed together – glue-eye, that's what Dr Marchant called it.

'Mummy, I think I may have glue-eye,' she said, but again the sound didn't come from her lips, and her cheek lolled against the wing of the chair.

'Fräulein, wake up, it's your scheduled time,' said Mummy, poking her again. Edie's head jerked up briefly, but her eyes remained fast shut and she smelled the wood smoke and felt the beckoning comfort of sleep. 'Fräulein!' A shout, and a swift slap to her cheek. Edie opened her eyes. In the place where Mummy's armchair should have been there was an empty space. The window was in the wrong place. And why was there an open suitcase on the table?

The present assaulted her in a rush. She was in Paris, in the *Sicherheitsdienst* headquarters in avenue Foch. And she'd just agreed to commit treason.

She saw Dr Goetz shifting from foot to foot, stroking his right hand as if the slap had hurt him more than her. 'Fräulein, it's time for your transmission,' he said, pointing at two large black-rimmed clocks above the fireplace. They looked like a giant's pair of spectacles, Edie thought, with the hearth a downturned mouth below. Under one clock was printed *Berlin* and under the other *London*.

The suitcase on the table was her wireless transmission set, aerial ribboning out of the window to where pigeons strutted and puffed on the grey slates. The sky was a small trapezium of pale blue. Edie remembered those two Molyneux dresses: sky-blue and dove-grey: not too showy, perfect for a young girl, Mummy had said. Afterwards they'd gone to buy her first proper handbag. Her lids began to flutter down again, like wings.

'Come now, Fräulein, Herr Kieffer wants *alles in Ordnung*,' said Dr Goetz.

'Everything in order,' came another voice from further across the room, translating. It was the interpreter. He'd been with her in that place. She remembered the water: in her mouth, in her lungs. Edie looked across the room and saw the interpreter standing beyond the fireplace, where shadows played. As she looked at him, he looked away. It was impossible to make out his expression. She remembered his voice in that place, throughout it all. His soft, strange accent.

Dr Goetz said something in German, his grey eyes like rain-washed pebbles, spittle flicking the corners of his mouth. His face was suddenly very close to hers. His pink fingertips jabbed at the piece of paper on the table next to the wireless set. The interpreter cleared his throat and explained that the questions were for Baker Street.

Edie stared down at the paper. The black type writhed like a row of ants in her over-tired gaze. 'Fräulein, it's time,' said Dr Goetz, at her shoulder.

Edie thought about Felix and Claude, and the tenderness between them. She thought about Justine, knitting socks for her husband in the labour camp. She thought about the little child she had glimpsed, looking wide-eyed from an upstairs window, the night she'd arrived. And then she remembered Bea, fallen on the railway track, and the little baby girl she'd left behind. That had been Edie's fault, hadn't it? She couldn't save Bea. But she could save Justine. She could save that one family, even if it meant working for the enemy.

She nodded at Dr Goetz and picked up the metal contact on the wireless set. Every dot and dash of Morse burned and stabbed, a reminder of her treachery. She asked all their questions, all their requests for names, grid references, Lysander drops and equipment. She used her correct code. She included the security check.

The fire had died down, the pigeons had flown away, and the sun swung behind the rooftops by the time she finished. Dr Goetz had stood behind her the whole time, his breath wet as seaside spray against her cheek as she worked. When she stopped, she drew breath and leant back in the chair.

'*Fertig?*' said Dr Goetz. '*Alles in Ordnung?*'

'He wants to know if you've finished,' said the interpreter, his voice still far away. Edie nodded and shivered. Someone's just walked over your grave, girl – that's what Bea would have said – a chill prickle right up her spine. She exhaled as if ridding herself of a nasty smell.

'Yes,' Edie said, 'it's done. *Alles in Ordnung.*'

Chapter 10

Gerhardt

'What did you think?' Gerhardt said. They had just seen *Die Grosse Liebe* with Zarah Leander playing the lead role. Norbert shrugged and pulled his cigarettes from the pocket of his long overcoat. Above them the white pillars of the *Soldatenkino* toppled like an over-iced cake, neon lettering flashing out into the dulling evening, and Gerhardt was reminded briefly of his little brother's birthday cake, frosted and studded with shards of glass after the night of the fatal raid on his home town.

It started to drizzle, cold drops percolating through the darkening skies. 'Did nothing for me, mate,' said Josef, holding out a hand for one of Norbert's cigarettes. 'Don't get me wrong, the Leander woman is lush, but I'm not really into that romance stuff.'

Gerhardt thought Zarah Leander was a little like the English prisoner – something about her eyes – but he didn't say that. Instead, he asked what the plan for the night was. It was his first proper night out in the city. Last time had been scuppered by the English girl's capture, but tonight they were all off together: he, Josef and Norbert. Josef had promised to show him the sights, and made it quite clear he wasn't talking about the Eiffel Tower and Notre-Dame Cathedral.

Josef winked at Norbert. Norbert checked his watch and shook his head. Gerhardt stared past them both into the damp wall of drizzle, where the painted streetlamps glowed like pale blue puffballs and black cars splashed intermittently through puddles. Other cinema-goers were spilling out into the street.

Gerhardt noticed a few civil service girls carrying their grey coats over their heads to protect their perms from frizzing. 'We could go where they're going,' Gerhardt said. He hadn't noticed whether or not the girls were pretty, but they were chatting and giggling as they scurried out into the evening. They reminded him of some of the girls from Hitler Youth he'd been hiking with last year, before he joined up.

He remembered the hot sunshine, and the high green hills, and pitching their tents by a clear stream. On the last night of the trip they'd all visited a beer cellar, and Lisel had let him kiss her, outside in the warm summer dark. He remembered pushing her up against the rough stone wall as the others walked ahead. Her breath had been hot and sweet and she'd let him undo the buttons of her blouse, gasped as he'd cupped her swelling breasts in his hands. He'd thought she was going to let him carry on, but at the last minute she'd said no, I mustn't, I'm so sorry, broken free and run off to join her friends. And he'd been left breathless, hard, frustrated. He couldn't hate her for it. He hated himself for not being more daring, not trying again with another girl, a girl who didn't care so much about God, marriage and parents. The problem was that the other girls weren't Lisel. He'd confided as much to Josef, just after he'd arrived, and Josef had laughed and said not to worry, Paris would make a man of him. Why suffer that kind of humiliation, Josef said, French girls were cheap. At that, Josef had rubbed his fingers together, as if chinking small change.

Gerhardt looked at the German girls, almost out of sight now, their voices no more than sparrows' twitters in the distance. He didn't really want to have to pay for it. He'd rather have a girl who liked him, who wanted him to do it. But he couldn't say that to Josef.

'Let's get something to eat first,' Josef said, throwing his cigarette into the street. It plopped and fizzled in a puddle by the kerb. 'We can have a nice steak and a few beers before heading on.'

'Steak?' said Gerhardt.

'Don't worry. Just don't ask any questions about what animal it's from. Tastes fine though, eh, Norbs?' Norbert nodded and did up the top button of his coat. Gerhardt followed his two colleagues out into the clammy chill of the late-winter evening.

Vera

Vera crossed the tail end of Oxford Street and reached Marble Arch. It was late, long past blackout. There was a momentary stilling of the wind as she passed under the cold stone archway, and then she was out in it again: tugging at her skirt, hissing down her neck. A taxi passed, speeding towards Bayswater; she thought of waving it down, but she had no money left in her purse – there never seemed to be any spare money these days. Silly of her to spend cash on presents for agents and the like, she rebuked herself, thinking of the solid-silver powder compact she'd given Yvette in the last moon period. But something like that could make a difference – one could hock a bit of silver, if one needed to raise funds urgently. Vera thought of her own precious earrings, and the overdue bills for the apartment in Nell Gwyn Court. But perhaps she could keep her diamonds a while longer?

Vera had waited late at work to check that the BBC announcers had voiced all the necessary messages on their French broadcast: *The lion has left the enclosure. The milk jug is between the sugar basin and the teaspoon,* and so forth. The radio chaps had started getting a little shirty about the volume of messages these days, not understanding that what to them was mere nonsense gave the French Resistance vital information about drops of weapons, explosives and rations. She'd had to visit Bush House, ingratiate herself, and stroke a few egos earlier that day. It was worth it, though: Vera imagined a group of *Maquis* huddled round a crackling radio set in an abandoned farmhouse, cheering at news of a weapons drop. *Mother is hanging out the washing* – that was the message they'd used for Yvette's drop, wasn't it?

She crossed into Hyde Park, taking the path towards the gun emplacements. Oak trees creaked like ship's timbers in the wind, and branches knocked against each other overhead. The moon, just a sliver, hovering behind her, periodically lit the path: a pewter line snaking forwards into the night. But when a cloud scudded across, the view blackened into shadows and Hyde Park was just a navy-grey sea of darkness. Vera stepped off the path and strode on.

There were occasional shouts from the girls manning the ack-ack guns, to her left, their voices caught and spat out by the wind. Vera thought again of Yvette, of the afternoon she'd first met her, when she'd walked her back to Hyde Park Barracks, where she was stationed with her ATS chums. Probably not up to your standards, Colonel Potter had said on the phone earlier on, telling her about the potential recruit that he had in his office, a bit of an officer's groundsheet – off sick with so-called 'appendicitis' at present, and we all know what that means, don't we? Shall I fob her off for you? But Vera had insisted on meeting the girl: a pale young woman with sandy freckles and red hair, who looked no older than a schoolgirl. And there'd been a spark of ferocity in those pale blue eyes, and despite her impeccable manners, she wouldn't be bossed about. During the meeting at Lyons Corner House and the walk along Oxford Street to Marble Arch, Vera had been reminded of herself at that age: naïve, eager to please, but stubborn, underneath it all – a fighter. At least, that was what she'd told Colonel Potter when she called him back to tell him she was sending the girl off for training immediately.

Now Vera skirted the perimeter fence of the anti-aircraft battery, and on into the blankness of the night-time park. One heard stories of what went on in London parks after blackout, but it didn't do to dwell on them. Needs must when the devil drives, she thought.

The ground was already limned with frost, but it wasn't yet frozen hard, and her heels sank into the earth, slowing her down. She'd have to clean her shoes when she got home, clean them herself, because the days of housekeepers, maids and stable boys were long in the past now. But one day, she thought, one day when Dick and I are married and he inherits

Felbrigg Hall – then the life I deserve will be mine again.

Vera pushed on, even though the moon was behind a cloud, and all that lay ahead was inchoate shapes in the gloom. When she reached the avenue of beeches, she paused, and then came to a complete rest underneath a large one to her right, listening to the bare twigs clattering against each other overhead. The moon reappeared, highlighting treetops like cobwebs: shivering, silver. She put out her right hand to feel the bark. There was nobody about. Her fingers moved over the tree trunk: rough and smooth, sharp places where old branches had broken off. Up and down and around she felt, as if she were reading Braille. Until she found the hollow: ah, that's it, there.

She needed to think. She reached into her handbag for her cigarettes and lighter. She had to cup her hand around the flame: the wind kept threatening to extinguish it, but eventually it caught – a flare of orange, shooting up like a tiny distress signal. She inhaled deeply, drawing in chill air with the warm smoke.

If Dick were here, would she ask him what to do? She exhaled, remembering all the earnest discussions they'd had when they'd first met on the cruise: setting the world to rights. She remembered the colours of the Mediterranean sunset, and the feel of Dick close to her, but not quite touching, as they watched the reflection of the lowering sun linking up with the ship's wake, like a pathway. But that was so long ago, now.

'What should I do, darling?' she said aloud, her voice mixed with smoke, snatched away by the wind. She turned, looking back the way she'd come, through the trees, past Hyde Park Barracks, to where the sickle moon rose in the cloud-dappled sky. Had the sun already set out there, and was Dick, too, gazing up at the moon, having a smoke, thinking of her?

She inhaled again and let go of her cigarette; it was caught by the wind and whirled away into the night. Dick wasn't here. And in any case, there were so many things she'd never be able to share with him.

She turned back to the tree, felt again round the broad trunk until she found the hollow, damp against her fingertips. She pushed inside. There it was. She pulled out the envelope, fat with what it contained, and thrust it deep into her pocket. As she checked her watch again, the moon went in, and the air-raid siren began its yearning wail. She broke into a run, heading for home, not looking back.

Gerhardt

Gerhardt wasn't sure exactly what he'd been expecting, but this wasn't it. Other than the pretty little waitress and the moustached proprietor, everyone was German. It didn't feel like Paris at all. He may as well have been in a workplace canteen, he thought, looking round the room. Everyone was in some kind of uniform: army, civil service or police. The waitress hovered like a hummingbird, the only splash of colour her orange-and-blue frock as she flitted between the grey throng of customers. The portly proprietor wiped his hands on a dirty white apron and smiled round the packed café. Someone played the piano in the corner. Gerhardt thought of the English prisoner. She played, didn't she? He thought about her supple pianist's fingers, and the tools on the table at place des États-Unis – he'd interrupted just in time. He frowned: Father would certainly think it wrong to feel sympathy for a terrorist. He pushed the image of the girl prisoner out of his head and focused on his first night out in Paris.

The steaks were good – he was hungrier than he'd realised – and the beer made his head buzz pleasantly. On the piano someone struck up 'Lili Marlene' and a few people clapped to hear the familiar tune.

'I don't know why the cheese-eaters hate us so much,' said Josef, wiping grease from his lips with a red napkin. 'Look at the business they get from us. If you ask me, we're improving the place.' He slapped the waitress casually on the behind as she passed by with frothing mugs of beer. 'You could have her if you want,' he said to Gerhardt, indicating the waitress's departing arse. Gerhardt looked as she scurried away between the tables. She was attractive enough, with black hair and high cheekbones. 'You'd have to wait until the end of her shift, though. And she's a bit of a fighter. I paid top whack though – cash and cigarettes, so she shouldn't have had any complaints. You had her, too, Norbs?' Norbert gave a grunt, which could have meant either yes or no, and took a huge gulp of beer. Josef said that Norbert was a dark horse, and slapped him on the back.

Gerhardt shoved extra potatoes into his mouth, even though he was already full. He didn't want to have to take part in this conversation. Josef had just said that the waitress was a bit of a fighter: did that mean he'd forced himself on her? Gerhardt had a vision of Josef following her outside after her shift, pinning her against an alley wall – and afterwards the girl weeping, scooping up cigarettes and coins from the gutter. Was that what Josef meant really?

Gerhardt wanted to lose his virginity, more than anything. He was nearly nineteen, after all. It was ridiculous that he still hadn't lost his cherry. But like that? That wasn't how he wanted it to be. He chewed the potatoes and fried onions and swallowed, the food going down his throat in a big fatty gobbet. It felt as if there was a cannonball in his stomach.

The piano player had changed melody now, thumping out something modern and jazzy, fingers stumbling over themselves on the out-of-tune keys. He thought again of the English girl, imagining her playing: slender fingers stretched over the cream keys. He imagined singing with her, but what? Stolz, perhaps? He thought about how after the song finished she'd turn and reach up with her pianist's fingers to touch his cheek. And she'd smile at him and say, 'Gerhardt.'

'Gerhardt! Mate – come back to us!' It wasn't her voice. It was Josef, nudging him in the ribs.

'Sorry,' said Gerhardt. 'Miles away.'

'Thinking about the waitress?' said Josef.

'Something like that,' Gerhardt replied.

At that moment the café door banged open. 'Beers all round!' came the shout as a cluster of men in Gestapo uniforms stormed in. The room erupted into a cheer.

'You got them, then?' Josef asked the tall, skinny one.

'Ach, Josef, we got them good. Those bandit bastards got what they deserved tonight and no mistake.' He grinned, white teeth a fissure in his chiselled face. 'Pierre, put it on the tab,' he shouted over to the proprietor, who nodded, grabbing beer glasses from the shelf.

Gerhardt made sure he was smiling too. Free beer, and the promise of losing his virginity later on: what hadn't he got to be happy about?

Gerhardt scraped his chair to one side to make place for the skinny Gestapo, who sat down between him and Josef.

The others clustered in. The table was tiny, and their knees all touched. A full, foaming glass of beer was placed in front of him, frothing head wobbling like a courtesan's coiffure. Gerhardt drank greedily. Whilst he drank, there was no need to talk.

The waitress was struggling with the rush. There were good-natured calls for her to hurry up. Her hair was coming loose, and patches of sweat showed in the armpits of her floral frock as she dodged and trotted round the packed room.

'Have they all been taken in, then, mate?' Josef said to the skinny one, who was wiping foam from his upper lip with the back of his hand.

'No. The brief was eradication. So all we had to do was find them and slot them.' He made a shooting gesture with the forefingers of his right hand.

'Good to get a bit of live target practice in,' sniggered another of the Gestapo boys – the one with the chipped tooth, sitting next to Norbert.

Gerhardt swallowed, put down his drink. 'But don't you need them for questioning?' he said. 'I mean, they'd have useful intelligence, surely?'

'Not necessary,' said the skinny one. 'Your boss told our boss he's got a double agent, a direct link with London now. Some girl transmitting from your place – you must know that – so he has no use for her colleagues.'

Gerhardt took a swig of beer. It tasted acidic. He wanted to spit it out. With an effort he swallowed, and looked at Josef. 'But Kieffer told the prisoner that he wouldn't kill her colleagues. They did a deal. I was there.'

Josef gave Gerhardt a look. 'Well of course he'd say that. What did I tell you about Kieffer: he doesn't like to get his hands dirty. If he said he wouldn't have her colleagues killed, then he wouldn't. Doesn't mean someone else wouldn't do it, though.'

Gerhardt remembered Kieffer giving his word, shaking the girl's hand. He remembered taking her up to Dr Goetz's room for her transmission, how she was dizzy with exhaustion, had kept slipping into unconsciousness. She had thought she was saving her colleagues' lives. He took another swig of beer to hide his dismay.

'A man and a woman,' the Gestapo bloke continued, recalling their triumph, 'coming out of Café Colisee. We got them down a side street.'

'Ach, but the woman was a fighter,' said the small man from across the table. And Gerhardt was reminded of the way Josef had talked about the waitress: she was a fighter, that one.

'So, Herr Kieffer gets the Gestapo to do his dirty work for him?' Gerhardt said.

'You catch on quick, mate,' said Josef sarcastically. 'It's just division of labour. We're the brains; they're the brawn.' He cocked a thumb in the Gestapo bloke's direction and laughed. 'Makes no difference really. We're all on the same side, mate. Isn't that right?' He held up his glass to chink it with the others'. Gerhardt joined in, clinking glasses, wishing the men '*Gesundheit*' and necking the rest of his drink. Even though there was a twisting in his gut and he'd begun to feel queasy. He laughed and joined in because, after all, what else could he do?

'Let's go,' said Josef. The café door banged once more behind them, letting out a gust of piano music, laughter and smoke. The Gestapo boys had stayed on inside, saying they'd join Josef later. Josef had made some comment about 'sloppy seconds' and everyone laughed. The ground shifted under Gerhardt's feet. An icy rain fell, but Gerhardt felt hot: hot and sick. 'This way,' said Josef, leading them into an alley. The ground undulated; Gerhardt struggled to stay upright. Too many beers, too quickly – he wasn't used to drinking like that.

His fingertips grazed the wet bricks of the buildings on either side. Norbert was breathing heavily behind him. Up ahead, Josef was bouncing off the sides of the alley like a garrulous ping-pong ball. 'Like to get there early, while the girls are still fresh, you know? Got a perfect one in mind for you, Gerhardt mate – blonde, a bit more mature, knows what to do: she'll show you the ropes, all right. Her name's Marie,' he called back behind him as they tumbled on into the darkness. The raindrops were like cool fingers tickling Gerhardt's neck as he struggled to keep up. But heat rose in waves up his chest and queasiness lapped his throat.

At last Josef stopped. There was a doorway in the wall on the right-hand side. The paintwork was peeling, but the brass doorknob was smooth and shiny from the touch of so many strangers. Josef knocked three times and the door opened to reveal a ferrety man, who looked them rapidly up and down before ushering them inside with an angry frown. Norbert slammed the door behind them.

Indoors it was almost as dark as the alley. Gerhardt had the impression of a dusty brown corridor and he could smell dried rose petals. He swallowed down another wave of nausea. The floor was still undulating. He put a hand out to steady himself on the wall. His palm touched bare plaster: gritty-dry. Josef was talking to the ferrety man, nodding and pulling out his wallet. He could still sense Norbert behind him, hear his panting breath. And then there was a woman. Her breasts were handfuls of dough that had been left to prove, rising out of the front of her too-tight dress.

He was too hot, sweating now, blinking raindrops and perspiration from his eyes. '*Schatzi*,' she said. Little darling – she spoke the German word with a French accent, running a long fingernail over his cheek.

His head spun. He gulped down a dribble of bile that had forced its way into his mouth. Her breath smelled of tobacco and peppermint, like their neighbour's back home: old Frau Schmidt, with her walking stick and her sausage dog, who he used to have to kiss in return for a sweetie if he met her in the street.

He tried to focus on her face. She had a black stripe in the parting of her yellow hair, and Gerhardt was reminded of a banana someone had given him, a long time ago, before the war, which suddenly struck him as funny. He gulped again as his stomach churned. He was about to lose his cherry to this banana-haired woman, who had breath like an old woman. It was a huge joke, really.

He opened his mouth to laugh, but what came out wasn't laughter, what came out was a stream of vomit: half-digested steak, potatoes, onions and beer, upchucked and acrid, mostly over himself, but also over Marie and the dusty-brown linoleum whorehouse floor.

'Sorry', he kept saying. 'Sorry'. *Entschuldigung. Desolé*. He said sorry over and over again, in English, German and French, trying to wipe the brown gobbets of sick off Marie's crêpey décolletage, his feet sliding on the vomit-slicked floor.

They threw him out into the alleyway. Norbert came too, silently helping him down the Métro steps, manoeuvring him round sleeping tramps. By the time they got back to avenue

Foch the ground had stopped moving, his stomach was caved out, and Gerhardt was just left with a thumping head and a raging thirst. Norbert shoved Gerhardt into his room and closed the door behind him, without a word.

Gerhardt fell into his bed; confused thoughts leapt and twirled. He knew there was something he had to do, but he couldn't think what. His beer-addled brain did him no favours. He could hear the English girl pacing the floor above him. They'd moved her up to the top floor now, to one of the little servants' rooms that had bars on the window, and no balcony (just in case, Kieffer said, especially now we've taken her handcuffs off). Every night he could hear her walking across the room and back, like a caged lioness, bare feet padding the boards until the early hours.

He was listening to her footfalls – there was something he needed to tell the English prisoner, but what was it? He would go up and tell her, if only he could recall what it was. Before he could remember, he slipped into a fitful sleep, already dreaming, the familiar dream-memory that had haunted him since he arrived in Paris.

The girl was waving from the kerb. The sunshine was so bright and her dress was white . . .

'I'm terribly sorry. I shouldn't have bothered you,' said the girl, beginning to turn away.

It was very hot now the car had stopped moving, even with all the windows open. The air was as thick as sugar syrup inside. 'Not at all,' said Gerhardt's mother. 'Does the Count usually pick you up?'

'If the car happens to be passing he occasionally gives me a lift into town. It's my lunch hour—' The young woman cleared her throat. 'He's a family friend,' she added . . .

Chapter 11

Vera

What silly impulse had brought her here, Vera thought, struggling against the wind. Last night she'd had two agents to see off: a man and a woman, who'd be working together in Metz. They were eminently suitable, both for the work and for each other. Vera sighed. Vicarious romance was all she had these days. But things will change, she thought, feet sliding on the muddy track, hair breaking free from her hairnet and flapping wildly at her shoulders.

The wind sliced like a rapier, cutting through her clothes and reminding her of the skiing holiday with Dick back in 1939: the blinding sunshine and the gasping beauty of it all and the two of them together, flashing through the blue-whiteness like a fleeting smile. He said he'd been impressed with her prowess. She wasn't like other women, he said. How she'd loved that, being admired. Her father had never admired her; he'd only ever been interested in her brothers Ralph and Guy. Girls were for fucking and fun – that's what her uncle always used to say, although he'd married Karen, their housekeeper, in the end. Vera wondered where they were now, if they'd managed to get away in time – nobody had heard from them since 1940.

She pushed a straggling strand of hair away from her eyes and strode on into the rushing stream of winter air. She must be nearly there now, surely? It's only a mile, the woman had said. Up the road. You can't miss it. A country mile, Vera thought, eyes watering. She checked her watch. She'd been walking for more than half an hour already. Hedgerows waved frantically, like crowds of commoners at passing royalty, and clouds swirled and fled overhead.

She'd asked her driver to drop her off in Cambridge after the airport send-off at Tempsford last night. It wasn't planned; it was just that seeing those two agents together had made her think of Dick, and how they'd be together, after the war. She'd taken the milk train to Norwich. She'd slept a little on the way, slumped like luggage between churns and sacks of mail; she woke in time to get off at North Walsham. From there she'd had to wait an age for the bus to Cromer. It being Sunday there was nowhere open for refreshments, and she'd survived the whole morning on just the flask of coffee she'd taken from Tempsford and her cigs.

The bus was crammed with soldiers and ATS girls, laughing and flirting their way to some ack-ack emplacement on the coast. Looking at them she thought of Yvette. She'd been in the ATS hadn't she? Vera remembered seeing her in that frightful khaki uniform and thinking that she'd make sure the French tailor found something that suited her skin tone far better for her drop into Occupied France.

Vera wondered whether she'd done the right thing with

Yvette's messages. Was Buckmaster correct? Had the girl really just forgotten her security check? Vera's face was pushed up against the cool glass of the bus window, and she drifted off to sleep again, thinking of that agent with the red hair. Her dreams were peppered with the stifled screams and laughter of the recruits on the bus. Except in her dreams it wasn't the hullabaloo of a coachload of soldiers and ATS, it became a party on the lawn at Crasna, and the laughter was her own, being teased and tickled by Friedrich until she'd begged for mercy, gasping out in German and English, *'Halt, bitte, Friedrich! Please stop, Ambassador!'*

Vera woke up before her stop, with dribble down her chin and a pain in her temple. She got off the bus by the village green and knocked on the door of a nearby house to ask the way. The woman who answered the door was surrounded by clumps of suspicious-looking children, a smear of coal dust next to her unsmiling mouth. 'They'll be in church by the time you get there,' the woman said accusingly after giving her directions. Vera said sorry for the bother and thank you so much for your help and didn't mention that she wouldn't be joining the Ketton-Cremers in church, didn't say the Ketton-Cremers might very well not even know she existed. Not yet, at any rate.

Vera pushed against the north-easterly, tired and hungry and wondering how the hell she would make it back to London today. How foolish she was to undertake this silly little quest. Then, suddenly, the track opened up, and there it was: Felbrigg Hall, family seat of the Ketton-Cremers and Dick's home.

It was even larger than she'd imagined, bigger by far than her own childhood home in Romania. In front of her was a huge two-storey Tudor edifice of brick and glass, with a sweeping gravel drive. A burgundy Ford Deluxe was parked outside the front door. She recognised it as Dick's, and she had to stem the impulse to run towards it. A thin line of blue smoke emerged from just one of the nine chimneys, whisked away into the wan sky. From behind the house she could hear the tolling of a chapel bell, calling the family to prayer. Vera wasn't sure if anyone else lived here with Dick's widowed mother. But in any case, they'd all be in church. It would be safe to go a little closer, just to look, without needing to bother anyone.

Her shoes crunched on the gravel. She looked in at the mullioned window to the right of the stone arch that framed the front door. She saw wooden panelling, oil paintings in heavy frames, a sweeping staircase with wrought-iron balustrades: everything as it should be. There was a particular portrait of a woman in blue at the bottom of the stairwell that caught Vera's eye: modern and severe. It would have to be replaced by something more in keeping, Vera thought – hadn't Dick mentioned a Gainsborough kicking about somewhere?

Vera imagined ascending the staircase after a charming evening entertaining. They'd have just waved goodbye to their guests at the front door, Dick's arm resting casually at her waist. 'I thought they'd never leave,' he'd whisper in her ear and his lips would graze her earlobe. After they'd shut out the night, he'd stay at the door a moment, letting her go on up first, watching appreciatively as her fingers trailed the smooth banister. She'd catch his eye, and they'd both know what the other was thinking, and he'd begin to follow her up the stairs to – where was the master bedroom? Vera looked up at the rows of windows. It must surely be at the front of the house.

She thought about drifting up from a four-poster and pushing thick tapestry drapes to one side to let in the morning sunshine and glorious parkland views.

Then a dog began to bark somewhere inside the house, and the spell was broken. If she tarried any longer someone would notice her, come to the door, ask what on earth she was doing here. And what could she say? I'm going to marry Dick, just as soon as I'm British, and he makes it home. I'm going to marry Dick, and all this will be ours.

Vera turned her back on the big house. But before she left, she paused to caress the smooth wine-coloured bonnet of his car and to remember that last summer before the war. He'd taken her driving in that car for her birthday, given her a collection of MacNeice poems, taken her to a hotel. 'June Thunder', that had been her favourite poem from the collection – the one she'd given to Yvette to use as her code.

The Junes were free and full, driving through tiny
Roads, the mudguards brushing the cow parsley,
Through fields of mustard and under boldly embattled
Mays and chestnuts . . .

She smiled at the memory. 'One day, my darling,' she said aloud. 'One day we'll have June thunder again.' And she forced her feet to begin the long journey back to London.

Edie

Even through the glass she could hear the tramp of boots on the road. The soldiers were marching along avenue Foch, just as they did every day, up the Champs-Élysées, round the Arc de Triomphe and all the way along the broad boulevard, almost underneath her window. She looked out between the metal bars – since her escape attempt she'd been moved to an attic room with a tiny barred window. It was sunny outside. The cream-coloured buildings rose up on either side of the road, and the ranks of soldiers passed with dark accuracy down the middle. Edie thought of mathematics classes with her governess, how she'd been taught to draw thickly ruled pencil lines underneath the answer. That's what they were like, the Nazi ranks, a triple underscore scratching into the paper-pale avenue.

She watched them, far below. Goose-stepping, that's what they called it, that funny way with the legs. Edie remembered how much trouble she'd had learning to march: all that shouting, the hours on the drill square in the biting wind. How much she'd hated it – and what she'd give to be back there, now. How had it come to this? Transmitting messages for the enemy, messages that London thought were from their own agents. Edie held on to the thought that she'd at least saved Felix and Justine. At least there was that. She sighed, as the sound of the parade died away.

There was a knock at the door, and she turned, but didn't answer. They could all just go to hell. The knocking came again, tentative, but insistent. She threw herself on the bed and covered her head with her pillow. But the knocking wouldn't stop.

'Go away,' she yelled, but she heard the door being unlocked and pushed open. She sat up to look. It was the interpreter, bringing a cup of coffee. 'Go away,' she repeated. 'Just leave me alone.'

He shut the door behind him, and walked across the room towards her bed, boots making the floorboards creak. 'I need to tell you something,' he said. As he reached the bed she jumped up, knocking the cup so it fell out of his hands: coffee all over his face, china smashed on the floor.

'I don't want it!' she screeched into his face, not caring that her spit hit his cheek, not caring about anything, and suddenly she was upon him, scrabbling and biting, tearing at him and his hateful SD uniform, not thinking, just hitting out wildly.

At first, stunned, he didn't respond, merely tried to block her, a look of surprise on his face. But then she caught him with a swift blow to his jaw, knocking him off balance, shouting that she hated him, him and his murdering friends. And then he responded, with a hard punch to her solar plexus, winding her and causing her to fall, landing on the shards of broken crockery. She tried to get up, gulping for breath, but he was on top of her, pushing her down. There was a sharp pain in her right cheek as something pierced the skin. She pushed back, struggling, but he was stronger, pinning her in place. She couldn't move.

His face was close to hers now: his lips half parted, he was panting. He kept her there, his body rigid above hers. A strand of his drenched hair had fallen forward, and twitched in time with his breathing. She'd never seen his face this close before. Coffee dribbled like dirty tears down one cheek. As she looked, she saw his pupils dilate, round and black as an eclipse. His face moved even closer to hers, his breath warm. Then he suddenly shoved her away and kneeled up. 'Do you want to get yourself shot?' he said at last, pushing the hair from his eyes and getting to his feet.

'Yes,' she replied, sitting up.

He was straightening his uniform. He stopped, shook his head, looked down at her. He held out a hand to help her up, but she ignored him. Instead she began to pick up the pieces of broken cup that lay strewn across the floor. 'Don't do that; I'll go down to the kitchen and get a dustpan,' he said. But she carried on, plucking the pale slivers from the spaces between the floorboards until there was a sharp pile of them in her right palm, like bones. She got up without his help. The broken crockery rattled as she threw it into the metal bin. The puddle of coffee was seeping slowly into the wood, like a bloodstain.

Then, looking at her, he said, 'Your face – come here.' She turned away, putting her fingers up to where he was looking. A splinter of china was wedged in the soft flesh of her cheek: it hurt when she touched it. 'Let me look at it in the light. Come.' He drew her towards the bed and sat down next to her, cupping her chin in his hand. She winced as he touched her cheek gently with a fingertip. 'You can't leave it like that,' he said, and before she could pull away he'd squeezed it, pinching it hard so that the shard of porcelain popped out into his fingers. He showed it to her. It lay like a baby tooth on the ball of his thumb. She put up a hand, rubbing the blood from her face. 'Hurts, doesn't it?' he said, and she noticed the purple-red bruise beginning to form on his jaw, where she'd punched him. He opened the catch on the window and flicked the broken china out between the bars.

'I won't say anything,' he said, closing the window. 'But if you made unprovoked attacks on other staff members, there would be serious consequences. At the very least they'd put the handcuffs back on you.' She saw him looking at her wrists, which were still encircled by pink-rawness where the cuffs had been, and had open cuts from where she'd been strapped into the chair in the cellar. He stayed sitting next to her. 'I'll get you another coffee,' he said, moving to get up.

'No,' she said. 'Don't bother. But what was it you wanted to tell me?' She looked down at his square-tipped fingers with their bitten nails resting on his trousers. She noticed the fabric dip as his hands tightened against his thighs.

'N-nothing,' he said. 'I should go.' The mattress shifted as he got up. He paused in the doorway. '*Adieu*,' he said, half turning, the slice of brown hair still wet from the spilled coffee. It was the way he held himself. It was his clumsy use of French.

At last she realised who he was: the soldier from place de la Madeleine that day.

The door slammed shut behind him, and she heard the key turn in the lock. Her fingers reached up to the tender place where he'd pulled the shard of china from her cheek and she closed her eyes.

Gerhardt

'Ach, she's a fighter, is she?' Josef said, winking at Gerhardt as they met at the bottom of the stairs.

'Sorry?' said Gerhardt.

'Your jaw,' said Josef, leering, eyes flicking up to the stair-well, and Gerhardt realised what he was alluding to.

'No, I just fell, that's all,' Gerhardt said, thinking about the struggle with the girl, and how he'd felt, holding her down, her face so close to his. He used to feel like that about Lisel. He wondered what Lisel was doing now. He wondered if she'd joined the civil service, as she'd said she would. She could be anywhere: France, Poland, the Netherlands. She could be anywhere, with anyone.

Josef shrugged, and Gerhardt could tell the driver didn't believe him. They began walking down the corridor together. He was on his way back to the clerks' office. He'd promised Frau Bertelsmann he'd help out with a backlog of filing. Josef had begun talking about some bandits who'd sabotaged a train near Metz. Gerhardt was only half listening, his mind still in the upstairs room, with the girl. He'd been about to tell her about her colleagues, that they'd been killed by the Gestapo. He couldn't stop thinking about it. The girl was only continuing to comply because she thought she was keeping her colleagues safe. It seemed wrong not to tell her the truth. But then again, if he told her, would she stop helping Kieffer and Dr Goetz with the radio game? What would they do to her if she ceased to comply? He'd even written to the Count about it, in a roundabout way, questioning the values and standards he should aspire to, as an officer in the Reich.

'Three hundred killed,' Josef said.

Gerhardt stopped outside the clerks' door. The scent of cigarette smoke mingled with coffee. There was the rattle of typewriters. 'What?'

'Three hundred of our boys,' Josef repeated. 'Those *Maquis* bastards. They could just have blown up the railway bridge, but no, they deliberately timed it so that a trainload of soldiers was halfway over when it went up.'

Gerhardt thought of the lads in compartments, joking, shooting the breeze. He'd come by train from Leipzig with a group of soldiers, fresh from training, full of bravado and banter.

'Some were killed outright in the explosion, but most drowned or were crushed when the train went into the river below,' Josef continued. 'They were on their way home on leave, for fuck's sake.'

'That's terrible,' Gerhardt said.

'It's more than fucking terrible, mate, it's evil,' Josef spat. 'And that's her lot.' He poked a finger up towards the stairs Gerhardt had just descended. 'Her lot will have supplied the arms and ammunition, organised it all – murderers!'

Gerhardt thought about the British bombers over Leipzig, and his little brother Franz, deep in the cold earth, because of them. He thought of the saboteurs who provided arms and ammunition to assassinate his comrades. No, he wouldn't tell the English prisoner about her dead colleagues. He didn't owe her anything. 'The only good Tommy is a dead Tommy,' he said to Josef. Let the *Funkspiel* continue for as long as necessary, put an end to the British and their killing ways.

Chapter 12

Vera

How could he, Vera thought, staring out across the sparse yellowed grass towards the bone-white mausoleum. How could Buckmaster ignore such clear evidence that their agents were in jeopardy, and yet still refuse to act? She wanted to shake him.

My darling . . . she wrote, turning her attention back to the aerogramme. It fluttered at the edges, where the breeze nagged. The ink bled through the thin paper and onto one of Buckmaster's old copies of *The Times* she had on her lap. She began again: *My darling Dick, I have good news. Very soon I shall be all yours!*

She paused, contemplating how to continue. For once she'd decided to give herself a proper lunch break, get out of the office and go to Paddington Square Gardens to sit in the sunshine and write to Dick, without the distractions of home or work to intrude. She tapped her pen against her lip, looking out over tree-lined grass, noting how the distant winter sunshine turned everything sepia. It was like looking at a memory.

She shifted, feeling the wooden slats of the bench dig into her buttocks. The park was empty. She was alone.

'It's just you and me, darling,' she said aloud, knowing there was nobody to hear. She began to write again:

I want to tell you about visiting Felbrigg. It was just as you described. Your car was parked outside. I felt the urge to run to it, imagined us racing off through the country lanes. Do you remember my birthday in June, when you whisked me away to that hotel? I remember driving along those tiny roads, the mudguards brushing the cow parsley. I remember the wind in my hair. And I remember that night, too. My best birthday present was you, darling. And there can be so many more birthdays like that, now the naturalisation process is nearly complete, and we can be married, at last, and not have to keep our love secret any more.

She wanted to write on, but found her mind snapping back to work, to the message on her desk waiting to be filed:

CIPHER TEL FROM BERNE. REPORT. YVETTE HAS HAD SERIOUS ACCIDENT AND IN HOSPITAL. FELIX AND JUSTINE GONE HOME. ADVISE FAMILY. CLAUDE.

Usually she and Buckmaster went through an agent's message together. Usually they agreed a response, before sending it back to the coders for transmission to the field. But Buckmaster had dealt with this one himself, not even bothering to mention it to her, simply leaving it on her desk for filing. As if she were nothing more than his secretary.

The message had come via a circuitous route, sent by an agent calling himself 'Claude', who had escaped to Berne, he said. Having a 'serious accident' and being 'in hospital' was code for being captured by the Germans. Moreover 'gone home' meant dead. Vera knew that – for heaven's sake, everyone knew that – and yet Buckmaster's looping pencil marks in the margins questioned the veracity of the report: *Who is Claude? Who are the Felix and Justine he refers to? No evidence this is genuine – no action required.*

Vera looked back at the letter she was trying to write. It was gushing with happiness and love. But the words on the page seemed very different from the reality of her life – a life Dick knew nothing about. She couldn't tell him anything about the work she did with Buckmaster and the Baker Street team: not now, not ever. Their marriage would be pocketed with secrets from the very outset. She sighed.

She'd tried, gently, to tackle Buckmaster about the message, bringing it up discreetly, before he went to lunch.

'I have some concerns about the information we're getting from the field.'

'Perhaps we could discuss this another time, Vera?'

'But there are implications for the Paris depot sabotage, not to mention the safety of all our agents.'

'I'm not sure what you're driving at.'

'If Yvette has been captured with her set, then the SD could be transmitting to us in her stead, don't you see? I had my suspicions when she transmitted without her security check – do you remember? – and I'm rather afraid this appears to confirm them.'

'Not at all. I think it's a red herring. Her messages have

been perfect – even encrypted in her "fist". Nobody could fake the particular idiosyncrasies of her Morse. Ask the coding chaps – it's like a fingerprint. No, the messages are definitely from her. This thing from "Claude" is just meant to frighten us, that's all.'

'What if she is working for the other side, Buckie? What if she's swapped sides?'

'But why would she swap sides, just like that?' Buckmaster said, chewing impatiently on his pipe stem.

'Why indeed,' Vera said.

There was a pause, where she and Buckmaster faced each other across the office, and neither of them spoke. There was nobody else in the room. She wondered momentarily whether Buckmaster could be deliberately affecting naivety. Was he really so credulous, or did he too have something to hide?

'How is the naturalisation coming along?' Buckmaster said, breaking the silence.

'The interview went well, I think,' Vera said.

'Do you suppose they'll need to speak to me, in support of your application?' Buckmaster said.

Was that a threat, she wondered, some sort of veiled threat, to keep her in line? 'I'm afraid I don't know,' she replied.

'Because I'm terribly busy at the moment. Taking time out for an interview would be inconvenient. I may not even have the time for it at all, if we can't progress things at work. If I get embroiled in some kind of communications technicality I certainly won't be able to take time off to go through your paperwork with the bods at the Home Office, d'you see? And it would be such a shame to put the dampers on it, when I know how keen you are to get matters concluded.'

Yes, Vera decided. He is telling me to pipe down and

comply. 'Well, if there is anything I can do to make things run more smoothly at work, then I shall of course do my very utmost to assist,' she said.

'Jolly good. You can make a start by filing those old messages from the field,' he said. So she did as she was told and tucked the slip of paper with the message from 'Claude' inside the manila file, thinking of Yvette – call sign Cat – and wondering where she was, and what she was doing.

Vera sighed again, and tried to concentrate on writing to Dick. *My naturalisation interview went well, and it should just be a matter of rubber-stamping it, barring some disaster,* she wrote. She thought of Buckmaster, chewing on his pipe stem: he could very well be a 'disaster', if she didn't continue to give him the kid–glove treatment. *But I think we're home and dry,* she added. *So you can feel confident in telling your mother all about us, at last, and we can finally make real plans for our wedding.*

She paused. The sun was a tiny white sphere, like a tossed tennis ball, thrown up to serve. The light glinted off her watch face, and she thought how the rubies in the Ketton–Cremer family engagement ring would also sparkle beautifully in the sunshine. Soon, soon. *When do you think they'll let you have leave?* she wrote. *I do miss you so. My sweet, my darling, my love.*

She looked up. A man in a long coat was entering the park gates, hat pulled low over his eyes against the sun. Vera signed the aerogramme, folded it and put it in her handbag. She'd send it out with the office post, later.

The newspaper still lay on her lap, spotted with blue ink that had bled through the airmail letter. Vera checked her watch, and took her notebook and pencil from her bag. The man had begun to walk down the path towards the mausoleum. She opened her notebook and wrote something down, pressing hard into the paper. Then she ripped off what she'd written, took out her lighter and burnt it. She had to cup her hands over the flame, and was left with just a tiny triangular slip of paper, blackened on one edge. She let it go, drift off like a daydream. The sheet on the top of the notepad was unmarked, but gouged by the impression of the pressed pencil marks. She ripped it off and placed it inside the old copy of *The Times*, on page seven, next to an advertisement for Andrew's Liver Salts. She folded the newspaper into a neat wedge and put it down on the bench next to her.

When she looked up again, the man had disappeared, out of sight behind the mausoleum. She checked her watch again. Just before she left, she opened the waxed paper packet of sandwiches her mother had made: plum jam, made with saccharine to save the sugar ration – vile. She took one bite, and threw the rest onto the grass, food for the scrawny pigeons that fell from the winter skies at the sight of it. She couldn't see the man anywhere.

She left *The Times* on the bench and walked quickly out through the park gates.

Chapter 13

Edie

'Tell them we've gone firm on the prototype depot sabotage,' the interpreter said, saying a date and looking over her shoulder. Edie wrote the request down on her pad as she sat wedged between the interpreter and Dr Goetz at the small table where they kept her wireless set. Dr Goetz said something else. 'And ask for more plastic explosives in the next drop,' the interpreter translated.

'Do you want to request specific amounts of armaments?' she said, looking up, pencil poised, as if the date she'd just written was of no consequence. But her mind was working. They were using her for this radio game – a *Funkspiel*, they called it – tricking London into believing that the French Resistance were planning to blow up the depot on the out-skirts of the city where a secret weapon was being developed. But once the date of the fictitious sabotage had passed, what then? Wouldn't Allied air intelligence see that the depot was still there? Wouldn't the War Box realise it was all a Nazi bluff? And what would happen to her, once the *Funkspiel* was over and the SD had no more use for her at avenue Foch?

Dr Goetz shuffled through a pile of papers. Edie looked up at the blurred grey rectangle of window, where two pigeons were cloudy daubs. One was puffing out its chest, pacing. She heard the faint flutter of feathers against glass. She caught the interpreter looking at her, three quarters on, and she returned his gaze. He had to sit close to her, close enough to see what she was writing on her pad, to check her coding to ensure she didn't include any hidden messages to London. He sat as close to her as a lover would in a darkened cinema: close enough to hold hands, to steal a kiss. He must have realised, as she had, that he'd carried her suitcase that day on place de la Madeleine. He must have recognised her. And what was it he'd almost told her, in her room the other morning? His eyes were such a dark brown that it was hard to tell where the pupil ended and the iris began, but she was sure the dark circle swelled, just as it had done when he'd had her pinned to the floor.

Then Dr Goetz waved a piece of paper in front of her face with a list on it, and the moment had gone. The interpreter watched her transpose her plain English into her code, so practised now that she no longer needed the copy of her poem, the one he'd found on the floor of her room the day she arrived. She reached for her wireless transmitter in front of her on the table; it click-hissed as she switched it on.

Dr Goetz's office was, as ever, stiflingly hot. A fire raged in the hearth, reminding Edie of her life before all this began. When Pop was home they'd always stoked the fire, and the smell of wood smoke had mingled with pipe smoke as he sat with his whisky and newspaper. What was it Pop used to say? Play up and play the game – yes, that was it. She began to turn her transposed text into Morse, tapping the dots and dashes that would speed all the way across to Miss Atkins and Major

Buckmaster in London, telling them to send weapons, rations for Resistance fighters – weapons and rations that would get harvested by German soldiers, late at night in French fields, and London would be none the wiser.

As she completed her transmission the men began talking across her. Despite her lack of German, she knew they were saying something about her, and about the *Funkspiel*. She listened, but the words still made no sense.

Outside the window one of the pigeons – the female – flapped away. The male, chest deflated, bobbed its head twice, and followed. She heard the word '*Funkspiel*' again, and the word '*fertig*'. Didn't that mean finish? The interpreter was asking Dr Goetz something now, and gesturing at her. Dr Goetz pushed his gold spectacles further up his snub nose and shrugged. Then he said something – it could have been a date, his pale hands flapping, indicating a going away.

It's about me, she thought, and the radio game ending, and going away, or being sent away. The interpreter had started to respond, and she strained her ears, trying desperately to understand something of what he said, but as he began, there was a knock at the door. The fat woman was there. 'Kieffer,' she said, panting, eventually continuing through uneven breath. Edie watched her cough out her words.

'Kieffer wants us both in his office immediately,' the interpreter said.

Vera

'I'd like to know what's going on!' Vera said, storming into the office. She'd spent half the night down in the shelter with

Mother because of an air raid that never materialised, and the start of a cold was making her throat feel as if someone had poured sand down it, like corn down a *foie gras* goose. Coming in to find Monsieur Dericourt canoodling with Margaret was too much to bear.

'Nothing, Miss Atkins,' said Margaret, red-faced, springing away from the pilot. There was a funny smell in the air: sharp.

'I was just showing Mademoiselle Margaret how to peel an orange,' Dericourt said, straightening up with a slow smile.

So that's what the smell was, cutting through the fusty office air: oranges. How long had it been since she'd last tasted an orange?

Margaret began wiping her fingers on a handkerchief. 'Monsieur Dericourt brought them with the agents' post,' she said.

'Indeed,' said Vera, forgiving Margaret, but still angry with Dericourt for invading her office.

'Everyone thinks you need a knife to peel oranges. Not so,' Dericourt said, turning to face Vera. 'Sometimes the best tool for the job is not the most obvious.' He held a dessert spoon in his right hand. Vera tutted, thinking that she didn't have time for this. But she couldn't help but pause, watching his capable left hand cup the plump fruit as he carefully pushed the bowl of the spoon underneath the orange peel. The zesty citrus smell intensified. She saw how Dericourt held the spoon upturned, so the bowl mirrored the curved outline of fruit, how he pushed the peel from the flesh, digging gently into the pithy white layer, following the swell of the fruit below until the peel was released in an unbroken, hollow sphere. He held up the inside, creamy and crenellated like a miniature moon. '*Voilà*.' Then he slowly peeled away the pith, tugging at the white skin with his fingertips until the fruit lay bare in his palm. 'Ah, now she's ready,' he said.

Vera could feel saliva rising in her mouth. She wrenched her gaze away from Dericourt and his party trick. Outside the windows the sleet pelted down, a grey curtain. Inside was the office clutter: desks, chairs, cabinets, telephone cables, lino floor, files and maps – all shades of brown and beige, everything dull and bland and so very British. Her gaze focused back on the naked orange in Dericourt's hands and she thought of the baking heat of Bucharest in summertime – long, long ago.

'Shall we?' said Dericourt, smiling that smile of his. Vera struggled to remember how Dick smiled. It was open and generous, she thought. But Henri Dericourt smiled as if he were withholding a secret.

He began to pull the orange apart, prising it open with his fingers. Juice ran down his wrist and his tongue flicked out to lick it off. Vera cleared her throat. She should really be getting on with her work and not engaging with this pantomime.

'Let's not get your fingers sticky again,' Dericourt said, leaning over to pop a segment directly into Margaret's mouth. Momentarily Margaret's lips closed over Dericourt's fingers, and her face flushed. Vera looked away. She heard Dericourt mutter something, and Margaret giggle. Enough of this. Vera strode over to her desk and sat down.

Dericourt had deposited the agents' mail on her desk. There were postcards, blueprints, maps, even canisters of film. Buckmaster had been right: having a pilot flying in and out of Occupied France during the moon period was a significant boon to their operational effectiveness. She rifled through the pile, making a mental note of which cells were using the new system of communication. Nothing from Yvette. Strange – she'd been transmitting clearly and regularly since that wobble with the security check. But what if—

'Mademoiselle?' Dericourt was in front of her now, interrupting her thoughts, and blocking out the watery light from the window. He held out the final segment of orange in his open palm. She wanted to refuse. But to taste orange again, after so very long – she reached out, but as she touched the fruit he began to curl his fingers over hers. She plucked her hand away, taking the slice of orange before he could catch hold.

'Thank you, Monsieur,' she said, holding the segment between thumb and forefinger. She looked up at him as she spoke. His teeth were a cream chink in his shadowy face. 'There's nothing here from Yvette or her cell,' she said, gesturing at the pile of post.

He shrugged. 'I pick up what I'm told and I deliver what I'm told, that's all. As you said, Miss Atkins, the less I know, the better.'

Vera could hear Margaret's typewriter; she'd be concentrating on work. The flesh of the orange segment was firm. It smelled divine. Vera tapped it against her lips, pausing before deciding how to respond. 'Sometimes I wonder whose side you're really on, Monsieur,' she said in a voice too low for Margaret to hear.

She saw his eyes narrow. 'I think we both know how to choose the winning side, don't we, Miss Atkins,' he said, before turning on his heel and abruptly walking off, slamming the office door behind him.

Margaret didn't look up. Her head was bent low over her work, and her fingers flurried at the keys.

Now Vera pushed the whole piece of orange into her mouth, gorging on the glorious swollen ripeness of it. But as she swallowed, the acidic juice caught the raw flesh of her sore throat and she found herself choking.

Damn that Dericourt. Damn him.

Edie

Kieffer, talking in German, strode towards them, arms outstretched. 'He's got some new music. He wants you to play for him,' the interpreter said. Edie nodded and went to sit down on the piano stool. The ivory keys were like teeth, running a smile through the octaves. The interpreter stood behind her. There was music on the stand; the title was in German. Kieffer grinned and nodded at the score. He reminded her of the Cheshire Cat from *Alice's Adventures in Wonderland*, always smiling. She wondered if he'd disappear when things got awkward, like the Cat did.

'Whenever you're ready,' the interpreter said. Her fingers touched the keys, and she began. It was an anodyne little tune: lilting, old-fashioned, but pleasant enough. It was only when the interpreter leant over and turned the page for her that she saw the lyrics, and then he began to sing. His voice, deep and complex, suddenly turned the bland little melody into something else: richer, sadder. Kieffer smiled as he stood watching them perform.

When they reached the end, Kieffer applauded them both, and said something to the interpreter, who told Edie that they were free to go. 'That's it?' Edie said.

'He just wanted to break the morning up,' the interpreter

said. 'He gets bored by mid-morning, needs a little boost.' Kieffer said something else, before going back to sit behind his desk. 'He wants us to perform for a s-staff party he's planning,' the interpreter added. 'He says we are to practise here every morning after your scheduled transmission is completed.'

Edie got up and walked past Kieffer towards the door. She paused in the doorway and turned to the interpreter who was escorting her out. 'What was the song called? What was it about?' she said.

'"Im Traum hast du mir alles erlaubt",' he replied. 'It's from a film where a young officer falls in love with a girl he shouldn't. It's a love song, about forbidden love.'

'And what does the name of the song mean?' she said. She caught his gaze then, and that's when she was certain: certain he recognised her too, remembered the rainy day at place de la Madeleine, before it all began.

'In the dream you allowed me everything,' he replied.

Gerhardt

Kieffer shunted them out of his office as if he were sending children out for playtime. Gerhardt followed the English prisoner out of the door and along the corridor towards the stairs, hearing the usual sounds of the building: the tap of typewriters as they passed the clerks' office, the flush of a toilet chain, someone whistling tunelessly, a door slamming, and the creak-thud of the girl prisoner trudging slowly back up to her room, with its barred window.

Except she wasn't really a prisoner any more, Gerhardt thought, watching the fabric of her blue dress sway as her slender legs pushed on up the stairwell. She'd stopped being a prisoner the day he brought her back from place des États-Unis and they'd undone her handcuffs, the day she transmitted back to her colleagues in London. She'd changed sides. What would the British call her now, he wondered, not a prisoner – a collaborator, a traitor, a double agent?

He watched her climb, leaning heavily on the banister, a broken shoe catching on the brown lino as she made her way slowly upwards.

At the top of the first staircase she hesitated, looking back at him, and he remembered the night when he'd talked her in off the ledge. He'd only done it because she was useful to them, but even so – he followed her as she continued to climb. Of course, it wasn't really her choice to swap sides. She'd thought she was doing a deal, saving her friends. Gerhardt felt a stab of guilt. She still didn't know what the Gestapo boys had done to her friends. If she were to know, what then? If she refused to transmit for Dr Goetz, stopped being useful and became instead a liability, what would happen to her then?

They'd reached the top of one flight of stairs now, and she wearily turned the corner and began to climb the next. Gerhardt followed. He had told her that the reason Kieffer wanted them to practise the song was for a staff party. What he'd failed to mention was the party was planned to celebrate the end of the *Funkspiel*, when her part would be played out, and she'd no longer be of any use to the SD here. Gerhardt, suddenly, inexplicably, felt as if he wanted to weep.

The stairs seemed to go on endlessly and pointlessly upwards, the wooden banisters smooth from the hands of so many tired servants over the years. At last they reached the top, the little dark corridor that contained her room. He followed her, seeing her safely to her door, as he had done many times already, and as he'd continue to do until – until when? How long would things carry on like this?

'Kieffer makes me feel like a performing monkey,' she said, waiting at the entrance to her room as he fumbled with the key in the lock.

There was nobody about, nobody to hear his disloyalty. 'I know. He does me, too.'

The door swung open. Now was the time when he'd let her go, lock the door behind her, go back downstairs to work on written translation. Or, if it wasn't busy, do some filing for the clerks and generally 'make himself useful' as Kieffer put it. (Kieffer said he'd been 'very useful' so far and had mentioned as much in a telephone call to Boemelburg, who had in turn told the Count. His father had written asking Gerhardt to detail precisely what he was doing that was 'very useful', claiming to be fascinated by the SD machine, telling his son to leave nothing out of his explanations.)

Gerhardt watched her go inside, wondering what she did there in the hours she spent alone between transmissions, what she thought about when she was ceaselessly pacing the floor at night. He began to close the door behind her, shutting out the slender silhouette of her that stood uncertainly by the little barred window. 'You can come in, if you want,' she said, half turning, catching his eye. 'Unless you have something else you have to do?'

Chapter 14

Vera

How horrid the Tube had been this morning, Vera thought, pushing up the crowded steps of Baker Street Station towards the patch of greyish daylight, squeezed and shoved by the rush of commuters. There had been an air raid last night – reprisal for the Berlin attacks, no doubt – and the Tube stations had filled up with sheltering families. It was like the Blitz all over again. One had rather thought Hitler was occupied elsewhere, but there always had to be a bit of tit-for-tat, she supposed. Vera reached the top and breathed in, but the air was thick with fog and traffic fumes. She frowned and began to hurry down Baker Street towards Norgeby House.

The dirty mist washed her face as she forged ahead. Buses streamed past in a red blur, splashing oily puddles in the gutter. There was a tug in her abdomen. Surely not that, not today? She ignored it and strode on. There was a nagging pain in her right temple – she hadn't managed to get back to sleep properly after that blasted air raid. A man in a bowler hat barged past, causing her to turn awkwardly on her ankle, a pain shooting up the inside of her calf. He didn't even pause to say sorry. He leapt onto the bus that had just disgorged passengers at the stop ahead, and the bus swerved away.

She saw the knot of bus passengers disentangling ahead of her on the pavement, and she recognised one, a head taller than the others, jagged gait: Buckmaster. Watching him, she thought of a stick insect she'd kept in a jar as a child: awkward legs scratching up against the glass. Her mother had told her to set it free, but she'd kept it there, tumbling about in its glass prison, until one day she'd come back from a hunting trip with her brothers to find it motionless: dead.

Norgeby House now reared up beside her. Buckmaster stepped underneath the curved glass awning and disappeared inside. She checked her watch. Yes, she was on time.

There was that tug again, deep down between her stomach and her groin. She closed her eyelids slowly, as if shutting out the world would shut out the pain. But there was no release. She pushed through the front door of Norgeby House and her heels tapped against the marble floor. She began to climb the stairs up to F-Section, thinking about Dick and wondering if he'd got her last letter yet. Sometimes the post took weeks. She tried to imagine what he'd be doing now: breakfast or flight checks or PT – he'd told her all about his routine – but she struggled to remember the time difference between here and there (was it two hours or three in wintertime?) and she struggled, too, to remember his face. For some reason every time she thought of Dick, his features were overlaid with the insufferable Dericourt chap's.

As she reached the doorway to F-Section, there was another insistent pull in her stomach, and she realised she couldn't possibly go in. Instead she wearily climbed the stairs to the second floor, to where F-Section shared ladies' lavatories with N-Section, the Netherlands arm of the SOE.

Her heels sank into the sea-green carpet as she passed the long mirror and went into the furthest cubicle and hung her handbag on the hook. She lifted her skirt, pulled down her knickers and sat down on the wooden seat. As she did so, the first wave of nausea came, a dull ache stretching across the whole of her lower belly. She leant forward and put her hands over her face, feeling the sweat begin to form at her temples. It will pass; it always passes, she told herself. A teaspoonful of bile surged up her throat, but she swallowed it back down. She let her urine pass in a hot stream. She wiped herself on the hard toilet roll, like baking parchment, and saw the red smear of blood on the slippery paper. She threw it down the toilet, frowned and checked her watch. What to do?

Just then, she heard the lavatory door open. Two women came in. She could just make out their feet beneath the cubicle door. The crocodile courts were Margaret's, her own secretary from F-Section, but the black patent pumps belonged to someone else, one of the N-Section girls. They were talking.

'So, how's tricks downstairs?'

'Oh, you know, same old. Everything needs doing by yesterday. I've had this toothache since last week, and no chance to even make a dental appointment.'

'Poor old you. Have you tried oil of cloves?'

'Yes, but it's just getting to that stage where – anyway, I mustn't complain. Oh someone's in that one—' The door to Vera's cubicle was nudged. 'It's fine, you go first, ducks.'

The other girl went into the stall next to her. Vera heard the swish of cloth as she pulled down her knickers and the stream of urine going into the pan. They carried on their conversation all the while. Vera kept quiet. It wouldn't do to make herself known. She needed to come up with a plan for how to deal with the curse, three days early and heavier than ever. Men just had no idea, she thought, waiting silently while the secretaries' pointless conversation rattled on.

There was the sound of the chain being pulled and the flush of water and the two girls swapped places. 'Huge palaver here yesterday,' said the voice of the patent pumps. There was the sound of a tap being turned on. 'Something about a spy down in your lot.'

Vera stiffened. Why would N-Section have intelligence on F-Section? What could possibly have alerted them?

'No!' came a muffled gasp from the cubicle next to her. 'I can't believe that, ducks. Really?' Vera heard the rustle of toilet roll being pulled.

'According to the chaps up top. I had to take down reams of shorthand about it all yesterday – thought my bally hand was going to drop off by the end of it. They even used the green telephone to call you-know-who.'

'Who do they think it is?' The toilet flushed in the next cubicle and Margaret's court shoes disappeared out of sight.

'They don't know – they just suspect. I've got to type up the internal report this morning, and then it'll be sent on up top for further action. It's about compromises in the field, how the security breaches can't all be coincidental, and so forth. Really, the spy could be anyone, out on operations, to do with the air transport, or even back here in Baker Street. It could even be you, Margaret!'

At this, there was the sound of laughter. 'If I can't even find the time to get a tooth filled, I'm hardly likely to get the chance to lead a double life,' said Margaret. 'I think it's all tosh. I can't imagine any of ours getting up to that kind of thing.'

Vera could picture them both, wiping their hands on the towel and primping themselves in front of the mirror, laughing at the impossibility of treachery. Sweet, pretty, young things – like that very young wireless operator she'd waved off during the last moon period: innocent. Just as Vera had been herself at that age, when she started working as a translator for the Pallas Oil Company in Bucharest. Just as she'd been when she'd met Hump at one of the German Ambassador's parties in Bucharest, and just as she'd been the first time she went for dinner with the German Ambassador himself: *Don't. Don't think about him. That book is closed, dear girl.* Vera bit her lip and waited.

She thought they'd never go, but eventually they did, leaving behind the scent of Penhaligon's English Fern.

Vera pulled her handkerchief from her jacket pocket and folded it in half, and half again. It had a lace edge, and her initials embroidered in the corner. It was a shame to ruin it, but what else could she do? She couldn't be late, couldn't do anything to upset Buckmaster these days. She placed the folded cloth in the gusset of her knickers, and pulled them up, hoping it would hold, sop the blood that had begun to gently seep from her. She smoothed down her skirt and picked her handbag off the hook. The pain twisted again in her stomach, but at least the nausea had passed.

One day, she thought. One day I will no longer have to suffer through this monthly misery. Instead of the blood and the sickness I shall have a gently rounded belly, and darling Dick's child, the heir to Felbrigg Hall, growing silently inside me. One day – one day soon, perhaps?

She took off her watch before washing her hands thoroughly under the cold water – the hot tap had never worked. The soap wouldn't lather properly, just slid in a creamish slick between her palms. But it would have to do. She needed to get on, couldn't be late, not with things the way they were. She dried herself on the damp hand towel and fixed the watch back on her wrist, before checking her fingers one last time – no, there was no blood on her hands.

Dericourt

'It's about the girl,' Henri said, trying not to look irritated. He hated the way Kieffer only talked to him in the kitchen doorway, as if he were no better than a servant. There was a crash of metal pans from inside and the muffled sound of German swearing.

'What about the girl?' said Kieffer.

'As you know, I've been delivering messages to London *en clair* from other agents in the network, but there's been nothing from her or the other agents in her cell. Baker Street is getting suspicious. If she doesn't write soon, they'll get wind of your little game.' He remembered Miss Atkins' face as she looked at the pile of post on her desk. She wasn't stupid, but, luckily, neither was she in charge of the outfit.

'Thank you. I'll see to it.' Kieffer held out the brown envelope. Henri didn't think it looked as fat as it should.

'I'm flying back to England again tonight,' Henri said, pulling out his penknife and slitting open the envelope. He hadn't mentioned it to Jeannot. She made it so difficult; it was easier just to disappear periodically. She'd only accuse him of having an affair – as if he had the time for such pleasures these days. He began to count the notes. His thumb flicked through the money; it was as he suspected. 'I think your accountant has made a mistake with my fee,' he said, knowing that Kieffer handled that side of things himself. 'This is not what was agreed. I'll wait here while you find the shortfall and get the girl to write something to London.' He handed the envelope back to Kieffer, noticing how his nostrils flared slightly as he took it.

'Very well,' Kieffer said, turning away. He didn't ask if Henri would like to wait inside. When he'd disappeared upstairs, Henri continued to stand in the doorway, leaning on the jamb, with the winter chill on one side and the blazing heat from the avenue Foch ovens on the other, one nostril breathing crisp garden air, the other stuffed with the scent of burnt fat and disinfectant. Caught on the border between two worlds, he pulled out his packet of English cigarettes and prepared to wait for his dues.

Edie

A knock at the door – she stiffened. It wasn't time for her scheduled transmission. What could they want with her? 'Come,' she said, realising as she did so that she'd said it like they did, leaving out the 'in': '*Komm*' – the German way.

The door opened. It was Gerhardt.

She had a name for him, now, her interpreter: Gerhardt Vogt. He'd been coming to her room after her scheduled transmission times, bringing her English tea, waiting whilst she drank it and taking the cup back to the kitchen again.

She knew more than his name from those brief chats – she liked hearing about him; it helped her forget herself, even just for the few minutes it took to drink her tea. She knew that his mother was South African, that his uncle was something high up in the Nazi Party and that his little brother had been killed by an Allied bombing raid on his home town. He never mentioned his father, though. When she'd asked, he just said that his father didn't live with his mother, that was all. She couldn't tell him anything about herself, of course, but there was some comfort in those stolen moments, and she found herself looking forward to them.

The clear Paris sunlight washed his dark SD uniform into a pale grey; it could almost have passed for an RAF uniform – if he'd only been born a few hundred miles west. 'Kieffer says you must write to London,' he said.

'I beg your pardon?'

'Your Miss Atkins is suspicious because she hasn't heard from you. Other agents have been sending messages back with the new Lysander pilot.'

Her mind worked quickly. How could they know that other agents had been using a pilot to deliver mail, unless— 'The pilot is a double agent,' she said under her breath as the realisation hit. Gerhardt walked towards where she sat on the bed. She felt the bedsprings give, and the warmth as he sat down next to her in his usual spot.

'And if I won't write it?' she said, looking out through the barred window to the bluest of skies, empty and endless above the Paris streets.

'If London becomes suspicious about you, then it could jeopardise the *Funkspiel*,' he replied.

Below the window, five floors down, was the patch of

garden where they'd brought Felix and Justine, blindfolded, at gunpoint. 'If I won't write, will Kieffer have my colleagues rounded up and brought in again?' she said.

He didn't answer. But he didn't need to. She knew there really was no choice any more. She pulled her gaze away from the brittle blue winter sky. 'I've brought a pen, and Kieffer says he'll reward you for your continued compliance – if you have any small requests?'

Edie didn't answer immediately, noticing how the sunshine slanted through the barred windows, making criss-cross patterns on the bare floorboards. She thought of the sheer drop below those bars. 'Very well,' she said at last, taking the postcard from him. On the front of the card was a picture of a little girl in a knitted pixie hat, pushing a basketwork doll's pram. She was reminded of Justine, and the little girl hidden away in the grandparents' farmhouse. Had Justine managed to go and see her? Edie wondered. After Kieffer released her, had she gone straight to the station and taken a train to the countryside to visit her little girl? Edie imagined Justine enveloping the child in a huge embrace on the station platform, burying her nose in the girl's soft brown hair. If I've done nothing else, I've saved that girl's mother, Edie thought.

She took the pen from Gerhardt. It was black, with a gold nib. 'I brought you my own,' he said.

'But I'll ruin the nib,' she replied. 'I'm left-handed, you know.'

'I know,' he said. 'So am I.' And his fingertips touched hers as the pen passed between them. He was so close to her on the bed. So very close. 'Kieffer told me to check what you write,' he said apologetically. But she didn't mind. It was almost a comfort, having him there.

Dear Miss Atkins, she began. The nib didn't scratch at all, used to the backwards slant of a left-hander. She'd written nothing personal since those hastily scrawled postcards Miss Atkins had asked her to write just before her departure: postcards that would still be sent out to Mummy and Pop at regular intervals. She wondered what Miss Atkins would do when the postcards ran out, Edie thought, recalling that day.

It had been one of those thick winter afternoons when a pea-souper had enveloped the capital, and she could still taste the sooty air in her mouth as she climbed the stairs to Room 43, Orchard Court – the grey block that looked out over Portman Square where Miss Atkins met up with her agents in London (not that you could see anything of the genteel square through the windows of Room 43: it was like looking out into a bowl of porridge).

Miss Atkins was alone in the room, sitting next to a green-shaded lamp, which cast a yellow light over a piece of clothing she was stitching. 'Pull up a pew,' she said, barely looking up from her sewing. 'I'm nearly finished here.' Edie knew what she was being asked to do. They'd talked about it in training: the need to reassure family, to preserve secrecy. There was a pile of unwritten postcards on the table next to her.

How are you? As you know, things are rather busy here, she wrote on the back of the card, leaning on her knee. How to carry on? If she intimated anything about her current situation, Gerhardt would see, and tell Kieffer. He was watching every word she wrote. That day in London, she'd asked Miss Atkins for advice.

*

'I'm afraid I'm at a bit of a loss. Could you help?' Edie had said. Miss Atkins looked up from her sewing. In the light from the table lamp her eyes were in shadow, but the beam caught her lipsticked lips: vivid claret.

'Keep it vague and general. If you give the impression that you're madly busy, that should help. And ask questions. You can fill them with questions and betray barely a thing about yourself,' she said, snipping off a thread with a minute pair of silver scissors. So Edie wrote, postcards and postcards, undated, with variations on the same theme: questions about Mummy's WRVS commitments, about Mrs Carson, Mrs Cowie, about her schoolfriend Marjorie, about Pop's job. She even asked about the weather, and signed each one with a breezy *Tallyho!* as if the war were such tremendous fun there was barely time to even think about home.

How is the weather in London? she continued. *It's glorious here – we've had blue skies for ages – not that I've had much chance to get outside, as you can imagine!* Could she, Edie thought. Could Miss Atkins really imagine the reason that she wasn't able to go outside? 'Do you think that's enough? I'm just not sure what to write,' she said to Gerhardt.

She'd said the same to Miss Atkins, that day, she remembered.

'Give your hand a rest for a moment, my dear girl, and try this for me,' Miss Atkins had said, motioning for her to stand. Miss Atkins came round the desk. She'd been sewing the cuffs of a woollen jacket, which she now slipped over Edie's shoulders. It was beautifully tailored, French-style, and fitted Edie perfectly.

'I want to show you something,' Miss Atkins said. Close up,

Edie could see the fine lines round her eyes where her face powder settled. There was a faint waft of scent: Chanel? 'Here, on the right cuff. Can you feel it?' Edie's finger found the spot where Miss Atkins pointed, where she'd just been stitching so carefully. There was a bump in the cloth, as if a button had been sewn inside. 'Your suicide tablet – cyanide – should you need it.' Miss Atkins' voice had the same brisk tone she'd used to describe the postcard messages.

Edie had worn the jacket back to her training centre that evening. She'd worn it on her flight out to France. And she still wore it, now.

Edie glanced down. Her right hand held the postcard. And her right cuff? Empty now – the suicide tablet had been removed when her clothes were laundered, the day they brought her in. Someone must have told them about what went on in London, in Orchard Court – maybe it wasn't just the Lysander pilot who was passing information.

'I'm afraid I have to hurry you,' Gerhardt said. 'The pilot is waiting downstairs.' It was time to end it: *Adieu, Yvette x*

She handed the postcard to Gerhardt and clicked the lid back on his pen. When he got up to leave there was a space next to her where he'd been, suddenly chill without him there. She looked up at him as she passed him his pen. And he looked down at her as he took it. The sun had shifted now, and his clothes no longer looked the wood-smoke-blue of an airman's uniform. But his face – those eyes, that mouth – his face still looked like the face of someone from home. He opened his mouth to speak and she wondered for a moment how it would feel to kiss those lips. 'Kieffer asked me to ask you if there was anything you'd like,' he repeated, '– a little token of thanks for everything you're doing here. He's very grateful. He says maybe lipstick or perfume? We can have someone sent to the shops.'

Edie looked over at the barred windows and as she did so shifted on the bed so that her fingers with their bitten-down nails were hidden between her thighs and the mattress. 'Oh yes, what a nice idea,' she said, as if the thought had only just occurred to her. 'Some cold cream and a manicure set, if you would.'

Chapter 15

Gerhardt

'Just take this up to the girl, would you? The black market guy left it earlier,' Josef said, and Gerhardt saw Frau Bertelsmann frown as he handed her the package. She'd only just come back from supervising the girl's bathroom trip and bringing down her supper tray.

'Let me,' Gerhardt said, reaching out a hand. 'I don't mind. It'll save your legs.' Frau Bertelsmann's frown morphed into a tight smile, but he barely heard her thanks as he bounded up the stairs, two at a time.

It was already dark, but he didn't bother switching on the lights, hurtling up the narrowing tunnels of steps until he reached her door, right at the top of 84 avenue Foch.

He was breathing hard from running up the five flights of stairs. Leaning against the wood, he could hear her pacing, as always. He knocked, before putting the key in the lock. The footsteps stopped, and he pushed open the door.

She was standing in the centre of the little room, ready for bed, in those funny striped army-issue pyjamas they made her wear. The light was switched off. She had the window open, and the chill night air washed in with the moonlight. As he crossed the threshold, Gerhardt felt as if he were stepping into an ice-cold ocean. She looked at him, but said nothing.

'I brought you these,' Gerhardt said, feeling suddenly foolish and awkward as he held out the tissue-wrapped package. 'It's those things you asked for, from Kieffer.' Her expression was blank, trance-like. But she blinked as she saw the parcel, and suddenly her features came to life again.

'Thank you. How kind,' she said. Their fingers touched as he passed the package, and he felt it again: just as he had when she'd written the postcard. He thought of that teacher in school who'd let them experiment with electricity: the moment when the copper wires connected, and the little light bulb buzzed to life. He felt that pulse of energy between them. She didn't pull her hand away, and they stood in the centre of the room, with the parcel connecting them.

'Kieffer says he wants you to feel comfortable, now you're one of us,' Gerhardt said. Why was he saying those stupid, formal words? Why couldn't he articulate what he felt?

'Kieffer is merely trying to salve his conscience,' she replied.

They weren't looking at each other but down at the parcel: a lumpen rectangle of paper, tied up with a bow. In the twilight, the paper was dun-coloured, the ribbon a dull garrotte. She hadn't moved her hands away; the package connected them. He gently began to move his thumb along the edge of her palm, the smallest of stroking movements. He couldn't look at her, couldn't speak. What he felt was too impossible to say.

They looked up at the same time. Her eyes, in the half-light, weren't blue at all, they were silver-grey, like twin moons. She opened her mouth, as if she wanted to say something, and he heard the intake of breath. And he wanted her to say it – to find the words he couldn't. But as she opened her mouth, there was a shout from the stairwell and a thump of approaching footsteps. 'Vogt, what the hell's taking you so long?'

Edie

He'd gone. He'd gone and she hadn't been able to say it: to say thank you to Gerhardt for being the only one here who treated her as a person – despite it all. It made no sense, Edie thought, as the lock clicked shut and the sound of his footsteps died away. It made no sense at all that the American GI last summer, who should have been on her side, could have been so cruel, and yet Gerhardt – her enemy – could be so kind. More than kind: she thought about their secret conversations, and the way he looked at her when she spoke to him. She thought about the moment that had just passed between them.

She slumped down on the hard mattress and undid the parcel. Her fingers worried the cords free and she pulled off the thin paper. There: a manicure set and a small pot of cold cream, just as she'd asked for. At last she had everything she needed.

The manicure set had a pale beige leather case that snapped open with a metal clasp like a coin purse. Inside were all the things an elegant Frenchwoman might need to do her nails: a stick with a rubber hoof to push back cuticles, a buffer covered with a soft patch of chamois, and a metal nail file with an ivory handle. She thought of Gerhardt's expression when she requested a manicure set – like a cloud scudding over the face of the moon. He knew she bit her nails. He knew, and yet he said nothing, still passed on her request, and delivered the package himself. Keep your best friends close, but your enemies closer – was that what Miss Atkins meant?

Edie stood up and took the manicure set over to the window. She knelt down. It was cold: the chill air seeped through the fabric of her pyjamas. From downstairs she heard a door bang, and men's voices, carried up towards her in the icy darkness. Three figures walked away from the front door and along the driveway: a skinny one, a burly one and – following behind – Gerhardt: she recognised him even from up here. She recognised his slight frame, and the taut way he carried himself. Their German voices drifted upwards to her open window. How different he sounded, speaking German: harsher, not like the Gerhardt she'd come to know. When he'd told her about his mother, he'd been speaking in English. And his voice had broken, words tearing softly apart, when he'd told her about his little brother and how he'd died.

The three men were at the gate now, but Gerhardt turned back and looked up at her window. He was so far away that his upturned face was just a tiny smudge of grey in the blue-black shadows. She raised a hand: quickly, furtively. 'Goodbye, Gerhardt,' she whispered out into the night, knowing nobody would hear her.

Only once they'd gone, voices and footsteps disappearing up avenue Foch, did she begin. She placed the edge of the nail file against the flaking paintwork of the bar nearest to the side of the window, and began to saw. Forwards and backwards, forwards and backwards: the paint chipped off and a small furrow began to appear in the hard iron bar. Forwards and backwards: she carried on as clouds skittered past the waning moon. A stray dog howled. Stars began to appear, one by one in the indigo sky. Forwards and backwards, metal on metal, until the nail file was hot and her finger had begun to blister. She swapped hands. She mustn't give up. There wasn't time. The air was colder now and the wind had started to rise. Through the open window she heard treetops clacking against each other and the breeze was sharp as lemon juice in her throat. She mustn't stop. There had to be time. She'd do what she should have done before, climb up, over the rooftops, get away, find Felix and Justine and tell them. Tell them what?

Tell them there was a double agent flying from London.

Tell them of her own treachery in 84 avenue Foch.

Tell them it was all for nothing.

Tell them to run, run before it was too late.

Tell them to run all the way to Grandmother's house.

The nail file felt awkward in her right hand. It was hard to find purchase against the slippery iron bar. She pushed harder. Then suddenly it gave, snapping under the pressure, and the end fell away out of the window, lost to the night. She was left with just a stump, a quarter-inch of metal attached to the ivory handle. She dug it down into the base of the bar where it met the windowsill. If she couldn't saw through, she'd dig out. I am not giving up; it doesn't end here, she thought, jabbing and gouging down. There had to be a way. There had to be. The stars began to blink out, and the moon hid behind a veil of cloud. Edie worked on in the darkness, knowing nothing except the jab-grind of metal against cement.

In the end the remaining piece of nail file snapped off. So she grabbed the bar, wrenching and heaving. But no matter how hard she twisted and pulled, it wouldn't budge. She was trapped. She was trapped and they'd see, in the morning, what she'd tried to do. And wouldn't Gerhardt be punished for letting her have the nail file? She remembered what he'd said when he'd pulled her in from the ledge: *They'd kill me if I let you die.*

She hung on to the bar a moment, feeling it cool under her palm, gazing out into the Paris night. Then she knew what to do. She turned on her light and went back over to her bed. There was the pot of cold cream. She still had the powder compact that Miss Atkins had given her. She found it now and clicked open the lid. She used the remnants of the nail file to dig a hole in the ivory-peach powder, then scooped it out and mixed it with a dab of cold cream. It was almost the same colour as the cement on the windowsill, once mixed with some of the gouged-out dust. She pushed the mixture carefully round the base of the bar, patting and pressing it down, and smoothing some onto the place where she'd sawed a hole in the metal. It wasn't perfect, but it was good enough, for now. Once the window was shut, it would barely show. She closed the window now, keeping out the biting night air. Behind the glass, the night was empty and black. She clicked off the light and fell onto the small bed, feeling the darkness push in on her wide-open eyes, lacking the will to even cry.

Gerhardt

He couldn't do it in the end. He'd made sure he hadn't had too much to drink this time, and they'd gone to a different brothel, to save embarrassment. And he had wanted to, but – Gerhardt berated himself as he walked along avenue Foch towards number 84. The wind had picked up now, whipping up icy dust and rattling the tree branches. He thought of *her* and how she'd waved at him, looking out of her window as he'd left with Josef and Norbert. Maybe that was why he hadn't been able to bring himself to do it, he thought, as the sleepy gate guard nodded him through:

The woman they brought him was brunette this time. Quite young, too: generous lips, melting brown eyes, and hips that swayed pleasantly as she led him along the corridor to her little room. Josef and Norbert had disappeared already. This is it, he'd thought, sitting on the shiny satin counterpane as she slipped out of the red dress and stood before him in just her stockings and heels. Then she'd sat on his knees and her buttocks pushed the key to the English girl's room against his thigh through the fabric of his trousers: he still had it in his pocket – they'd been in such a rush to get out that he'd forgotten to give it back to Frau Bertelsmann. The Frenchwoman began to undo the buttons of his uniform, slowly, one by one. When she got as far as the third button he tried to kiss her, but she put a finger on his mouth. The red-painted nail was very long, scratching his lip. No kissing: it was one of the house rules. In frustration he buried his face in her hair, but it smelled wrong, somehow: peppery and dank. She didn't smell right. She didn't smell like – like the English girl. And that's when he knew. He knew he couldn't go through with it, couldn't lose his virginity to a French prostitute. It wasn't what he wanted. What he wanted was – was something that he couldn't have.

He'd paid the woman the full price, anyway, apologising as he buttoned up his clothes and left. She'd smiled, pecked him on both cheeks, said something in French that he couldn't understand. He'd been cold, trudging back through the curfew-empty streets, with the wind working its way down the nape of his neck. He'd been cold, but hot too: hot with frustration, hot with anger at his inability to control his emotions.

He closed the front door of 84 avenue Foch behind him and began to climb the main stairs, feet clomping, echoing through the marble-floored hallway.

He ran up the stairs to his room, not bothering to turn on the light, and threw himself onto his bed. He lay there for a while, fists balled, letting his breathing slow: anger, frustration and unsatiated desire squashed into a tangled ball in his gut. The Frenchwoman had been there for the taking. What was the matter with him? Why couldn't he be a man about it? He banged his head backwards, denting the pillow and staring up into the blackness towards the ceiling. Above those wooden boards, just above his head, that's where the English girl was. But she'd be asleep now, wouldn't she? The wind rattled the shutters of his room, as if the night were trying to break in.

She wouldn't even be there, but for him, he realised. If he'd told her what he knew, that her colleagues had already been shot, she wouldn't have agreed to continue with the *Funkspiel*. She wouldn't be transmitting her daily messages, coming down with him to Kieffer's office to play the piano. She would have been taken away, to one of the camps Josef talked about.

The wind died down again, and the room was silent. That was when he heard the floorboards starting to creak above his head, the sound moving to the other side of the room, and then back again. She was awake – pacing above him. If he told her the truth, he'd be putting her in danger. But what kind of man lied to a woman he cared about?

He stood up, and half ran towards the door and on up the stairs to the attic floor where her room was. He knocked first, then put the key in the lock. She was standing in the middle of the room, almost exactly where he'd left her, hours earlier. This time he didn't hesitate. 'Your colleagues are dead.'

Edie

'I'm so sorry,' Gerhardt said.

She looked at him standing there in the doorway in his half-buttoned uniform, like a ghost. 'How?' she said.

'Shot,' he replied, his voice thick and low. 'But not by us, by the Gestapo. I'm so sorry.'

Felix and Justine, bullet holes leaking blood, expressions blank in death, sprawled on a dirty kerb somewhere in the Paris back streets. It was too easy to imagine. 'When?'

'I d–don't know.' He hesitated. She noticed his stammer had returned. 'Not long after Kieffer had them brought in. I should have told you. I feel disloyal for not having said. But I thought if I told you . . .' His voice trailed off. His arms hung limply at his side. She couldn't make out the expression on his face. The distance between them seemed vast.

All that time she'd been playing along with the *Funkspiel*, thinking she was saving them, and they were dead. The fig-leaf of humanity she'd clung to was gone. Justine: dead. And what about little Violette? It was unbearable. All this time she'd spent on their wretched radio game and she was nothing better than that Lysander pilot: a double agent and a traitor. 'Thank you for telling me,' she said, wondering why he had. She should have known – had she known, in her heart?

'What will you do?' he said, and she watched him take half a step towards her, across the bare boards.

'I don't know,' she replied.

'Will you stop cooperating? Because if you do, if you're no longer any use to them, then Kieffer will have you sent to Karlsruhe.'

He took another step forward as he spoke, arms raised, reaching out to her, but he still seemed so far away. She didn't care about being sent to a German prison camp, not now everything was over. But she realised that if she withdrew her cooperation, Kieffer would want to know why. And she couldn't let on that it was Gerhardt who'd told her the truth; she couldn't implicate Gerhardt.

'They'll have me sent to Karlsruhe anyway, once the *Funkspiel* is over,' she said.

'No,' he said. Another step – he was closer still – if she reached out now she could almost touch him. 'My uncle is very influential in Berlin. I'm sure I can persuade him to find some kind of propaganda position for you, in broadcasting. You know, like the one you British call Lord Haw-Haw has. I could get you away from here. I could keep you safe. I can help you, I'm sure I can.'

Edie took a step back now. She shook her head. She saw his hands move up towards his face, and heard the sound of his breath quickly escaping: a cross between a sigh and a sob.

She took two quick steps towards him across the rough boards and was there. She reached up and put her arms round his neck and leant into him, then lifted her face to meet his.

Gerhardt

He could smell the soft, musky scent of her as she pulled him close, her hair smooth against his cheek. And for a while he just held her there as the moonlight frosted the barred window and the winter wind sighed in. They didn't kiss, not at first, just held each other close – so tight it almost hurt: her fingertips squeezing his shoulder blades through his jacket, his hands feeling the warmth of her flesh underneath the thick cloth.

He closed his eyes, shutting out the metallic moonshine, burying his face in her hair. It felt like finding something precious that had been lost for a long time. He could feel her heartbeat, synchronised with his own: in-out, in-out. Eventually she shifted her head, moving her hair away. His lips grazed her cheek, powder smooth, and then their lips met.

There was no awkwardness. She kissed him the way he'd always wanted to be kissed: her soft lips, the taste of her – it was like slaking a thirst. He ran his fingers down her back, feeling the curve of her body beneath the harsh fabric, moving his hands downwards.

'Are you sure?' he said.

'Now,' she said, tugging his shirt from his trousers. 'Now, if only now.'

They fell together onto the thin bed, limbs tangling: the taste of her. 'Your name,' he said, lips against her neck, hands running over her smooth skin. 'I can't do this without knowing your real name.'

'Edie,' she said, her arms pulling him closer in. 'My name is Edie.'

Afterwards he remembered thinking how easily they fitted together: her head resting in the space underneath his shoulder, arm lightly across his chest, their sweat slowly drying as their skin began to cool. He wanted to tell her he loved her, but sleep came suddenly, like a drug, before he had the chance to say it. And with sleep came the memory-dream.

The girl was waving from the kerb. The chauffeur pulled the car in beside her. The girl walked over to the car and leant in towards the open window, smiling. Her broad mouth had lots of very white teeth. 'Yes?' said Gerhardt's mother.

'Oh, I do apologise. I thought this was the Ambassador's car,' said the girl, her smile dropping away.

'It is,' said Gerhardt's mother. There was a pause.

'I'm terribly sorry. I shouldn't have bothered you,' said the girl, beginning to turn away ... The chauffeur got out and held the door open for the young woman. Gerhardt shuffled along the seat to make room for the extra passenger. The leather was hot and sticky in the gap where his shorts ended. The young woman got in beside him. She smelled of perfume, but not the same one as his mother's, muskier somehow. She shook hands with his mother, both of them leaning across him. He looked beyond the briefly clasped hands, out through the windscreen to see Hans, the chauffeur, furling up the black-and-red swastika flag that hung from the stubby flagpole on the car bonnet so that it no longer showed ...

Edie

He should never have left the door unlocked, Edie justified, disentangling herself from Gerhardt's sleep-heavy limbs and sliding out of bed. Her pyjamas lay in a heap where she'd left them in her urgency. Now she pulled them on, glancing back at the bed where Gerhardt lay, chest gently rising and falling with the rhythm of sleep. She paused to pull the blankets up to his chin, smoothing them down so he'd stay warm. And she let herself smile at what she'd done – at what they'd done together, alone in the night.

It had been so different, she thought. That time with the American he'd pushed and held and forced and it had hurt. And afterwards she'd felt dirty and empty and dead inside, as if he'd stolen her soul. But this was so different, like a gift. Like springtime, when colour starts to seep out into the world, and the air gets warm. It was like that, inside her, now.

She almost couldn't go through with her plan. All she wanted to do was slip back under the covers with him, lose herself in the warmth and the scent of his body next to hers, the luxury of togetherness. But she forced herself away, across the room towards the door. This was her chance. There wasn't much time.

She padded down the narrow servants' staircase, the lino smooth-cool under her bare feet. Somewhere a clock chimed three times. Round the corner and along the corridor: she knew the way. Here: she tried the door handle. Her fingers, still bruised and sore from wrangling with the nail file on the bar, wouldn't grasp properly, and at first she thought the door was locked. But when she tried again there was a click and the door gave. She was in Dr Goetz's room. The windows were shuttered, and it was very dark without the moonlight, but she knew she couldn't risk turning on the lights. However, she also knew that her own wireless transmitter would be open on the table, ready for her morning transmission. She closed the door carefully behind her and made her way across the floor: five steps diagonally to the table, the wool of the rug soft beneath the balls of her feet. She pulled out her chair without making a sound, then sat down and reached forwards to click on her machine. The wind shook the shutters, making her jump. She told herself to calm down as she listened for the familiar throaty hiss as the transmitter came alive. She reached for the contact and began, practised enough now to create, transpose and code a message in her head, without needing to write anything down.

She knew what she had to say; she knew what she had to tell Miss Atkins in London. She had to trust that Miss Atkins would do the right thing, at last.

For a moment, when she heard the voices outside, she was going to carry on. Because what did it matter if they found her now? It was all over anyway. All she hoped to do was salvage something from the mess, stop London being an unwitting player in the Nazis' radio game. But, as the front door banged shut downstairs, she realised that, if she was caught here, they'd check to see how she got out of her room, and they'd go up and discover Gerhardt there in oblivious sleep. And what would happen to him if he were caught in the English girl's bed, when the English girl was down in Dr Goetz's office sending messages back to London? She doubted if even the influential uncle could save him then. So she shut down the machine and ran upstairs to her room, launching herself at the sleeping figure in the bed and shaking him awake. 'Quick, the others are back. Leave and lock the door behind you!' He staggered up, bundling up clothes and boots, and was gone, the key clicking in the lock.

She fell into the warm space Gerhardt had left behind, fitting her own body into the hollow he'd made, and wishing he were still there to share it with her. She shut her eyes, listening to the soft sounds of his footsteps and the thud of his colleagues' boots. Yes, he made it back to his room in time; she had saved him.

She thought about what she'd managed to send. What would Miss Atkins think when she read it? Would it make any difference, now? She sighed and waited for the release of sleep.

Chapter 16

Gerhardt

'Not so fast, young man.' Kieffer strode out of his office, putting out a hand to stop him. Gerhardt had been late for breakfast and was on his way upstairs. It was time for her morning transmission. He had to be there. He had to find out what course she'd chosen, now she knew that her colleagues were dead. Was there a chance that she'd go along with his plan, say nothing, and that he could persuade the Count to put in a good word for her with his friends in Berlin? Was it really possible? There had been no time to talk when he'd had to rush back to his room last night, and he hadn't had a chance to see her yet today. 'Boemelburg's asked for you. I've just got off the phone with him. He's back in Paris for a few days on a special assignment and needs an assistant. You can drive, can't you?'

'Yes,' Gerhardt said. 'But—'

'I thought so. That's good. I'll get Josef to take you straight over.'

But *she'd* be waiting for him. He needed to see her. 'What about the *Funkspiel*?'

'We can manage. Dr Goetz speaks some English, as you know. In any case, it's merely a matter of continuity now. We don't require any further information. The testing is almost complete at the prototype depot. They will shift the whole thing out for production in a new location any day now. We can spare you, Vogt, don't worry.'

He felt as if he were caught at a checkpoint, Kieffer's arm a barrier to a forbidden zone. 'Should I pack some things?' he said, thinking that if he was allowed past to get to his room, he could at least slip away to see her.

'No, I think you should go immediately. Boemelburg was very insistent. We can always send Josef over with some luggage later.'

It was impossible.

'Yes, sir,' Gerhardt said, turning to go back downstairs.

Edie

The pillow still smelled of him. No regrets, she thought, luxuriating in the memory. No regrets either for what she'd done with Gerhardt or for the message she'd secretly sent back to London afterwards. Even though she hadn't completed it, it might be enough to warn Baker Street. She thought of Felix and Justine. Nothing could bring them back. But she'd done the right thing, at last.

Edie lay back on the bed, waiting. He'd be here, soon, knocking on her door and taking her down to the coding room for her scheduled transmission. In the distance she could hear the barking shouts of the morning parade and imagined the grey uniforms swirling round the Arc de

Triomphe and down avenue Foch. He always came at this time. And after doing the usual transmission work, they'd go down to Kieffer's office, and play and sing for him, practise the song he'd had them preparing for some staff party he was planning.

So long as London didn't respond to the message she'd sent secretly last night. Miss Atkins would understand the intent, wouldn't she? Edie had to put her faith in Miss Atkins; there was nothing else she could do. She didn't want to think about what would happen next, after the *Funkspiel* was over. For now there was just this morning, and him, and that would be enough. The sunshine was a warm block of yellow across the centre of her body as she stretched out, waiting.

There was the sound of the key twisting in the lock – odd that she hadn't heard his boots on the stairs. And odd, too, that he hadn't knocked, as usual. But perhaps after last night he'd decided to dispense with that formality.

The door opened to reveal Frau Bertelsmann, frowning, red-faced from the climb, jerking her head to request Edie follow her. Edie pushed herself out of the sunshine. Where was Gerhardt?

Gerhardt

Gerhardt breathed in icy air mixed with petrol fumes and his boots crunched on the driveway. He got into the back seat and slammed the car door behind him. Josef's pointy face regarded him in the rear-view mirror.

'I didn't see you at breakfast,' he said.

'I was late; I overslept,' Gerhardt replied as the car lurched backwards up the driveway.

'We called in for you, but the girl said you'd gone.' Gerhardt felt a sudden lurch of fear. They'd been up to her room? Then he realised that Josef was talking about the French prostitute in the brothel. Josef waggled the wheel with one hand as they manoeuvred out of the wrought-iron gates. 'What time did you get back?'

'I don't know,' Gerhardt replied. 'A little before you, I suppose. I heard you coming in.' It wasn't a lie. He had heard them coming in. He'd heard their footfalls on the stairwell as he slipped into his room and under the covers, naked and cold, with his bundled-up uniform and boots in a pile on the floor. And he'd waited, holding his breath until he heard them going to their own rooms. 'I didn't notice the time.'

They swung round into the street. 'And did you do the deed?' Josef asked. The sun hung like an overripe fruit to the right of the Arc de Triomphe, the sunlight syrupy-yellow. Black figures were clustering beneath the monument, like ants. Gerhardt could hear muffled shouts in the distance. 'Bugger, I forgot about the morning parade,' said Josef, jamming the gears and turning the car round, away from the gathering ranks of soldiers. 'Well, did you?'

'Yes,' said Gerhardt, not looking at Josef's face in the mirror, turning instead to look at the lines of uniformed men, beginning their inexorable march down avenue Foch behind them.

'I told you Paris would make a man of you, mate,' Josef said as they accelerated away in the direction of the Bois. And Gerhardt remembered that other car, that other time as they sped away.

The girl was waving from the kerb . . . The chauffeur pulled the car in beside her . . . He looked beyond the briefly clasped hands out through the windscreen to see Hans, the chauffeur, furling up the black-and-red swastika flag that hung from the stubby flagpole on the car bonnet so that it no longer showed.

The roads were bumpy and he was shunted alternately into his mother and the young woman as they coasted a succession of potholes and sped into town. He looked up at the young woman as they drove: her brown hair was a smooth, neat curve against her pale neck, reminding him of the carved wood on the balustrade at his father's house here in Romania. It was very different from his mother's hair, which was fair and wispy, pinned up in a bun that was forever coming loose, so strands played across her cheeks and her brow . . .

'So, how long are you with the big man for,' said Josef, interrupting his thoughts.

'I don't know,' Gerhardt said. He was thinking now of *her*. Would she transmit as normal this morning, or would she refuse because of what she now knew about Kieffer's duplicity concerning her dead colleagues? Even if she did comply, continue with the *Funkspiel*, it was almost over. Kieffer already had a celebratory party planned. Would he be back by then? Would he have a chance to see her again?

He turned his head to see the buttercream mansions of avenue Foch slide past. The Arc de Triomphe was a breached dam, the military parade a river of grey chasing them down a gulley.

'Kieffer didn't say when I'd be back,' he said.

Edie

Dr Goetz waved her inside and motioned for her to sit down. 'Vogt has gone,' he said in clipped, heavily accented English. 'Today we work together.'

Edie nodded and sat down. The chair next to her, where Gerhardt usually sat, was empty. The air tasted stale and musty on her tongue. Dr Goetz rifled through a stack of paperwork and made a snuffling sound as he pushed his spectacles up his nose. A car started up in the driveway outside.

Why had Gerhardt gone? Where had he been taken? She couldn't ask Dr Goetz: her very curiosity could be incriminating. Edie's breath was dry in her mouth. She brought a hand up to touch her lips, chapped and sore from last night's kissing. She could hear boots outside, tramping down the avenue Foch, increasing in volume as the morning parade approached.

What if London responded to her secret message, like they'd done when her security check had been left off? What if word came back that she should stop sending riddles in the middle of the night and keep to her scheduled time? Then they'd know what she'd done. Would Kieffer have her sent to a prison camp, or would he just have her shot?

The sound of boots outside got louder as the soldiers marched directly underneath the window.

Gerhardt was gone, and she was alone.

Vera

The message had come through on Yvette's frequency, in the middle of the night. Vera stared at the slip of paper in her hand, willing an answer to emerge. She stood up and walked over to the window, pausing to look down at the roofs of red buses and black cabs, beetling down Baker Street in the rush hour. Through the glass the traffic noise was just an echoing growl.

They'd had a postcard from Yvette. Buckmaster said that was proof that she was fine, despite the strange message from 'Claude' that they'd received. And the girl had been trans-mitting regularly, with her fist, keeping to her scheds – until now, until this broken message, sent hours ahead of time. Vera turned away from the window and began to pace back towards her desk, fanning her face with the slip of paper. What could it mean?

The office door banged open and Buckmaster was there, shaking off his umbrella. 'Vee, you're in early. Are you well?' he teased. But she'd made certain she'd been in early every day since he'd agreed to sponsor her naturalisation, even on the mornings after airport send-offs, and she failed to see the funny side.

'Quite well, thank you,' she lied. She still hadn't managed to kick off that dreadful cold. It felt as if pebbles were wedged under her jaw and her ears were stuffed with tin foil.

Buckmaster had started to undo his coat buttons and was glancing down at his diary, which lay open on his desk. 'Buckie, I've had a rather worrying message in from Cat—' she began.

'Good Lord, not this again,' he said. 'What does it say?'

'It's not what it says, exactly, but what it doesn't say.' Vera held out the slip of paper, but Buckmaster didn't see it, his eyes scanning his daily schedule as he began to slip off his trench coat.

'Let's get Dericourt on to it, then. He has excellent contacts in Paris. I'm sure it's nothing, but if it will put your mind at rest, then we can get our man to clear this up, once and for all.'

'But, I'm not sure that Dericourt—' she began, but couldn't finish because Buckmaster's phone rang and he picked it up. Vera strained to listen, watching the expression on his face change from polite concern through consternation and finally to panic. 'Yes, of course. I'm on my way, sir,' was all he said, before hanging up. He began to do up his coat again. 'I need to be somewhere else rather urgently. Whatever it is, it'll have to wait, Vee.' He grabbed his umbrella and was gone.

Vera was left alone in the office, still holding the slip of paper. She paused for a moment, then folded the message up and put it in her pocket. Perhaps it was best not to rock the boat, not to give Buckmaster any cause for irritation. Not with all that other hullabaloo going on with the internal investigation. Not now she was so close to being home and dry.

Gerhardt

'I thought you needed me for some translation work as well as driving,' Gerhardt said, looking down at the Paris streets unravelling below them. The icy railings were sticky-cold beneath his bare hands. Why did height make you want to launch yourself out into it and fall, he wondered, as a seagull arced below them. And he thought of *her* that night, at the window when they'd first brought her in. Had he really saved her?

'All in good time, my boy,' Boemelburg said, his voice half strangled by the wind that whipped through the metal girders that criss-crossed above and below. 'Your uncle told me he'd

wanted to take you here when you were down for the interview, but there hadn't been the chance. I said I'd be happy to
compensate.'

'How kind,' Gerhardt said flatly. He didn't remember his
father mentioning anything about visiting the Eiffel Tower.
All he'd talked about was the need to communicate. 'Write,
every day, no matter what. Tell me everything. Even the
things you won't tell your mother – especially the things
you won't tell your mother!' Gerhardt had written, dutifully,
sending pages and pages in the diplomatic bag that went up on
the night train from Paris. Even yesterday, before he went out
with Josef and Norbert – before he'd come back again to *her*.

He looked down at the blue-grey swirl of streets and the
velvet twist of the Seine, tugging the city seawards. Would
he write to his father today? Would he tell him about leaving
the whorehouse and finding himself in bed with an English
agent – and finding himself in love with an English agent, that
too? He leant out into the chilling wind and Paris shifted and
spun below him. No, he wouldn't write today, and he wasn't
sure when he would write again. He felt a sense of release as
the air eddied and whipped. Uncle, father, mentor: whatever
Count von der Schulenburg was, Gerhardt wanted nothing
more to do with him.

'Now, smile!' Boemelburg said, and Gerhardt saw that he'd
taken out a small Kodak camera. 'Some snaps for your uncle,'
Boemelburg said. Gerhardt looked into the camera lens, imagining his father's stern face behind it, instead of Boemelburg's.
He couldn't bring himself to smile. 'You look very serious,
for a boy on a sightseeing trip,' Boemelburg remarked. 'But
no matter. I'll take some shots of the view. Look, you can see
Notre-Dame over there.' The camera shutter clicked. 'Isn't

that Sacré-Cœur? It looks so small from up here!' Boemelburg pointed the brown box in different directions and continued pressing the shutter. 'Now, where is that prototype depot that this *Funkspiel* has been all about? Can we see it from up here?'

Gerhardt shrugged, wondering why on earth his father would want a photograph of the depot centre roof. But at Boemelburg's insistence he remembered the grid references from the transmissions, and was able to point out a nondescript red-roofed building, towards the east of the city. Boemelburg clicked the shutter a few more times. 'You do get a remarkably good view from up here,' he said. 'It's almost like being in an aeroplane. Now, let's get back down to the bottom and take some pictures of the pretty French girls on their bicycles – your uncle would like that.'

Gerhardt could taste moisture in the wind. Clouds covered the morning sun now, and the air was empty grey. He followed Boemelburg towards the lift. 'Oh, and your uncle gave me something to give to you,' Boemelburg said, turning back. 'Don't let me forget.'

'Yes, sir,' Gerhardt said, not caring about the Count and his pointless missive, whatever it was. The sky was darkening, the weather coming in. 'How long am I to be assigned to you, sir?' he asked as they entered the lift.

'As long as it takes,' Boemelburg replied. The lift doors closed, partially shutting out the daylight. Machinery clunked and whirred.

Gerhardt thought of *her* face in the darkness, as he'd caught a final kiss before racing back to his room. Edie, that was her real name. Nobody else knew – another secret they shared, along with their stolen night together: invisible cords, binding them.

But would he ever see her again, he wondered, as the lift dropped, and they plummeted earthwards.

Vera

'A word, Vee.'

Vera sighed, not bothering to check her watch. She was already late.

'Buckie?'

'Um – perhaps in the meeting room.'

She nodded, and they walked along the corridor together. Buckmaster held the meeting-room door open for her, and she stepped inside. The air was cold and stale, the windows blacked out already, even though it was still early. Like a tomb, Vera thought, clicking the light switch. Buckmaster closed the door behind him.

'You're aware of the internal investigation?' Buckmaster said.

Vera perched on the edge of a table, one leg hanging with studied casualness. She had known about it long before he had, thanks to the gossip in the ladies' loos. 'Naturally. They spoke to me yesterday, dear boy.' They had all been sent for an 'informal chat' up in N-Section. Luckily, Vera had been well prepared, thanks to the silly secretaries and their washroom indiscretions.

'This is rather awkward,' Buckmaster said, teeth working his unlit pipe stem. 'The thing is, Vee—'

Oh God, no. They couldn't have anything on her. She had been so careful. They'd grilled Margaret for longer than her, for heaven's sake. Margaret ... surely not Margaret?

Vera thought of the secretary blushing and whispering with Dericourt that time. What had Dericourt said to her? What had Margaret told them in her interview?

Vera looked up at Buckmaster. Beneath his unkempt brows his eyes showed – what? Consternation? Anger? Disappointment? Usually she could read him like a book, but today that book was closed.

'I'm so sorry,' he said.

She couldn't bring herself to respond. It was all she could do to keep breathing.

'It seems you were right . . .'

What? What was he saying? Vera clasped her hands in her lap.

'. . . about Henri Dericourt,' Buckmaster continued.

Vera exhaled, let her clasped hands part.

Buckmaster was frowning, pulling his pipe from his lips. 'I can hardly believe it myself, but apparently he's been seen visiting avenue Foch. It looks like the SD is running him.'

Vera tried to keep her face a blank page as she formulated a response.

'And the evidence?' she said.

'There have been sightings on more than one occasion.'

'Just circumstantial, then?'

Buckmaster nodded.

Vera slowly closed her eyelids and opened them again, mind working furiously in the moment of blindness, thinking of that broken message from Yvette, calculating repercussions.

'I had absolute faith in Dericourt, but it appears you were right to mistrust him,' said Buckmaster.

'How do we know it's not just black market?' Vera said and watched as Buckmaster's brows shuffled upwards. 'I've never been a fan of Monsieur Dericourt, as you know, but shouldn't a charge of treason be based on a bit more than someone being seen to visit an enemy building? A man like that has fingers in all sorts of pies. He brought oranges into the office,' she continued, remembering the fragrant acidic rush and the sticky sweetness on her fingertips. 'He could very well be a supplier of Nazi kitchens, but that doesn't necessarily make him a double agent, does it?'

'I hope you're right, Vee. But in any case, they're going to take him in for questioning,' Buckmaster said.

'Surely not today? I've got agents to send over. It's the first clear night we've had in ages,' Vera said. Buckmaster looked uncomfortable. 'Oh Buckie, why are you telling me this now? It's all set up. Cinema and Fox have both been told they're flying tonight, and the weather's set to change again tomorrow, the Met boys say.' Vera pushed herself up off the edge of the table. Buckmaster was a head taller than her. His eyes – now she looked closer – weren't hiding anything except exhaustion and worry. 'Can't you stall them?' she said.

Buckmaster cleared his throat. 'Well, as you say, the evidence is only circumstantial and there could be some perfectly valid reason. I'll ask for an extra couple of days. But not a word, Vera. This can't get out.'

'Absolutely, dear boy,' Vera said. 'But thank you for keeping me up to scratch on this.'

'Not at all,' Buckmaster said, reaching out and resting a hand on her arm. 'Thank you, Vee, for being so gracious about all this.'

Vera let herself lean in towards Buckmaster: pipe smoke, old tweed, and Imperial Leather soap. She lifted her face towards his. 'Don't be too hard on yourself, Buckie. We don't know anything for certain. There may be a reasonable explanation for it all.' She stood on tiptoe so that her cheek just grazed his; she felt the roughness of his stubble beginning to come through. 'Whatever the outcome, Buckie, I'm totally onside; you'll always have my absolute loyalty.'

Edie

The moment Kieffer took the gun out, Edie knew it was all over. London must have responded to the message. She had thought Miss Atkins would understand the cryptic words, but she'd been wrong. The game was up. I'm so sorry, she thought, not expecting forgiveness, but acknowledging for one final time all the wrong she'd done. She closed her eyes.

But there was no blinding flash, no sudden oblivion. Instead there was a click, and when she opened her eyes she saw that Kieffer had merely opened the barrel.

They were standing in the middle of the little garden. Anxiety contracted her vision; all she could see were Kieffer's hands turning the pistol over. The metal caught the weak sun and gleamed dully. He was saying something in German and Edie automatically turned, looking for Gerhardt, for translation. But Gerhardt wasn't there. It was just her and Kieffer, and the sly-eyed driver, leaning up against the black Citroën, smoking, watching from a distance.

Edie watched Kieffer insert bullets. He rammed the barrel shut. Edie thought: Maybe now, maybe this is it, but this time she didn't close her eyes, instead looked skywards, through the skeleton trees, up into the grey winter sky. Something rustled in the bushes near by and she saw two pigeons rise, spiralling giddily through the naked branches. Kieffer grunted. There was a loud crack. Edie jolted, but felt nothing. She saw one pigeon fall: spinning, flailing. She was reminded of the time they'd shot down an enemy plane, back on the ack-ack guns, how the wreckage had twisted, curled in orange flames, screaming as it fell.

There was the softest thud as the pigeon landed, and the frantic flap of wings as its partner escaped over the Paris rooftops. And Kieffer laughed, pleased with himself.

Edie looked. The shot pigeon had landed between them. Edie heard distant hand-clapping: the driver applauding his boss's hit. But Kieffer hadn't killed the bird outright. It jerked and twitched like a dying fish, making strange choking sounds. Blood began to seep from its beak, ribboning crimson onto the yellow-green grass.

She heard Kieffer say something in German, looked up at him smiling his white-teeth smile, pointing at his gun, gesturing upwards. It was incomprehensible, but she knew what he meant: *Such a nice day, and I've got a new gun, just thought I'd try it out – makes a change from piano recitals, eh?* He's showing off, she realised. I'm just a girl to show off to, to admire him for being such a fine shot.

She looked back at the bird, silent now, but still twisting slowly, being wrung out by death, still trapped in its suffering. She noticed the stone near her feet. It was quite large – large enough. Kieffer was calling to the driver, who shouted back. Neither of them noticed her pick up the rough pyramid of rock, and walk forwards, lifting it high, ready to strike.

Chapter 17

Vera

Vera's heart was high in her chest as she walked down Park Lane. She felt truly alive. Above her the sky was ice blue, clear as glass. Such a beautiful day – glorious, one would say. Exactly the kind of day you'd want for a wedding, Vera thought. Winter was almost over. She could feel it: there were crocuses round the tree stumps in Hyde Park. Was that what she'd say to Dick's mother over lunch? She imagined their conversation: *How lovely to meet you. Dick's told me so much about you. Isn't the weather splendid today – would you and Dick like a winter wedding?*

Vera gasped in the cold air. She was beyond joyful: Dick's mother had asked her for lunch at the Dorchester, and that could mean only one thing, couldn't it?

She paused momentarily to take in the hotel's façade, ranks of windows studding the curved concrete like buttons on a uniform. Eisenhower's suite was on the first floor, wasn't it? She wondered which was his balcony. Her feet tapped on the paved pathway up to the hotel entrance. A man in a top hat and a frock coat held the door open for her as she approached.

The British: such class, even in wartime, Vera thought. And she'd be British soon. She'd written Dick as much, and he, in turn, must have contacted his mother. The entrance hall was tiled with grey and cream marble slabs, slippery as an ice rink. White statues wreathed with gilt edged the curved floor. Vera took a deep breath and checked her watch. She was a little early, but no matter. She was hardly likely to be late, couldn't concentrate on anything at work once she'd had that phone call this morning.

> *Hello, is that Miss Atkins?*
> *Yes, speaking.*
> *This is Dick's mother. I'm staying at the Dorchester for a few days. Are you free for luncheon?*
> *Yes, of course.*
> *Shall we say 12.30?*
> *It would be a pleasure—*

Vera hadn't quite finished speaking when there was the click of Dick's mother hanging up. A very brief conversation, Vera thought. But then, she considered, older people often weren't comfortable speaking on the telephone. It would be different when they met in person, wouldn't it?

Vera paused at the doorway to the restaurant, realising that she didn't know what Dick's mother looked like. He'd never shown her photographs of his family, hadn't even talked about them much. Her eyes scanned the windowless room, brimming with tables of immaculately dressed women and portly men. She wasn't sure what to look for, other than a woman in her late fifties. Would she be matronly and dimpled, or tall and athletic, like Dick? 'Does madam have a reservation?' came a voice in her ear.

'Naturally, my dear boy,' said Vera. 'Ketton-Cremer, thank you.'

She turned to watch the man check the open ledger on the plinth. 'Ah yes, 12.30. This way,' he said. She noticed his Italian accent. She wasn't the only one to dodge the intern-ment camp then, Vera thought. She threaded behind the maître d' to a small table underneath a fresco of a dancing woman. There was a lamp with a crimson shade on the table, casting light upwards in a rosy aura. The maître d' held out a chair, and Vera sat down. He said a waiter would be with her shortly. Vera looked out over the full room, hearing the voices rise and fall like sea breaking on the shore, watching the waiters in their long white aprons flow and eddy all around. A menu appeared like a wave crest, water sparkled into her glass. There was the chink of cutlery against crockery, the trill of intermittent laughter. Smoke drifted up towards the ceiling, and everyone who was anyone was here in the bomb-proof restaurant in the safest hotel in London. But where was her future mother-in-law?

Vera's stomach rumbled. She should look at the menu, take care to choose something suitable. It wouldn't do to dribble gravy down one's chin in front of Dick's mother. But first maybe a ciggie, just to calm herself. She opened her cigarette case: Dick's dear face half hidden behind the row of Sobranies. She plucked one out, revealing a little more of his open smile.

As she picked up the lighter, she noticed a woman approach-ing her table: tall with dark, greying hair parted in the middle of her forehead, and wearing an indigo-blue dress. She walked with care, deftly sidestepping chair legs and champagne buckets, as if negotiating her way across a packed dance floor. Vera dropped her lighter, and stood up, her leg bashing the table so that cutlery clattered. This was it. Here was Dick's mother, shadowed by the Italian maître d'. 'Lady Ketton-Cremer, what a pleasure,' Vera said, thrusting herself forward. A look passed across the woman's face, a cloud passing over the sun, and then was gone. She didn't smile, merely held out her hand, which Vera grasped. The fingers were long and cold. Vera noticed she had large black pearls drooping from her earlobes and a matching necklace: not showy, but expensive.

'Shall we?' Dick's mother indicated their table. The maître d' pulled out her chair and she lowered herself slowly into the seat. Vera sat back down. The maître d' bowed, and was gone, replaced immediately with a waiter. 'Gin and tonic, please,' Dick's mother said, and Vera asked for the same. The waiter floated off.

They faced each other across the small square table, and Vera could see the family likeness. Dick had inherited his long nose and high arched brows from his mother. But her eyes were hooded and pulled down at the edges, and her mouth was a thin, hard line. She looked a little French, Vera thought, with that hair and those eyes. She couldn't possibly be, though, could she? Dick said that his English lineage went back centuries – some long-dead ancestor had been given Felbrigg Hall by Henry VIII, hadn't he? – and that was why it was so important that she should be British. The Lady of the Manor couldn't possibly be some foreign johnnie, he'd said. That was just the way of it. But Vera was British now, or as good as. The paperwork would be through any day, she was certain of it. And she'd be able to say as much to Dick's mother.

'Dick must have told you about me,' Vera said, breaking the silence.

'A little,' his mother said, still not smiling. The waiter came back with their drinks. Vera took a sip, then offered a cigarette from her case to Dick's mother. 'No thank you,' she said. Vera asked if it was all right if she smoked. 'Well, everyone else seems to be,' came the reply. Vera lit her cigarette. This wasn't quite what she'd had in mind. Dick's mother seemed actually quite cold. But perhaps a little light conversation would help. They'd be best of friends by the time the dessert trolley came round, and she'd be able to write about it to Dick, later.

'Are you up in town for anything special?' Vera said, tapping ash into the china ashtray.

'I have some affairs to sort out,' said Dick's mother. She took a sip of her drink before continuing. 'Of a personal nature.'

'And does the family always stay at the Dorchester when they're in town?' said Vera. Dick's mother nodded, her gaze wandering somewhere to the side of Vera's left shoulder. The waiter came back and asked them if they were ready to order. Dick's mother said they'd have the consommé followed by the lamb. Vera thought it an excellent choice for them both. The waiter took the menus from them and left.

'I know we've never met, but I feel I know you,' Vera said. 'Dick was forever talking about his family home. Felbrigg Hall is very close to his heart, Lady Ketton-Cremer.'

'Mrs Ketton-Cremer,' Dick's mother said, staring directly at Vera, a frown forcing through her wide brow. 'I don't know what Dick told you, but there's no title attached to Felbrigg.'

"No, of course not. My mistake. I must have got confused because Dick said—'

'Dick said a lot of things to a lot of girls, I'm afraid,' his mother interrupted. Vera felt herself flush. 'The Ketton-Cremers are merely country squires, my dear. There's a coat of arms, and local duties, Justice of the Peace and so forth.' Dick's mother waved a hand as if indicating a list of Ketton-Cremer functions. Vera nodded. What was it Dick had said? He'd talked about Felbrigg Hall, and his inheritance, and about her being Lady of the Manor one day. She hadn't bothered to check Debrett's. Now she felt foolish.

The waiter arrived with the consommé and swished the napkin onto her lap. The soup was very hot. Vera blew carefully on it, and sipped from the side of her spoon. Of course it didn't matter that Dick wasn't actually going to inherit a title. There was still Felbrigg Hall, and there was Dick, with his car and his plane. There would still be skiing in the winter, yachting in the summer, shooting in the autumn, and love and laughter all year round, wouldn't there? The faux pas about the title was an embarrassment, but it didn't matter. She sipped her soup in silence until the bowl was spotlessly clean. Dick's mother didn't appear hungry, and barely touched hers. The waiter took their bowls away.

Dick's mother clasped her hands in front of her on the thick white tablecloth, and Vera noticed how her fingers were knotted with arthritis. She noticed, too, the flash of rubies and diamonds on the ring finger of her left hand, next to her wedding ring. The skin on her hands was pale and blotched, like the dripping Vera's mother kept in the larder.

'I expect you're wondering why I asked you here,' said Dick's mother as they waited for the main course to arrive.

'I have an idea,' said Vera, leaning forward, wondering whether it would be entirely appropriate to reach out and put her own hand over her future mother-in-law's at this juncture.

'Do you?' said Dick's mother, her frown returning. She chafed her palms together.

'Naturally, Dick has written to you about us, and our plans to marry when he's home, and he'd like you and me to meet. And I have to say it's my absolute pleasure to finally get to know—'

'Oh heavens, no,' said Dick's mother, cutting Vera off. 'Dick's dead, my dear.'

The room suddenly contracted, as if all the knives and forks had been pulled inwards, as if Vera herself was a magnet, attracting all the sharp metal objects in the vicinity.

'But we're engaged,' Vera said.

'I'm very sorry. I thought you knew. They said there'd been a letter.'

'We're getting married,' Vera said in a whisper.

Just then the slaughtered lamb arrived.

She didn't quite know how she got through the main course. Later she recalled the smell of roast meat, and the feeling of food, hard as cardboard, grazing her dry throat. There was the sound of a woman laughing loudly again and again at the next table, and Dick's mother saying something in a low voice about a cheque. Knives scraped against plates. Smoke curled, mingling with the smell of gravy. Vera gulped down the rest of her drink and smoked three cigarettes in quick succession. Dick's mother said something about a meeting with the family solicitor, probate, due process. The walls of the windowless restaurant felt suffocatingly close. Main course plates were taken. They both waved away the dessert trolley. Vera asked for a strong black coffee. Dick's mother asked for the bill to be put on her room number. Vera felt as opaque and brittle as the tiny cups that came with the coffee pot. If someone was to hold her, she'd simply crack.

'Perhaps it's for the best,' Dick's mother said at last as Vera drained the last of the coffee. 'After all, he could never have married a Jewess.' Vera stiffened. 'Your father's name was Rosenberg, was it not?' said Dick's mother. Vera didn't nod, simply stared at the woman, who was folding her napkin into a neat triangle and placing it on the table in front of her. How on earth had she found out? 'You see, this way, at least Dick didn't have to let you down. You have the memory of your affair, and of course the five hundred pounds he left you, which will arrive in due course. But I would never have sanctioned the marriage. A Jewess in Felbrigg Hall? No, that would never do. So it's for the best, don't you see?'

Vera stood up. The restaurant doorway seemed very far away, but she swam towards it, like a diver returning to the surface, gulping for breath as she finally reached the cool grandeur of the hotel atrium.

Dick was dead.

The letter was waiting for her when she got home. It was the earliest she'd come home for months, not even mid-afternoon. But she hadn't been thinking straight, running out of the hotel, across Hyde Park – going to ground. She had barely closed the front door behind her when there was Mother, gesturing to the sideboard, wiping floury hands on her apron. 'You said the other day that you might have some news, so when that letter came, I decided to make frogs-in-the-morning,' she said, nodding in the direction of the letter, before going back through to the kitchen. 'I wasn't expecting you home so early, though.'

The wireless was on, the BBC orchestra playing an insufferably upbeat rendition of 'Smoke Gets In Your Eyes' and the smell of frying apples wafted into the hallway. Vera peeled off her gloves and undid the fastenings on her fur, hesitating to shrug it off – she felt so cold. She walked over to the sideboard.

Miss Vera Atkins, said the neatly typed letters on the front of the beige envelope. She wondered if one of her fellow typists from the secretarial college had typed that. Most likely – they all seemed to end up somewhere in Whitehall, marrying Mr Brown types and later on getting holed up in mock-Tudor mansions in the Home Counties. Vera hadn't wanted to end up like them, with their quotidian little lives. She'd wanted more, deserved more. And that was what Dick had offered, hadn't he?

She picked up the envelope and went through into the lounge. She put it down next to the pot of white hyacinths on the windowsill, glancing briefly outside to where figures scurried, buses trundled, everyone skirting the bomb crater as if by ignoring it it would simply cease to exist. She sighed and checked her watch, turning away from the window.

Vera remembered the time she'd brought Dick here, the only time, when her mother was away in Winchelsea. He'd said there was hardly room to swing a cat. He'd said that if he had to live with his mother in a place like this, he'd probably end up throttling her. And they'd laughed. Then Vera had asked Dick when she'd get to meet his mother, and he'd said all in good time, darling, puffing on his cigar, and looking out of the window. And she hadn't wanted to press things further because it was his last day of leave, so instead she'd said but you haven't come all the way here to swing cats, have you? And she'd pulled the cigar from his lips and twisted her arm up and round his neck, and then, right here – they hadn't even made it as far as her bedroom – Vera shivered, remembering the softness of his lips, the rough stubble, and the cool feel of the floorboards underneath her haunches. My sweet, my darling, my love, he'd said. And it had felt like a promise.

Vera went over to the gas fire and knelt down to light it, the flames jumping out to burn her fingertips. The air smelled of gas and hyacinths. She took off her coat and laid it over the arm of the chaise longue. Then she picked the letter up and began to open it, slowly tearing apart the gummed edges, like prising open a secret. She pulled the sheet of paper out and opened it up. After glancing at it, she let it fall from her fingers; it rested like a blown leaf on the windowsill.

There was a clatter as her mother came in, carrying a tray with a pot of coffee and a plate of apple pancakes. She put it down on the circular occasional table, next to the armchair. 'Here, let's sit down and you can tell me your news,' she said. '*Kaffee und Kuchen*, just like the old days. Remember how we always had frogs-in-the-morning when we visited your cousins in Vienna?' She smiled, patting the seat next to her.

'I don't have any news,' Vera replied, appalled. Why had she mentioned anything to her mother? Then she picked the letter back up and passed it across. 'It's only this.'

When her mother looked at the paper, her face broke into a grin. 'But that's wonderful. Your naturalisation certificate – you're as British as I am now. You're safe; we're all safe: you, me, Ralph and Guy. I'm so happy. Wonderful, wonderful.' She started to pour the coffee. 'But how strange, I thought it was something else altogether.' She looked up at Vera. Vera looked away. 'I thought it had something to do with that man you've been seeing,' her mother continued.

'Why ever would you think that, Mother?' Vera said.

There was a knock at the door. Her mother moved to get up, but Vera told her not to bother, glad of the excuse to get away from the clatter of crockery and the desperate cheer. The hallway was dark and cold. She opened the front door. It was only Mrs Littlewood: hair like candyfloss and smudged lipstick. 'Postman delivered this to the wrong door, dearie,' she said, holding out an aerogramme. 'I thought you'd want it soonest – your mother said you were expecting some news.'

Vera took the tissue-thin paper and put it in her pocket. She didn't recognise the handwriting. 'Thank you. Won't you come in, Mrs Littlewood.' Anything to relieve her from the pressure of a conversation with her mother.

'Oh, I wouldn't want to intrude.' Mrs Littlewood's pink lips twitched.

'Not at all. It would be a pleasure. Mother has just made some apple pancakes. It's an old family recipe – we call them frogs-in-the-morning. Do come in and try some.'

'Well, if you're sure?'

Vera nodded, standing aside so the front door was wide open, and Mrs Littlewood bustled inside. Vera ushered her into the lounge. 'I've invited Mrs Littlewood to join us – it's been so long since we've had her round,' said Vera, ignoring her mother's raised eyebrows. 'Do sit down,' she said. 'I'll just pop into the kitchen for the extra things.' Vera's face felt as if it were cracking with the effort of smiling.

She went through to the kitchen, pulling a teaspoon and cake fork from the drawer, and taking a side plate and cup and saucer from the cupboard. Her hands were shaking so much that she dropped the cup. It smashed on the tiled floor. Her mother called out, asking if everything was all right, and Vera replied that she'd be through shortly. She put the things down next to the sink and took the aerogramme from her pocket, tearing it open.

Dear Miss Atkins

I am sorry to have to tell you that Dick was killed in action during an attack on the airfield. It is unbearable to think about, and I know it will grieve you very much. The RAF will have already contacted his family, but he asked me to write to you personally, in the event of anything happening to him. He gave me two addresses for you, work and home, but given the nature of this news, I thought you'd prefer to receive it at home. He was a very special friend, a good man, and my heart goes out to you at this time.

It was signed by a Wing Commander Edward Montague. Vera thought that this must be the 'Gu' Dick had referred to in his letters.

So it was true. It was like someone taking out a thick black pencil and underscoring her grief: Dick is dead. She crumpled up the aerogramme and stuffed it into her pocket, like a used handkerchief. Then she took out the dustpan and brush and swept up the broken china. It wasn't just her hands shaking now, her whole body seemed to convulse. But she wouldn't allow it. No, she would not give in.

'Vera, dear, are you sure you're all right?' Her mother's voice was laced with twin strands of concern and impatience.

Vera checked her watch. She went back to the lounge and took her coat from the end of the chaise. 'You may as well use my things,' she said to Mrs Littlewood, who had taken off her slippers and had her stockinged feet stretched out towards the gas fire. 'I have to go, now.'

'But you've only just got back,' said her mother.

'Is it to do with that letter, dearie?' said Mrs Littlewood, turning to look at her.

But Vera didn't answer either of them. She pulled on her coat, checked her watch, and left, slamming the front door behind her.

Very Mayfair, madam, Vera thought sadly, catching sight of herself in a passing bus window. In her fur coat and red pillbox hat she was still the epitome of pre-war glamour. She was still the woman Dick had fallen in love with. But what did that matter, now?

The acidic sunshine squeezed all the colour out of the houses in Burlington Gardens. The Arcade was still a tumbledown mess from the Blitz. The air smelled dirty, thick with fumes and dust. Her teeth clenched, eyes pricked, hot with unshed tears. She walked quickly, as if trying to escape her own shadow, which slid along paving stones and crept up brickwork beside her.

She was gasping for a ciggie, but she'd left hers on the table at the Dorchester, along with – no. She paused, realising – the photograph of Dick, the one of him in his RAF uniform. She should go back. But risk running into Mrs Ketton-Cremer? No, it was more than she could bear right now. She began walking again, almost at the junction where Savile Row cornered into Vigo Street. She'd get this over with first, and then go back to the Dorchester.

She stopped on the kerb opposite number 1 Savile Row.

There it was, four floors of British establishment, white stucco peppered with London soot, Union Jack flipping idly from the flagpole above the entrance: Gieves & Hawkes, military outfitters. She waited for a taxi to pull out of the junction, then crossed over to the other side.

As she did so, she noticed a man swing round the corner from Vigo Street. They arrived at the outfitters steps at the same time.

'Oh, it's you,' she said.

Dericourt

'Miss Atkins, what a pleasure,' said Henri. He hadn't expected to see her. He'd been under the impression that she spent her whole working day holed up at Norgeby House, not even breaking for lunch.

She'd reached Gieves & Hawkes just before him, and already had one foot on the bottom step. He had to tilt his head up slightly to meet her gaze; she had the high ground. 'Been off making friends in Piccadilly, have we?' she said, inclining her head in the direction from which he'd come.

'Not at all. I've been having lunch with Monsieur Humphries at his club,' he replied. Let her imply that he'd been visiting prostitutes if she wanted. But they operated in the same milieu; he was her equal, and she knew it.

'Hump?' she said, and he saw her eyebrows rise. 'I didn't know you two were acquainted.'

'I thought everyone knew Hump,' he said with a shrug.

Her face, in the bright afternoon light, looked old, he thought. The candlelight of the send-off dinners at the airfield was more flattering to a woman of her age. Here in the unforgiving sunshine he could see every wrinkle, and the way her lipstick bled into the smoker's lines at the edges of her mouth. 'I thought you'd be in Tempsford,' she said.

'I shall be, later. The Met boys say it's set fine for the night. But I had some errands to run in town.'

'Indeed,' she said, running her eyes up and down, as if scanning his outfit for something. 'Well, so do I. Good day to you, Monsieur Dericourt.' She turned and began to walk up the steps.

Henri walked up behind her, and they reached the glass doorway together. It was taped up into diamond shapes, reminding him of old-fashioned leaded windows, like the ones in the big house. He supposed his mother still worked there – what else was there for her? He still hadn't been back to visit, despite landing the little plane so close to the family home.

'Are you following me, Dericourt?' Miss Atkins said as he reached past her to push open the door. His arm brushed her back. He felt her shiver. 'Because I have an appointment to pick up my WAAF uniform, my dear boy.' Ah, but she was hard, he thought, every syllable like a rap from an impatient teacher's ruler.

'I, too, have an Air Force uniform to pick up, Miss Atkins,' he said, following her into the outfitter's. Touché.

Vera

Vera was aghast. 'But you're not British!' she said, the words falling from her mouth before she could stop herself, thinking of all the compromises she'd had to make to get her precious naturalisation granted, and qualify to wear her WAAF uniform. 'You're no more British than—' she began.

'I'm no more British than you are,' the odious Dericourt broke in. How dare he?

She looked round. An assistant was hunched over, measuring a piece of fabric against a metal ruler that was fixed into the counter top. He took out shears and Vera heard the material tear and fall. The clock on the wall tick-tocked, and Dericourt smirked, before continuing, 'Because I was in the French Air Force and we worked together with the RAF in Syria. So they agreed to let me have a uniform, because we're on the same side, really.'

It is not the same side, Vera thought. How could they possibly allow this charlatan to wear the same uniform that Dick had.

The man on the counter unfolded himself and asked if there was anything he could help them with. Dericourt gestured to Vera and she explained that she was here to pick up the WAAF uniform she'd been measured up for. She gave her name, and he opened his fat leather-bound order book, pulling a bony finger down the page and nodding when he'd found her details. 'Here it is,' he said. 'And I remember you, sir.' He smiled at Dericourt, showing a line of uneven teeth, like tombstones. 'One moment, please.'

He disappeared through the doorway behind the counter, leaving Vera standing awkwardly with Dericourt. She watched the minute hand on the clock jerk forward a notch. She could hear Dericourt breathing, next to her. The shop was suffocating, all polished wood, plush and woollen uniforms. Hurry up, she thought. Please hurry up.

Eventually the man reappeared with two large paper bags.

There was some confusion about whose they were. They had to pull out clothes, check which one had a skirt and which trousers, swap bags. It wasn't meant to be like this. It wasn't how she'd envisioned it at all. She'd imagined writing a long letter to Dick about how well she'd got on with her future mother-in-law, and enclosing a picture of her in her new WAAF uniform. It would have been perfect. Now it was all ruined, all of it. She sighed, taking the correct bag, thanked the assistant, and prepared to leave.

'But madam must try it on first,' the man said.

'I'm sure it will be fine. Your tailors have an excellent reputation,' Vera replied. Let me go. Please just let me go, now.

'If the fit isn't perfect it will reflect very badly on Gieves & Hawkes, madam,' the assistant said.

Vera sighed again. 'As you wish. Then I shall try it on.'

Dericourt

He could hear everything: the soft swish as she hung up her coat. He imagined her taking off that ridiculous hat of hers and hanging that up, too. She'd be bare-headed now: her hair was a rich dark brown, like good coffee – no greys that he'd noticed. She'd be beginning to unbutton her suit jacket, he thought, wondering what she was wearing underneath. The black velvet curtain between their cubicles trembled.

She'd expected him to be a gentleman about it, to let the lady try on her uniform first. But he was no gentleman. The cubicles were intimately close: just the plush cloth between their two undressing bodies. He heard another soft brush of material: she was hanging her jacket up. What next?

He undid his own jacket and slung it on one of the brass hooks, loosened his tie, and looped that over, too. He began to unfasten his shirt, thinking of her slender fingers unhooking pearl buttons on a silky blouse. The swish of her removing her top coincided with her sigh. He pulled off his own shirt, and threw it on the back of the chair in the corner. He heard her clear her throat. He looked down at the gap between the cubicle curtain and the burgundy carpet. He saw her skirt fall, heaping up, and the spikes of her heels sinking into the carpet pile as she stepped out of it. He let himself imagine her legs, firm and smooth, stocking tops girdling creamy thighs. He bent over to undo his laces, and kicked his shoes into the corner.

His RAF uniform was waiting on the seat of the chair, a neat pile of grey-blue wool, the colour of the undersides of clouds. He hadn't checked his rank, wondered what they'd given him. He told them he was a *commandant* in the French Air Force, so he should have got squadron leader with the British, surely?

He undid his belt buckle and began to unhook the fly. The partition curtain shivered again as the Atkins woman nudged the fabric from the other side. She'd be down to her underwear now, he thought. What kind of style did she prefer? She had quite an athletic frame for a woman of her age: good muscle tone, strong haunches. He imagined her playing tennis, like the girls at the big house that he'd watched as a boy, hiding in the bushes on those long summer afternoons when he should have been at school – they'd never guessed he was there.

He stepped out of his trousers, and slung them over the chair back with his shirt, thinking about what colour underwear Miss Akins wore: virginal white or sinful black? No, less obvious, he thought: a tricky shade of something that was neither one colour nor the other, like coral or turquoise. He glimpsed again the black points of her heels, moving around inside her cubicle. He imagined her in just underwear and heels. She wasn't much older than Jeannot, he guessed.

He heard her cough, clear her throat again, and the swish of cloth as she began to dress. She's uncomfortable with this. Good, let her sweat.

He reached for his uniform. The wool on the trousers was a little rough, but they fitted well enough. Of course he'd never be able to wear the uniform to fly in. It would be kept for him to wear at the airfield, for the send-off dinners – and for when he was out and about in Britain. It would be very useful to be able to blend in with everyone else. And Miss Atkins would blend in, too, he thought, putting on the cotton shirt. They would both look just the same as everyone else.

He picked up the RAF jacket, and checked the insignia. Pilot officer: never mind – he shrugged it on. He could hear Miss Atkins putting on her own jacket in the next-door cubicle as he leant over to push his shoes back on. He wondered what rank they'd given her. If she were just an NCO, she'd have to salute him. Ah, that was a pleasant thought. He was smiling as he pulled aside the curtain and came out into the shop.

Vera

Why wouldn't he leave her alone? The Dorchester was ahead of them. All she wanted to do was go and get Dick's photograph back. It might already be too late. His mother might have seen it and taken it. The waiter might have pocketed the cigarette case. But there was a chance. There was still a chance.

'What is it you have to go to the hotel for?' Dericourt said, making it sound as if it were she who was pursuing him, not the other way round.

'I left something precious behind at luncheon, and I was rather hoping it would still be there,' she replied, not looking at him, staring straight ahead along the pavement, willing the hotel to get closer. She increased her pace and the Dorchester slowly magnified.

'Perhaps I can help you find it,' Dericourt said.

'No. No, thank you. I can cope.'

It was the only photo of Dick she had where he was on his own. All the others were snaps of him in a group: taken at après-ski parties or fancy-dress balls. She thought again of Mrs Ketton-Cremer: *Dick said a lot of things to a lot of girls, I'm afraid.* But Vera had been more than just another one of Dick's girls, hadn't she? They'd had an agreement. He'd promised – what exactly had he promised? Five hundred pounds, he'd left her in his will. Enough to buy a little flat somewhere, Vera supposed. She thought of Felbrigg Hall, and blinked rapidly, blotting everything out.

'There's no need for you to escort me, really,' she said as Dericourt kept pace with her. He moved briefly into her slip-stream to make way for an old lady with a stick approaching from the opposite direction. Then he was at her side again.

'I have to go back to the hotel anyway,' he said. 'I need to check out.'

Of course, Dericourt was staying at the Dorchester. Dericourt always stayed at the Dorchester – and Vera still hadn't got to the bottom of who picked up the tab for his little jaunts. But how dreadful, she thought now, as they reached the path towards the front entrance. There's no escape.

They reached the revolving doors together. At least we're both in uniform, she thought. People will take us for colleagues, nothing more.

She left Dericourt behind in the ice-rink entrance hall. At the restaurant the maître d' recognised her, despite her outfit change. 'We found these at your table,' he said, holding out the almost-empty cigarette case and lighter. She flipped the case open. There. There he was, smiling, looking straight at her: *My sweet, my darling, my love.*

'Thank you,' she said, fumbling for her purse, for the man deserved a generous tip. But she had her other clothes in the Gieves & Hawkes bag, and her handbag as well. Things tangled. The maître d's fingertips glanced off the sleeve of her WAAF jacket. No need, he said with his Italian accent. It was a pleasure to be able to help someone who was doing so much for the country.

'You're too kind,' Vera said, turning away so he couldn't see her face grimace with the effort of withholding tears.

There was a smattering of afternoon clientele taking tea: plates of éclairs and scones, sandwiches in white triangles like starched collars. Vera's eyes scanned the room, taking in all those people who were laughing, smoking, eating, drinking, as if everything was just tickety-boo. As if life was one long merry-go-round and nothing was happening in North Africa, Russia, the Far East. As if nothing was even happening just a hundred miles away in Occupied France.

Thanking the maître d' again, and turning to leave, Vera thought of the agent codenamed Yvette. She thought of the compromised messages, the cipher from 'Claude', the nagging feeling of unease she had every time she saw a code come in with the call sign Cat. All those clues she'd chosen to ignore, but to what end? Dick was dead, and the war was everywhere. It was all for nothing.

The cigarette case was still open in her palm, and she took one last glance at the photograph of Dick with his open smile. But instead of love, all she now felt was guilt. She shut the lid, put the case in her pocket and walked out of the restaurant.

In the entrance hall Henri Dericourt was still waiting for the lift. Vera swerved to avoid him. But there in front of her, by the revolving doors, engaged in conversation with the door-man, was Dick's mother. It was too much. Vera turned. The lift pinged and the doors slid open, and she followed Dericourt inside before Mrs Ketton-Cremer could see her.

'Miss Atkins,' Dericourt said as the lift doors closed behind them. 'Did you find what you were looking for?' She couldn't bring herself to respond. There was the heart-sinking rush as the lift rose, and with it an unbidden sob escaped her mouth. She put a hand up to stifle it, and her fingers felt the hot wetness of tears. No. I will not cry. I will not give in. 'Ah, Miss Atkins.' His breath at her neck, his arms round her shoulders.

The sobs jerked up like vomit and the tension gripped her forehead like a vice. 'No, no,' she choked out. Her insides disintegrating, mouth pulled, lips curled, jaw squeezed. 'No!'

But his arms: warm, strong – the feel of the fabric of his Air Force jacket.

To be touched, to be held, that was all.

Dericourt

'Come, chicken.' Henri found himself speaking to Miss Atkins as if she were Jeannot. 'Come,' and he led her from the lift towards his room. He unlocked the door and ushered her inside. She was still sobbing: loud, tearing sounds. Once he'd shut the door, he embraced her again, stroking her back, not saying anything.

In the end, it was her lips that found his, surprising him with the depth of passion: tongue, lips – biting, sucking. She tore off his new uniform, stripping him naked. She kept her own clothes on, and her eyes closed, even as she pushed him to the floor, and straddled him. He plunged into her. She rode him harshly, angrily, tears streaming blindly down her face. But her sobs were replaced by cries of pleasure as her back arched and she was gone, screaming out another man's name.

She slipped off him, finished, eyes still wet with tears, falling back onto the hotel rug: hair mussed, lipstick smudged, WAAF skirt hoicked up, showing her suspender belt, the ripped gusset of her knickers. He pushed himself up, looking at her there: in that moment she was his. With a few quick strokes he was done, an exquisite vinegar surge, splashing all over the shiny brass buttons and the rank badge. Ah, Miss Atkins.

Henri propped himself up, sleep-dizzy with the rush of it. He looked down at her, chest rising and falling under the blue-grey wool. She was a handsome woman, still. And the best fuck he'd had in a long time. Her hair fell away from her now-impassive face. She'd stopped crying.

'Nice earrings,' he said, noticing them as he found his discarded trousers and grappled in the pocket for cigarettes. 'Diamonds?'

'Naturally,' she replied, opening her eyes.

They regarded each other for a moment across the length of her uniformed body. His cock lay flaccid and useless on his thigh. He lit a cigarette and inhaled. She propped herself up, held out a hand, and he passed it over. They shared the cigarette between them, drag after drag, not speaking. He reached for the marble ashtray from the bedside table and placed it on the floor between them. It was she who took the final drag, and as she ground out the butt, she spoke. 'If you like my earrings so very much, you can have them. But in return I need you to do something for me, Monsieur Dericourt.'

Chapter 18

Edie

'I need the salt,' Rosa said. Edie reached for the salt cellar. Her handcuffs jinked as she passed it awkwardly over. They'd cuffed her since the incident with the pigeon in the avenue Foch garden with Kieffer.

She closed her eyes, smashing it down again and again, not wanting to see the pulpy black-redness oozing out. She remembered how her wrist was caught, held high. There were shouts. She dropped the stone; it thudded down. She opened her eyes and Kieffer was staring at her, wide-eyed, smile gone. Had he thought she was going for him? The driver, who'd run across to grab her, now wound her arm up behind her, and pushed her back towards the front door, past the remains of the pigeon, its skull smashed like rotten summer fruits on the damp grass. 'I couldn't bear to see it suffering,' she'd said, trying to explain. But they couldn't understand her English. She wanted them to know that all she'd tried to do was release the dying bird from its pain. She wanted someone to understand her, she thought, as they shoved her back indoors. She wanted someone – she wanted Gerhardt.

She shook her head at the recollection. Life had been bearable here with Gerhardt. But now he was gone, she just wanted an end to it.

German voices hissed and buzzed round the table, making Edie think of the radio at home when it was turned up too loud but not tuned in properly: dissonance. As usual she joined the drivers and gate guards down in the belly of the house for lunch. Rosa kept her head down, barely acknowledging Edie. *I need the salt* were the only words she'd spoken since their few words that first morning.

They had a dish of soft brown-grey lentils, with a sausage shoved on top. Edie watched as Rosa slipped the sausage off her dish with one hand, whilst shaking salt with the other, deft as a pickpocket. Edie wondered who the sausage was for – how many mouths was Rosa feeding on her cleaner's wage? Rationing in Occupied France was worse than in Britain. Children here were stunted, starving. No wonder Justine had left her little girl out in the country. Oh God, Justine.

Edie's fingers fumbled awkwardly with her fork as she cut her own sausage in half, speared it, and placed one half on Rosa's plate. Nobody saw. Nobody took much notice of her these days: she was just another cog in the SD machine. And nobody had noticed that today her place had been laid with both a knife and a fork. She looked at the knife, half hidden under the right side of her dish. It had a pointed end and a serrated edge, like a steak knife.

Rosa gave her a grateful look, and gobbled up the half-sausage. Edie brought the remaining half to her mouth and took a bite. It was succulent, good. The food at avenue Foch got better every day. Edie wondered what price Kieffer paid the black marketeers, and how many ordinary French families were going short to make up for their gluttony. Around the table the SD staff were laughing, talking, scraping dishes, gulping coffee, engrossed in their own lunchtime world. Only Kieffer's driver shot her an odd look as he sparked up a cigarette. But then someone made a comment and he broke his stare, turning away to reply.

Edie dipped the rest of her sausage into the lentils, leaning forward as she did so. She felt for the knife – there – and slid it into her lap, where it lay in a dip in her skirt. She shut her legs and the knife was hidden in the invisible pleat between her knees. She carried on eating the lentils: they were the same consistency as the mushy peas she'd had once from the chippy on a night out with the ATS girls, ages ago. The problem now was how to secrete the knife. Her pockets weren't big enough: it would poke out. She needed to get it up her sleeve. But how to do that without anyone seeing?

Rosa then did something that at first seemed very strange. With her left arm she swept the salt cellar off the table and onto the floor, with such force that it smashed into pieces, the salt a snowdrift in miniature, and shards of broken glass fanning all over the tiles.

There was a moment of silence, then the gabble-shout, finger-pointing, chair-scraping hullabaloo of it all, everyone looking at Rosa. Everyone looking at Rosa, and nobody noticing Edie, who slipped the knife up her sleeve, pushed the remains of her uneaten food away, and calmly got up to leave the table, before anyone had even thought to find a dustpan.

*

Edie tried, but the knife slithered in her fingers and she couldn't get purchase against the bar. It slipped to the floor-boards below the window. The handcuffs made it almost impossible to coordinate her hands. She paused to kneel on the knife to conceal it, thinking she'd heard someone coming, but the sound of footsteps went past her door and on down the corridor. She breathed again, shifted her knee off the knife, caught it in her fingers and began again.

This time she managed to get the serrations to catch in the ridge where she'd already begun working with the nail file. But the iron bar was hard and the paintwork slick with the cold-cream-powder mix she'd used to disguise her previous attempt to get through. It slipped from her grasp again. As she leant over to pick it up she noticed how the avenue Foch garden was hushed and still, apart from the treetops etching the violet sky. Edie remembered seeing Gerhardt leave, that night when he'd gone out with the others, and how he'd come back up to her room in the middle of the night. She thought of what they'd done – would she see him again? No, it was a stupid thing to hope for now.

She grasped the knife. The handle was cool and solid in her hand as she started again the awkward twisting thrust of metal against metal. She felt the cold caress of the wind on her skin – the rain was coming. The knife caught, and she sawed, pushing the metal hard, making slow progress through the iron bar at her window. Her handcuffs clinked and pulled painfully against the flesh of her wrists as she worked, all the while imagining the door banging open, a pistol pointing at her head. But nobody came, and she worked on uninterrupted as the light began to fade.

She remembered how Gerhardt had barged in when she

really had tried to escape, just after they'd caught her, when she was still in the unbarred room on the third floor. She hadn't even known his name then. She'd thought of him as just another Nazi, and she'd hated him. When had things changed? When Kieffer had asked them to practise for the recital together, or before that? She remembered the touch of his hand on her shoulder that first morning in place de la Madeleine – he'd always been there, right from the beginning, helping her. But now he was gone, she thought, sawing harder, feeling the metal warming with friction.

The rain came suddenly, like a drop scene, blotting out the garden, hissing softly downwards. Gerhardt was gone, and soon she'd be gone too. Her fingers worked at the metal: pushing, pulling. She imagined the moment when she would be able to wrench the bar from its socket and push through to the window ledge. She imagined stepping off, falling into the blackness. And at last the twisting guilt would disappear, like someone flicking off a light switch.

Gerhardt

The Métro carriage was full of the usual stench of smoke and urine. Gerhardt slumped down, taking in his surroundings. He was the only German in the compartment. Eyes stared, but as soon as his met them, slid away. Unspoken hostility hung like fog in the fetid air.

At the next stop more passengers got on, hurrying home before curfew. There were no more empty seats, so they stood, hanging like butchered meat from the ceiling bars. There was a young woman, pregnant belly pushing up against her dress, lifting the hem at the front to show skinny knees. She had a basket on one arm, full of muddy potatoes, and with the other arm she clutched the hand of a little boy – he couldn't have been more than four or five: black knitted cap, chapped red cheeks, wide-eyed in the forest of legs that surrounded him. The woman's hair escaped in tendrils from her knotted headscarf. She put the basket on the floor next to her. Like an exhausted medusa she hissed quiet instructions to the boy, who let go of her hand to hold on to a seat back, whilst she reached up to grab one of the bars.

Gerhardt pushed himself out of his seat, gesturing for the woman to take it. For a moment she looked grateful, began to move: a stuttering half-step in his direction. Then, expression hardening, she shook her head. The train jerked out of the station, darkness closed around them as they hit the tunnel. 'Madame,' he said, pointing to the empty seat. She didn't even respond, turned her head away. Gerhardt looked around the carriage, glimpsing the nods, hearing the rustle of whispers, and imagined that they were approving of the poor woman's defiance of the filthy Boche, even in her condition, good for her.

The train rattled through the tunnels, and Gerhardt continued to stand next to the empty seat. The little boy was still hanging on to the back of a seat, feet sliding as the train swerved round a corner. There was a hole in his left shoe, a small brown-socked toe showing through the torn leather. Gerhardt smiled at him, and the boy began to smile back. Gerhardt pointed at the empty seat, raising his eyebrows. If the mother wouldn't sit, then surely the boy?

'*Non!*' the woman shouted at her son, and he shrank back, face flushing. Gerhardt felt an answering rush of angry embarrassment, watching as the boy turned to stare out of the window at the brown-black tunnel walls streaming endlessly past. In the train window Gerhardt could see the boy's reflection, eyes wide and black, mouth turned down at the corners. The mother sighed, slowly sweeping a hand over her pale face. And Gerhardt stood, swaying in time with her, next to the empty seat.

Struggling out of the Métro was like waking from a nightmare. A gust of wind billowed the huge flag hanging from the Arc de Triomphe. In the rainy darkness the red-and-black swastika was just a mess of grey on the heaving fabric. Sleet pelted down from the pulpy sky. Gerhardt pulled his collar up and began to stride along the pavement towards avenue Foch, towards her, and it felt like he was going home.

Dericourt

'Good to see you,' said Henri. 'It's been too long.' He wondered where Boemelburg was taking him. Before the war they used to meet up at Boemelburg's place out beyond the Bois. There'd been a very good cook there: pretty, too – Francine, wasn't it? But since his promotion Boemelburg no longer lived in Paris. They'd probably go somewhere decent – maybe Maxim's. It was a shame he hadn't invited Jeannot, but her charms would be wasted on Boemelburg, in any case.

'Yes, yes, it's been a while,' said Boemelburg, speeding up, but failing to change gear, so the car sounded as if it were continually clearing its throat. 'I hear that you're a regular visitor to avenue Foch these days?' He had to raise his voice a little, over the straining sound of the engine.

'I'm often there when I'm not flying. These days—' Henri began.

'Yes, yes, I know all about your little British secrets,' Boemelburg interrupted. His fat hands held the slender steering wheel as if it were a neck he was slowly throttling the life out of.

'Of course you do,' Henri laughed. 'I'm sure you know more about what I've been doing than I do myself, you old dog!' Flattery: flattery and humour, that was the way. Even Boemelburg wasn't immune.

'Perhaps I do,' Boemelburg agreed, and Henri could hear the smirk in his voice. The rain was coming down harder now. It was almost impossible to see what was outside the car. Boemelburg suddenly skidded to a halt as a woman in a bell-shaped coat stepped off the kerb in front of them. Her face was silver-white in the headlights' glare as she swished past like a flick of his mother's old besom broom. The cold and wet always made him remember his childhood, Henri thought. 'How is Kieffer treating you?' Boemelburg continued, pulling away.

Henri paused, not answering immediately. 'Kieffer is not as generous with me as I'd hoped,' he replied. He looked out of the window, but through the sheeting rain it was hard to tell where they were. Although Boemelburg seemed sure of himself, driving slowly and deliberately onwards through the night-time Paris back streets.

'And in return, you are not as generous with him as he'd hoped, not so?' Boemelburg said. Henri stole a sideways glance at him, but the German's eyes were fixed on the road ahead, and his droopy profile gave nothing away.

'I'm keeping to the arrangement,' Henri said.

'And what are you keeping for yourself?' Boemelburg let the steering wheel glide through his fingers. This time Henri did not reply. Boemelburg was a friend, of sorts. They'd had good times together, before the war. Nevertheless ... 'Don't underestimate Kieffer,' Boemelburg added. Henri reached in his pocket for cigarettes. 'I wouldn't bother,' said Boemelburg, noticing. 'We're nearly there.' So Henri left the cigarettes in his pocket. He frowned; he'd wanted a smoke.

'You promised diamonds,' said Henri, struggling with irritation.

It was Boemelburg's turn to laugh. 'You sound like a little boy demanding sweets. But you know we're all subject to wartime rationing these days. No sweeties for you, little boy!' Henri felt Boemelburg's hand land heavily on his thigh, causing Miss Atkins' earrings to prick his flesh through his trouser pocket. 'I hear there's a Madame Dericourt now,' Boemelburg said.

'Yes, Jeannot is very well, thank you,' Henri replied, realising as he did so that Boemelburg hadn't actually asked after his wife's health. He could feel Boemelburg's thick fingers through the fabric of his trousers. He thought of Jeannot, tucked up under the bed covers for warmth with her ridiculous knitting, and the smooth-scented skin of her neck.

'Did you see much of you-know-who, when you were in London last?' Boemelburg said, lifting his heavy palm and returning it to the steering wheel.

'A little. He hasn't changed much. He's losing his hair on top, but he's as elegant as ever.'

'We are all getting older, aren't we? Time and tide, isn't that what the British say? Here we are.'

Henri wondered which restaurant they were going to. He

wasn't sure exactly where they were. The car slowed down and came to a halt. Through the dark windscreen he could just make out a tall apartment block opposite. It looked depressingly familiar. 'You know where I live?' he said.

'I know where everyone lives. Besides, as we're old friends there should be no secrets between us,' said Boemelburg. The engine was still running.

Henri refused to be wrong-footed. If Boemelburg had merely driven him home, instead of taking him out to dinner, he could still turn things to his advantage. 'Of course there should be no secrets. Do come in. Jeannot will be so excited to meet you. I have a bottle of Calvados, and some cigars, so we can make a night of it.'

'I would love to, but I have a prior commitment,' Boemelburg said. 'However I shall be here a little while longer and Kieffer told me he has something planned – some celebration to do with the success of his little *Funkspiel* – I'm sure you'll be invited and we'll see each other again soon.' Boemelburg made a soft buzzing sound with his fleshy lips. 'Which reminds me. Kieffer wants the English girl to look decent for the recital he's planning – she plays the piano rather well, apparently. I've said I'll ask Coco for something. Would you mind picking it up from the Ritz and delivering it to avenue Foch for me? You can expect the usual remuneration,' Boemelburg added.

Henri nodded. He was tiring of all this: Miss Atkins, Boemelburg, the SD, the SOE – everyone wanted something from him. Ah, but the money was good. He thought about the leather satchel in the wardrobe, stuffed full of high-denomination notes: it was time he took another trip to Zurich – get it somewhere safe, before something happened.

Henri opened the car door and got out into the pelting rain. Icy water immediately drenched his bare head and ran down his neck. He slammed the door and stepped off the kerb. Even at this time, cars occasionally sped along the back street, using it as a rat run between busier main roads. One passed now, splashing through a puddle in front of Henri and soaking his trousers. Boemelburg pounded the driver's side window. 'It's dangerous. Be careful crossing to the other side,' he called through the glass.

Henri nodded and dodged out past another speeding vehicle. *Be careful crossing to the other side*? What kind of a warning was that?

Gerhardt

He'd almost reached number 84 when the car drew up on the kerb beside him. The window wound down. 'Get in, Vogt.' It was Boemelburg, leaning across the passenger seat.

Gerhardt's eye's flicked up at the headquarters building. He could just about make out her window. Was she looking out? Could she see him? 'With respect, sir, I thought you'd given me the night off,' Gerhardt said. He saw Boemelburg's scratchy brows shrink into his furrowed forehead in surprise.

'Yes, quite so. It is your night off, and I'm taking you to dinner. Unless you have other plans?'

Gerhardt hesitated. Plans? What could he say? 'If it's all the same to you, sir, I'd really rather just stay here tonight. I promised my uncle I'd write, and I'd like to get the letter off in the diplomatic bag this evening.' Gerhardt looked through the sheeting sleet into Boemelburg's squinty gaze.

'Dear boy,' Boemelburg said, 'you can write to your uncle tomorrow and tell him all about the marvellous dinner you had at Maxim's with Coco Chanel and von Dincklage, which will make far more exciting reading than the usual SD gossip – what's the news at the moment, I wonder? Frau Bertelsmann's bad back, or what kind of stew they had for dinner or some such? Not so?'

'It's a very kind offer, but—' Gerhardt began, making a move away from the car. Five more paces and he'd be at the gate; twenty more paces and he'd be at the front door; five flights of steps and he'd be outside her room. So close.

'Vogt, get in the car for heaven's sake. The rain's coming in through the window and the seat's getting all wet. I've got a dinner date with Chanel and von Dincklage and you're my plus one. You will charm Coco, and she will love you, and von Dincklage will be jealous. It will be very amusing. Now come along,' said Boemelburg.

Gerhardt looked up again at the pale looming shadow of the headquarters façade: so close – this could be his only chance. 'Sir, I don't mean to offend, but I'm going to have to decline your very kind offer on this occasion—'

'I do hope you're not disobeying an order, Vogt?' Boemelburg's voice was suddenly sharp and hard, like the tap of a conductor's baton.

Gerhardt tore his eyes away from the tiny barred window that was her room and looked back at Boemelburg's puffy face. 'No, sir, it's just that—'

'Good,' Boemelburg interrupted. 'Then you'd better get in.'

Gerhardt did as he was told, sitting down in the passenger seat and slamming the car door. Boemelburg revved the engine and crunched into gear. 'Wouldn't you like me to drive, sir?' Gerhardt said.

'Not at all, dear boy. Why would I ask you to drive for me on your night off?' Boemelburg said. He released the hand-brake and they skidded away.

Gerhardt looked ahead into the sluicing windscreen, hearing the squeak of the wipers, smelling the stale scent of cigar smoke. He closed his eyes against the darkness, letting the familiar memory take over.

The girl was waving from the kerb . . . The chauffeur pulled the car in beside her. Gerhardt looked questioningly up at his mother, who shrugged. 'Hans must recognise her. Or perhaps she's in trouble,' she said . . .

'Where shall we drop you?' said Gerhardt's mother. The young woman said anywhere, here will do, so Gerhardt's mother tapped Hans on the shoulder, and the car came to an abrupt halt on a piece of waste ground near the railway station. The girl got out without waiting for Hans to open the door for her.

'Shall I pass on your regards to the Count?' Gerhardt's mother called out through the window as Hans put the car back into gear.

'Yes, do,' said the young woman, smoothing her palms down her skirt.

'Remind me of your name again, dear,' said his mother, and the girl opened her mouth to reply . . .

'It's in the glove compartment.' Boemelburg's voice broke into his thoughts.

'I'm sorry, sir?'

'That package your uncle gave me. I keep forgetting to pass it on. It's in the glove compartment.'

Gerhardt clicked open the little hatch in the dash. Inside was a paper parcel tied with string. He took it out, turning it over in his hands. He could feel the waxy nub of the von der Schulenburg seal on the reverse. Why had his father used the family seal? Why had he given it to Boemelburg instead of posting it? Gerhardt cracked the wax and opened the package. Inside were two sheets of smooth, thick paper, one that looked like a form of some sort, and the other a letter, but it was so dark in the car that it was impossible to read what was written on them. There was also a leather box. He could make out *Patek Philippe* in embossed gold lettering on the hinged lid. He snapped it open: a watch – an expensive one, too. He remembered the day when he'd been late for the interview – his father's angry face. He pulled the watch from the case and turned it over in his hands. There was something engraved on the back. He rubbed a forefinger across the chill metal: the outline of a shield containing three four-clawed arms – the von der Schulenburg crest.

He put the watch on; it felt heavy, like a shackle on his wrist. He put the papers back in the glove compartment, telling himself that he didn't care what the Count had to say. All he cared about was the impossibility of seeing *her* again. What difference could anything from his father make now?

Vera

Vera's legs scissored through the chill as she crossed the Mall. To her right St James's Park unravelled in faded brown and green. And up ahead – she checked her watch and strode on faster – up ahead were the vast cream blocks of Horse

Guards Parade. It was twilight already. The air was cool and heavy: even the smoke from distant chimney pots slumped, unable to lift to the darkening skies. Men and women in various uniforms were starting to spew from the War Office buildings, bumping past her as they hastened homewards before blackout. Buses and bicycles sped past. Vera fought forwards against the rush-hour tide, ignoring the tightness in her chest, and the thoughts that flitted like disturbed bats in a cavern:

Dick is dead.

Someone knows all about you, Vera Rosenberg.

Dick is dead.

If they know your real name, what else do they know?

Dick is dead.

My precious darling, my love, my life.

A Jewess in Felbrigg Hall? No, that would never do.

Dick is dead.

Filthy Jewess, dirty Boche.

Dick is dead, dead and gone.

Through the fog of her thoughts, Vera carried on up Birdcage Walk, the War Box looming larger and larger ahead of her as she walked. A flock of geese suddenly rose from St James's Park. They made just a small 'V'-shape, like the chevron on a sergeant's uniform, no more than seven birds at most. The flock flew, honking, right over her head, and then swerved, turning north-west, towards Buckingham Palace and beyond. The sky was purplish in the early evening light, like a bruise coming out.

Vera crossed the road, dodging traffic, and reached the sandbag-clad entrance. Two marines were on duty on either side. She paused at the doorway to remind herself: she was

British now, part of the armed forces, she had important information to pass on, and she wouldn't be fobbed off.

Inside the doorway a puffy major with a salt-and-pepper moustache looked up from his desk. 'Full name, rank and nature of business,' he said, pointing at the ledger in front of him.

'My dear boy, I don't have time for any of that nonsense,' said Vera. 'It's a matter of extreme urgency.'

Chapter 19

Dericourt

'What do you have for me, *chéri*?' Jeannot's voice fluted along the hallway. Henri was cold and wet. It was pelting it down outside. Why did she always demand presents? Miss Atkins' diamond earrings pricked at his flesh from inside his trouser pocket.

'Nothing,' he muttered, putting the carrier bag down next to the front door. He'd had to hang about in the Ritz to collect it, whilst that Chanel woman finished her business with her German lover, and then, on the way back, the skies had opened. He couldn't face trudging down avenue Foch in the rain. And anyway, Kieffer wouldn't thank him for handing it over dripping wet.

Jeannot appeared in the bedroom doorway, swinging on it as if it was a lamp-post and she was a street girl. She had that grass-green frock on that he'd bought her in Marseille. But her waist was thickening, he noticed, seeing her swaying there. The buttons were pulling at their holes. She was starting to show her age. He took off his soaked shoes.

She skipped over and flung her arms about his neck, planting a cherry-drop kiss on his damp cheek. 'Leave me; I'm drenched,' he said, shrugging her off. He wanted to get out of his wet clothes. As soon as the rain cleared, he'd have to go.

'You don't care about me,' she said, pouting. That was his cue. That was where he was supposed to tell her that of course he loved her, more than anything, and to make love to her, urgently, up against the wall, or on the hallway floor. But he was worn out. Dear God, he was bored of being treated like an errand boy. All this to-ing and fro-ing between London and Paris, the meetings, the debriefings, having to remember what he'd said and to whom. His leather satchel might be full of high-denomination banknotes, but his body was running on empty.

He sighed, pushing past her and into the bedroom. 'Would I be here if I didn't care?' he said, taking off his jacket and hanging it over the back of the bedstead.

'What kind of an answer is that?' she said, and although he heard the dangerous waver in her voice, he lacked the energy to dole out the endless flattery and placation she needed. 'Well?' She followed him into the bedroom, standing so close he could smell the dusky rose scent of her perfume. He turned away, beginning to unbutton his shirt. 'Are you ignoring me, *chéri*?' she whispered.

'I can't do this now, chicken,' he said. He had to get changed. Through the window he could see the rain was beginning to ease. There was a curved prism of rainbow, sliced apart by the roofs that forced up into the dark grey sky.

'Don't speak to me like that!' she said.

'Like what?'

'Like I'm not important. Like I'm nothing to you.'

'Of course you're important, it's just—'

'Who is she?'

'I don't know what you mean.'

'Oh, you think I'm stupid? In and out at all hours.'

'I've told you, it's my job, chicken. My life's not my own these days. When the war is over I will be all yours again, I promise.'

It was following the usual pattern, and he should have expected it, but the sting of her palm on his cheek was still a surprise. He caught her wrist, held her fast. She had that look on her face: the colour high on her cheekbones, her pupils darkly wide. *She wants me to push her down, pin her arms back, and fuck her until she screams. That's what she wants.* He let go of her wrist. 'I'm sorry, chicken,' he said. He wouldn't play her games, not now, not today.

'Sorry?' And she was on him again: scratching, pulling, ripping at his shirt, screaming about how much she'd given up for him, how badly he treated her, how he didn't care. He held up his arms to shield himself, but she was relentless: all teeth and nails and the high-pitched screech of her voice and in the end he couldn't help it. He struck out, hard, and she staggered back, banging her shoulder against the wardrobe.

They regarded each other, panting, across the dusty floor-boards. Her head dipped. 'It's for her, isn't it?' she said, mouth agape, lipstick smeared.

'What?'

'In the bag. You've bought a present for your floozy, and you have the temerity to bring it here!' She gestured through the open bedroom door into the hallway, where the Chanel bag rested against the wall. So that was it. He breathed out.

'I just picked it up from Madame Chanel's suite in the Ritz,' he said: start with the truth and work sideways. 'I have a contact who's very close to her.' (Still true: Boemelburg was friends with von Dincklage, Coco's lover.) He saw Jeannot begin to relax: her shoulders lowering, her chin rising. 'I was going to take it somewhere else, but then the rain came down, and I didn't want it to get ruined,' he continued. 'I never thought I would be able to get you a real Chanel dress, since Coco closed her shops, but I had this opportunity and I took it. It was going to be a surprise, for your birthday.' A tear began to make slow progress down her chalk-white cheek, reminding him of a painting of a sad Pierrot clown he'd seen once, and he knew he was on solid ground. 'But perhaps we could cele-brate your birthday early, chicken?' He collected the bag from the hallway and presented it to her. She squealed, and held the midnight-blue velvet outfit up against herself, but before she could try it on, he began to kiss her. He made love to her quickly, bending her over the foot of the bed. Afterwards, he lifted her onto the counterpane and helped her pleasure herself to release. Then he kissed her forehead and her eyes shut like a doll's as she slipped into a doze.

He changed into dry clothes. The rain had slowed to a patter on the windowpane. He could no longer take the Chanel dress to avenue Foch, but there must be an old frock of Jeannot's that he could substitute? He opened the wardrobe and rifled through the hanging clothes. There was a black evening gown with ruffles that he hadn't seen her wear since Marseille. She'd never notice its absence.

On the bed Jeannot sighed and turned in her sleep, clutch-ing the Chanel dress like a teddy bear. He leant over and cut out the label with his penknife. Then he took a needle and thread from Jeannot's workbox and quickly stitched the Chanel label into the home-made gown. After all, who would know? Who would care?

From the breast pocket of his jacket he took out a square of silk. Anyone who'd glimpsed it over the last few days would have thought it was a patterned handkerchief, nothing more – hide in plain sight, that's what all Miss Atkins' precious agents were taught. He tacked the material inside the bodice of the dress with large, swift stitches that would be easy to rip out. Nobody would think to look inside the dress, would they? That fat Frau in avenue Foch was almost too lazy to wipe her own arse – she'd never check. What more did Miss Atkins expect? He was a man, not a magician, he thought, biting through the cotton with his teeth. It was all he could do.

Henri slipped out of the apartment with the Chanel bag, closing the door quietly behind him. He didn't want to wake Jeannot. He didn't want to say goodbye.

Edie

The handcuffs fell open. Frau Bertelsmann took them and handed her the bag: *Chanel* it said on the front. Inside was a black dress. Edie pulled it out: silk taffeta, with ruffles on the sleeves and down the side of the skirt, like the fronds of some kind of undersea growth. She looked at the label. It did indeed say *Chanel,* but it was stitched on a little skew-whiff, as if the seamstress had been in a hurry, and the dress stank of stale smoke and heavy perfume. Frau Bertelsmann said something in German and Edie understood she was to put it on. Edie stood up and held it against herself. It was too long, and there were yellowish stains under the armpits, from the sweat of the previous owner.

It was a re-run of that first night when Frau Bertelsmann had strip-searched her, with Gerhardt standing, tense at the window. The Frau watched, arms folded, as Edie shivered out of her day things. But this time there was no Gerhardt, awkward, fists balled on the window ledge. And this time, the Frau helped her on with the evening dress: zipping up the back, patting down seams. The silk lining was slippery and ill-fitting over her chest, gaping slightly: the dress had been made for a plumper woman. The Frau pawed away a speck of fluff on Edie's bodice, and then nudged Edie ahead of her, out of the doorway, carrying the handcuffs like a prize.

Down they went, past Gerhardt's room, past Dr Goetz's office, all the way down to the first floor. The air was cold against her exposed throat and shoulders, which rose from the slashed neckline of the rustling dress.

She'd watched the staff party preparations from her window that afternoon – vans delivering crates of champagne and pallets of food – as she'd continued to work away at the bar on her window. It was taking days longer than she'd hoped, because she had to stop and hide her work when there were mealtimes or transmissions, but she was almost finished now. She'd thought she might be able to get through tonight, when they were all busy at their soirée. But it seemed Kieffer had other plans. Edie remembered how she and Gerhardt had been encouraged to practise that song – 'Im Traum hast du mir alles erlaubt' – would she be playing it tonight? Would Gerhardt be there?

The lights were blazing and from inside Kieffer's office there was the sound of voices and clinking glass, and the smell of cigar and cigarette smoke. She stopped in the doorway, at the point where the cool corridor air met the warmth of the crowded room.

There they all were, the people she'd come to recognise during her time here: the typists and the clerks she'd seen drifting in and out of the building from her attic-window vantage point. Over there was the rat-faced driver and the portly head of security, and beyond them the wireless-detector boys, laughing over some joke or other. Dr Goetz stood beneath the chandelier, pale as an overexposed photograph in the brightly lit room. And there was Kieffer, at the centre of it all, arms extended.

Behind her, Frau Bertelsmann huffed, and prodded her, so she almost fell, stumbling forwards into the crowd. For a moment the room fell silent. Everyone stopped talking and looked at her. Edie's eyes skittered round. Was Gerhardt here? Had Kieffer recalled him so that they could perform together, as he'd planned? She looked and looked, but no, he wasn't here. It was too much to hope for.

Kieffer's Cheshire Cat smile faltered momentarily at the sight of her, but quickly repositioned itself on his face. He waved her over to the piano. The uniformed Germans parted before her as she made her way. She sat down on the stool, and Kieffer said something to the crowd.

There was a moment of dislocation as she settled her fingers over the ivory keys. She was above herself, looking down at the jewel-bright room and the clotted grey figures. She was looking down on the girl, pale face drooping like an arum lily, and the crumpled blackness of her dress. She heard the word 'British' and the word 'Führer'. She heard the word 'Coventry' and a ripple of laughter ran round the room.

The *Funkspiel* was over. They'd get rid of her anyway,

tomorrow. Where would Kieffer send her? To Fresnes Prison near Paris, or straight to Karlsruhe? Or would he just let her go, set her free like he had Justine and Felix, to provide sport for the Gestapo boys? Would jumping and breaking her neck be any swifter than being shot? She wasn't sure – but at least that way she'd have some control. She'd had plenty of time alone up in her room with the dinner knife, picking up where the nail file had failed. Nobody had thought to check on her, too busy congratulating themselves on the success of the *Funkspiel* and preparing for their precious party. The bar was almost sawn through now. She was nearly ready. Just as soon as she could get this performance over and done with.

'You are to play the Beethoven.' Dr Goetz's voice suddenly loud, hissing in her ear, and she was back inside herself again. There was no music on the stand. She knew what she had to do: Kieffer wanted her to play the Moonlight Sonata, just as she had on that first night, when she was still trying to convince him that she was a piano teacher. She paused, looking up, raising her hands, seeing Kieffer's smug grin across the room. And for a moment she wondered if her decision would have been different if Gerhardt had been there. Would she still have chosen to jump? No, it was too late to hope for Gerhardt. She let her hands fall.

But it wasn't Herr Hitler's favourite she played as her fingers crashed down onto the keys. It was three quick 'G's and a long 'E' flat: Beethoven's Fifth, the opening chords echoing the dot-dot-dot-dash of 'V' in Morse: Churchill's 'V' for Victory. She saw Kieffer's smile slip: this wasn't what he'd expected. But to interrupt now would be to lose face. He nodded, as if this were exactly what he'd expected, as if he weren't aware of the powerful irony of it. However, a few minutes later, at the end of the first movement, when her hands rested momentarily, he began to clap energetically. Taking their cue from the boss, the others joined in. She saw him mouth something to Frau Bertelsmann, who bustled over and shoved her off the piano stool.

Edie felt numb, allowing herself to be pulled up, out of the room and into the corridor, barely hearing the applause.

Back in her room, Edie stood by the bed, hearing the key turn in the lock and the Frau's footsteps disappear. Edie clasped and unclasped her hands. Then, with a large swift movement, threw her arms wide. In her haste to get back to the party, the Frau had forgotten to handcuff her. With her hands free, what she planned to do would be easier.

Through the barred window Edie saw people starting to spill out into the drive – off to a fancy restaurant, no doubt, to carry on their celebrations: hadn't Dr Goetz said something about the Lucas Carton? She'd need to wait a little while longer, couldn't afford to get caught. She thought again of Gerhardt as she listened to the sound of footsteps and voices in the driveway, and cars driving away into the night: he wasn't here to save her this time. Suicide: such a slippery word. Would anyone at home ever find out? What would Miss Atkins tell her parents once the pre-written postcards ran out, she wondered.

Outside the clouds parted to reveal the moon: a thick wedge of yellow, low in the sky – it was right at the tail end of a moon period. At last it was curfew-quiet and she was ready.

Gerhardt

He'd never had French champagne before, Gerhardt realised, as they stood clinking glasses to the success of the *Funkspiel*.

Last time he'd been here the Count had ordered red wine. He remembered the rainy afternoon of the interview. It had been the depths of winter and he'd stupidly left his coat behind. It was the day he met her – before he even knew who she was, or what she'd come to mean to him.

'Shouldn't we be toasting the man who's made all this possible?' said Josef from the end of the table.

'You mean Vogt?' said Dr Goetz, watery eyes blinking behind his glasses. And Josef said no, not the interpreter, Herr Hitler, of course, without whom none of them would be in Paris at all, and everyone laughed, lifting their glasses again – to the Führer.

There was a scraping of chairs. As they sat down, Boemelburg apologised to Kieffer for their being unable to attend the staff party: he had kept Gerhardt busy listening in on bugged telephone conversations between Coco Chanel and von Dincklage – but he didn't mention that to Kieffer.

'Seriously, though—' Dr Goetz turned to Gerhardt as they settled back down at the table. 'I couldn't have played this radio game without you. Your input has been invaluable – right from the moment the girl arrived. You managed her so well.' Kieffer was sitting opposite them, smiling into his champagne glass as if remembering a secret, and Dr Goetz caught his eye. 'I was saying, Major, how useful Vogt has been.'

'Indeed,' Kieffer said, lifting the glass in Gerhardt's direction.

'What's that?' said Boemelburg, leaning into the table from his place at the window, away from the black sliver of night that pierced the drawn curtains behind him.

'Dr Goetz was just saying how vital young Vogt has been to the operation. A commendable recruit,' Kieffer said.

'Ah yes, Vogt.' The security chief's face was pinkly porcine in the candlelight. 'I do apologise for stealing him from you these last few days, but you seem to have managed very well without him. A successful completion of this little *Funkspiel*?'

'Absolutely,' Kieffer replied. 'Even as we speak, the British think that their people are laying explosives in the prototype depot, ready to blow in the early hours of the morning. Instead, thanks to Dr Goetz and Vogt's excellent handling of the English agent, we have captured all their explosives and ammunition, and the prototypes will be moved to a new location for large-scale manufacturing tomorrow. By the time the silly British realise they've been duped, the new weapon prototype will be long gone, even if they do decide to send in the bombers.' Kieffer waved his champagne glass as he spoke.

Boemelburg nodded. 'I'm glad it's working out so well for you here in Paris, Kieffer. It sounds like you've hit the ground running.'

'Thank you,' said Kieffer, smiling. 'But of course you left me with an excellent team to work with.'

'I wouldn't normally recruit new staff just as my replacement was due in post, but I can see it has worked out rather well,' Boemelburg said, turning to Gerhardt. 'When I met you here with your uncle I must admit I had some doubts about your suitability for the role. You seemed like a bit of a daydreamer to me. But when you recited that poem, just like an English gentleman – what a voice you have – I knew you wouldn't be a wasted resource. And I see now, from your success at avenue Foch with the English girl, how right your uncle was to persuade me.' Boemelburg was tucking a napkin between the soft fleshy folds of his neck and his starched white collar as he spoke.

'What poem?' Kieffer said, looking over at Gerhardt. 'I know some English poetry myself, as it happens.'

'K-Kipling,' Gerhardt muttered. It felt as if they were all looking at him.

'Let's hear it then,' said Kieffer.

'I really don't feel—' Gerhardt began.

'Ah, yes, why not? I'd like to hear it again,' said Boemelburg.

'C'mon, mate. It'll be a laugh,' Josef chipped in from the far end.

'I'd really rather not,' said Gerhardt.

'But Boemelburg would really rather you did,' said Kieffer. His finger and thumb were pressed so hard into the stem of his champagne glass that they were white with pressure. 'Stand up, Vogt, and let's have it.' To cheers and table thumping, Gerhardt stood.

He looked out beyond Boemelburg's stodgy outline, through the chink in the curtains and beyond. *'If you can keep your head when all around you are losing theirs . . .'* he began. The last time he'd stood up to recite this he'd seen two figures passing outside. But this time outside was just a black mirror, reflecting back. *'If you can walk with crowds and keep your virtue . . .'* he continued, looking out into the sliver of darkness, remembering that day, before it all began. He'd thought she was just a scared French girl with a heavy suitcase, as he battled through the rain and traffic to carry her luggage up the steps to the room. And when she'd shut the door, not thanking him for his trouble, he hadn't been upset. He'd been more worried about the impression he'd make on Boemelburg, and his chance for a career with the SD. *'If you can fill the unforgiving minute with sixty seconds' worth of distance run . . .'* He remembered saying *'Adieu'*, as the door slammed shut in his face. He hadn't expected to even see her again. He hadn't known she'd become the most important person in his life: Edie. His Edie.

'And – which is more – you'll be a man, my son!'

There was applause and table thumping as Gerhardt turned his hazy focus back into the room. He could see waiters flocking forward with the first course. Boemelburg was motioning for him to sit. But if he sat down? If he sat down there would be four more courses and more champagne and speeches. The applause died away, and the waiters were there with the tomato soup, red circles on white china: surprised mouths in powdered faces, just like the expensive-looking Frenchwomen he'd noticed on his first visit. 'Sit down, Vogt,' Kieffer muttered, a smile frozen on his drawn lips, nostrils flaring.

What would Kieffer do with *her*? Gerhardt wondered. What would happen now that the radio game was over, and now that she knew her colleagues were dead? If only he could see her, just one last time.

'I'm so sorry,' Gerhardt said. 'I feel unwell. If you don't mind I'll just go outside and get some fresh air.' He didn't wait for their remonstrations, but strode quickly out of the restaurant, plucking his overcoat from the stand on the way. He felt like a catapult, stretched back, shivering with tension, ready to release.

The keys to Boemelburg's car jingled in his pocket as he stepped out onto the street.

Vera

'Just pause a moment, would you? There's something I have to attend to,' Vera said to her driver. As it was a Saturday evening she'd been picked up from home for the airport run. There wouldn't be anyone about at this hour, Vera thought, slipping out of the car. Baker Street was almost deserted. Her heels tapped the pavement. The moon kept dipping behind clouds, so she walked between blindness and clarity until she reached the entrance to Norgeby House.

'Good evening, Miss Atkins.' A voice in the gloom. She almost jumped in surprise. 'Burning the midnight oil?' But it was only old Godfrey, the night guard.

'I'm afraid so, dear boy. Time and tide, as they say,' she replied, closing the door behind her.

'Time and tide.' He nodded at the out-of-hours register.

'Oh, I'll only be a moment,' she said. 'Something I forgot.'

Godfrey grunted and turned his attention back to the racing pages of the *Mirror*.

Vera began to climb the stairs, the metal banister chill beneath her hot palms. Six mornings a week she climbed this staircase, barely noticing it, but tonight she felt weary, had to stop and catch her breath halfway. She looked down at Godfrey, who was licking the tip of a pencil and then carefully circling racing tips highlighted in the pool of yellow light from the lamp on the front desk. She carried on upwards. F-Section entrance was locked, but of course she had the key, kept safe on the key ring with the silver sickle moon that Antelme had given her before he left. They were very sweet with their gifts, the agents. She sighed, turning the key in the lock, and pushed the door open.

She didn't turn the lights on immediately, but instead walked blindly into the space, sensing the edges of things, until she'd reached the windows and checked that all the blackout blinds were shut. Then she walked back and switched on the lights, and everything turned opaque and yellow: mustard floors and amber desks and the dark brown telephones like crouching insects.

She went over to the locked metal filing cabinet behind Buckmaster's desk. The padlock was cool to the touch. She had a key for that, too. She lifted the lid. Inside were the records of all the decoded messages from agents in the field: all the requests for supplies, ammunition, and all the grid references. All the little personal messages home: *Tell my darling wife I love her and can't wait to meet the new arrival* – that kind of thing. She sighed again.

Vera's long fingernails flicked quickly through the alphabet. 'C': here she was – agent Cat, codename Yvette Colbert: Edith Lightwater. She took out the folder and went over to her desk, flicking on the lamp to create a slab of cream light. She sat down and opened the file. The first few messages had been fine. She just needed to find the one that Jenkins had alerted her to, the one with the missing security check. Vera licked her fingers and rifled through the pages, like a bank teller counting notes. Here it was.

She remembered the day the message came through. She'd been sure the girl was compromised, even then. But she'd let Buckmaster bully her into ignoring her instinct; because of the naturalisation certificate she so desperately needed, because of Dick.

Vera took out all the slips of paper from there onwards. Messages of treachery, betrayal: treasonous, perhaps. If anyone found out that the SOE had continued transmitting to a compromised agent ... and if Cat ever made it home, and the authorities found out what she'd done ... No, it wouldn't do. Tonight there'd be an end to it.

Vera put the papers to one side of her desk and the others back in the filing cabinet and locked it shut. She knew they were the only copy. The SOE was all about action, nobody cared a hoot about record keeping – that was what happened when you put superannuated Boy Scouts in charge, Vera thought, going back to her desk.

Monsieur Dericourt – he wasn't a Boy Scout though, was he? She lifted her right forefinger to her earlobe, felt the fleshy dimple where one of the diamond earrings used to be. Could she trust Henri Dericourt to do her bidding? She sighed, told herself she'd done the best she could, under the circumstances. Friedrich had given her those earrings, that night, long ago. Dear, dear Friedrich. He'd done the best he could, too.

Vera's ashtray was empty. She made a point of emptying it every night, along with the contents of her waste-paper basket. She took a cigarette out – the last of the Sobranies from home – and saw Dick's face looking up at her. She flicked on her lighter. But instead of lighting her cigarette, she picked up the top sheet of paper from the pile and let the flames lick the edge until they caught. Then she clicked the lighter shut and held the lit piece of paper above the ashtray, so that the ash and smuts were neatly caught in the obsidian dish. When it was almost burnt, she lit another sheet with the dying flames, repeating the process again and again, until all the coded records were gone. With the final lick of orange-blue flame she lit her cigarette, swilling the smoke around her mouth and exhaling with a rush of blue-grey. The black dish was almost full of ash now, a dark circle in the centre of the silvery lamplight. She sat, staring at it, finishing her smoke. Then she reached into her pocket and pulled out the crumpled aerogramme that still lay there – Wing Commander

Montague telling her with heart-breaking kindness that her lover was dead.

She stabbed the burning tip of her cigarette into the centre of the crumpled ball of paper and dropped that, too, into the ashtray, watching it burn from the inside out, glowing like a lunar eclipse. The scrambled words caught the orange-blue flames, blackened, and were gone. She took one last puff and stubbed the fag out, too. Then she spat, a gobbet of saliva into the centre of it all. It wouldn't do to go starting fires. She picked up the ashtray and threw the contents into the bin next to Buckmaster's desk. It could be his mess to clear up on Monday morning.

Chapter 20

Edie

She'd waited as long as she could. It was time. She got off the
bed and smoothed down the bedcovers – no point in making
extra work for Rosa, even now.

Edie knelt down on the bare floorboards and clasped her
hands together, closing her eyes. She asked God for forgiveness, with no expectation of receiving it. Who could forgive
her for what she'd done – or what she was about to do?
She asked him to bless and protect her parents, at the same
time wishing they'd never find out the truth of it all. She
dwelt, briefly, on the life she'd had. She was aware of how
privileged her upbringing had been, and she'd always had
the notion of honouring that privilege with a duty to do her
bit for the greater good: first the ATS, now the SOE. But
doing the right thing had always ended up so very wrong.
She thought of Bea, dead on the railway tracks, and of Felix
and Justine, shot by the Gestapo. Nobody could ever forgive
her for that, could they? By ending it all now, at least she

wouldn't ruin anyone else's life. At least it would all be over.

She got to her feet, and began to work the bar at the window backwards and forwards. Crunchy bits of broken plaster mixed with the powder-and-cold-cream camouflage. She was reminded, suddenly, of meringues in Eton mess pudding, and a long-ago summer party at her friend Marjorie's house. But that part of her life no longer felt real, it was like someone else's girlhood grafted onto her own.

The bar came free. She managed to stop it falling: it would have made a noise. She couldn't afford to be discovered, like last time. She remembered how Gerhardt had talked her in from the ledge of the room below, thinking she was suicidal. How she'd despised him, as merely 'one of them'. But now she was 'one of them' and she despised herself. She wondered how Gerhardt would react when faced with the news of her death, but maybe he'd never find out.

She put the bar on the bed and began to push herself out through the small gap she'd created. The air outside was chill, but not freezing; she could smell the beginnings of foliage – spring was on the way. She managed to get her head and shoulders through sideways, and looked down at the little patch of grey below. Five storeys: that should be high enough, even though the ground was no longer hard with ice.

She tried to pull herself through the gap, but her arms were pinned, stuck. There was still a little cold cream left in the jar on the windowsill, so she slathered it on her arms. That should do it. The now-empty powder compact lay next to the cold-cream pot. She picked it up and slid it inside her dress, where it was smooth against the skin of her chest. She didn't know why she took Miss Atkins' compact – maybe it was just to have something with her in her final moments, something from home.

She tried again, head outside, then shoulders, sideways. The splintered window frame caught her right arm, scratching, and the remaining bar squeezed her left, and for a while she thought she wouldn't make it. But she heaved and struggled, inching through until at last she was almost free. All around the grand houses in avenue Foch had shutters closed like unseeing eyes. She scrabbled with her feet against the bed, one hand clinging to a bar, the other resting against the stucco wall of the house. She wanted to jump, not fall. She realised that if she put one hand up a bit higher, she could reach a drainpipe that ran down the side of the building, and she could then pull herself up, have a moment of steadiness, before plunging into the darkness. She was just pulling her legs out, clinging onto the guttering, when the sirens went off.

Searchlights suddenly raked the night sky. Reflexively, she looked up. The gunner girls had been taught to look up to the skies when the raid began and she'd been one of the best spotters in the battery. Beyond the sirens' yowl a distant hum was already audible. But she couldn't see the planes, yet. Her gaze was just falling back from the night sky when she noticed a line of palings wedged into the side of the roof edge – they must have been built in for chimney sweeps – a kind of ladder going upwards.

Her hand still grasped the drainpipe and her hips were almost through the window now. The siren pulsed in her head like a migraine. She looked down and the ground swayed dizzily below. She looked up again at the palings beyond the drainpipe.

She kicked her legs free from the window and, clinging to

the drainpipe, scrambled to get them onto the ledge. It was time to end it all.

But instead of jumping, she twisted her body, reached out, and began to climb: upwards and away.

Gerhardt

Gerhardt clicked the key into the ignition and the engine snarled awake. He noticed that his hands were shaking as he shoved the car into gear.

You stupid, reckless boy, ruining your life over some silly girl – he could almost hear the Count's voice in his ear. *You'll get yourself shot, and then what will become of your mother? Two sons lost to the war – you stupid, reckless, boy.* Gerhardt set his jaw and released the handbrake.

He looked in the rear-view mirror, but there was nobody there. How long until Boemelburg and the others began to question his continued absence? The tangled Paris streets unravelled ahead of him in the car headlights as he turned the wheel, heading back to avenue Foch, and to her. He drove on, mind tumbling, spinning like the car wheels on the cobbles.

It was only as he turned into the boulevard Haussmann that he heard the sirens start, and looked up into the wailing skies. There was a procedure – they'd get her from her room and take her down into the cellar for the air raid, with the others. He wouldn't be able to be alone with her, but at least he'd see her, one last time. He pushed his foot down harder on the accelerator.

There was a crash overhead, the sky orange-white and the

car slewing sideways, and he sheared up the Champs-Élysées, the Arc de Triomphe seeming to slam from side to side of the windscreen as he struggled, turning into the skid. The air was thick with smoke and noise. As he wrested control of the car and pulled away again he saw a redhead in a black evening gown, skittering suddenly out from a side street.

Edie

Edie let go, pushing herself off the low wall and into the darkness. The skirt of the stupid dress flew up like a duff 'chute, and for a moment her face was encased in rustling black fabric like raven's wings. She hit the ground and the dress flapped down. There was no time to pause. Three rooftops she'd clambered over: twisting, slipping, leaping. She'd made it further down avenue Foch, but the palatial terrace ended here. She ran the length of the long garden, grabbing handfuls of the slippery skirt to stop herself from tripping up. The air was razor-cold, her breath steaming as she went.

The sirens were still shrieking, and in the background the drones of the bombers, getting louder, buzzing in. The moon was up, lighting the path to the gate. Stars swung like blown kisses as she stumbled onwards. There was the sound of a dog barking somewhere near by. She just needed to get through the gate. The wrought iron curled upwards, tangled loops of metal. She looked for the latch, but it was locked, the padlock cool as an ice cube beneath her fretting fingers. So she started to climb, toes scrabbling against the slippery curlicues. Momentarily she was astride the gate. She glanced back at the building. The windows were shuttered, but the dog was barking frantically. Searchlights played against the navy sky. She let herself down by her hands, landing awkwardly. She broke into a run, stumbling along the kerbs.

The back street careered behind the big houses: dustbins, high walls, potholes, broken paving stones. Her mind raced faster than her feet: it wouldn't be safe to try to find anyone from the network. No, she'd have to keep moving, right across the city, find her way to the catacombs where the Resistance had their headquarters.

The sirens abruptly stopped, but the sound of the planes was vast, inside her very bones. Flak from anti-aircraft guns splashed orange against the sky, but the planes roared on. The streets were a grey-black bruise of abstract shapes jarring against each other in the night. She had to stop for a moment under a lamp-post, coughing, gulping for breath, eyes watering, nose running, the cold air piercing her lungs. She needed to cross a main road soon. She'd be exposed, but there was nothing else for it.

As she began to run, there was an enormous thudding crash as the first bomb dropped, knocking her off the kerb. She landed, winded, in the gutter, the skin scraped from her palms.

Edie gasped for breath, pushed herself upwards, head spinning, ears stuffed full of sound. The air was thick with explosions now, an almost constant thudding roar, and the sky lit up like dawn. She staggered on. The raid was a chance. Nobody would notice the girl in the black dress, running through the night. *All the way to Grandmother's house . . .*

Through the maelstrom of furious sound she didn't hear the car approach from behind until it skidded to a halt beside her, a shiny black door opening right in front of her face.

They weren't going to catch her that easily. She sprinted towards an alley.

Gerhardt

In an instant she was gone, running along the kerb, past the blackened windows, red hair flying like a hunted fox's tail. He threw himself out of the car, gave chase, boots pounding the paving stones. She went to ground down a side alley, where he managed to grab the slippery fronds of her dress. It ripped as he caught her, but it was enough to slow her, and he got hold of her arm, pushing her up against the damp bricks of a wall, catching her there. 'Edie, stop – it's me,' he said, his chest heaving with the effort of the chase. He loosened his grip.

'They told me you'd gone,' she said. He could barely hear her voice over the cacophony of the air raid.

He let go of her and they looked at each other. Close enough to touch, but not touching. He'd only wanted to see her, one last time. He hadn't thought—

'So you've got me. Now hand me in. You'll probably get some kind of medal from your blessed Führer for this,' she said, interrupting his thoughts, breathing fast, warm air like mist from her parted lips. He wanted to kiss her.

'I can help you!' He had to shout above the noise. The air smelled burnt.

'Don't bother. You'll get us both shot, and what's the point of that? Hand me in or let me go, Gerhardt.'

Hadn't the other night meant anything to her? It had meant everything to him. 'But we've got a chance, don't you see?'

In the chaos of the air raid, it would be an age before anyone noticed they'd gone. There was hope, wasn't there?

Edie

'Why couldn't you have just left things as they were, stayed on your own side?' she yelled, wanting to reach out, to fall into his arms. But he'd let go of her now, and the bomb-blasted air was a wedge between them.

'I couldn't do that. Could you?' He shifted towards her. 'It was you who—'

'I know.' She shook her head, remembering how that night she'd pulled him to her, how it had felt. 'I shouldn't have.'

'But you did.' He was closer still now. She felt the rough brick against her bare shoulders. She saw his hand reach out towards her. Why was he doing this? It was madness. She shook her head again. If she could convince him she didn't care, she could at least stop him from being implicated in her escape. She could save him from what they'd do to him if they knew.

'I only seduced you so that I could send a secret message to London,' she said. She saw his eyes widen in surprise. 'You left the door unlocked, remember? And when you slept I went to Dr Goetz's room and transmitted to Baker Street, to Miss Atkins at Norgeby House. How else do you think they knew to call this air raid in? Miss Atkins would have gone straight to the War Box once she knew the truth about the *Funkspiel*.'

He took a step back then. 'No,' he said. 'No, that's not true.'

'Yes, Gerhardt, it is. What, did you think I'd fallen in love with you? You, a Nazi, for God's sake? Don't be naïve.' She began to walk away.

He reached out and caught the top of her bare arm, fingers circling, and she was reminded of the mob of wireless-detector boys, how they'd held her tight, the day they captured her set. 'Prove it,' he said. 'Kiss me one last time and prove that you don't care, and then I'll let you go.'

She yanked her arm free. 'Very well.' She leant in and tipped her face up to his, meeting his lips, intending to prove to them both how very wrong he was, so that at least he could save himself. But it was impossible to pretend, even now – especially now.

Chapter 21

Gerhardt

'I can't take you to the catacombs – the Resistance will shoot you on sight. We'll have to get out of the city and head north. Maybe we can make it to the coast,' she said, as the Tuileries sped past to their left. To his right the lamp-posts and trees that bordered the Seine were a parade marking time. It was impossible that she was here in the car with him. It was impossible that he'd swapped sides to be with her. But when he'd kissed her in the alley off the Champs-Élysées, she'd kissed him back. And there was no hiding how they both felt. 'Turn left here!'

'There is no left turn,' he shouted as another crack split the sky orange-white.

'Here!' She leant over and shunted the steering wheel so the car skidded left across the carriageway and through an archway in the walls. Without the sudden flare of the explosion they would have missed it. The façade of the Louvre flicked past his periphery and they were through another archway and out the other side. The brakes shrieked as he spun the wheel. The sky crackled with flak. There was a rhythmic roar as more bombers surged in over the city. 'Head towards Sacré-Cœur,' she yelled.

Had she really called in the air raid? A memory flashed through his mind: Boemelburg taking all those photos from the top of the Eiffel Tower ... *It's almost like being in an aeroplane* ... photographs to send to his father. But Count Friedrich Werner von der Schulenburg was a committed Nazi, wasn't he? Those rumours about what had happened with that spy in Romania had never been proven. Christ, there was no time to think about that now.

Gerhardt's knuckles were tight as a vice on the wheel, jerking and grabbing for control as the car powered on: fast, faster, between the high ranks of buildings towards place de l'Opéra. The planes were roaring in from the north, right overhead, over the golden avenging angels that stood astride the opera-house roof. Pigeons rose in an incandescent flurry, their wings strafing the windscreen as they fled. And his hands jarred, turning the car away from the flock, away from rue la Fayette, and onto boulevard des Capucines.

'It's the wrong way,' she yelled. 'You're going the wrong way. Turn round!' There was another crash. He glimpsed flames and falling masonry in the rear-view mirror. He accelerated forward until the road opened out. And there in front of them was the familiar slab of marble, rising up in front of the windscreen: L'Église de la Madeleine. The car swerved and spun as his foot hit the brakes and they skidded to a halt, just missing the beggar woman who'd staggered out into the road. Gerhardt saw her sway off in the direction of the church. But as he pushed back into gear, he saw people spilling out of the Lucas Carton restaurant, pointing at the car, shouting, breaking into a run.

'They've seen us,' he said as he lifted his foot off the clutch. 'They must have checked your room when the air raid started, and phoned the restaurant to tell Kieffer you'd gone.'

'Stop the car and tell them you captured me when I was trying to escape. It's not too late to save yourself.'

'No.' He pushed his foot hard down on the accelerator and headed away from the scurrying figures. As he forced the car up through the gears, he looked into his rear-view mirror and glimpsed car headlights flickering on. And through the fog of noise from overhead there was another sound – of a car engine revving up, wheels skidding, as Kieffer began his pursuit.

Edie

Edie saw the flash of headlights behind them, heard the screech of tyres, felt the surge as Gerhardt accelerated and the roads untangled in front of them as they fled. She was thrown from side to side as he turned, and turned again, trying to lose Kieffer's car.

'This way,' she said, recognising a route through the maze of streets. Kieffer's car was fast, but she knew Paris better. 'No, up there, to the left!' and the car wheeled down a side street narrowing like a tunnel in front of them. Had they lost Kieffer? She turned and saw twin beams slip down the high walls as a car cornered into the street behind them.

'He's coming,' she yelled above the stuttering rumble of another wave of planes. They shot over a crossroads and began to climb a hill, the streets pulling beneath the wheels, a line of bare trees to one side. The road was steep; the car seemed to slow. She looked behind again: Kieffer was gaining on them.

At the brow Gerhardt had to swerve to avoid a parked car, jolting off the opposite kerb. Blistering thuds from overhead as more bombs dropped: dust in her nostrils, ringing in her ears. A barefoot woman in a ripped cocktail dress staggered out from a burning building, and Gerhardt jerked the car away.

Edie turned back to look behind them: dust and smoke like fog, but the car headlights were still there, following closer now. How to lose Kieffer?

'Faster!' she yelled. The Moulin Rouge was a dull red blur as they flashed past at dizzying speed, so fast it felt like falling, and swerved to another small side street, up a dark avenue piled with trees and buildings, the road narrowing, suffo-catingly tight. She looked back. The headlights were closer. Kieffer was gaining on them. They juddered over cobbles.

Through the haze of smoke and dust she glimpsed the white dome of Sacré-Cœur. The road split, and the car wheeled right. Her torso hurled against the car door.

Gerhardt

'Not this way, we'll end up at the church,' she shouted, but it was too late. Gerhardt's mind scrabbled. Could they run into the Sacré-Cœur, claim sanctuary? Above them there was the sudden scream of a British bomber being hit by German flak, the roar of it spilling, spiralling, breaking apart: flames and shrapnel hurling downwards – an orange flare bursting across his rear-view mirror. There was a crack-crash, a different sound from a bomb dropping: sharper, closer.

'He's been hit,' she said. 'Kieffer's car's been caught by shrapnel.'

The little mirror showed the red-and-white curl of flames and grey wash of smoke in the street behind them. He chicaned round the side of the Sacré-Cœur and through the skinny alleyways behind, doors scraping against the high white-washed walls. They screeched round corners and bumped over cobblestones, away from the bombs and the falling buildings, away from Kieffer's burning car: escaping.

Edie

Eventually the corridors of stone and concrete opened out. Edie began to notice railway sidings, a field. Buildings became separate shadowy blocks, rather than a jumble of piled masonry. She glimpsed the bruised line of the horizon; Paris was almost behind them. The sky was still roaring fury as Gerhardt twisted the wheel, taking them out of the junction and on towards St-Denis, but the road was empty, and wide and straight ahead. 'We're free,' she whispered, daring to believe it to be true as they drove away from the exploding light and into the safety of the night.

The thundering buzz of bombers was quieter now. She could hear the sound of their car's straining engine. And another sound? She glanced behind, but all she could see was the blackened scar of road leading back to the wounded city. There were no other headlights worming behind them – there were no other vehicles at all. She must have been imagining it.

Gerhardt

'*Halt!*' he saw the soldier mouth, the headlights turning his face limelight-white in the dark. One arm was outstretched, the other cradled his weapon. There was no way round: buildings either side, concrete pillars and a white-painted wooden barrier blocking the way ahead. There was no time to hide her. There was no time for anything. The soldier began to walk towards them.

There was no point trying to burst through the barrier. It would only prove their guilt. He couldn't bring himself to look at her as he slowed the car to a standstill in front of the wooden palings. He wound down the window and held out his pass. A bored-looking corporal took it. 'You know it's after curfew,' he said, torch beam flicking over the ID card and into the car.

'Who's the girl?'

'It doesn't matter who the girl is.'

'I need to see her identity papers.'

'No, you don't.'

'I can't let you through.'

'Yes, you can.'

'I'm under orders.'

'So am I.'

Gerhardt felt as if he couldn't breathe. This was it then, after all they'd gone through, caught by a jobsworth soldier stagging-on at a minor roadblock. The torchlight wavered in front of him as the man shone it in her face. 'It doesn't matter who you are. My orders—'

Gerhardt turned towards her and pointed at the glove compartment. He couldn't risk talking to her in English.

She reached forward. He heard a click and the rustle of paper, saw her hand reach into the beam of light, holding something out. The torchlight dropped away as the soldier took it.

Gerhardt watched the soldier's torch flicker over the paper, saw his square face frown as he read and reread the words. Then he handed the sheets back to Gerhardt in the car.

'*Alles in Ordnung*,' he said reluctantly. 'Untersturmführer von der Schulenburg, you're free to go.'

Edie

Breathe, she told herself. Just breathe. She watched Gerhardt jerk the car into gear and they rolled through the lifted barrier, accelerating away from the roadblock. She looked down again at the papers she'd passed over, but the German writing made no sense. What was written there? she wondered. Why had their passage through gone so smoothly, even though she had no papers herself?

'Where are you taking me?' she said.

'What are you talking about?'

'Why was that so easy, back there?' She remembered what he'd said that night in her room. 'If this is a way of getting me to Berlin to do propaganda work for your uncle, you need to know that I won't—' she began.

'He's not my uncle,' he interrupted.

They were approaching a crossroads .

'Whoever he is. I'm not going to—'

'He's my father,' Gerhardt cut her off again. 'Count Friedrich Werner von der Schulenburg is my father. He never married my mother, never openly acknowledged me as his child. Nobody knows.'

'That soldier knew. He called you von der Schulenburg when he waved us through. Gerhardt, if you're trying to save me, don't. I don't want to be saved. I don't want to carry on playing games, switching sides, pretending. Let me go.' She pulled the door catch.

He put a hand out to stop her. 'I can't let you do that.'

No. She wasn't going to Berlin to work for his father and become part of the Nazi machine. She wrenched herself free and reached again for the door. 'You'll have to shoot me to stop me.' She saw him make a grab for his holster. 'My God. You really will,' she said, pausing with the door just ajar, cold air streaming past. She'd thought he'd rescued her because he cared about her, but could it be that she was just a trophy to impress his estranged father with? She felt strangely unafraid as she waited and he held the pistol in one hand, the steering wheel in the other. She wasn't going to run. She'd been a dead woman walking since the moment she landed in France. Why postpone it any longer?

But he tossed the gun in her lap. It lay inert in the folds of her black dress, dragging the fabric down between her thighs. They'd reached the crossroads now. He pressed the brake, and the car drew to a halt. 'Why would I kill the woman I love?'

Gerhardt

'You didn't let me finish,' Gerhardt said, putting the car into neutral. 'I couldn't let you leave without telling you I love you.'

She shook her head, opened the door a fraction further. 'I

think you're better off without me,' she said. 'You don't owe me anything, you know.'

'But I do. I owe you everything. I have never felt like this about anyone before. If you'd told me a few weeks ago that the Count would accept me as his son, I would have felt overjoyed, but everything has changed now,' he said, looking out over the flat fields of Picardie, dark and empty as the sea.

'Everything?'

'Being with you changed everything,' he replied, looking down at the gun where it lay in a dip on the skirt of her dress. The car door was still open a crack, the night air seeping in. 'I won't stop you from leaving, if you think that's the right thing to do. But take my gun, at least. You'll need it.' The last thing he wanted was for her to go. But she'd been a prisoner long enough. She deserved her freedom.

'Everyone who gets close to me gets hurt in the end,' she said, picking the gun up from the folds of her dress, holding it high, pointing it in his direction. He could see down the barrel, into her eyes – not blue, but grey in the darkness. Her finger caressed the trigger.

Edie

'You say you love me, but you know nothing about me, except my name,' she said, holding the pistol, remembering her weapons training in the Scottish Highlands. She met his gaze along the barrel of the gun.

'Tell me,' he said, looking unblinkingly back at her.

'I used to be a soldier,' she replied. 'I watched a man drown and did nothing to save him. I had to get rid of my baby before it was born. I saw my best friend killed, and it was my fault she died. I volunteered to come out here as an escape from those three deaths. I thought I could – God, how stupid I was – I thought I could somehow expiate that guilt by doing undercover work here. But then your Gestapo boys murdered my colleagues, and now you, you, you—' Her voice was breaking with the effort of containing her sobs, the weapon wavering between them.

She lowered the gun, took her finger from the trigger. 'I'm so scared I will just destroy your life, like I destroy the lives of everyone who comes into contact with me.'

He put his arms round her, and she let him. 'I do love you,' she said. 'It's unbearable.' She pushed the gun back into his holster as he pulled her towards him.

Gerhardt

'What now?' Gerhardt said as they sped on through the French countryside. When he'd left the restaurant he hadn't thought beyond going to avenue Foch to tell her he loved her. And now here he was in a stolen car with an escaped English agent.

'Keep going,' she said. 'We might make it to the Channel before dawn.'

'And then?'

'We find a boat, and we hope that the tide is on our side.'

They needed to get to the coast, to find a friendly fisherman and for the seas to be calm and clear, she said. And then where – to England? He'd be thrown in jail, of course. To neutral Ireland, perhaps, if they could find someone willing to take them that far? It was possible: there was still a chance.

The road was straight and empty, running ahead of them

into the darkness. He caught her looking at him and glanced back. 'I'll have to ditch my uniform,' he said. She nodded. He turned his attention back to the road. 'And we'll need to pay for the boat. I've got my watch. It must be worth something.'

'I have a solid-silver powder compact,' she said, 'and you have your watch. Together, they might just save us.' When he glanced sideways he could see that she was biting the edge of her thumb.

Far in the distance behind them he thought he glimpsed a single beam of light: a motorbike? Who would be out on a motorbike after curfew, at this time of night? In any case, it was kilometres behind them, away over the darkened fields. Gerhardt fixed his eyes on the road ahead and drove on.

Edie

Edie decided to take the mirror compact from its hiding place in the bodice of her dress, thinking to feel the weight of it, gauge how much it might be worth. But it was caught on something snagging on the dress, and when she tugged, a piece of cloth came too. Except it wasn't a torn strip of lining that she pulled out, it was a thin silk scarf, patterned with lines and swirls. She almost disregarded it, let it slip to the floor. It was the compact she was interested in. But just then the moon came out from behind a cloud, shining full into the car, and she saw that what she held in her hands wasn't just a silk handkerchief.

'Look at this,' she said. Gerhardt turned his head as she held it out. 'A map.' The screen-printed patterns weren't mere decoration, there were blue swirls of rivers, grey ribboning roads, black-dotted fence lines, and there, marked in red ink with a cross, was an 'L'.

'L' for 'landing strip'.

'L' for 'Lysander'.

They were approaching another junction. There was a choice: north-west to the coast, or north-east, to Picardie. Gerhardt began to feed the wheel through his fists, sending the car left. 'Not that way,' she said. 'We need to head towards Aisne and find a landing strip in a field near Château Thierry.'

The engine growled as they turned right, away from the coast. She glanced back the way they'd come. What was that? She thought she could see a single point of light in the far distance, but when she looked again it was gone. She must have been mistaken. They'd lost Kieffer, and there wouldn't be any other vehicles on the road at this hour, after curfew, would there?

Gerhardt

Between them they worked it out. The double-agent Lysander pilot who supplied black market goods to avenue Foch: he was the key. She said she knew he'd been the one who brought the fake Chanel dress because she'd seen him arriving with the bag, watched from her vantage point as she sawed through her window bars in the lonely afternoon. It was a British map, screen-printed silk. English agents used them all the time, she said, grinning in recognition; it was exactly the same as the ones they'd used in training.

'But how do you know it's not a trap?' he said. 'How do you know whose side this pilot is really on?'

'It could be a trap, you're right. The pilot could betray us. But I think Miss Atkins is behind this. And I think we can trust her.'

Gerhardt thought about this 'Miss Atkins' and wondered how her influence could have extended across the Channel, and why she cared so much about this particular agent of hers. But he said nothing, because, after all, what choice did they have?

Once they'd found their way from the map, they held hands as he drove along the wide road, feeling the warmth of the connection between them. The moon shone down, lighting up the way as it cut between fields and sky. And he was together in the car with the woman he loved. Driving, driving away. In his rear-view mirror he could just make out a few final volleys of flack over Paris, drifting skywards like sparks. And for a moment he thought he heard the sound of a car somewhere in the distance behind them, but told himself it was probably just his ears still ringing from the air raid. He let his mind drift and the memory-dream reach its conclusion:

The girl was waving from the kerb . . .

The chauffeur pulled the car in beside her and furled up the black-and-red swastika flag that hung from the stubby flagpole in the car bonnet so that it no longer showed . . .

The girl got out without waiting for Hans to open the door for her . . .

'Shall I pass on your regards?' Gerhardt's mother called out through the window, as Hans put the car back into gear.

'Yes, do,' said the young woman, smoothing her palms down her skirt.

'*Remind me of your name again, dear?*'

The woman opened her mouth to reply. '*Miss Rosenberg –
Vera,*' *she said.* '*Do pass on my regards to Count Friedrich von
der Schulenburg. And thank you again for the lift.*'

He wondered who she was, Vera Rosenberg. And he wondered what happened to her, after that long-ago midday in
Bucharest.

Chapter 22

Dericourt

'And when are you going to bring your new wife to meet me?'

Henri prodded the dying embers with the poker, not answering his mother. Never, he thought. She can never meet you. I've told her you're dead.

From outside there was the faintest crackle of distant flak, no louder than twigs burning in the hearth. Paris, just one hundred kilometres south-east, would be blazing tonight, he knew. And Jeannot was there.

His mother finished sweeping the stone floor, opened the back door and swished the detritus outside. There was a sudden blast of icy air as she did so, and the firelight flickered. He poked again at a charred log. Deep inside it was still orange-red. Jeannot sometimes wore lipstick that colour; it made him think of her lips. Ah Jeannot. He sighed.

His mother locked the door and hung the keys in their usual place on the nail. There was a grunt from upstairs: a muffled, angry voice. 'I should go to bed,' his mother said.

'Your father doesn't like it if I stay up too late. In any case, I have to be at work for six.' She took off her apron and hung it over the banister. 'Tell me again about your wife, and I can imagine her when I'm going to sleep, or when I'm scrubbing the steps tomorrow,' she said, pausing on the bottom stair.

'She's small and pretty, like you, Maman,' he said. His mother smiled at this, and made an absurd coy gesture, tilting her head and lifting a hand to her straggled hair. Maybe she had been pretty once.

'And her personality? Her character?'

'Sometimes happy, sometimes sad,' Henri replied. When he'd left their apartment she'd been sobbing uncontrollably. She'd lashed out at him when he'd gone to kiss her goodbye. He'd locked the knife drawer, taken the key. He'd taken her shoes, too, scooping them from the corridor floor on his way out. She wouldn't be able to hurt herself, or go anywhere without her shoes. As for the bombs, they weren't aiming for the city, only for the weapons depot. She should be fine, shouldn't she? She should be safe until his return, by which time the moon would be waxing and she'd be returned to a giggling sprite.

'Well, goodnight, son,' his mother said, turning to go. In the firelight the grey in her hair looked rose gold. Henri pushed himself out of the rocking chair and went over to her, kissing her on both her paper-dry cheeks.

'Goodnight, Maman,' he said. As he pulled away there was a sharp prick of metal against his thigh. He put his hand in his pocket and pulled them out. 'I nearly forgot. I have a gift for you, Maman.' He opened his palm to reveal the twin stars nestling there.

His mother gasped, put a hand to her mouth. 'Henri, are they really—' She couldn't even say it.

'Yes, Maman, they are really diamonds. Diamond earrings. For you.'

'But I couldn't possibly—'

'Sell them, if you want. Sell them and use the money to stop working. Or wear them to church on Sundays. I don't mind. They're yours.' He took her hand away from her mouth, turned it to make a cup, and tipped the diamond earrings into it, closing her fingers shut.

'I don't know what to say. Thank you, son.'

He couldn't look at her face, knowing there'd be tears in her eyes. He couldn't cope with her tears. 'Don't thank me,' he said. 'For God's sake, don't thank me for anything. Now go to bed, or Papa will be angry with you.'

He turned away, back to where the empty rocking chair waited, and then sat down, head in hands, listening to her footsteps going upstairs one-two, in tune with the in-out of his breathing. He stayed like that for a long time, hearing the creaking timbers as his mother padded across the bedroom and slipped into bed beside her husband. Eventually it became quiet in the little house, and Henri judged it was time. He wouldn't sleep by the fireplace, as he'd done as a child with his two elder brothers, jostling on the hard floor for the place closest to the still-warm embers. He heaved himself slowly out of the rocking chair, ran a hand through his hair, and pulled on his flying jacket. Then he took the door key off the nail, and unlocked the door. The cold air was a slap in the face. He wondered if anyone would be waiting at the landing strip? No matter – he'd done what he'd had to do. It was time to go.

Edie

'She won't budge,' Gerhardt shouted above the throb of the Lysander engine, as he shouldered the landing strut.

'Let's try again,' Edie replied. Because what was the alternative? It was a small miracle they'd got this far, made it to the airstrip on the outskirts of the market town. Even given the chaos of the bombing raid and its aftermath, word would be out by now: Boemelburg's car missing, she and Gerhardt gone. No roadblock soldier would wave them through, regardless of Gerhardt's prestigious family connections. And the pilot wouldn't risk flying in daylight. They'd be stuck. As stuck as the Lysander's landing gear was in the muddy field. She shivered, bitter-cold, even though Gerhardt had given her his coat to wear.

Winter was on the cusp of spring, and the icy French fields were beginning to thaw. The hem of the stupid evening dress clung to the cloddy earth as she turned to look up at the cockpit. The pilot gave the thumbs-up from inside the cab, the engine roared, and they tried pushing again, but the wheels spun deeper into the claggy quagmire, flicking mud over them, but not moving the aircraft forward an inch.

The Lysander's engine died down to a judder and then stilled. The pilot got out, booted feet sinking in the white-flecked earth as he joined them. The skies were stilled, British bombers long gone. There was nothing but the faint rustle of the hedgerows and the distant tweet of a waking bird. Soon it would be dawn, creeping from the east, overtaking them. The pilot took out a cigarette. 'I can point you in the direction of a safe house in the village,' he said. 'But you can't stay with me.' His cigarette tip was like tracer fire. The smell of his smoke in the night air reminded her of Miss Atkins, and of that long-ago night in Tempsford when she left for France.

They couldn't go to a house in the village. Who'd take on a uniformed German on the run with a British traitor? They'd both end up getting shot, sooner or later. '*Eh bien*, we can't stay here,' the pilot said, shrugging and flicking ash into the mud.

'No, we can't,' Edie said, taking off Gerhardt's coat and flinging it in front of one of the plane's wheels. 'This might give it some purchase – one last try,' she said to the pilot. 'Please.'

'All right then,' he said, 'one last try.' He was just about to get into the plane when they all saw it: in the distance, where ebony became indigo and the slender moon was sinking towards the horizon, moving across the dark flank of the valley's edge: a single amber light, travelling at speed. A motorbike?

As the light wavered closer, bouncing off hedgerows and into ditches, illuminating the winding country road, they could hear the buzzing sound of an engine. But it didn't sound like a motorbike.

'Let's go,' she said. The pilot nodded and tossed his cigarette away before clambering into the cab. He turned the ignition. The engine roared back to life, and the rotor daisy-wheeled in the darkness. She leant against the strut, heaving forwards, willing it to move. She could see Gerhardt pushing from the other side. The plane's wheels kicked and skidded against the half-thawed ground and the thrown-down overcoat.

The vehicle was closer now. She could make out a moving shadow fast approaching. No, it wasn't a motorbike. It was a car with only one headlight working, and something wrong with its engine, cough-choking up the road in the wrong gear. She thought about Kieffer chasing them through the streets of Paris. His car had been hit by shrapnel, but what if it hadn't been burnt out? What if it had just been damaged? She thought of the soldier at the roadblock – he'd seen which way they went. Picardie was flat and open and there were no other vehicles on the roads – it would have been possible for Kieffer to make out their distant tail lights and follow them, follow them all the way here to the makeshift airstrip in the muddy field.

The Lysander wheels still spun uselessly. 'It won't work,' the pilot shouted from the cockpit window. Edie saw the car coming to a halt by the gate at the end of the field. Above the sound of the engine she could just hear shouts: German. What was that? A whirring crack across the night – a shot, then another. Black figures oozing out of the car towards them across the field. It was Kieffer – of course it was Kieffer.

She pushed as hard as she could against the strut, and fell into the mud. The plane had lurched forwards, finally catching on the fabric of the coat. They were at last clear of the rut. Gerhardt's hand was there, helping her up. Could they do it? Bullets buzzed past like angry hornets. The plane had begun to move, bumping slowly at first, but with increasing speed over the pitted earth. They sprinted to the ladder and Gerhardt shoved her in front of him into the hatch. She hurled herself inside, hitting something hard, winding herself. She caught herself up, turned in the little cab to see a dark line of Linden trees, rearing up out of the grey fields outside the window.

'Gerhardt!' Edie shouted. Where was he? He'd been behind her on the steps. She looked through the hatch – but outside was a jostle of moving space. She couldn't see him. The pilot rammed the revs up and the plane surged. She could hear more shots. Where was Gerhardt? She turned back to the hatch. He was there, on the ladder, but not yet inside, and the plane was already nosing upwards.

Edie fell to the floor. She reached out into the rushing darkness through the open door to catch Gerhardt's hand, grabbing his wrist, heaving him into the cab. The Lysander finally lifted free as Gerhardt struggled inside. Their bodies tangled together, and they held each other tight as the plane angled up. A bullet shot through, cracking the glass. They ducked as more shots came. The pilot swore and the plane shot up at an even steeper angle, wheels kissing the treetops as they rose.

Edie looked through the open hatch as the ground sank away below. The pilot banked, the sinking moon slipped sideways. She could see the earth, lit up by the single beam from the car headlight, with the strewn handful of uniformed men looking upwards. The ploughed field was cross-hatched with the imprint of the plane's wheels and there, she could just glimpse, Gerhardt's discarded SD coat in the mud, and next to it – what was that? – a tiny silver dot: Miss Akins' powder compact, which must have fallen out when she stumbled in the mud.

The wind was roaring past the open hatch. Edie pulled away from Gerhardt, caught the door handle, and heaved it to, shutting out the angry night. Eventually the sound of shots died away. She leant forward and tapped the pilot on the shoulder. 'Thank you,' she said.

He shrugged. *'De rien.'*

'Can I ask you a favour? When we land in Tempsford, would you be able just to give us a moment together, before you call in the military police?' she said. Of course Gerhardt would have to go to prison in England – what other option was there? – but maybe this French pilot could be persuaded to let them have a few minutes of privacy to say their good-byes first.

'I'm not sure if the Swiss military has a police force,' he said.

'I beg your pardon?'

'I have an appointment with my bank in Zurich,' he said, nodding at the leather satchel that lay next to him on the seat. She could see banknotes spilling from the top. 'But I think a trip to Switzerland might suit us all, don't you?'

'Yes!' she said, sinking back into Gerhardt's embrace. Switzerland – glorious, *neutral* Switzerland – just a few flying hours to the east.

Outside the plane's cracked window the horizon was a gilded line. They were running into the dawn, the darkness at their back a tailwind, driving them onwards. She was still holding Gerhardt's hand, his palm against hers, as the pilot lifted the little aircraft higher still, and France fell away like a bad dream. *'Adieu,'* she said aloud, as they headed for a distant constellation of fading stars. *'Adieu, Yvette.'*

Vera

The car was waiting in the usual place to take her back to London. Noticing Vera approach, the driver got out and opened the door. The weather was closing in now, a nondescript blanket of drizzle that blanked out the moon. Vera nodded her thanks to the driver as she got into the back seat. The engine was already running and the car pulled off, wheels skidding slightly on the damp gravel as the driver put her foot down. Vera was lurched to the side, and tutted. Then she took out her cigarettes and offered one to the driver, who said, 'No thank you, ma'am.' That was new, thought Vera, the 'ma'am', and no more silly chit-chat, either. Everything had changed since she got her WAAF uniform. A speck of ash fell on her skirt, and she brushed it off, feeling the damp wool beneath her fingertips and remembering the feel of it from another uniform, another time. When she'd last seen Dick he'd been in uniform. She could still remember the feel of his lips, soft and urgent against hers. She inhaled again, swilling the smoke around in her mouth. His breath had tasted of good cigars and single malt, she remembered. She shook her head and exhaled. That book was closed now. Closed off like so many others. The car jolted along the farm track. Vera looked out of the window but there was only a grey nothingness outside. She hoped the flight had outrun the weather front. That new agent wouldn't be able to get any sleep if there was too much turbulence, and she'd need to be rested, keep her wits about her on arrival.

'How did she seem to you?' Vera said, leaning forward to address the driver, who was changing down a gear as they approached the junction.

'The agent? Oh she was lovely,' said the driver. Yes, Vera thought, she was lovely: curly chestnut hair and a broad grin – the whole of F-Section had fallen in love with her. But she hadn't meant that. What Vera meant, but couldn't let herself say out loud, was, 'Do you think that girl really knows what she's let herself in for?' Vera thought back to the moments before the plane took off, after she'd checked through the agent's clothes, made her empty her pockets of anything incriminatingly British – they'd found an old bus ticket – and given the final pep talk. It's not too late to back out, she'd said, as she always did. Remember that you are a volunteer, and if you don't think you can hack it, we can send another agent in your place. But the girl said she was fine, she was quite sure, wanted to do her bit. They always said that, Vera thought, inhaling and listening to the swish-scrape of the windscreen wipers. Why did they always have to say that? She'd given the girl a silver powder compact, just like the one she'd given Yvette. Before hauling herself into the fuselage, the girl had turned and waved. '*Au revoir*,' she called, hand fluttering. '*Au revoir*, Miss Atkins.' And Vera lifted her hand in salute. '*Adieu*,' she called back, as the plane's engines coughed into life. '*Adieu, dear girl*.'

Epilogue

1947: Wuppertal, Germany

'They tell me your trial is scheduled for tomorrow. It would appear I caught you just in time.' The man looked up as she spoke. The cell door slammed shut behind her. Vera heard the key in the lock and the guard's shuffling feet in the corridor. The man stood, chair legs scraping on the flagstones. He held out a hand, which Vera ignored. 'I am the intelligence officer from the French Section of—'

'Miss Atkins, what a pleasure. I have heard so much about you.'

Still the proffered hand.

'I am not here for pleasantries, Herr Kieffer.' She glanced from his hopeful face up to where a square window was cut into the wall, shedding a meagre wedge of daylight into the bare room. The air was stone-chill and smelled of a mixture of disinfectant and old urine from the chamber pot by the door. Friedrich would have ended up somewhere like this, she supposed, had he not been executed for his part in the assassination attempt on Hitler, back in 1944. She sighed and checked her watch. 'We don't have much time. I merely require some information from you.' It had been many years since she'd spoken German; her mother tongue felt like a mouthful of pebbles.

'Of course. There is nothing that I haven't already shared with my lawyer, I can assure you, but please take a seat, if you would like to talk.' He gestured to the solitary chair.

'I would rather stand, thank you.' She faced him across the small room: chair and small table on one side, bed on the other, and the yellow-white light from the high-up window. Her hand drifted up to one of the pearl earrings she wore these days, creamy and smooth as the moon. 'I just want to know what happened to Yvette, in the end.'

She watched his face carefully as he answered, checking for a tell-tale flicker of expression crossing the brow, or an unbidden finger tapping the side of the nose, but there was nothing. 'Yvette?' He shook his head. 'No, I don't recall anyone of that name.'

'A convenient lapse of memory.'

'Not at all. I remember other women agents who passed through avenue Foch: Madeleine, Paulette, Simone . . .' He gestured to suggest a list. 'I recall twelve or more – should I list them all? Would you like to write them down?'

Vera said no. She had all their names written in red on the first page of her notebook, underneath the heading *Missing Presumed Dead*. She'd always thought that such a terrible verdict, no comfort for the families at all. But the names were ticked off now, dates and places of death, along with certain details of what the Nazis had inflicted on them – all except one:

Edith Lightwater: codename Yvette Colbert – call sign Cat.

'Some were easier to turn than others. But most were useful to us,' Kieffer continued. 'Remarkable that the women often held out longer than the men, don't you think? But they all gave way in the end.'

'Gave way?'

'You are not suggesting I did any of your agents any harm? They were treated properly when they were with us. They were well fed; we even managed to procure English tea and cigarettes for them.'

Vera thought of Henri Dericourt. She didn't doubt there was English tea and cigarettes at 84 avenue Foch. 'And then, afterwards, once they ceased to be of use?'

'When they had outlived their utility, they were sent to a prison in Karlsruhe. The commandant was a personal friend, and he assured me—'

'At Karlsruhe the women were sent on to the camps to be tortured, raped, and tossed into the ovens to burn,' Vera interrupted.

'No. No, but Fritz said . . .' Shock mangled his tidy features and he slumped down onto the bed, with his head in his hands.

Vera sighed. 'Herr Kieffer, if one of us is going to cry, it is going to be me. Please stop this pantomime immediately, and look at this.' She held out a photograph and placed it in his hand. 'This is the agent we called Yvette Colbert. She was the first female wireless operative we sent over. Her call sign was "Cat", which you would know very well because your Dr Goetz ran a *Funkspiel* with her. Look closely. You do remember her, don't you?' He stared down at the gloss-grey rectangle in his hand. 'There are no records of her in Karlsruhe. What happened to her, Kieffer? What happened to Yvette Colbert?'

'If I tell you, will it affect the outcome of the trial?'

'I am not a lawyer; I cannot say. But your trial starts in the morning, does it not? And I shall be dining with the prosecution team this evening.' She wasn't lying. Let him make of it what he wanted. 'Now look again at this photograph and see if it jogs your memory.'

He turned his face up towards her, and he looked tired, tired and older than his forty-seven years. 'Yes, of course I remember her,' he said. 'She was the first. But we kept no records of her time with us. She was erased from the files.'

'Because?'

'Because she escaped.'

Vera exhaled in a sudden rush, not realising she'd been holding her breath. 'You destroyed the evidence of her because the *Funkspiel* was a failure and the agent escaped, and it would have been an embarrassment to have such a blot on your counter-intelligence copy book?'

'Not exactly,' Kieffer said. 'It's true that as time went on we were under pressure to get the agents in, and turn them. Berlin always thought that the French networks were the most dangerous – the Führer took a personal interest – but in those early days mishaps were tolerated. However, when Yvette escaped we were directed to "lose" the information about her, which is why, when you asked, I denied knowing her – I suppose I was still obeying orders.' He broke eye contact with her, and his head dropped.

'It was hushed up,' Vera said, looking down at the hunched man on the prison cot. 'But why?'

'It was because of one of our interpreters. He escaped with her – he was very well connected, related to von der Schulenburg. You might know of him: Count Friedrich von der Schulenburg?'

'Yes, he was known to us,' Vera said, giving nothing away. Kieffer held out the photograph and Vera took it from him without touching his fingers. 'What happened to Yvette and the interpreter?'

'They got away in a small plane with Dericourt. Boemelburg was confident he had him in his pocket, called him his "super ace", but I never trusted him. I always knew he'd let us down, one way or another. Afterwards, the message came from Berlin that there was to be no kind of investigation or anything of that sort, and I can only think the boy's uncle intervened, to save the scandal. There were other agents, other opportunities – we were very busy, for a while. The incident with "Yvette" was just brushed under the carpet and forgotten about.'

Vera took out her cigarette case and flipped it open. She pushed Yvette's photograph back underneath the serried ranks of Sobranies, where she'd been keeping it. So Dericourt had done what he said. She hadn't believed him – he always told people what they wanted to hear – until now. She held out the open cigarette case to Kieffer. 'Would you like one?'

He looked up, and smiled, and for a moment he looked his real age – looked like the handsome charmer he must have been, lording it over the *Sicherheitsdienst* in Paris. 'It's been a while since I had one of these.' His smile faded. Vera clicked her lighter and lit their cigarettes. Close up his skin had a yellowish tinge, and stubble was starting to break through.

She should have been feeling happy, Vera thought, straightening up and swilling the smoke around her mouth. She should have been feeling a kind of joyous relief that she had finally achieved what she set out to do. She had come all the way out here to Germany, at considerable personal expense – funding the trip from Dick's legacy – to find out precisely what had happened to all the women agents who had been in her charge, and been marked down as still missing at the end of the war. She had a leather-bound notebook in which she'd made notes over the past few weeks, detailing for parents, children, husbands and fiancés what had happened to their loved ones, and hoping the information – however awful – would at least help them close a book on the past.

The others were all dead, but Yvette had escaped. And Vera realised, with a jolt, that what she felt wasn't happiness on Yvette's behalf, it was the acid-sting of jealousy: the girl ran off with her lover, leaving her past behind her. What Vera wouldn't give to pull off that little stunt. She exhaled, hating herself.

Kieffer tapped ash onto the stone floor. Vera cleared her throat. 'I think I have what I need. I shall leave you now.'

He looked up through the haze of smoke. 'You don't need me to sign a deposition for the lawyers?'

'That will not be necessary.' She walked the three steps to the cell door and knocked to be let out. 'Don't trouble yourself to get up.' Out of the corner of her eye she saw that he already had. He was moving towards her. His cigarette was in his left hand, and he held out his right to shake hands goodbye, in the German way. She slid out of the door and nodded at the guard to slam it shut. Her footfalls echoed down the long corridor as she strode towards the exit, not looking back.

Outside the June heat burst onto her skin. The streets were a mess of rubble and late blossom, the clouds toppling like falling masonry in the darkening sky. Vera ground the remains of her cigarette into the dirt with the tip of her brogue. She paused at the top of the prison steps by the waiting gallows, the noose twitching in one of those sudden scuds of air that presages a rainstorm. Distant lightning flashed like a sword from a scabbard. A warm gust dislodged a lock of hair from her WAAF cap. And as she reached up to push it back, she noticed that her cheek was wet with tears.

Author's Note

Although *The English Agent* is entirely fictional, certain real-life characters provided a catalyst for the story:

Romanian-born Vera Atkins was an agent handler for SOE's F-Section during the war. Anyone who has read Sarah Helm's excellent biography *'A Life in Secrets – the story of Vera Atkins and the Lost Agents of SOE'* will know how much I am indebted to her.

French pilot Henri Dericourt flew agents into Occupied France for the SOE. Robert Marshall's *'All the King's Men'* provided invaluable information on Dericourt's wartime exploits.

Other instances where a real-life namesake was used as a stepping-off point for the creation of a fictitious character include: Maurice Buckmaster (F-Section head), Hans Kieffer (SD chief), Richard Ketton-Cremer (RAF pilot and heir of Felbrigg Hall), Count Friedrich Werner von der Schulenberg (German Ambassador to Romania and Russia), Charles Fraser-Smith (inventor of 'Q-gadgets' for SOE), Josef Stork (Kieffer's chauffeur), Dr Josef Goetz (SD's radio game mastermind), Karl Boemelburg (Kieffer's predecessor), and Jeannot Dericourt (Henri's wife).

*

Many of the settings in *The English Agent* are actual wartime locations:

In London, SOE's Headquarters were at Norgeby House in Baker Street. Meetings with agents took place at Orchard Court on Portman Square. Sabotage equipment was developed and stored in the Natural History Museum (where there is now a commemorative plaque honouring the agents and their contribution to the war). Vera Atkins shared an apartment with her mother at Nell Gwyn House on Sloane Avenue. The Dorchester Hotel was reputedly bomb-proof due to its robust construction and was therefore popular for wartime visitors, if they could afford it (Allied Forces Supreme Commander Dwight D Eisenhower had a first-floor suite).

In Paris, the SD's Headquarters were at 84 avenue Foch, and the so-called 'house prison' was in place des Etats Unis.

If you're interested in discovering more of the books and DVDs that helped inspire *The English Agent*, a comprehensive list can be found on my website: http://clareharvey.net

Acknowledgements

A huge thank you to those who offered advice, support and encouragement, but especially to my mum, Anne Harvey, who knows far more about bridge than I do!

**SIMON &
SCHUSTER**

Clare Harvey
The Gunner Girl

Bea has grown up part of a large, boisterous Kent family.
But she hasn't heard from her soldier sweetheart in months
and her mother is controlling her life. She needs to
take charge of her future.

Edie inhabits a world of wealth and privilege,
but knows only too well that money can't buy happiness.
She wants to be like Winston Churchill's daughter,
Mary, to make a difference.

Joan can't remember anything of her past or her
family, and her home has been bombed in the Blitz.
Desperate, she needs a refuge.

Each one is a Gunner Girl: three very different women,
one remarkable wartime friendship of shared hopes,
lost loves and terrible danger ...

Paperback ISBN: 978-1-4711-5054-8

PRICE £7.99